HOMELAND IN
MY HEART

The Conquest series

an Indian saga **volume two**

James G. Landis

HOMELAND IN MY HEART

VOLUME TWO OF A SEVEN-PART SERIES

An Indian saga of Meas and his struggle
to preserve his homeland as he meets
with settlers, traders, pirates, governors,
Mennonites, soldiers, slaves, traitors, and his
own native people.

–as told by Owechela, a master Lenape storyteller

"The truth shall make you free!"

ISBN: 978-1-943929-18-4 soft cover
978-1-943929-19-1 hard cover

Illustrations by Coleen B. Barnhart

Printed in China

TGS001247

Published by:
TGS International
P.O. Box 355
Berlin, Ohio 44610 USA
Phone: 330.893.4828
Fax: 330.893.2305
www.tgsinternational.com

Dedication

Doris Heatwole Landis

My dear wife who:

» encouraged me to keep on writing for more than forty
  years.

» had the courage to attack my pet phrases and the wisdom
  to make them better.

» flattered me by asking if parts of this story were really true.

» petted me along and provided my daily comforts.

» cheered me uphill and downhill to the finish line.

» actively promotes the book and me.

– James G. Landis

Overview of The Conquest Series

AMERICAN HISTORY THROUGH INDIAN EYES

James G. Landis

LENAPE HOMELAND ✦ Volume I
This story tells the early history of the Delaware Indians and the coming of the white man to the Delaware River Valley as witnessed by Lenape heroes.

HOMELAND IN MY HEART ✦ Volume II
Recounts the life story of Lenape sage, Meas, as he staggers through the events that engulf him in his homeland in the Delaware River Valley.

TOMAHAWKS TO PEACE ✦ Volume III
Glikkikan, a renowned Delaware war chief and famous orator, brings to light the hidden causes of what is commonly known as Pontiac's Rebellion.

UNDER ATTACK ✦ Volume IV
Details fierce White attacks against all Indians and the heroic attempts of Christian Indians to remain quiet and peaceable throughout.

WAR CHIEF CONQUERED ✦ Volume V
An Indian saga recounting Isaac Glikkikan's struggle to give up his former life as an influential chief, prophet, and orator and find peace in his heart.

BLACK CLOUDS OVER THE OHIOLAND ✦ Volume VI
A story of duplicity and the betrayal of the Delaware nation and the Moravian missions during the Revolutionary War.

THE FINAL CONQUEST ✦ Volume VII
Isaac Glikkikan remains stedfast in his faith amid conflict, deportation, and starvation, and at last finds a permanent homeland for his people.

Contents

Maps and Illustrations. ix

Foreword x

Credits. xiii

Timeline xvi

» **v o l u m e   t w o** «

Homeland in My Heart

Chapters

Prelude 1

1. » Meas and the Vision Quest (1655-1657). 3

2. » Meas–the Trader (1657-1658). 25

3. » Meas and Cool Water (1658) 63

4. » Meas–the Defender (1658-1659). 101

5. » Meas–the Interpreter (1661-1663). 123

6. » Meas–the Sage (1663) 165

7. » The Spirit of Tamenend (1664) 219

8. » Finale (1664-1682). 257

Cast of Main Characters. 316

Place Names 319

Fiction, History, and Truth. 320

Bibliography 324

About the Author 330

Maps & Illustrations

Maps by James G. Landis

CQM201 - The Lenape River and the Lenape Bay 6

CQM202 - Southern Maryland. 24

CQM203 - Northern Maryland 122

Illustrations by Coleen Barnhart

CQ201 - "Who am I, Dutch or Lenape?" —Meas 10-11

CQ202 - "I trow that Lord Baltimore does not enjoy this
land half as much as you and I." —Meas. 42-43

CQ203 - Cool Water Seeks the Singer 72

CQ204 - "Could youth last, and love still lead." —Meas and
Cool Water. 89

CQ205 - Three Barrels of Maize for One Good Gun. 109

CQ206 - Meas Lifted the Treaty Aloft That All Might
Watch It Burn. 158-159

CQ207 - They Saw the World, Not as It Was, but as It Ought
to Be —Meas and Friend Dreamer at the Soul Meet 177

CQ208 - "We carry the Spirit of Tamenend in the Land
of the Dawn." —Meas and the Lenape 198-199

CQ209 - "You have deceived yourself!" —Meas to the
Commander (Sir Robert Carr). 287

CQ210 - "Now, I too, possess the homeland in my heart!"
—Glikkikan in Peace Valley. 314-315

Foreword

I first conceived of The Conquest Series as telling you the compelling life story of a famous Lenape war chief named Glikkikan. The scanty records tell us Glikkikan murdered an infant, led his warriors to near triumph at Fort Pitt, and as an orator for the Delaware Indians, defended the right of his people to keep their heritage and their homeland. Glikkikan converted to Christianity, became a preacher of the true Gospel, and died a martyr in the bitterness and strife of the Revolutionary War.

These bare details of Glikkikan's life lie before us as only a skeleton. They are only dead history, a scanty collection of names, dates, and events. My task in The Conquest Series is to breathe life into Glikkikan's dried bones and give him a face you can see, a heart that throbs, and a soul that lives.

If your pulse would beat with Glikkikan's in Volume III, *Tomahawks to Peace*, you must learn to walk in his moccasins through Volume I, *Lenape Homeland*, and Volume II, *Homeland in My Heart*. You must learn of Glikkikan's past—what he believed, his culture, his heroes, his doubts, his fears.

In Volume II you will listen firsthand as Owechela tells the tale of Sage Meas to Glikkikan, a grandson Owechela is preparing to be a spokesman for the Lenape people.

As you listen to the tale, you will wonder with Meas at the purpose and meaning of life, as he, a half-breed orphan, struggles to find himself.

You will tremble with Meas and Cool Water as their love forces them to rise above hate, fear, and prejudice.

Your passion will rise with that of Meas at the crass immorality of the Dutch and the English as they fight to steal Meas's homeland in the name of God and the King.

You, with Meas, will feel the soothing words and songs of Friend Dreamer Plockhoy and his band when they come to the Siconece, and you will be jarred by the senseless ravages of lusting rulers upon those same unresisting settlers.

You will admire Meas's courage as Meas accuses a British lord of shameless lust, theft, and murder; overpowers the commander's defenses; rescues his own wife; and sets up a slave refuge in his homeland.

Like Glikkikan, Meas, and Tamenend, perhaps you, too, will come to treasure the Land of the Dawn in your heart.

This story claims a unique role in the historical record. It presents the whole drama as seen through Lenape eyes—the eyes of smart, thinking, and rational men—and not as commonly portrayed by white historians: dumb brutes and ignorant savages.

Even most of the early artwork meant to portray to white people this ingrained bias of the observer. In contrast to early drawings, the artwork in The Conquest Series is intended to convey a sympathetic print of Lenape Indians as men created equal to any white man, not the image of some primitive ape-man.

The Conquest Series is not a dead recording of Lenape history, but a carefully crafted story, true to the historical record, in which every character struggles with the same passions that still tug at our own hearts today.

After you weep and laugh as you follow the trails of the heroes in this story, you will never think the same way about the history of the Delaware Indians ... or about your own life. For the themes—right and wrong, good and evil—that you will ponder are timeless.

Credits

Bringing this book into print required the help and cooperation of many people, a large portion of whom will remain unseen and unknown. We pause here to pay these quiet supporters our special thanks for holding up the arms of those who receive the recognition.

Captain David Hiott of the *Kalmar Nyckel* gave special time to explain seventeenth-century navigation instruments and sailing methods. Judy Hentkowski and Barbara Meyer of the *Kalmar Nyckel* Foundation reviewed portions of the text and made valuable changes.

Cousins Harrison and Libby Myers journeyed with us to their old home farm bordering Neshaminy Creek in Peace Valley, Bucks County, Pennsylvania, and showed us the lay of the land around Owechela's wigwam.

The following folks were a vital part of the research in Volume II as well as in Volume I—Michael Depaolo at the Lewes Historical Society, Lewes, Delaware; Mike Dixon at the Elkton Historical Society, Elkton, Maryland; Ed Chichirichi at the Delaware History Center, Wilmington, Delaware; Brian Cannon and Cindy Snyder at the New Castle Courthouse Museum, New Castle, Delaware; Lois Burkholder at the Menno Simons Historical Library, Harrisonburg, Virginia; and Dr. Peter Craig, F.A.S.G., Washington, D.C. I owe them my thanks.

Coleen B. Barnhart used her native skill and professional touch to make the artwork masterpieces depicting the story.

And with all due respect, I acknowledge the touch of the Almighty upon this series. I bow before Him.

The Conquest
series

volume two Homeland in My Heart

An Indian saga

of Meas and

his struggle

to preserve

his homeland

as he meets

with settlers,

traders, pirates,

governors,

Mennonites,

soldiers, slaves,

traitors, and

his own native

people.

–as told by Owechela,
a master Lenape storyteller

History with a heart and a face

Homeland in My Heart Timeline

Historical Notes		Story Timeline	
European Thirty Years' War begins	1618		
Dutch & Mengwe declare Lenape Peacemakers	1621		
New Amsterdam becomes Dutch capital in the New World	1625		
		1631	Dutch settlement at Swanendael
		1632	Indians destroy Swanendael; Meas is born
Swedes come to Lenape River	1638		
European Thirty Years' War ends	1648		
Stuyvesant takes Lenape River for Dutch	1651		
		1655	Meas's Vision Quest begins
Lenape commandeer Mercurius	1656		
Death of Mattahorn	1657	1657	Meas's Vision Quest ends
		1658	Meas trades with Dutch
		1658	Meas buys Cool Water
		1659	Meas trades for guns
		1661	Meas as treaty interpreter
		1663	Friend Dreamer comes to Siconece
Duke of York overpowers Dutch in America	1664	1664	Charles Calvert visits Swanendael
		1664	English destroy Swanendael
		1665	Lenape take Matennecunk Island
		1673	Yellow Dogs raid Siconece
		1675	Slave refuge destroyed
Bacon's Rebellion and burning of Jamestown	1676		
William Penn visits Pennsylvania	1683		
William Penn returns to Pennsylvania	1700	1700	Glikkikan's birth
		1705	Owechela tells the story (1705–1708)

Prelude – 1711

Narrated by Glikkikan

I am Glikkikan. I like my name. It has a musical tapping sound to it. GLIK-ki-kan. It sounds good. My grandfather, o-wee-CHEE-la, gave me this name, and it means "the foremost sight on a gun barrel."

When I had seen only five winters, Owechela had seen more than eight tens of winters. Owechela, a once great chief, now lived by himself in a wigwam near the top of the hill above Neshaminy Creek.[1]

Owechela was so old. He had actually talked to William Penn, the great MEE-kwan[2] as the Lenape call him. I shall never get to see the great Miquon because the last time he came to our homeland was the year I was born.[3]

At his wigwam above ne-SHAM-i-nee Creek, Owechela first told me, "Glikkikan, a long long time ago, the Great Spirit gave us our homeland. If we would keep it, we must treasure our homeland in our hearts. If we do not treasure this land in our hearts, the Schwanneks[4] will take our homeland and drive us away." For a long time I didn't

---

[1] Located in Peace Valley Park near Dublin, Pennsylvania.
[2] *Miquon* meaning "quill" or "feather" in Lenape was a play on the English "pen."
[3] William Penn last visited Pennsylvania between December 1699 and November 1701. Glikkikan's date of birth is unknown, but my research would place it around 1700. Therefore I have chosen to use 1700 as the year of Glikkikan's birth throughout the series. —JGL
[4] Pronounced "SHWAN-neck." A derisive term meaning, "salt beings" or "bitter beings," and generally referring to all bad white people.

understand what he meant by "treasure the homeland in my heart." How does one treasure a homeland in his heart? I wondered.

When Owechela said "our homeland," he meant the land all along the Le-NAH-pay-WEE-he-tuck from its source to the Salt Sea. The white man named this river after a governor of Virginia who never even saw it: River De-La-Warr. I still call it the River of the Le-NAH-pay.

My homeland was far more than just the place where I was born. To me it was the place where I grew up as an innocent child reveling in the wonder of life. It was the land where I hung my heart of love without fear of hunger, sickness, or war.

I loved my homeland. It was a good land where my people were all around me. When I say "my people," I mean more than my father and mother and brothers and sisters and grandfathers and grandmothers. I mean the people of our nation who spoke the same tongue we did, dressed the same way we did, had the same black hair and the same black eyes we did, and who worshipped the same manitos[5] we did. Our people shared the same ancestors and the same heroes.

I call my people the LEN-nee Le-NAH-pay, which means "real men." Some say it means "original people," but "real men" comes closer to its full meaning. Because the Lenni Lenape and many, many related tribes far to the north, the west, and the south of us sprang from the Lenni Lenape, the other tribes call us Grandfather. We in turn call them Grandchildren.

The Lenni Lenape pass all their beliefs, history, and traditions on from generation to generation by teaching apt young boys all the lore and learning of the Lenape. My grandfather, Owechela, chose me as one of those special boys and began to teach me everything he knew about our past.

I revered Owechela partly because he was so old, and partly because he was the world's best storyteller. But my favorite story of all the ones Owechela told me was the legend of my other grandfather, MEE-as. This tale, then, is the story of Meas as Owechela told it to me.

[5] Spirits. Pronounced man-NEAT-toes

Meas and the Vision Quest

As told by Owechela

The land at Siconece[5] where the mouth of the Lenape Bay opens into the Great Sea is some of the best land in our homeland. The creek emptying into the bay at Siconece might be called an ordinary river, for no other river in the bay can compare with it for usefulness and convenience. The water in the creek is about six feet deep at the entrance to the bay and about two hundred paces broad. With canoes one can travel up the creek for a distance of two hours. Within the creek lie two small islands, the first quite small, the second about a half hour in circumference, lying a distance of half an hour from one another. The latter is a distance of about an hour from the mouth of the creek. At the first island, and sometimes toward the second island, the creek again widens out to two hundred paces broad. Both islands nestle under a blanket of beautiful grass, especially the second island. In the shallow muddy soil around these islands grow the very finest oysters. After the islands, the creek fades into a great saltwater marsh.

[5] Siconece in the Lenape tongue was the same place the Dutch called Swanendael and the Whorekill. Present-day Lewes, Delaware.

On higher grounds to the west of the Siconece Creek and the Siconece Marsh, rich black soils grow the finest maize and beans and squash ... every year.

Ever since the massacre at Swanendael,[6] the Schwanneks wanted this land again. It commanded the bay; it sported a pleasant climate; and the richness of the land yielded such bountiful crops. But no Europeans dared to settle there. All feared the Lenape who lived on the land.

Notable among the Lenape dwelling in a mainland village near the upper island were three sons of Eesanques's youngest daughter: Koketotoka, Meoppitas, and Meas. Koketotoka was the eldest of the three brothers and the chief of the village.

Meas was the youngest of the three brothers, but he was different. Yes, Meas had the same stalwart build as his brothers, the same black hair, and the same dark eyes, yet he did not quite look like them. His nose was narrower and his cheekbones not quite as high. His looks were not the only thing different about him. Meas would not settle down. He was a roamer. Even at twenty-four winters, Meas had not married.

Meas loved ships from an early age and spent many a day perched on the high dunes along the coast watching the ships at sea. Where did they come from? How did they work? Where were they going? He asked many questions of his mother while he helped her plant the maize, the beans, and the squash. They spent many hours tending and harvesting the crops together.

Glikkikan, it wasn't the right thing for a Lenape boy to be working in the fields, but I told you Meas was different. And there was a good reason why Meas didn't mind the taunts of the other boys. His mother often walked with him to the ruins of the old dormitory at Swanendael and sat with him there. Then while they looked out over the sea, she told him stories of the ships and the men who sailed

[6] The massacre at Swanendael took place in 1632. The time referred to now is 1657.

them; stories of the settlers who came to capture the whales and to build homes; stories of traders who exchanged furs and skins and maize for looking glasses, needles, knives, kettles, beautiful garments, and a host of dazzling adornments such as she loved. The tears always came to her eyes when she told of the rum and the death of her father and the deaths of thirty-two Dutchmen, and then the tears would overflow into sobs when she added, "the death of ... your father. He was one of them."

The sickness claimed his mother when Meas had seen only twelve winters. Before she died, she removed a palm-sized piece of copper from around her neck and handed it to Meas. Inscribed on one side stood a tawny cat with two arrows in its paw; on the other side crawled a tiny tortoise. Meas studied the medallion, then placed the copper chain around his own neck. Neither Mother nor Meas said a word; both understood.

Meas spent the next years learning the lore of the woods and the sea. He fled from the presence of other people and sought solace in the study of the living creatures that surrounded him. At times he went for days without eating, and he often prayed, as he had been taught, that he would receive a vision. None came. Day after day and night after night he wandered without specific purpose. He stayed at one place as long a time or as short a time as he wished before moving on. But he always moved on.

Meas wandered restlessly over the land between the bays[7] until he knew every stream and creek, every hillock and depression, and almost every tree, plant, and animal in the land of his birth—his homeland— while he sought to learn from the life around him.

He reared his head back to stare at the rack of the mighty oaks towering high, and then with a sigh he bent down to look at the rook of the raccoon within it. He paused to admire the beauteous attire of the lily and the trumpet vine, then stopped to dine on raspberry,

7 Delaware Bay and Chesapeake Bay.

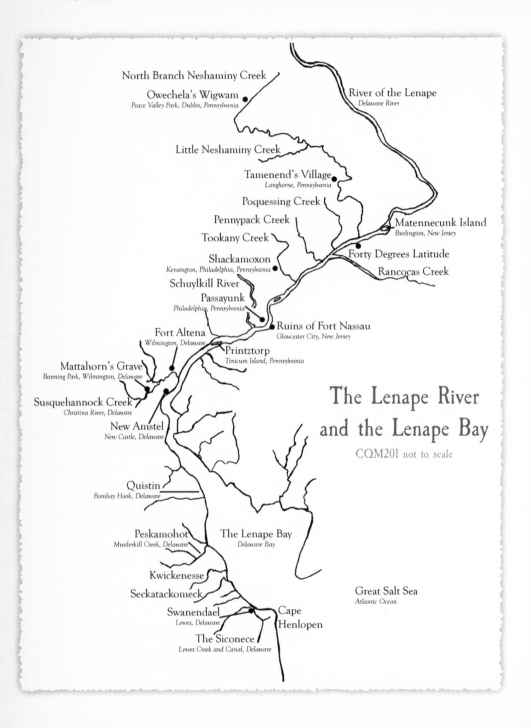

North Branch Neshaminy Creek

Owechela's Wigwam
Peace Valley Park, Dublin, Pennsylvania

River of the Lenape
Delaware River

Little Neshaminy Creek

Tamenend's Village
Langhorne, Pennsylvania

Poquessing Creek

Pennypack Creek

Tookany Creek

Matennecunk Island
Burlington, New Jersey

Forty Degrees Latitude

Shackamoxon
Kensington, Philadelphia, Pennsylvania

Rancocas Creek

Schuylkill River

Passayunk
Philadelphia, Pennsylvania

Ruins of Fort Nassau
Gloucester City, New Jersey

Fort Altena
Wilmington, Delaware

Printztorp
Tinicum Island, Pennsylvania

Mattahorn's Grave
Banning Park, Wilmington, Delaware

Susquehannock Creek
Christina River, Delaware

The Lenape River
and the Lenape Bay

CQM201 not to scale

New Amstel
New Castle, Delaware

Quistin
Bombay Hook, Delaware

Peskamohot
Murderkill Creek, Delaware

The Lenape Bay
Delaware Bay

Kwickenesse

Seckatackomeck

Great Salt Sea
Atlantic Ocean

Swanendael
Lewes, Delaware

Cape
Henlopen

The Siconece
Lewes Creek and Canal, Delaware

blackberry, strawberry, and cherry, and if that wasn't enough, he could stoop down to pick from the rick on the forest floor beechnut, chestnut, hickory nut, walnut, and grape. While he ate, he continued to gape at pines so straight and slim, at bulging beech with silver bole, at varied maple with limbs that embraced so much space in the fight for right to air and light amid the giants tall, and he could not help but see the ash and the buttonwood that also strove to hove their limb above their lesser kin.

And of the lesser kin Meas found much closer to the ground jolly holly and dogwood good, alder, sassafras, and hornbeam, vying for space to take their place in the life that rose above them. He noted the tangle when the grapevine tried to strangle the trees it would smother with its deadly cover. Then he cut the vine that did dangle and twine, and swung free in a glorious arc of liberty.

Where the creek ran free to the sea, there on the Siconece, herring, mackerel, halibut, and pike could swim from the ocean rim to prim in its waters fresh. And along its shores willows could sprout in a bout of confusion and profusion.

But Meas did not miss in the earnest of his quest to find his rest, that if beaver the stream did clog, forth from their work came a lifegiving bog, and from it came reed and feed for duck, goose, heron, muskrat, fish—bass, perch, catfish, and eel—and fisher and mink and otter, a panoply of life amidst the toil and strife.

And Meas saw that in it all, the strife of life did never cease. Bear, wolf, and panther prowl and growl about seeking something to devour in the hour when they might hungry be. Eagle, hawk, kite, and owl wait high up in the sky for just one dash below when in a flash he has his meal in tow. A turkey, a partridge, a quail, or a pheasant can eat a meal most pleasant of seed or bug or grain before he too must strain to flee or he will eaten be. And if perchance in life the eater is not eaten, the buzzard and the crow watch from a tree, and pray that they may prey upon him too.

In his travel to the north, Meas's mind brought forth the question,

"Is life then only death and dearth?" and then he saw the miracle of birth.

The deer brings forth her young and licks it with her tongue before it staggers to its feet and suckles on her teat. How does the fawn know where to go to find its treat?

For four long weeks a duck must wait while nearby swims the drake, before ten ducklings through the shells will break. How does she know that she must sit and wait?

A frog does not wait at all; she has the gall to wander off instead, where'er led, and let her thousand eggs begin without their legs. How does she know to lay a thousand eggs abed?

As Meas zigzagged through the forests and marshes and back to the bay, he knew not what to say. Could life be always sad and drear with never a word of cheer for a burdened heart with many a tear?

And then he found that many a sound did abound with joy and cheer. For many a warble and many a song burst from the woods and meadows around him. Warblers, thrushes, and wrens nearly shattered their breasts to do their best and give voice to the joy within them.

Then he went to the bay to watch the porpoises at play as together they leapt, and the rhythm they kept ere the water them swept, and they did it again and again. It had to be fun to make such a run with such grace and beauty, and one might note that as they ran the race with so much grace, out of duty they did it.

Then he saw the whale spout, and he wanted to shout as the monster gave vent to the water it sent spewing and roiling upward. For Meas knew now that joy like the spout comes from within and not from without.

Meas knew now what life was about, within and without. Within hid the heart, without lay the home. For wherever he might roam, his home would never depart from his heart, his homeland there by the Siconece.

Meas spent years continuing his Vision Quest. He moved along the bay listening to the sea. He studied the birds of the sea and learned the meaning of their cries and movements. He watched the clouds and the winds and the colors of the sky.

Gradually he began to understand the moods and fits of the sea and the bay. He watched the occasional ship dancing by on the bay, always remaining discreetly hidden. He wandered north along the shore of the bay as far as Canaresse[8] where the trees became short and scrubby. Then Meas straggled inland zigging and zagging aimlessly back and forth, generally to the south, until at last he arrived once more at the ruins of Swanendael.

Meas threw himself on the grass where his mother had told him so many stories, the spot where she said the pole with the coat of arms of Holland had stood, the spot where her father had been murdered in a pool of blood, and the spot where his mother now rested. All around that spot bloomed a small white flower that Meas knew came from Holland.[9] There Meas lay troubled and restless as his mother's stories came back to him. Meas himself knew not what he sought. He knew only of the restless longing in his spirit.

He pulled the copper medallion from his neck and held it in front of his eyes where he could study it. There was the tortoise, the revered symbol of the Lenape and the symbol of its head clan. His mother was the daughter of the great Eesanques. She had imparted the blood of chieftains to her sons. He turned the medallion over. There was the tawny cat with the arrows in its paw. What did it mean?

Suddenly Meas sprang to his feet. He knew now what he sought. "Who was he?"

---

[8] Meaning "thickets" or "little trees." In Dutch "little trees" was *Boompjes*. Today the place is known as Bombay Hook.
[9] The flower was the lily of the valley.

"Who am I, Dutch or Lenape?" –Meas

Koketotoka was in a foul mood for several days after he sobered up. "If I ever get my foot on the head of Two Tongue Sander Boyer,[10] I'll crush it in the dust," he growled. Meas and Meoppitas tried to calm him down.

"Sachem Koketotoka, you did not have to trade with him. You did not have to drink his watered-down rum. You knew he was going to cheat you by cupping his hand when he measured out the powder. You did not have to accept his stretched-out duffel. Why did you trade with Two Tongue? Why did you not wait for Falling Leaf before you sold all your skins to Two Tongue?" Meas scolded. "What you should have done was knock a hole in a keg or two of his rum as soon as he sailed up the Siconece."

"Sachem Koketotoka," Meoppitas pleaded, "do you not see? The rum is ruining us. Look at the village: dirt, hovels, hunger, sickness. Yes, many are sick, many are weak. Many suffer, many sleep. Meanwhile, brave and good men like you sell your spirit to the demon in the rum and then lie around on the ground like pigs wallowing in the mud. If you were not my brother, I could not talk to you so freely. But our situation is desperate. You have squandered some skins on enough rum to make the whole village drunk. For the rest of the skins you have bought some powder that

CQ201

[10] This was the same Dutchman who served as translator for Governor Stuyvesant when he bought land from Mattahorn. The man had a Swedish wife and a bad reputation among the Swedes.

you may go out again next winter and hunt more skins to trade for more rum. You are no better off than the Schwanneks' slaves who labor in the fields for a day's bread."

"Sachem Koketotoka," Meas argued on, "can you not see? Will you trade a few quarts of rum for the lash of the master's whip? Would you not rather be free on the Siconece to hunt and fish and trap than hoe tobacco in a Schwannek's lap? What will we do on the winter morn when the days grow cold and short? What will we eat? What will keep us warm?"

"Brothers," Koketotoka replied, "you do not need to punish me with the lash of your words. The wound in my flesh festers and hurts. You do not need to poke your finger in the hole and probe around. That only makes it sore. But if you would see the wound heal, you must feel gently and touch it lightly with herb and balm.

"Brothers, our situation is bad. Our plight calls for action. But what can we do? We must have the guns and powder. We cannot go back to bows and arrows. We must have kettles and knives, needles and metals. Who wants to go back to things made of stone and bone and clay? We must have the colorful duffel so light and bright. Who wants to go back to the weight of furs and skins to cover our bodies and beds?

"Brothers, the Schwanneks hook us like perch and pike on their trade goods. We may thrash about and try to do without them, but in the end, the Schwanneks will fry us in their pan and drive us from our homeland.

"Brothers, you speak of the sad condition of our village. It is the Schwanneks who have done it. The Schwanneks bring the sicknesses. The Schwanneks bring the rum. The Schwanneks bring the guns. Then when we are weak, when we are drunk, the Schwanneks take our skins, the Schwanneks take our maize, and if it had not been for Swanendael, the Schwanneks would also have taken our land and killed us or driven us away. Schwanneks," he hissed.

"Brothers, the weight of the Schwanneks crushes my spirit. Oh, that

I might again soothe my troubles with rum and feel its power flowing through my body. For then nothing is too hard for me. Then I am strong and can whip the Schwanneks with one patch of thorns.

"Brothers, Meas and Meoppitas, today I must not think such wicked thoughts. Today I am sober and able to reason. What do you think? If enough Lenape and Susquehannock sachems talk to the Dutch commander at New Amstel, will he keep the traders from cheating us and make that all traders must pay one price for a beaver? Would he force the traders to stop selling liquor to the Lenape?"

Meoppitas blew a lot of smoke before he responded to his brother's questions. "Our village indeed is in a sorry plight. Perhaps a manito has placed his curse on us. Perhaps we should hire a medicine man to carry off the evil spirit or at least drive it away. We must do something. If we tell the Dutch commander how Two Tongue has cheated us, it may be that he will punish Two Tongue and keep it from happening again. It is only a journey of several days from here to New Amstel. I will go with you if you want to try complaining to Commander Alricks. I have heard that he is as nervous as a turkey hen sitting on a clutch of eggs. He worries about the Swedes; they're too friendly with the savages. He worries about the Susquehannocks; they might trade with the long knives. He worries about the Lenape; they might kill the Dutch. He worries about the English; they want to claim the lands along the Lenape River. I don't think it will do much good, but if you want to go talk with Jitter Hen, I will risk it."

Meas listened in stolid silence while Meoppitas gave his opinion on Koketotoka's proposal to plead their cause at New Amstel. He listened carefully to what his elder brothers were saying. Silence again ruled the wigwam, and many a curl of smoke drifted upward before Meas spoke.

"Brothers," he said at last, "I am but a youth. I sprout only the feathers of a fledgling, and my wings have never yet been tested by flight. What I say cannot be trusted to lift our village out of squalor and debauchery. But is it not true that when the hare is caught in the snare, he must free himself? He cannot wait for the fox or the hunter to come along and release him. He must struggle and jump and squirm to break loose from the noose, or he will surely die in the trap. And would it not be better yet, if the rabbit had any sense at all, for him to avoid sticking his head in the noose? Perhaps we are already caught in the Schwanneks' trap. Perhaps it is too late to break loose. Yet I am quite certain that if the Schwanneks have set the liquor trap, they will not spring us from it."

Here Meas glared at Koketotoka. Then he went on. "If you want to be free from the curses of the evil spirit in the rum, you must do it yourself. If you will but stave in the ends of the kegs as soon as Two Tongue brings them to you, I assure you that he will never bring another keg close to you. And if you do not like the wares that Two Tongue offers you for your furs, sell them to Falling Leaf. Save yourself. Do not count on Jitter Hen to spare you. Remember, he is but a poult of Strutting Turkey.

"Nevertheless, I will go with you to New Amstel. Perhaps the squab's judgment is bad. Perhaps not all Dutchmen are like Two Tongue. Maybe one will arise to save us from our own stupidity.

"I shall go with you to New Amstel, but I shall not return with you. I thirst for knowledge of these Dutchmen. I would learn their tongue and see what sort of men they be. I must know of what sort of man I have been born and what sort of man I am. I own no wife and child, so I will leave my homeland here on the Siconece and wander for a time along the River of the Lenape. When my thirst for knowledge of my father has been quenched, I shall return to the Siconece."

Falling Leaf and Meas hit it off like identical twins. Nearly the same age, youthful, strong, much the same build and height, and wearing much the same kind of clothing, they often could have switched places in the canoe, and no one would have known the difference, except that the blue eyes and blond hair of the Swede contrasted with the black hair and dark eyes of the Lenape.

There were other differences as well, but one would have had to watch and listen more closely to observe them. Falling Leaf could get by quite well in five different tongues: Swedish, Dutch, English, Lenape, and Mengwe. Meas spoke only the Lenape. Falling Leaf never felt ill at ease in any culture or place. As long as there were people around, he was at home in New Amsterdam or in a wigwam village. Meas much preferred the songs of the forest and the sea to the voices of people. Falling Leaf had seen the world. Other than a peep sight of the world from the lips of his mother, Meas knew only the forest and the heritage of the Lenape.

Both welcomed each other's company, Meas for a guide to introduce him to new worlds, Falling Leaf for an able friend to assist him in his trading and for someone with whom to talk, the latter reason being the more important.

One day while camping on the eastern shore of the Chesapeake, Meas said to Falling Leaf, "Tell me how you learned to speak so many tongues. Is it possible that I, too, can learn another tongue?"

"Oh, easily, my friend. Easily. If I can do it, you surely can. Do you hear the sound of yon whippoorwill? Mock him."

Falling Leaf stopped while Meas whistled a perfect replica of the whippoorwill's call. "Meas, that is perfect. Now let us pretend that a crow has just discovered a hunter in the woods and wants to warn other crows of the danger. Can you tell me in crow language of this discovery?"

Instantly, Meas began an alarming array of caws changing in rapidity and intensity, drawing out some calls into a hoarse rasp while ending others in staccatos.

"Stop!" Falling Leaf laughed. "I fear we shall have the whole woods full of crows tormenting us during the night. I see you already know two languages, Lenape and Crow. Meas, how did you learn Crow?"

"Falling Leaf, I do not know how I learned Crow. I did not even know that I knew Crow. If you tell me it is so, I must know Crow.

Caw! Caw!" A triumphant smile played on Meas's face. Then he shrugged. "I guess I just grew up with it."

"Meas, do several more calls for me: the catbird, the mockingbird, and the ruffed grouse."

Meas gave the scolding cry of the catbird followed by its pleasing song. He followed that with the entire repertoire of the mockingbird plus a few other birds he chose to add. Then he stopped. He looked puzzled. "I do not know the song of the ruffed grouse."

Falling Leaf thought a moment, then continued his lesson. "Of course you do not know the sound the ruffed grouse makes when it drums. His home is in the mountains farther north. I wanted to see if you could do as well with an unfamiliar sound as you did with the other calls. Never mind the grouse. A turkey call will do as well."

Meas cut loose with a series of turkey gobbles.

"As I thought," added Falling Leaf as he continued his schooling. "You will have little trouble learning other languages. You have learned to listen well to the sound, and then you have practiced mocking it until the bird itself is fooled into thinking you are one of its family. This is what you must do to learn another tongue. Listen. Mock. Listen. Mock. Listen to every rise and fall in pitch. Listen to every sound. Make sure that you are hearing the sounds. Then mock them. It does not matter if you sound as sick as a young crow when you try it; try it anyway. Others will laugh at you. That's all right. You will sound funny to them and probably to yourself. Laugh and then mock their laugh. That is the way you have learned Lenape and Crow. You see, old pal, there's nothing to it for someone who already knows two languages to learn a third or even a fourth. Meas, which language did you want to learn?"

"Dutch," Meas answered quickly.

Falling Leaf asked no questions and showed no surprise at his friend's unusual interest. He only said, "Very well. Starting tomorrow morning and every morning thereafter, I shall speak nothing but Dutch to you. The rest of the day we shall converse in Lenape.

"Now I would like to change the subject and ask a question of you. Mayhap, Meas, you tire of my constant chatter, and so I will give you a chance to speak. Did you not mention to me that you were along when the Lenape chiefs met with Jitter Hen Alricks?"

"Yes, I was along with Meoppitas and Koketotoka and a number of other Lenape chiefs about a year ago when they went to New Amstel and met with Jitter Hen," Meas offered. Then he stopped.

"Go on," Falling Leaf urged. "What did the chieftains want Jitter Hen to do? This matter is of large interest to me. Tell me all you know."

"Koketotoka wanted Jitter Hen to fix the price of a beaver so that it would be the same for all the traders," Meas added. "Koketotoka thought this would stop the traders from cheating the Lenape when they traded with them." Then Meas stopped again.

"Meas," Falling Leaf went on, "you do not need to be afraid to open your heart and loose your tongue. It is only you and I here, and I shall not harm you. What do you think of the request? Would a fixed price stop cheating? Did Jitter Hen agree to it? What did he say?"

Meas hesitated before going on. "Falling Leaf, I have never spoken to anyone of this matter, but since you ask, I shall trust the matter to you. Before I came to New Amstel for the meeting with Koketotoka and Jitter Hen, Koketotoka and Meoppitas and I had a falling out. Two Tongue Boyer came to our village with watered-down liquor and gave Koketotoka and Meoppitas enough liquor to craze them. Then he sold them enough liquor to make the whole village drunk. After that, he traded with them for their skins until there were no more skins left. Then Two Tongue left the Siconece.

"Koketotoka is no longer the proud chieftain he once was. Now he is only a shadow of the former noble man he was. Now he is always ashamed of himself when sober and a tyrant when drunk. Liquor has ruined him. As long as Koketotoka wants liquor, he will get it. He hunts and fishes and traps all year now only so he can trade for more liquor next year.

"No, I do not think a fixed price will stop cheating by the traders. But I am only a pup and Koketotoka is the headman of the village. He will not listen to me. When the pig stops wallowing in the mud, Koketotoka will stop drinking. Koketotoka knew you would have given him more for his skins, without the brew, if he had waited. But that is the problem. He wanted the liquor. And there are so many like him in the village. Even the women crave the stuff."

"What did Jitter Hen say?" asked Falling Leaf. "Did he offer to stop selling liquor to the Indians to save them from self-destruction?" Falling Leaf let out a chuckle.

"No, Falling Leaf. Jitter Hen told us that it would be impossible for him to stop the sale of liquor to the Indians or to fix the price of beaver. But there was something funny about this whole council. Falling Leaf, do you know who the interpreter was? Two Tongue Boyer. And when Jitter Hen started talking about stopping the sale of liquor to the Indians, his roly-poly officer just laughed and laughed. He thought that was really funny."

"Truly? Meas, you tell a wild tale. The officer you speak of is none other than Lieutenant Alexander d'Hinoyossa. The Lenape call him Fat Pig. Fat Pig laughed because he likes to drink brandy and wine as much as the Lenape. The tale is told of him that one night he was tippling in New Amstel and started shouting, 'Down with Stuyvesant. Down with the council. Down with the Dutch. They treat me badly. I've a mind to do as one Minnewit, the uncle of Hendrick Huygen did. He introduced the Swedes here when the Company treated him badly.[11] I will go and fetch here the English or them from Portugal, the Swede or the Dane, what do I care whom I serve? The English or the Swede or the Dane or the devil ... what do I care ... or the devil or the English ... what do I care?' Fat Pig roared out his drunken song while he danced tipsily around the tavern and then out into the street

11 After the Dutch fired Peter Minuit as head of the Dutch West Indies Company, Minuit went into the employ of the Swedes and founded a Swedish colony on the Delaware.

still singing lustily ... 'or the devil or the English ... what do I care ...?' Nobody laid a hand on him.

"No, Meas. I don't think you'll get any liquor laws passed when Fat Pig is propping up Jitter Hen's arms."

Falling Leaf laughed again as he pictured Fat Pig roaring down through New Amstel shouting his drunken chant.

Then Falling Leaf sobered up. His body grew tense and his voice hardened. "Meas, the trade laws are another matter. Do you know that Two Tongue has had to raise his prices three times in one year to match my prices? Already the price of the pelts has gone up by one-third in just a year. Two Tongue is very unhappy. The Dutch do not like it that I, a Swede, am forcing them to pay more for their pelts. Of course, they would not like it if the English jacked the prices up on them either.

"Jitter Hen has come up with a solution that will stop the rise in prices. He has already set the prices of skins to be in effect as soon as I return from this trading journey:[12]

— One beaver, two strings of wampum.
— One bearskin, two strings of wampum.
— One elkskin, two strings of wampum.
— One otter, two strings of wampum.
— One deerskin, one-hundred-twenty wampum.
— Foxes, catamounts, raccoons and other to be valued accordingly."

At this point Meas broke in on Falling Leaf. "And just how does Jitter Hen think he can possibly keep you from paying three strings of wampum for a beaver?"

"Ah, Meas. Jitter Hen, Two Tongue, and Fat Pig are very cunning. There are several ways they will control it. First of all, the Dutch can make wampum much cheaper than the Lenape. They use iron tools to drill the holes and iron tools to polish the beads. The resulting wampum is far more uniform and prettier than that made by the stone

[12] Prices established at New Amstel 10 January 1657.

tools of the Lenape. There is no limit to the amount of wampum the Dutch can make as long as the Lenape accept it as payment for their skins. Why, the Dutch could as easily pay four strings of wampum for a beaver as two strings. The cost of making wampum is negligible. The question is, What can the Lenape and the Susquehannocks buy with the Dutch wampum? Can they buy the same number of guns, matchcoats, kettles, and knives as they did when they traded beaver directly for them? Meas, do you think the Lenape and the Susquehannocks will accept the Dutch wampum as payment for their skins?"

"Falling Leaf, the Lenape and the Susquehannocks will not accept the false wampum of the Dutch. Do you think we are only stupid savages who cannot think? Who among us would be so foolish as to trade valuable skins for worthless beads? Even a child can see through that one. That will not work."

"But, Meas, if the Dutch insisted that you must take the false wampum in payment, what else could you do?"

"Falling Leaf, we could trade with you or other Swedes or maybe even the English. I would prefer trading with you anyway because we trust you."

"Thank you, Meas, for your confidence. I do always try to have a clean heart, and I shall try to be worthy of your trust. However, the second part of Jitter Hen's plan will make it very hard for me to trade as before. The new law says 'no persons shall go to the Indians, by land or water, to trade with them, or offer them gifts by sailing up and down the river.' If I want to continue trading anywhere on the Lenape River, I must buy a license from Jitter Hen that will permit me to trade. Besides that, the new law states that if any trader pays more than the decreed rate of exchange, on the first offense he will have his license suspended for one year. On the second offense he will be severely beaten, and on the third offense he will be expelled from the colony.

"The third part of this managed-trade plan restricts trade to New

Amstel where it can be carried out under the watchful eyes of Jitter Hen and Fat Pig and Two Tongue. Now, Meas, before you get too excited, let me tell you that the reason for restricting trade to New Amstel is to protect the Indians from unscrupulous traders who would cheat them in trades or sell them liquor. Like little children, the Indians need Jitter Hen and Two Tongue and Fat Pig to watch out for them. Meas, it's a mockery. Those three will watch out all right ... for their own pockets.

"Meas, the hour is getting late, and we must turn in for the night. Tomorrow will be a long day, and the Dutch lessons start in the morning."

"Yes," Meas agreed, "we must rest. But there is still one question I must ask of you, Falling Leaf. What will you do when the new law is in effect?"

"Meas, I do not yet know what I will do. The Dutch have pursued me before and thought they would put an end to me. But the woods are large, and I have many friends among the Lenape and the Susquehannocks. Jitter Hen and Two Tongue have many enemies because they have cheated and beaten others at will. Even the Dutch do not like them. And there are the English who would relish the thought of taking over the trade on the Lenape River. Meas, remember, the Dutch must first catch the fox before they can kill it.

Narrated by Glikkikan

"Owechela," I asked, "why did the Great Spirit not send the vision to Meas? Was it because he was part Dutch?"

"Glikkikan, Meas did receive understanding even though it was not in the form of a dream. When a young man goes on a Vision Quest, he only presents himself to the Great Spirit and asks for a dream. He can fast. He can beg. He can wait. But he cannot command the Great Spirit to send him a message.

"Glikkikan, when the time comes for you to go on your own Vision Quest, you should remember the legend of Isadilla."[13]

Once upon a time there was a great Lenape sachem who was known for his wisdom in the council and his great success in war. This Great Sachem had only one son named Isadilla. As Isadilla grew up, the father very much wished Isadilla to distinguish himself among his people by performing some great feat.

When Isadilla reached the proper age for him to retire into some solitary place and submit himself to a long fast, the Great Sachem determined that his son should fast for twelve days. The longest fast on a Vision Quest that anyone remembered had been for a period of nine days. Some ambitious youths had gone several days longer than the nine days, but none had survived the attempt.

The Great Sachem of the Lenape believed that his son, so noble, generous, and brave, should show his supremacy in everything by fasting for twelve days and thereby hold a greater claim to the blessing and protection of the Great Spirit. The Great Sachem built a little lodge in the forest and furnished it with skins for Isadilla to lie upon during the hours of his trials that he might not become weak from exposure to sun, wind, rain, or cold.

Isadilla began his lonely vigil lying upon his bed of skins in his little lodge in the forest. Each morning his father visited him and encouraged him to persevere for twelve days. The ninth day came and passed, also the tenth. On the morning of the eleventh day, Isadilla was dying of weakness. His full rounded muscles had shrunk and withered from the effects of

[13] This story is adapted from *Legends of the Delaware Indians*, by Richard C. Adams.

the dreadful ordeal.

"Father," said the youth, "I have fasted eleven days, a longer time than man ever fasted before. The Great Spirit is satisfied. Give me something to eat that I may not die."

"My son," said the Great Sachem, "tomorrow I will bring you some venison. Fast until then that your name may become mighty among the great sachems of the Lenape."

The Great Sachem returned to the little lodge the next morning before the sun had risen. He brought the most savory food. But when he looked in the lodge, Isadilla lay still upon his bed of skins and another youth with golden wings and a halo of light around his head was painting Isadilla's breast vermilion and his body brown. Then Isadilla changed into a strange and beautiful bird, flew through the door, and perched on a nearby limb.

"Father, farewell," said the bird. "The Great Spirit saw I was dying from hunger and sent a messenger for me, and now I am changed to this bird. I will always preserve my love for man and will build my nest and carol near his dwelling."

Every morning after that, during the lifetime of the Great Sachem, a robin sang from a limb of the large oak tree that overhung his wigwam.

"Glikkikan, learn from Isadilla. Do not let pride or ambition try to force fame upon yourself. In your own Vision Quest, remember that if the Great Spirit favors you with a dream, it is the light within the dream you seek, not the dazzling glory of the vision."

"Owechela," I said, "your story about Isadilla did not answer my question about Meas. Did the Great Spirit withhold the dream from Meas because he was part Dutch?"

"Glikkikan, the Great Spirit does what he wills. But a man's race is determined by more than the color of his skin or by who his father is.

"Glikkikan, listen well and you shall learn how Meas found out that anyone can be a Lenape if he holds the Spirit of Tamenend in his heart."

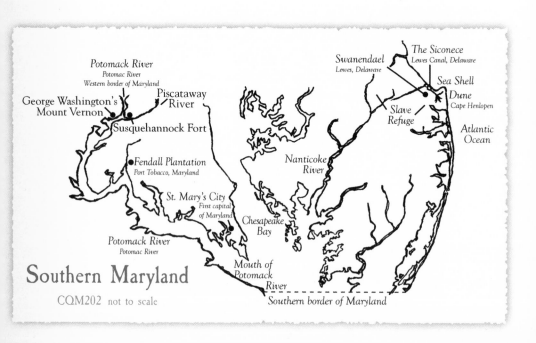

Potomack River
Potomac River
Western border of Maryland

George Washington's
Mount Vernon

Piscataway
River

Susquehannock Fort

Fendall Plantation
Port Tobacco, Maryland

St. Mary's City
First capital
of Maryland

Chesapeake
Bay

Nanticoke
River

Swanendael
Lewes, Delaware

The Siconece
Lewes Canal, Delaware

Sea Shell
Dune
Cape Henlopen

Slave
Refuge

Atlantic
Ocean

Potomack River
Potomac River

Mouth of
Potomack
River

Southern border of Maryland

Southern Maryland

CQM202 not to scale

Chapter 2 — 1657-1658

Meas—the Trader

As told by Owechela

True to his word, Falling Leaf began his Dutch lessons the next morning. The two friends took their time going about the morning chores of frying several perch and a rabbit Meas had managed to snare. Falling Leaf patiently named the different utensils and the parts of his body, while Meas mimicked the words.

The sun was already well up in the sky before the two launched their canoe once more. They guided the canoe ever southward without stopping once to relax. Late in the afternoon they passed the mouth of the Patuxent River. Toward evening the two beached their canoe on the western shore of the Chesapeake Bay. Falling Leaf sprang from the canoe, grabbed his pack and gun, and motioned Meas to do likewise. Then he set off to the west on a well-traveled trail through the woods.

After a five-mile hike through the woods, they came upon a small town. "Meas, welcome to St. Mary's City, the Capital of Maryland," and Falling Leaf spread his right arm toward the town while bending his torso toward Meas. Then Falling Leaf headed straight toward the largest building in the town, a long double-hipped roof affair that gave the appearance of two buildings jammed together into one without a street to separate them.

"What are you doing?" Meas gasped.

"I only wanted to introduce you to the new governor of Maryland," Falling Leaf answered nonchalantly. "It is only fitting that we should welcome him to the area. Perhaps he will want to know more about the land and the people he governs. And by accident or providence, his interests and our interests may happen to converge."

Two soldiers stood guard at the gate. "What do you wish?" one soldier asked suspiciously as he eyed the rough garments of his two strong visitors.

"We wish to visit the governor and help him attain peace throughout his province," Falling Leaf responded grandly.

"Do you not think you have arrived rather late in the day for such a great undertaking?" the soldier queried.

"Ah, but the night is young," Falling Leaf retorted.

"I'll see what I can arrange," the soldier said and departed.

"Meas, I don't see how the water is drained off where the two roofs come together," Falling Leaf commented. "It will always have to be a problem with that building to keep the water from rotting the timbers out. I've never seen anything quite like it. You see, Meas, the governor and his servants live on the side of the building with two chimneys rising through the roof peak, and the citizen lawmakers of Maryland meet on the other side where the one great chimney rises along the side of the building. Again, there has to be a water problem on the back side of that chimney."

After a lengthy stay at the mansion, the soldier returned. "We will accompany you in now," he announced, "and you can tell the governor himself the lofty nature of your business."

Falling Leaf and Meas followed the soldiers to the double doors near the wide chimney. A porter opened the doors, and the four followed him into a high-ceilinged council room. Candelabra lit the room with a soft sparkling light. A newly lit fire crackled in the huge fireplace.

Falling Leaf left his musket and pack at the door, chose a well-padded chair next to the fire, and seated himself upon it. Meas, too, left his pack and gun at the door and seated himself on the floor beside Falling Leaf. Falling Leaf motioned Meas to take a chair. "Stand to your feet when the governor enters," Falling Leaf said tersely. The two soldiers stood at attention at the door.

The governor entered unencumbered by the robes of office. He bore a relaxed and somewhat casual manner that put his visitors at ease even as they rose to their feet. He studied his strange visitors thoughtfully. Meas and Falling Leaf waited. Without introducing himself or asking for the names of his guests, Governor Fendall stated, "I am glad to see you are old friends who have come for a visit." He turned to the soldiers. "We will not need your services here," he said pointedly.

Then Governor Fendall stepped forward and held out his hand to Falling Leaf. "Josias Fendall," he said. "Just call me Josias."

"With pleasure," said Falling Leaf. "I am Lasse Cock. My friends call me Falling Leaf. 'Tis my enemies who call me Lasse Cock, and it seems that name has earned some well-deserved notoriety ... for doing good."

"How so?" Josias wondered. "Usually it is evil that gains fame for the doer. But come now, introduce me to your savage friend," said Josias as he eyed Meas carefully.

Falling Leaf spoke quickly. "This is Meas. He is a Delaware Indian from the place the Dutch call the Hoerenkill or Swanendael. His mother was a chieftain's daughter, the daughter of the great Eesanques whom the Dutch killed. His father was a Dutchman whom the Delawares murdered in retaliation for Eesanques's death. Sort of 'tit for tat,' you might say."

"I see," Josias observed. "I've learned one can never quite trust the savages." Josias smiled and motioned both his guests back into their chairs. "You have already brought me the most interesting news. Have you had any refreshments?"

"None since morning," Falling Leaf replied.

"Then we shall have something immediately," the governor replied, and he left the room at once.

When the governor returned, he edged his chair close to his guests. "Now," he resumed, "Falling Leaf, you were saying that you have gained notoriety for doing good deeds. Would you care to explain why this is so?"

Falling Leaf laughed. "I can tell you some tales, but perhaps you will have to tell me why it is that supposedly good men do evil and then hate those who do right. Just for a starter, why would traders who sell the Indians rum and then buy their goods at half price hate me? I do not sell rum to anyone and always try to pay the Indians a fair price for their skins. I can't figure it out."

Now it was Josias Fendall's turn to laugh. "Falling Leaf, you are not that dumb," he chuckled. "You remind me of the jester in the King's court. He is a fool only in name, with his jokes packing the meanest barbs. Surely you can see that if the trader cheats the Indians once, they will avoid him the next time. And if the Indians know an honest trader, they will surely favor him with their skins and maize."

"True," said Falling Leaf. "But if the Indians choose to favor me with their trade, how does that make me an evil man?"

Josias clucked his tongue several times. "Do you have a license to trade with the Indians?" he asked thoughtfully.

"A license from whom?" Falling Leaf sneered. "From God? From the Pope? From Luther? From Calvin? From the Indians? From Jitter Hen Alricks? From Strutting Turkey Stuyvesant? From the Assembly of XIX in Amsterdam? From King Charles I in London? Or from your Lord Baltimore? A license from which one will make me a good fellow?"

"Falling Leaf, you truly are a son of this wilderness. You concede no honor to anyone, but scorn kings, councils, pope, and archbishop. Do you also scorn God?"

"Josias, I do not scorn God. I scorn those who claim to be speaking for God or to have authority from God while openly doing what is wrong. As you say, Meas and I have not been formed by the senseless drivel of clerics and priests, men who bend the truth to any shape they wish and mold right and wrong into a mud pie. Meas and I do what we know to be right and good, and no king or pope or council can change right and wrong. Josias, is it not so?"

"Are we not straying from the question of from whom you should get a license to trade?" A light knock on the door interrupted Josias. "Gentlemen, our refreshments have come."

Josias arose, went to the door, and opened it. "The ladies have chosen to join our company and share the meal with us," he said as he ushered three buxom ladies into the room. Each of the three carried one tray.

Falling Leaf and Meas rose to greet the ladies. Josias introduced them. "This is Mary, my wife. The older girl of seventeen years is Margaret. Her younger sister of fifteen is Maria."[13] He held out his hand, pointing to Falling Leaf while he said, "Falling Leaf," and then with the other hand he motioned toward Meas and said, "Meas." All six made a slight curtsy.

"Now," said Josias, "we must enlarge the circle of chairs so the ladies can join us. Mary will sit next to me, Margaret will sit next to Falling Leaf, and Maria will sit beside Meas. Mary is teaching the girls the housekeeping skills of the settlement, rather than trying to make English ladies out of them. We shall now taste and see how well the girls have learned the day's lessons."

Then Josias added, "In honor of our heavenly Father, let us pray.

"Creator God, maker of the heavens and the earth, the sea and all that in them is. We thank you for this our daily bread and ask that you would bless it. Amen."

"All right, Josias," Mary began as soon as the prayer ended. "You will need to set a good example for our guests. What do you think of this

---

[13] Both Margaret and Maria are imaginary characters.

bread? And the butter and the honey?"

"I think you had better hold your honey bread over the tray when you eat it or the honey will drip on your lap," Josias warned. "Falling Leaf, could you not entertain the ladies with a story or two while we eat together?"

"I will be glad to regale you with a story or two in exchange for the repast," Falling Leaf offered. "It is a shame, though, that you do not know the tongue of yon Meas so that you could listen to his native oratory. When Meas tells a story, even a blind man can see the vivid scenes he paints as his words brush across the canvas of the mind. His imagery powers into the picture he paints, filling every scene with florid details. Over the centuries, the Lenape have honed the art of storytelling to the finest edge it can carry, and Meas is the best. Nevertheless, since you cannot understand Meas, you will have to put up with my simple tales."

Four heads bent forward, and eight eyes fixed on Falling Leaf while he told them the story of Swanendael.

Suddenly Maria sprang to her feet. " 'Tis a mouse right beside my leg!" she shrieked. She looked under the wooden chair for the culprit, then seated herself again beside Meas.

Falling Leaf resumed his story. He barely got started again before Maria jumped up on her chair shrieking. Then Margaret hollered and started stomping around the bottom of her chair until she, too, like Maria, sprang up on the chair.

Meas placed a hand on Maria's arm to steady her while she danced about on the chair. The rest of the crowd scurried off into a far corner of the dark room, stomping and kicking as they tried to kill the offending mouse. Soon all quieted down and the tiny mouse was heard no more.

Meas helped Maria down from the chair, then turned to face Falling Leaf. "What was the excitement all about?" he asked.

"Didn't you hear the mouse?" asked Falling Leaf in surprise.

"I did not hear any mouse," Meas answered.

Falling Leaf looked at Meas closely, and the two of them burst into open mirth. "It's good no one stomped on the mouse," Falling Leaf laughed. "Meas might have picked you up and run away. I tell you, he can do a perfect mimic."

There were no further distractions while Falling Leaf finished the story of Swanendael.

"How far is it from here to Swanendael?" Margaret asked.

Falling Leaf translated the question for Meas, and after a brief talk answered, "It would take about three days of travel by canoe. First, one goes east across the bay, then follows the Nanticoke River to its source. From there it's about another day on foot. Meas knows the whole area better than you know the veins on your own hands."

"Did you not say Swanendael is a very lovely place?" Margaret continued. "Why have no Christians ever settled there since the massacre?"

"Margaret, look at yon savage Meas. He is a prime specimen of the Lenape. Do you see how strong he is? How cunning? How mean his eyes? How sharp his teeth? He is really gentle as a kitten, but when aroused, he can be as dangerous as a panther. Do you have any idea how much Meas loves his homeland?

"Many Europeans covet the land on the Siconece. But all are fearful that one day, if a settlement were made, the natives may do to them again as they did to those first settlers at Swanendael: kill them all. There is nothing to such nonsense. I have learned to deal justly with the Lenape, and I know they will stay true to a friend better than any European nation has ever done. England and Holland go to war. They make peace. The ink on the treaty barely dries before one side or the other is at it again—stealing, robbing, plundering, looting—on some pretext that supposedly justifies their holy war. Let me stop this tirade. The Indians I have dealt with are more trustworthy than nine out of ten so-called Christians. What puzzles me is why they do not rise up together and throw out all the Europeans.

"I have a question for Mary. Earlier you said that you wanted Margaret and Maria 'to learn housekeeping skills and not grow up to be just English ladies.' Why is that?"

Mary had her answer ready. "Because Maryland[14] is our home. We are never going back to England, to the unending struggle between Papist and Protestant, Crown and Parliament. One day you are rich and everything is fine. Next week you are in jail and may lose your head. If you don't lose your head, you may get out of jail the following year. Again, you may not.

"We are Protestants. I know the Calverts set Maryland up to be a haven for Catholics, and during the times when Catholics are hunted in England, they have found a refuge here. At other times the Catholics have been strong, or should I say more ruthless, in England. In those times, many Protestants, even many from Virginia, have found respite in Maryland. However, even in Maryland the struggle between Catholic and Protestant continues. The Assembly passed a religious toleration law, which offers toleration to all religions.[15] The Calverts, as owners of the country, struggle to make Catholic ways, I mean their intolerance, dominant. With Cromwell as Lord Protector in England, Protestants will be all right in Maryland, but if the King ever returns in England ...

"You asked why I teach Margaret and Maria housekeeping skills instead of allowing them to be pampered and petted by servants. Work never hurt anyone, and I have never yet seen a bit of knowledge or skill that one possessed that did not come in handy some time or the other, all the more so in Maryland. I want these girls to know the worth of honest toil and the dignity of doing good. They shall not be conceited lilies who bloom but for a day and think that all the world must fawn before their beauty, while the next day they droop uselessly

---

[14] The original grant was made by Charles I of England in 1632. The province was named after his wife Mary who was a loyal Catholic. Cromwell beheaded Charles I in 1649.
[15] An Act Concerning Religion or Religious Toleration Law passed Assembly 21 April 1649.

into the water and vanish.

"Falling Leaf, you have opened the door to a mother's heart, and I shall let its desires bubble out. I want that each of these girls might marry an honest man of character who knows right from wrong and falters not at the truth, not some English squire who will forever be chasing his head to save it from the pope or the king. Not some ..."

Here Mary noticed that Meas had lifted his hand to signal Falling Leaf and she stopped abruptly. Meas spoke briefly to Falling Leaf and then Falling Leaf translated for the group.

"Meas hopes the kind hostess will not be insulted if he does not drink the wine offered to him. Liquor has been the death of his grandfather and the ruin of his brothers. He does not wish liquor to destroy him. He wonders if he might have some fresh water instead."

Maria sprang up instantly. "I will fetch him some well water," she offered hopefully.

"Would it be safe for Maria to go by herself to the well at this hour?" Mary wondered.

"Would it be safe if Meas went with her at this hour?" joked Josias. "What would happen if just one wag saw them alone together ... at this hour? Why do we not all walk over to the well together and taste of its coolness?"

Maria slipped out immediately and rejoined the party carrying a two-quart pitcher. She led the way with Meas in tow to guide him along the path. Meas held Maria's hand to keep her from falling as she tripped excitedly along. Margaret and Falling Leaf followed gaily behind Maria and Meas, with Mary and Josias walking further back in a more subdued manner.

At the well Maria drew a bucket of water. Meas prepared to scoop water up in his hands and slake his thirst. Maria laid a restraining hand on his shoulder, then motioned him to one side away from the well. Maria scooped her pitcher full of water and motioned Meas to kneel on the grass before her. At once she began pouring copious amounts of water down over his bronzed head and face. Meas sputtered till he caught on, then began washing his face and hands and arms as Maria splashed ever more water over his head. At last he jumped to his feet and pointed to his open mouth. Once more Maria had him kneel. This time she poured the liquid into his cupped hands and he drank until satisfied.

"It is equal to the water from the fabled Fountain of Youth at Swanendael," Meas said reverently. Falling Leaf translated for the group.

Maria triumphantly handed the pitcher to Margaret and then faced Meas while they waited on the others to get their drinks. "Maria," she said and pointed to herself.

"Maria," he repeated. "Meas," he said and pointed to himself. She had no trouble repeating it. Then he pointed to her again and said, "Cool Water." Maria pointed to the well. Meas shook his head. "Cool Water," he said again and pointed to her once more. This time she pointed to herself and repeated, "Cool Water."

The others refreshed themselves by simply drinking from the pitcher, and then the group began a leisurely stroll back to the assembly hall. Meas noted that during the pause at the well, Falling Leaf had acquired a smooth walking stick and a blade of coarse grass to chew on. Meas wasn't sure what his friend was up to, but he suspected some trick to compensate him for his mouse prank.

Sure enough, as Meas and Maria dallied along the path, the tall grass beside Maria started moving. It caught Maria's attention, and she stopped to see what it was. A slow hissing sound emerged from the grass. "Meas!" she screamed, and jammed into his body with such force that she shoved him off the path. She clung tightly to him while her frightened pleading kept beseeching him. "A snake! A snake!"

Falling Leaf sprang into action. In a tremendous flurry of strokes, he flailed the grass beside the path from which the hisses continued to sizzle. At last the sounds started moving off in the grass away from the path. Falling Leaf chased the hisses with loud whacks until his pursuit stopped at the creek.

"That's kind of scary," Falling Leaf declared on his return. "I always like to carry a stick when I'm in the woods, and it's sure good I had one tonight. Now that the scare is over, let's get on back to the house." So saying, Falling Leaf and Margaret led the way back to the house.

At the entrance to the house, Mary said, "It's time now that we ladies said our goodbyes. I can speak honestly for all three of us and say that you both have charmed us with your visit. Come to St. Mary's again ... soon." Mary Fendall shook hands with each of the two guests, then disappeared into the living quarters.

Margaret shook Meas's hand while he politely said, "Margaret, thank you."

When Maria stepped up and held her hand out to Meas, he clasped it in both his big strong hands and looked gently into her eyes. "Cool Water," he said, "thank you."

Maria paused briefly, and then responded. "Meas, come again." Then she tipped her head forward slightly so that her bonnet brushed across his shirt as she danced from the entryway into the living quarters.

Josias ushered Meas and Falling Leaf back into the assembly hall, and once again they sat together in a tight semicircle. "The ladies have been a most refreshing diversion," Josias began, "but I hope we may parley on several matters before you depart. You do not yet know this, but it is my wish that you be some distance from here when morning light breaks on the eastern shore. As far as the soldiers, the servants, and Philip Calvert are concerned, you two have been here only on a friendly visit. Nothing more. Do you understand?"

"And I can truthfully tell everyone that we have been pleasantly entertained, even Meas," Falling Leaf added. "Now, because Meas cannot understand what we say, and because we have some traveling to do before morning, could Meas stretch out on the floor and get some rest while we talk?"

"Certainly. We can get some blankets and perhaps a pillow for him if he likes," Josias offered.

"No. No. He will be fine on the floor with his pack." Falling Leaf explained the situation to Meas. Meas picked up his pack, stretched out on the floor and was soon fast asleep.

Josias leaned forward in his chair toward Falling Leaf. "Falling Leaf, there are a number of things you must understand about my situation. Three years ago a radical Protestant cabal succeeded in wresting the Maryland government away from Lord Baltimore. Only this year has the right to govern Maryland been restored to Lord Baltimore.[16] His hold on power is still tenuous enough that he dare not appoint a Catholic governor to run the colony. He appointed me governor and then appointed his half-brother, Philip Calvert, councilor, court justice, principal secretary, and judge of probate. So you can see that Philip is here to make sure that Lord Baltimore's wishes get carried out. I want you to understand that whatever you and I agree on does not necessarily have the backing of the Maryland government. It may not happen. There is only so much I can do.

"One of Lord Baltimore's urgent aims is to assert authority over the whole territory granted him in the Royal Charter to his province. As Lord Baltimore interprets this grant, it includes all the land between the south bank of the Potomack River, north to 40° latitude, and as far east as the Delaware Bay. Do you know where 40° latitude is?" Falling Leaf shrugged. "Can you find out and get the answer to me?" Falling Leaf nodded.

"Another matter. I have just recently received a complaint that a number of bondmen who still owe twenty pounds to their bondholders have escaped from Virginia plantations. The Virginia government seeks the assistance of the Maryland government to

---

[16] The second Lord Baltimore, Cecilius Calvert, son of the first Lord Baltimore, George Calvert.

capture these escapees and return them to Virginia. We think they probably have fled to the Dutch and will seek asylum there."

"Is twenty English pounds the exact amount owed by the servants?" queried Falling Leaf.

"That is the exact amount owed or at least claimed to be owed. But you know property owners can exaggerate their claims in these cases ... and often do. The Dutch have the same problem with Dutch bondmen who tire of their slavery under Dutch masters. Sometimes a bondholder will continually charge a bondman with some petty theft or neglect in the performance of his service and thus get his term of service extended. I probably wouldn't blame half of them for running away at the first chance to flee. The Dutch want the Maryland government to return their runaways to them, but we feel bondmen seeking asylum in Maryland should be tried in a Maryland court before we return them to possibly unjust masters.

"Another matter. A growing number of seemingly random Indian attacks are terrorizing Susquehannock and Delaware villages as well as European settlers along the northern borders of the Chesapeake." Falling Leaf sat bolt upright.

Josias continued. "The latest information we have is that five Maryland Indians have been killed by Oneida Mengwe warriors for being friends to Maryland and the Susquehannocks. Settlers everywhere are inflamed. The settlers cannot tell the difference between a friendly and an unfriendly Indian, and they want to kill all the Indians. Any small incident such as an Indian shooting a white man's dog for biting him threatens to blow up into an all-out war. Falling Leaf, do you have any idea what can be done to prevent such flaming carnage?"

"Governor Fendall, I am honored that you solicit my humble opinion. May I ask, why did not the Maryland Indians defend themselves when the Mengwe warriors attacked them? If the Maryland Indians knew who the attackers were, and they apparently did, why did they not pursue the Mengwe and punish the war parties until they sued for peace?"

"Falling Leaf, I am told that Mengwe warriors are the most treacherous and accomplished of Indian peoples when in battle. Even the threat of a Mengwe raid brings other nations to the council fire ready to sue for peace."

"Nonsense, Governor. Nonsense. Old wives' tales. I trow I would rather have yon sleeping Meas on my side than three of those cowardly Mengwe you fear ... if both sides carried the same guns.

"Do you not yet see, Governor? The Maryland Indians and the Susquehannocks fear the Mengwe because the Dutch are supplying the Mengwe with guns. They urge them to raid and plunder the enemies of the Dutch. The Dutch wish to weaken the Delawares and the Susquehannocks so they can control all the fur trade of the Chesapeake and the Delaware watersheds. The Susquehannocks do not fight back because they do not have guns.

"And why do they not have guns? Because Maryland and Virginia have treated the Indians so cruelly they are afraid that if they sell the Indians guns, the Indians will fall on them rather than bow and scrape before them in abject submission. If Maryland made a treaty with the Susquehannocks and armed them, the Susquehannocks would keep the Mengwe from raiding Maryland Indians or Maryland settlers. It goes without saying that Maryland settlers must be fair in their treatment of all Indians."

"Falling Leaf, there is much sense in what you say. But how do you think such a major shift in policy might be arranged?"

"Governor Fendall, I am just a backwoods trader that fears not the wrath of the pope or the king. My only concern is to make sure the deeds I do in the day do not keep me from sleep at night. You know better than I what is in the purview of the Maryland government and what will allow you to sleep at night."

"Falling Leaf, you place a great load on my shoulders that I would rather someone else tote. Let us think for a moment. If we were to find someone who could search out the king of the Susquehannocks, Maryland could negotiate a peace treaty with him in exchange for arms. Then somehow we would have to push a bill through the Maryland Council to pay for the guns."

Falling Leaf shook his head. "Friend Josias, you do not understand. The Indians do not have 'kings.' A chief does not gain his position by sword point and gunsmoke. He is chosen to lead a village because of the respect the people in that village have for him and his leadership. A village chief will always obtain the counsel of his councilors and the agreement of the people before agreeing to a formal treaty.

"No one chief can speak for a region or a certain group of Indians in that region. If one Indian sets himself up to be 'king' in the European sense, do not trust him. Working out a peace treaty with the Susquehannocks or, let us say, a 'mutual defense pact,' will take much travel and many moons before agreement can be reached. And the arrangements will have to be made by someone who knows the Mengwe tongue. The Susquehannocks speak Mengwe and not the Algonkian tongue used by the Delawares.

"You know that no bill promising guns to the Susquehannocks will ever make it through the Maryland Assembly. It would be far easier to get a bill through the Council and the Assembly to kill all the Susquehannocks than to arm them. Do you not think so?"

"Ah, Falling Leaf, sometimes the truth is hard to bear. Is there no solution then that may stop an Indian war from falling upon us? Is there nothing we can do?"

"Josias, I am hesitant to speak for the danger I fear it poses to you and your family. Nevertheless, I will speak and you may make the call. I have a close friend who speaks well the language of the Susquehannocks and who has traded with them for many years. You have never met him and do not know anything about him. But if a gun shipment intended for the Maryland militia happened to turn up several hundred guns short, and those guns were made available to my friend to 'sell' to the Susquehannocks, he might in the process of time arrange a mutual-defense 'understanding' between the Susquehannocks and the people of Maryland."

"And what kind of pay would your friend wish for the danger he would place himself in on all sides? Surely you know that one slip of the tongue or the foot might result in death."

"Aye. Aye. I have thought of that. Do not a few bitter herbs mixed with the meat make the stew more tasty? For his pay in this dangerous adventure, my friend would like to have a license to trade with the Indians. The license would of course have to be issued by the government of Maryland."

Josias Fendall rose from his chair and stretched out his hand to Falling Leaf. "Easily done," he promised. "Your friend shall have his license."

Falling Leaf rose from his chair and took the extended hand. "Take good care of Mary, Margaret, and Maria. And should the need arise, how shall I contact you?"

"Let Meas bring your notes to Maria. You trust him explicitly, do you not?"

"With my life," Falling Leaf said simply.

Falling Leaf shook Meas awake. The two grabbed their packs and their guns and disappeared into the night. When the morning light began to break over the eastern shore, the two were far out on the Chesapeake. Meas pulled steadily on the oars keeping his rhythm and propelling the canoe forward with long, powerful strokes. Falling Leaf relaxed easily in the other end of the canoe.

"Falling Leaf," Meas said, breaking the long silence, "I would like to learn English instead of Dutch."

Falling Leaf feigned surprise. "What could have brought on such a swift change in your tongue?" he mocked. "Maybe a mouse and a snake?"

The two friends laughed. "What was Mary telling you last night when we headed for the well?"

"She was telling me what kind of men she wanted the girls to marry. She wants the husbands to have black hair except where they pull it out on their face and forehead. Each one must have black eyes. They must be tall and strong, about thirty years of age ..."

"Falling Leaf, I think you would like a dunking in the Chesapeake this cheery morn," Meas teased. Then he asked more seriously, "How did the visit go after I went off to sleep?"

Falling Leaf groaned. "Josias is a good fellow, but he knows nothing about Indians. He still sees everything like a Schwannek.

"Meas, look at this beautiful bay and all the surrounding land. On a clear day you can scarcely see across the bay, and it is impossible to see either end of the bay if you are floating in the middle. How much land is there between the south side of the Potomack River and 40° latitude?

"I do not know where 40° latitude is, but let us imagine it goes north as far as the top of the Chesapeake Bay. Is that land full of people—Indians or Schwanneks? If you owned all that land, would you be fighting with your neighbors over the land between the Chesapeake Bay and the Delaware Bay too? Yet that is exactly what Lord Baltimore wants to do. It is as though the Schwannek reaches for yet another glass of liquor even as he reels and staggers from the swill he has already swallowed."

"Falling Leaf, has last night's wine addled your mind?" Meas stopped paddling. "Look at the bay. Do you see the expanse of water? Let its vastness rest your mind. Listen to the land. Do you hear its harmony and rhythm? Let its music calm your troubled spirit. Breathe the air. Let its freshness sweep over you. This land is all yours. It is all mine.

"I know not this Lord Baltimore, but I trow that he does not enjoy this land half so much as you and I. And the day will come when neither we nor he shall enjoy it at all. Let us revel in the land today. Tomorrow we can no longer conquer its beauty." Meas laid his paddle

CQ 202

on his lap, and the two sat together in the canoe, entranced in an enchanted land.

Slowly Meas began to speak, haltingly at first, backing up and relining a few times, then satisfied with the sound and the thought, he went further. Falling Leaf studied Meas and then listened while Meas's words added to the spell of the surrounding grandeur.

Cool Water

Today I may drink from the cup of life,
I may draw from the bottom swallowing sorrow and
    strife,
I may sip from the top of the foam and the froth,
Or I may stir the cup and drink it all up.
But what I want is only Cool Water.

I cannot drink from yesterday's cup today,
I have already poured it out along life's way.
I splashed some on the sand as I carelessly played,
I dipped some for a friend as he stumbled and swayed.
But when I drank what was left, it was Cool Water.

"I trow that Lord Baltimore does not enjoy this land half as much as you and I."   —Meas

Nor can I borrow from the cup of tomorrow
Any healing for suffering and sorrow.
I cannot expend the morrow's cup on a hurting friend,
Nor on tomorrow's cup myself depend,
All I have to spend today is today's Cool Water.

At length, Meas picked up his oar and resumed paddling. Then he said casually, "If you want to know where 40° latitude is, I can tell you. The captain of the *Kalmar Nyckel* told Mattahorn that 40° was north of Tinicum Island. Strutting Turkey told Mattahorn that where Neshaminy Creek enters the Lenape River is very close to 40° latitude."[17]

"Meas!" Falling Leaf exclaimed. "You are a genius. That means Lord Baltimore claims the land as far west as the Lenape Bay plus all the land on the western shore of the Lenape River from Swanendael to beyond Fort Altena. Oh, Meas! This will be great sport to watch the great Lord choke and gag while he tries to stuff that much more land down his gluttonous gullet."

Meas wavered, "I must confess it amuses me to watch the great blue heron push his long neck in and out and snatch his head back and forth as he struggles to get his meal down. What I fear is that it will not be such great sport to be the frog swallowed by the heron.

"Falling Leaf, grab your paddle and give me a hand. I do not like the look of the sky or the feel of the air. It looks to me as though a bad storm will break upon us from the east in only a few hours."

The storm Meas forecast, though intense, soon passed on and the travelers continued their journey toward Meas's home, Koketotoka's village on the Siconece. English lessons began each morning and

[17] The actual reading includes the present city of Philadelphia, Pennsylvania.

continued till noon. The pattern was always the same—talk, mimic; talk, mimic; talk, mimic. The lessons never seemed to last long and always covered objects and activities familiar to Meas. Meas progressed rapidly.

Falling Leaf and Meas arrived at the village rested and fresh on the fourth morning after leaving St. Mary's City. It had been an easy trip for them, with Meas often taking time to point out special little plants and animals he had discovered during his Vision Quest. The two shared these rare delights together. Meas could easily have wandered ... for a month ... or a year. But Falling Leaf pushed onward. He had made a bargain and he aimed to keep it.

Meas and Falling Leaf found things in a frightful state at the village. In a tempestuous fit the storm had tossed sixteen forlorn Schwanneks onto the cape. Somehow Koketotoka and Meoppitas discovered them and took them to their village, where they shared with the survivors what food and comforts they had.

Neither the villagers nor the survivors could explain a word to each other, and by the time Meas and Falling Leaf arrived, the village had deteriorated into an armed camp.

"Koketotoka!" exclaimed Meas when he found his bleary-eyed brother. "What is going on? The Lenape do not treat strangers as enemies. We do not treat a visitor in our midst as a prisoner of war. Why do you stand over them with guns and bind them with ropes? Why do you not treat them as friends and help them on their way?"

Koketotoka glared at Meas and Falling Leaf through swollen eyelids. "Get out of here," he growled. "Let me alone."

Falling Leaf and Meas made their way to the dejected captives. "Hello," said Falling Leaf as he moved quietly among them. He placed his hand on each one as he spoke. "I am Falling Leaf. Everything will be all right now," he reassured them.

"How so?" one woman screamed. "I had rather hoe tobacco five more years than be caught in this den of savage—" Suddenly she caught herself. Someone had spoken to her in English, and it was not just part of her dream. "Sir, can you really help us?" the woman begged.

"If you will calm down and answer a few questions, I will see what I can do to help you. As it is, it looks like God alone has brought you here, and God Himself may have to rescue you. Where did you come from and to where did you want to go?"

"God did not bring us here," the woman said tartly. "Those two shifty-eyed scalawags tied to yon tree brought us here. They took our passage money and intended to dump us off here and flee. God did send them here, and they should suffer many stripes," the woman noted sarcastically, "but those two sneaking scamps brought us here and not God. We be but the poor of the earth, and God knows we have suffered twice for our sins already. We do not deserve another stripe. Check them over and see if they don't have five shillings apiece on them. That's right, three and one-half pounds sterling."

"That may sound like a steep price for your fare," Falling Leaf agreed, "but they have risked much to bring you here, and as of now twenty pounds sterling might be useless to them. I suspect that if they were caught anywhere from here to Virginia they would swing freely. Where did they promise to take you?"

"We came from down Virginia way, and they promised to set us off in a beautiful land the Dutch had bought from the Indians thirty years ago."

"What is the name of the place?" pressed Falling Leaf.

"Swanendael, the Valley of the Swans. I think it is such a beautiful name," the woman mused.

"Do you know Dutch?" Falling Leaf asked. The woman shook her head. "Madam, the Dutch also have another name for the place. They call it Whorekill. And I have big news for you. You have arrived at Whorekill regardless of who brought you here."

"Oh, what a horrible name! Oh, what a horrible place!" And then a thought struck the woman. "Do you ...?" She tried again. "Do you mean these beastly savages are going to ...?" But the woman just couldn't get it out.

"Then you do not wish to stay here?" asked Falling Leaf. The woman shook her head vigorously. "If you do not want to stay here in this beautiful land, where would you like to go?"

"I cannot go back to Virginia," began the woman slowly, "and I am afraid Maryland would only turn us back over to Virginia. I guess I will still try my luck with the Dutch. Do they not have a city called New Amstel? Might we go there?"

"Madam, why do you not wish to go back to Virginia if that is where you are from? Or perhaps you would like to return to your home in ... I shall guess Ireland?"

"Aye, you're a good guesser. But, nay, I shall never return to Ireland except they carry me there in a box. I have suffered much in Virginia, but I am still alive and there is yet a better life to live than in Ireland. For a poor one such as I, even hope is dead in Ireland. And can you not spare me the bruises of telling why I have fled the tobacco fields of Virginia? Sometimes I wondered if 'twould not be better to be a black slave than a white bondwoman. Spare me.

"Nevertheless, if it will help you, the fourteen of us, by the reckoning of our bondmen, owe twenty pounds sterling to Virginia masters. By our reckoning, we owe nothing. In the minds of our masters, the harder we work, the larger the debt grows. And now that we have run away, if our Virginia masters can ever get their hands on us again, the rest of our lives will be short, but horrible."

"Madam, do you speak only for yourself, or do the rest of your companions all share your same feelings?" inquired Falling Leaf. He did not need to wait for an answer. A chorus of sighs and murmurs and yeas from the thirteen huddled by the cookfire in their rags gave assent to the woman's plea. One man boldly declared, "I'm with her 200%."

"Very well. I shall try to see what I can do to arrange a trip for you to New Amstel. Is anyone sick or do any of you need care? How about food and drink?" Falling Leaf again stepped around to examine each prisoner. Despite their worries, they assured him that they had survived the wreck without any broken bones and were in "pretty fair health."

Meas, Meoppitas, and Falling Leaf now stepped off to one side to sort things out. They walked easily along the bank of the Siconece.

"Meoppitas," Meas asked, "why are these people so rudely held?"

"When we first found them, the fourteen were ready to kill the two you found tied to the tree. Then when we brought them here and gave them food and tried to care for them, they tried to turn on us and kill us. If I had not caught two of them trying to stab Koketotoka, drunk, of course, he would already be dead. It's so confusing. Why do they want to kill us when we rescued them? What in the world shall we do with them now?"

"Meoppitas," inquired Falling Leaf, "could you tell anything about the boats that brought these people here? Did all the people survive the wreck, or were some of the people lost in the wreck? It seems strange to me that none of the fourteeen have any broken bones, bad bruises, or cracked heads."

"No," said Meoppitas, "we found nothing on the shore except drenched survivors—no dead bodies, no wreckage, no supplies. How do you explain it?"

"Did the two have any silver on them?"

"Oh yes. They had quite a pile between them. Seventy coins to be exact. We took it from them, and Koketotoka guards it well."

Falling Leaf's mouth fell open. Meas seemed unfazed. "Then Meoppitas and I must talk to Koketotoka," he said. "Falling Leaf, why do you not amuse yourself with a visit to Swanendael and the cape while Meoppitas and I spend some time with Koketotoka? We have a number of things we must work out, so you have plenty of time."

Then Meas added in English, "Goodbye. I love you. Thank you. Come again." The two friends smiled at each other and then Falling Leaf continued down the Siconece while Meas and Meoppitas turned and walked slowly back to the village.

"Meoppitas," Meas asked, "are you ready to be the village headman? Koketotoka is drowning himself in a sea of liquor. I fear he shall die before he succeeds in downing all the liquor he can get."

"No, little brother, I do not wish to be the headman. It is a rock too big for me to lift. And if the rock should fall while I am trying to lift it, it will crush my foot."

The two walked quietly back to the village and then into Koketotoka's wigwam. Meas and Meoppitas sat cross-legged on the dirt floor before him. All three stared silently at each other. Koketotoka would not meet the eyes of his guests with his own, but evaded their pitying, quizzical looks in his direction.

Finally Koketotoka broke the silence. "Is that you, little brother? Have you come home at last?"

"Yes, elder brother, it is I, Meas. But the one my eyes see is not my elder brother. What I see is but the empty skin and bones of a once noble brother. His spirit has flown away to the source of the Lenape River and there wanders restlessly, awaiting a summons to return to the Siconece.

"Elder brother, have your eyes been pasted shut with matter for so long that you cannot see? Let me pry open your eyes and wipe away the matter, and I will show you what is happening. Your children waste away without purpose. The women grow weary and hungry without food or care or love. And at childbirth they have not the strength to bring forth.

"The old men no longer dream of Tamenend or Eesanques or Mattahorn, and if they do not dream dreams, they cannot tell them to the young men. Strength and honor hide from the young men, for they have no spirit and care only for the pleasures of the moment.

The young maidens sing only the songs of death and mourning in the Land of the Dawn. The sachem fails to pray the ancient prayer of the Lenape.

"Elder brother, like a body racked by unremitting fever, our village wastes away. Some are leaving. Some are dying. Some remain in body, but they are dead of spirit. All the time fewer and fewer people are left to hunt and fish and tend the fields of maize and squash and beans. Even now the Schwanneks sit in the trees or circle overhead waiting for us to die so they can pick our bones.

"Koketotoka, where is the spirit of Eesanques who rallied his people to defend this treasured land?

"Koketotoka, can you not call back your spirit from the far reaches of the Lenape River and follow it once more? Meoppittas and I shall await your decision."

No one disturbed the three brothers while they sat waiting. No one even thought of food. Occasionally, they passed a pipe from one to the other and smoked it for a time. The afternoon passed and slid on into the night. Late that night Koketotoka rose from his seat and left the wigwam without saying a word. Several more hours passed before he returned.

When Koketotoka entered the wigwam again, he smelled of newly cut grass and the aroma of pine needles. His skin shone as it glistened with fresh oil. He resumed his seat, and once more the three brothers took turns smoking as the pipe passed from one to the other. Then Koketotoka tapped the ashes from the pipe and placed it in his pouch.

Koketotoka rose from his seat and led the way out of the wigwam. Then he turned to the east where the morning light broke its pact with the darkness of night. Koketotoka raised both arms toward the light and extended the longer two fingers of each hand while pinning the two shorter ones with his thumb. He began to chant:

Great Spirit,
Maker of the sky, the earth, the sun, the moon,
Keeper of the spirits of the fish, the birds, the animals, the trees, the
stones.
Guardian of the Four Winds,
Thank you for bringing light again to the People of the Dawn.
Thank you for sending fire to warm our houses and cook our food.
Thank you for bringing water to inspire the ground and to quench our
thirst.
Thank you for the ground to grow the maize and the deer to give us
meat.
For the ancient song of the Lenape,
For the everlasting sun that rises this day,
I, Koketotoka, a sachem of the Lenni Lenape, thank you.

When Koketotoka had finished his chant, he took a small pinch of tobacco from his pouch with his left hand and sprinkled it on the ground before him. Then he stood motionless with his right arm still raised and his two fingers pointed toward the horizon.

Meas and Meoppitas slipped quietly away to get some rest.

The village was not the same place when Meas awoke at noon. Some women were preparing food. Some were gone working in the fields. Several men worked at repairing wigwams while others fished. The prisoners had been moved to a clean spot and seemed more content with their lot. Children played along the Siconece while Meas bathed. One old man entertained several young boys under a tree, telling them stories.

Before long, a warrior showed up and told Meas that Koketotoka wished to see him. Falling Leaf and Meoppitas were already there when Meas arrived. Koketotoka bade Meas enter and be seated with a simple sweep of his hand while he continued his conversation with Falling Leaf.

Soon Koketotoka turned to Meas and said, "Little brother, this is what I have decided to do with the prisoners. I want you and Meoppitas to go to New Amstel as quickly as you can. Tell Jitter Hen Alrick that the late storm has tossed fourteen prisoners upon us. Tell him that the prisoners claim to be runaway bondservants from Virginia, but that they also thought their destination to be Swanendael. Tell him we are uncertain why the English might be wanting to send runaways to Swanendael. The prisoners tell us they wish to seek asylum among the Dutch at New Amstel.

"Koketotoka is uncertain what to do with the prisoners. He is thinking of sending them back to Virginia if the Virginians will pay him a decent price for the trouble he has incurred upon himself. You have traveled with Falling Leaf and watched him trade for several years. By now you should know how to trade with the Dutch. I want twenty-eight pounds of good British money for the release of the fourteen prisoners."

"And what shall I demand for the two?" asked Meas.

"We are not yet certain what to do with them. But for now do not mention those two to the Dutch."

"How shall I tell them to pay us? Will they not want to see the prisoners before they give us the money?"

"I will let you work out the details of the exchange with Jitter Hen. Falling Leaf will stay here with me to find out more from the two weasels who brought the prisoners here. See what you can do."

As Meas and Meoppitas rose to leave, Falling Leaf called out, "No English class today."

"Goodbye," Meas answered. Then he pointed to Koketotoka. "He good chief."

Meas and Meoppitas spent the next two days traveling overland to New Amstel. Here Meas again knew the land very well. This time he felt impelled to push forward. Koketotoka had said, "As quick as you can."

When Jitter Hen Alrick found out Meas and Meopittas had arrived from Swanendael to see him, he had them graciously cared for, laid aside his other activities, and called for Fat Pig, Two Tongue, and several other officials to come to his headquarters. When all was in readiness, he brought Meas and Meoppitas into the courtroom.

Meas told of the storm-tossed visitors from Virginia who had been cast upon their shores by the storm. He made sure that Jitter Hen understood Koketotoka's uncertainty as to exactly how or why the supposed refugees had arrived at Swanendael. Then he gave them Koketotoka's decision. Koketotoka would return the fourteen prisoners to Virginia if Virginia would pay him enough for his trouble.

Fat Pig jumped right in. "Had Koketotoka named any price that he might accept from the Virginians?"

"Yes, in fact he had," admitted Meas, "but I am not sure Koketotoka would want me to divulge this information to the Dutch. And what difference does it make to the Dutch anyway since the bondmen owe their debts to the Long Knives and not to the Dutch?"

Fat Pig laughed. "And just why would Koketotoka send you and Meoppitas here if he did not think we might be interested in paying for the release of the captives? Koketotoka must be far brighter than his half-brother." Here Fat Pig turned a knowing glance toward Jitter Hen and Two Tongue.

Meas waited for the smirks to disappear from the faces in the courtroom. His face betrayed nothing of the sting of Fat Pig's barb. "There is no doubt that Koketotoka is far brighter than I," he parried. "For he is a true Lenape and I am but half Dutchman." Meas waited for his thrust to sink in. "Nevertheless," he continued, "being half Dutch has a nice side. When I am among the Dutch, I am treated civilly as being next of kin. Therefore I shall return your kindness and tell you that Koketotoka will take thirty-six English pounds in exchange for the fourteen prisoners."

Jitter Hen choked. Fat Pig gasped. "Now we know you're crazy," sputtered Fat Pig. "Not even shipwrecked dukes would be worth that much. Tell Koketotoka not a shilling more than twenty pounds." Jitter Hen nodded his head in approval.

"Then I shall tell Koketotoka the Dutch were not interested in the prisoners, and he shall have to let them go to Maryland or Virginia."

"Why would Koketotoka offer them to Maryland?" Jitter Hen asked quickly.

"Because both Maryland and Virginia seem very interested in what happens on the Siconece, and both seem very anxious to obtain Koketotoka's friendship," Meas answered at once.

Things seemed to stall for a few minutes, and then Two Tongue came up with an idea. Jitter Hen, Fat Pig, and Two Tongue put their heads together and talked in low tones. Then Jitter Hen broke the silence. "We have decided to make Koketotoka another offer, one that we believe will appeal to him. This is our best and final offer. We will give twenty-one pounds of good silver and one barrel of our finest rum in exchange for the fourteen prisoners. That is one and one-half pounds per captive plus several pounds worth of rum."

Meas did not hesitate. "Friends, I am delighted to tell you that Koketotoka will not allow one drop of liquor in our village ... ever again. And I warn you that if you or anyone else brings a drum of liquor into our village on the Siconece, Koketotoka will stave the end in. And as far as the captives go, Koketotoka's best offer is two pounds per head. I will give you till first light of tomorrow morning to decide. Then Meoppitas and I shall return to the Siconece."

Fat Pig glowered. "Of a truth he is one-half Dutchman, probably three-quarters Dutchman. Meas should be working for us," he joked.

"Not so fast," Two Tongue butted in. "Meas is a liar. Koketotoka likes his rum better than you, Hinoyossa. And it will take more than this lying savage to convince me Koketotoka has turned dry."[18]

---

[18] In 1657 a storm wrecked two boats on Cape Henlopen. Fourteen survivors were ransomed from the Indians by Dutch officials. The actual ransom price is not known.

The next morning the Dutch agreed to pay the twenty-eight pounds sterling for the fourteen captives. Fat Pig and Two Tongue Boyer then floated Meas and Meoppitas down the Lenape River to Swanendael, where they exchanged the silver cargo for the runaway debtors.

As the ship sailed away with the captives, Meas stood there holding the bag of silver coins. Falling Leaf clapped him on the back.

"Meas! What a splendid job! Meoppitas told me how you twisted Fat Pig's tail and made him squeal. A full-blooded Dutchman could not have done it better. To extract twenty-eight pounds sterling from Dutchmen is drawing maple syrup out of an oak tree. Why, they had sooner parted with twenty-eight of their teeth."

"Why did Jitter Hen and Fat Pig want the captives so badly?" Meas asked.

"Meas, the Dutch sell thirty to forty thousand beaver a year by controlling all the trade along the Lenape River. This includes the beaver that come from inland through the Susquehannocks. They do not want Maryland or Virginia to siphon that trade off through the Chesapeake Bay. Neither will the Dutch allow Maryland or Virginia to control the trade on the Lenape River by establishing a fort on Cape Henlopen or at Swanendael. Mark my word. The Dutch will sing any song and pay any price to keep the English from building a fort at Swanendael.

"I think the Dutch will soon restore the fort at Swanendael so they can exclude the English from all the trade on the Lenape River. And if the Dutch have a fort once again on the cape, they will feel able to protect settlers at Swanendael. It is only a matter of time and ... of who gets there first."

"Falling Leaf," asked Meas, "have you explained this to Koketotoka?"

"Meas, I did not need to explain it to Koketotoka. He knows. All we need to do now is help Koketotoka carry out his plans. He will lead us. You can be proud of your brother."

"And what might the plans of Koketotoka be?"

"Meas, we will have more time to talk as we journey. Koketotoka has given us a job to do. You and I must deliver the two weasels to the governor of Maryland, none other than Josias Fendall. Might you be interested in visiting St. Mary's City?"

"Certainly. When do we start? I am anxious to see Cool Water again."

"We will start our journey by morning light."

As soon as all was in readiness, the two prisoners, bound together by ropes, marched on ahead while Meas and Falling Leaf followed a short distance behind on the familiar trail.

They were barely out of earshot when Meas returned to the subject of the day before. "Falling Leaf, what are Koketotoka's plans? I suspect they have something to do with me."

"You are right. Koketotoka wants to establish a trading post on the Siconece, and he wants you to run it."

"Falling Leaf, that's impossible. No Lenape has ever run a trading post. We are only hunters and fishermen."

"Meas, maybe it's true that no Indian has run a trading post such as the white man runs. But the Indians ran far-flung trading networks long before the white man ever came. Why cannot a Lenape run a trading post?" And Falling Leaf added with a twinkle in his blue eyes, "Remember, Meas, you are one-half Dutchman and a very shrewd one at that. I think Koketotoka has a wonderful idea. With a little help from the Dutch and the English and maybe a Swede or two, your post should prosper."

"Falling Leaf, you tell me the Dutch will help me because I am half Dutch. I can believe the Swedes may help because you are my friend. But why would the English want to help me?"

"Meas, it is very simple. You will have an English wife. But really, you misunderstand why anyone will trade with you. People do not trade with each other because they are relatives or of the same race. They trade because each of you values what the other person offers more than what you own. Take, for example, a fine deerskin. Let us say that you have a fine deerskin. You can go out in the forest at any time and kill another deer to obtain another deerskin. On the other hand, your wife does not have a copper cooking kettle. So I, the trader, come by your wigwam to visit you. I have a copper cooking kettle. You agree that if I give you the copper kettle, you will give me the deerskin. I know that if you give me the deerskin, I can trade it for two copper kettles when I get back to my supplier. So we are both very happy with our trade. You did not trade with me because you are my friend, although it is nice to trade with friends, but you traded with me because I had a copper kettle you wanted more than you wanted the deerskin. You were very happy. I was happy."

"Falling Leaf, where is your copper kettle? I will soon have you the deerskin. Let us trade."

"Ha! Ha! You are a Dutchman sure enough. You would snap up a copper kettle too cheap. My proposed trade was only to show you why people trade when they are free to do so. It is not always so simple. Perhaps your wigwam is four days' journey from New Amstel where they would also trade you a copper kettle for a deerskin. You would surely trade with me because I have it right there and you would not have to deliver the deerskin to New Amstel. But suppose that if you took the deerskin to New Amstel, Two Tongue would offer you the copper kettle plus a pint of liquor in exchange for your deerskin, what would you do then?"

"Leave town."

"Excellent! That would be the best thing you could do. Alas, many would take the liquor and wind up paying two or three deerskins for the kettle. So you will not take the liquor, and you will trade with me for just one deerskin. But what if you are the trader and you know that the Indian will not trade with you without the liquor. Would you then sell him the liquor and take two deerskins in the trade?"

"Falling Leaf, I could not sell my brother the liquor at any price. Some things are worth more to me than a copper kettle or two deerskins. If I knew that I would destroy my friend and bring his wife and children to utter ruin, it would haunt me night and day. Is not killing another with a bottle just as much murder as plunging a knife into his heart? And is not taking an extra deerskin from a man when he is drunk just as much stealing as taking a deerskin from him when he is sober?"

"Meas, you are right. I believe the same and do not trade liquor. You must know that I do miss many trades because of liquor's mighty power. And no matter how many deerskins I might gain and how much land I might own, I will not sell liquor. But there is another side. Because I do not sell liquor, there are many Indians who trust me. They know I will not steal from them, so they favor me with their trade. So not selling liquor has two sides to the trader. It makes trading more complicated than just swapping a deerskin for a copper kettle.

"There is another thing that tangles up a trade. Suppose Two Tongue put a gun to your head and said, 'Give me two deerskins for the kettle.' Now what would you do, Meas?"

"I suppose I would give him the deerskins. But I would try to trade with someone else the next time."

"And suppose Jitter Hen would not allow you to trade with anyone else. Suppose Jitter Hen required all traders in your area to have a license from him or else he would lock the trader in jail. And suppose that to get the license to trade, you have to buy your goods from Jitter Hen and sell your skins to him. What would you do in that situation, Meas?"

"I do not know. Maybe nothing. During my Vision Quest I did nothing for many years. I enjoyed that, except for the loneliness. A wife and children would not take that much if we lived as the Lenape used to live. Maybe I would do nothing."

"You had better not get a wife and children if you want to live on nothing," said Falling Leaf.

"I believe I can provide for a wife and many children," Meas assured Falling Leaf. "But I have a more urgent problem. How are we going to get these two weasels ahead of us across the Chesapeake Bay?"

"Meas, you surely recognize the two chaps ahead of us as the ones who brought our good fortune to the Siconece, do you not?"

Here Falling Leaf jingled the heavy bag of coins slung over his shoulder. "Twenty-eight pounds!" he clucked.

"I can help you carry your heavy burden if you like. Or we could split it," Meas offered. "Whatever happened to the seventy shillings the woman claimed the two weasels stole from the passengers? Koketotoka was guarding it."

"Koketotoka gave it back to the two. Koketotoka said it was the only honorable thing to do if these men had justly earned it; 'twas theirs. He would not steal from guests who had done him no harm," said Falling Leaf.

"The weasels claim they were traders hired by Virginia planters to deliver fourteen bondmen to Koketotoka's village. I think they are nought but lying pirates caught by Virginia and ready for the noose. Someone probably offered to slip the noose for the two if they would deliver fourteen bondmen to Swanendael.

"Virginia probably holds some more of their mates in a dark gaol to secure delivery. If anything goes wrong with the voyage, which it has, it's the noose for the lot and nobody in Virginia will know anything about any settlement at Swanendael. So we aim to give those two a truth test and see if they're lying or not."

Meas laughed. "Is it simple?"

"They devised a truth test in Maryland so they could tell the difference between a Catholic and a Protestant. It works like this. The accused kneels on the floor. They place a pot of gold right in front of him, but just beyond his reach. Then the one being tested is told to pray for five minutes and ask God to judge him. While the supplicant prays, the examiner noisily takes the coins out of the pot and carries them to another room. When the five minutes are over and the prayer is ended, the judge gives the verdict.

"If the supplicant closes his left eye when he prays, he's Catholic. If he closes his right eye when he prays, he's Protestant. If he prays with both eyes open, he's lying. If he prays with both eyes closed, he's telling the truth. If the supplicant is Protestant or Catholic, he's lying half the time, and the other half he's telling the truth."

Falling Leaf laughed heartily at his own joke. "We shall see. We shall see," sang Falling Leaf as they trudged along.

"Falling Leaf, you mentioned earlier that I would marry an English wife. Is that possible? Do you really think Mary would allow Cool Water to be my wife and live with me on the Siconece?"

"Meas, I see it is time to turn from jesting to more careful talk lest I unintentionally wound my friend. Who can tell what a woman might decide? If I could understand a woman or the mother of one, I might already be hitched up myself.

"Meas, might it not be far easier for you to take a dusky swallow than a white dove? Cool Water does not know Lenape, and she might become very lonely on the Siconece. The Schwanneks would have nothing to do with her if she married you. Life could be very hard for Cool Water and for you and even for your papooses."

"Falling Leaf, let me tell you a few things," argued Meas. "It is not uncommon among Indian peoples to take captives in war and marry them to replace a loved one who has died from sickness or been killed in battle. We have blood from many different nations among us. I myself am evidence that there is white man's blood mixed with the blood of the Lenape. The Lenape will accept Cool Water if I bring her to the Siconece. She will be one of us."

"Meas, what you say is true. Cool Water would be accepted by the Lenape. But what I am telling you is also true. Cool Water and you both will be hated by the Schwanneks if you take her home to the Siconece with you. In the eyes of the Schwanneks, it is one thing for a white man to have an Indian woman. That's not so bad. But it's quite another thing for an Indian man to marry a white woman. Schwanneks think that for a savage heathen to be so proud as to marry a white woman is a disgrace to the whole white race. Meas, I warn you, if you marry Cool Water, you will be hated by the Schwanneks, and Cool Water will be scorned by them for marrying you.

"Nevertheless, if it is the white dove you want, I will ask Mary for you. Unless, of course, you want to try out your own English when you propose to carry Cool Water off to the Siconece."

"Falling Leaf, I can learn English and I will." Meas said no more for some time while he made his way through the forest. When the shadows began to lengthen and the whole group began to tire of the journey, they came upon the bank of the Nanticoke River at exactly the place Meas and Falling Leaf had left it two weeks before.

Then Meas spoke once more. "Falling Leaf, it is the white dove that I want. I will leave the dusky swallows for you to choose from. And if, like yon two weasels bound by ropes of our making, the Schwanneks be so bound by ropes of their own making that they must hobble through life in hatred and unhappiness, there is nothing I can do about it. But Cool Water and I will 'cut the vine that does tangle and twine, and swing free in a glorious arc of liberty, there on the Siconece.' "

"Meas," Falling Leaf asked, "are we not coming to the slip where we stowed our canoe?"

"Yes," Meas replied. " 'Tis very close. But do you not wish to leave the canoe hidden till morning? We may have to find another larger one so we can all cross the Chesapeake together."

"No, Meas. Launch the canoe so that all lies ready to whisk us away on a moment's notice. I sense danger in yon two weasels and feel the truth test shall be upon us before the morning light."

Narrated by Glikkikan

"Owechela, Falling Leaf was a real friend to Meas, wasn't he?" I asked. "Falling Leaf understood the ways of the Schwanneks and the ways of the Lenape. He did what was right and treated everyone fairly. He was a good man.

"Owechela, do you think Falling Leaf carried the Spirit of Tamenend in the Land of the Dawn?"

Owechela pondered the question in silence for a long time before he answered me. "Glikkikan," he said, "that is a very hard question for me to answer. In many ways Falling Leaf and Meas were alike—kind, honest, fair, just, and intelligent. But in many ways they were very different in race, heritage, learning, and values.

"Glikkikan, you ask, 'Did Falling Leaf carry the Spirit of Tamenend in the Land of the Dawn?' It is hard to see into the heart of another and to feel of his spirit. Usually, we may judge a man's spirit only by what he does.

"Glikkikan, listen well and see if you can tell. When the red man be forsaken and all his land be taken, will Falling Leaf with the red stand firm? Or will he to his own return?"

Meas and Cool Water

As told by Owechela

Falling Leaf busied himself setting up camp and preparing an evening meal while Meas went for the canoe and brought it to the bank of the campsite. Falling Leaf arranged the campsite so that the prisoners slept only ten paces from the canoe while he and Meas slept seventy paces beyond the prisoners. At dusk he carelessly threw the twenty-eight pounds of silver on the ground beside his pack. Falling Leaf checked the short rope that bound the ankle of one prisoner to the ankle of the other. The rope showed no signs of fraying, and the knot seemed taut. He and Meas seated themselves comfortably on the ground facing the two weasels. The weasels sat on a log with their legs bound together by one arm's-length rope. They shifted uneasily on the log while they cast furtive glances at their captors.

"Okay," Falling Leaf began, "the moment of truth has come. As you two can probably guess, we have a problem. The canoe will only hold two and there are four of us here. What are we going to do? Do either of you have any ideas?"

Neither captive spoke. "Well," Falling Leaf mused, "what are the possibilities? I guess we could shoot the weasels, take their seventy shillings, and be gone. That would be an end to our problem."

"Not a good idea," said the weasel with the bushy Blackbeard, bald head, and bulbous nose.

"I wonder why it would not be a good idea to rid the world of such vermin," Falling Leaf continued as though thinking to himself. "Probably Blackbeard[19] and Neck Scar have taken many a life when it was convenient and in their power. And what is a life anyway? Only a bullet or a blow and it is over. Buzzards or fish eat the dead and they are gone. The woods and the sea are large, and dead men cannot defend themselves. Who cares about these two? Would not two villains dispatched be a good riddance and the world a better place for their disappearance?"

Here Falling Leaf broke off his musing in English and spoke to Meas in Lenape. "Be on your guard," he warned. "The weasels are desperate and may try anything."

Meas rose to his feet and moved between the two and the canoe. He took his tomahawk in his hand.

While Falling Leaf talked to Meas in Lenape, Blackbeard spoke a few words to Neck Scar in a tongue Falling Leaf did not understand.

Falling Leaf continued his musing. "I know fourteen ransomed bondmen would be most happy if they were assured these thieves had disappeared and seventy shillings were returned to them. But why would I return the shillings to the bondmen? I could more easily keep the seventy shillings than return them. Who would ever know? Who would ever care?" Falling Leaf closed his eyes, deep in thought.

Blackbeard interrupted Falling Leaf's reverie. "Perhaps killing someone is not as simple as you think. Even though the victim may be helpless before my knife or gun, there is still something awful about killing a man. 'Tis true that I have taken the lives of several men, but

---

[19] Edward Teach, a notorious pirate (1680-1718).

still, 'tis not an easy thing to do."

"Tell me more," said Falling Leaf. "Do you not think it would be a simple thing for me to allow Meas to cleave your skull with his tomahawk and take your scalp in sweet memory of his valor?"

At this suggestion Blackbeard and Neck Scar both twisted around for one glimpse of the powerful Meas towering behind them in the gathering gloom. They quickly stared straight ahead at Falling Leaf, who lay in front of them nonchalantly chewing on a blade of grass.

"Yes. I mean nay," said Blackbeard hastily. "It is not an easy thing to kill a helpless man. Somehow that last cry for mercy, that last look of fear, haunts one long after the deed so drear."

"And why does the deed worry you long after the helpless one is dead? Would it be easier for me to kill you in a fair fight if we both held guns and knives? Would it be easier for me to take your life if I pointed a cannon at you and blasted you apart from another ship?"

"Aye," said Blackbeard hopefully. "It is easier on one's conscience that way."

"But what if I have no conscience?" insisted Falling Leaf. "Conscience is only a constraint of the mind brought on us by religion. One only has to shake off the shackles of such upbringing, and then he is free to kill at will."

"That is not so," argued Blackbeard. "Only a fool will argue that a man can kill another innocent man and not know that he is doing wrong. I swear that such a deed will haunt him till the fires of hell engulf him."

"Come, come, Blackbeard. You are letting fear craze your mind. The Lenape, like Meas there, know nothing about hellfire. See, hell is only a warp of your mind, a product of your upbringing. I still think the best thing to do is to murder you two and make off with your ill-gotten shillings."

"Well," said Blackbeard, "I see there is no hope for us. God will deal with you, and may He have mercy on us."

"Do you believe in God?" inquired Falling Leaf.

"God! I cannot escape from Him. No matter how hard I tried, the knowledge of right and wrong pursued me, and I could not evade this dastardly guilt when I murdered and lied and stole. Now I fear God has sunk my ship and hell awaits me, for I have not done what I knew to be right."

"Blackbeard, I believe now you are telling the truth for the first time since we met. So there are several things I would like to know before Meas knocks the wind out of you. How came you to Cape Henlopen?"

"Ah! Perhaps there is a chance we are worth more to you alive than dead," Blackbeard suggested. "And if that savage killed me now, you would never know the answers to your questions. You would never obtain the ransom I am prepared to pay for my freedom."

Falling Leaf cut Blackbeard off. "Now you are lying again. Answer my questions and then Meas may bargain with you for your life. But I will warn you that your scalps may be worth more to Meas than a ton of silver."

"I see I have nothing to gain or lose by telling the truth," Blackbeard continued. "Since you two savages fear neither God nor man, you had just as well do your deeds in ignorance and burn in hell with us. I shall tell you nothing."

"Nay, Blackbeard," Falling Leaf corrected. "I do believe in God. And Meas, the savage heathen, believes in a Great Spirit who rules the world. His scruples about what is right and wrong exceed your own. Do you not have the seventy shillings with you because Koketotoka gave them back to you as a matter of principle? If Meas and I kill you two, it will simply be to execute God's wrath upon wicked sinners. As you have already suggested, none of us can escape the judgment of God."

"Do not judge us so harshly," Blackbeard went on. "Until you sail the sea in the boat with us, you do not know what you yourself would do when the gale hits you. We be not such wicked fellows as you imagine. We be only privateers who exact tribute from other shippers. We do nothing different from what the Dutch, the English, the French, or the Spanish do every day. The only difference is that privateers swear allegiance to no king or queen or parliament.

"If our ship is stronger than the one we stop, the other ship grants us a portion of their cargo. If the other ship's officers refuse to cooperate, we simply take a portion of their goods in payment for our services. Is that not the way ships from all nations operate? The only difference is that privateers do not go through the pretense of saying it belongs to the King."

"What is the difference between a pirate and a privateer?" Falling Leaf asked.

"It is the same difference as exists between a tyrant and a king," Blackbeard continued. "The privateer is reasonable, whereas the pirate is not. Often the privateer assists the trader by protecting him from the greed of kings of other nations. For example, Virginia planters grow tobacco. They must sell it in Europe. The English King says that all Virginia and Maryland planters must ship their tobacco on English ships. Then the King of England demands a part of the shipment. Neck Scar and I assist those planters in getting their tobacco on Dutch bottoms, which require no tax. Do you not think the planters gladly pay us for our service?"

"Indeed, you pull on my heartstrings," Falling Leaf offered. "I see nothing wrong with evading the English robbers. But if you privateers be such good fellows, why does your conscience bother you?"

"We do not assist only in the tobacco trade. There are more dangerous business ventures. There are arms shipments. There is slave trade. There is rum traffic. Sometimes things go wrong, and then you just do what you have to do. Ugly things happen. Like at Cape Henlopen."

Blackbeard stopped. Falling Leaf had somehow lured him in further than he wanted. But then he added, "We needed a base at Swanendael to assist us in our business. The Virginia planters were willing to give up their bondmen ... till the storm messed it all up. Who can argue with God? And we have done penance. We have paid many a pound, many a ducat, many a guilder to priests who absolved us of our sins."

"Blackbeard, when you paid the priest to absolve your sins, did you feel better?"

"Yes," answered Blackbeard. "I felt better after the priest prayed. But still I doubted. Would God honor the prayers of the filthy priest enough to forgive me of what I knew was wrong? Oh, I suppose 'tis money well spent," said Blackbeard carelessly. "Perhaps the priest's prayers may appease God's wrath a little."

"Blackbeard, perhaps God would be pleased if you changed your wicked ways," suggested Falling Leaf.

"It is too late, you heathen murderer. Even now you hold a tomahawk over my head and then piously suggest that I change my ways." The scorn dripped from Blackbeard's voice like pine pitch from a gashed pine.

"I'll tell you what I'll do. I'll give you the seventy shillings to return to their rightful owners. After you have killed us, you cannot keep the money. You must give it back to the fourteen bondmen the Dutch ransomed." A crafty smile played around the corners of Blackbeard's mouth.

Falling Leaf jumped to his feet. "A wonderful idea," he exclaimed. "Meas will be glad to deliver it. And what else would you like to straighten out before your departure?"

"There is nothing else," said Blackbeard as he and Neck Scar rose to their feet in the dark. In a perfectly timed motion, Blackbeard jumped to the other side of Neck Scar, while both of them whirled around and lunged past Meas. Blackbeard snatched the tomahawk from Meas's hand as he shot past, and the rope that tied the two desperadoes together threw Meas face forward on the ground. Blackbeard cleft the rope with one chop of the tomahawk, and the two raced to the waiting canoe. Rapid splashes of the paddles soon faded into the distance till silence again mastered the night.

Falling Leaf rolled Meas over on his back, gently shaking him. "Wh-h-a-a-t hap-p-pened?" Meas asked as he rolled his eyes upward and tried to focus them on Falling Leaf.

"It appears that you only had the wind knocked out of you by a fall," Falling Leaf said as relief oozed out of his every pore. "And we have found out that it is best not to play with cornered weasels. At least the truth test worked quite well," Falling Leaf joked. "Blackbeard and Neck Scar both closed their left eyes when they were praying. They're Catholics."

"Where are the two weasels?" Meas asked.

"Meas, for some unknown reason they left in an awful hurry without their packs or the seventy shillings. I think they will return ere the morning light to pick up their goods. As a precaution, we will move our camp some distance before we doze off. We will leave their goods and the seventy shillings right here beside the river."

"Falling Leaf, do you not wish to watch for them and grab them when they return for their goods? I can easily wait a bit downstream and snatch the canoe away from them when they return."

"No, Meas. What would we do with Blackbeard and Neck Scar if we caught them again? Dead dogs are of no use to us. Prisoners bound with ropes or chains only bind the jailer down to watch them. But a dog set free will love you all his life. I suspect these two privateers may even be the means of helping us carry out some of our plans.

"In my mind it is quite certain they will return. These two do not want to be caught on the Chesapeake in a canoe. They want to get back to the Delaware and their real master, Fat Pig. Just wait and see. By morning light we shall have our canoe back and be ready to continue our journey to St. Mary's City. What a relief! I had no idea what we were going to do with those two weasels. Now they have admirably solved our problem for us."

Sure enough, the next morning the canoe was again back at its mooring by the campsite, and lying in the same spot it had lain the night before was the bag of seventy shillings—and Meas's tomahawk.

Meas and Falling Leaf took their time fishing and cooking a huge breakfast. English lessons continued. Meas delighted Falling Leaf by recounting much of the discussion from the night before. Meas asked some questions on things he had not understood so that he could get the meaning of the entire conversation. "Maybe if I had not been so intent on what you were saying," Meas said, "I would have been ready for the weasels when they rushed me."

"Meas, do not fret. Things have turned out very well. By tomorrow night we shall be in St. Mary's City. Have you a speech ready for Cool Water?"

"Yes. Do you remember the piece I made when we were crossing the Chesapeake several months ago? If you will help me learn the words in English, I shall recite it to the group in English. And I shall be gathering flowers and vines all day to make her the prettiest bouquet she has ever received."

"Meas, if you tell them the poem, 'Cool Water,' I am sure they will all be impressed. I believe it will be almost as beautiful in English as in Lenape, and I hope the meaning will not be marred by the translation. What sort of flowers did you have in mind to gather? If we are going to make a lot of detours and stops, we had best get started or it will be another week before we get to St. Mary's City."

Meas and Falling Leaf failed to find the Fendalls at St. Mary's City. But inquiry soon told them to head on up the Potomack River for a three-day paddle.[20] Where the river swings sharply to the north and then veers quickly back to the south, they would find another small

---

[20] Nearly fifty miles upriver.

river emptying into the Potomack. The two were told to enter that river and they would find a new port not far from Governor Fendall's plantation.[21]

Meas and Falling Leaf easily found the Fendall plantation on the morning of the third day. Everything fit the description—the dock, the newly cleared fields, the growing tobacco, and the plantation houses and barns. Meas swung the canoe into the shore near the boat dock where he and Falling Leaf quickly hid it in the swamp. Then they eased their way through the trees toward the house.

Meas saw Cool Water first. She worked alone in the garden off to one side of the house. Cool Water bent over the bean rows, carefully snapping the full, ripe beans from the vines and throwing them into her white apron before dumping her gathered handfuls into the basket she dragged along. Meas stopped and watched her. A white bonnet capped her black tresses. A long yellow dress neatly shielded her arms and body as she worked. Her movements were quick and strong as she moved down the row. And she was singing. Her clear, sweet, high notes were like those of the lark and the warbler. Over and over she seemed to sing the same lines, not always a complete thought, but always ending with the same words and notes.

Meas edged closer to the garden, but remained hidden and still. He listened. Then he began whistling the same tune Cool Water sang. Cool Water stopped singing and stood up straight. Her black eyes strained to pierce the shadows from which the sound came. Meas whistled the strain one more time and then stopped. He waited.

Cool Water edged closer to the trees. Then she began to sing again. This time she sang all the lines:

> But could youth last, and love still lead,
> Had joys no date, nor age no need,
> Then these delights my mind might move
> To live with thee and be thy love.[22]

---

[21] Port Tobacco, the first seat of Charles County. Governor Josias Fendall created Charles County from St. Mary's County by proclamation on 10 May 1658.
[22] Words written by Sir Walter Raleigh. Set to music by James G. Landis.

Cool Water seeks the singer.

While Cool Water was still holding the last high note, Meas began whistling the entire song. Cool Water moved quickly into the trees toward the sound. She had trouble spotting the source of the sound, for it moved ever deeper into the trees. At last she stood in an open meadow. Suddenly Meas stood in front of her. As far as she could tell, there was no movement. He just stood there looking down at her.

"Cool Water," he said. "Song beautiful. Sing again."

And this time Cool Water astounded Meas by answering in halting Lenape, "I will sing it again if you will help me."

In answer Meas stepped closer and looked down into her dancing black eyes.

Cool Water blushed and then began to sing. At first she kept her eyes on the ground, but on the last line she lifted her eyes up to his and locked them there while she held the final high note longer and longer and longer. Meas whistled along with her. He, too, held the final note until it seemed it must simply collapse.

Meas and Cool Water both stopped together and drew in a deep breath. As soon as Meas could get his breath back, he asked, "Cool Water, where you learn Lenape?"

"We have an Indian slave boy on the plantation," Cool Water said hesitantly. "He is teaching me his words."

"Josias have Indian slave boy?" Meas asked.

"Yes. And black slaves too," Cool Water answered unhappily. "In Captain Fendall's eyes every person is worth so many pounds of tobacco ... or so many acres of land. Even I. I am equal to one hundred pounds of tobacco or fifty acres of land. Land! Land! Land!" Cool Water fumed. "Happiness of an orphan Indian boy means nothing to Captain Fendall. Or of black slaves. Or of servants. Or of me. Only land and tobacco." Cool Water's black eyes burned.

Meas studied her calmly. "Go," he said at last. "You go to garden. Work. Maybe someone say, 'Indian boy steal white girl.' Bad news. White man bring guns. Kill Meas."

"To hear that I have been stolen away by Meas would not be bad news," said Cool Water cautiously. "I have been anxious for you to come back. I have even dreamed of running away and finding you."

"Cool Water!" For the first time Meas's voice rose in alarm. "You do no such thing. Where you go? How you find me?"

Cool Water placed both hands firmly on her hips. "Oh, it would not be hard to find Swanendael, that lovely spot on the Siconece." She twisted her one bare foot in the sandy earth and spun around till she faced east. Standing on tiptoe and waving one hand toward the east, she proclaimed, "I have found out that every native on the eastern shore of Maryland knows an orator-poet from the Siconece. I would find you. I am not helpless. I have made plans," Cool Water said determinedly.

Then she spun around again and faced Meas. She stood very close to him now, but his face did not twitch, nor did his eye flicker. "Getting to the Siconece is not what worries me," she whispered. "What worries me is, what if I get to the Siconece and find out that you do not want me? What if there is some beautiful Lenape girl that you wanted instead of me?" Her big black eyes searched his face for some sign of assurance. Meas gave none.

At length Meas laid one hand on her shoulder. "Come," he said again, and led the way to the edge of the woods. She followed him. While still hidden in the shadows, he turned to face her again. "You work," he commanded. "Pick beans. Pick squash. I go. Talk to Soft Heart. Maybe she let Cool Water go. Talk to Captain Big Field. Maybe he sell Cool Water."

Meas watched Cool Water walk dutifully back to the garden. She neither turned nor waved before she once again bent over the bean rows. She sang no more as she worked.

Meas found Falling Leaf leaning against a tree. A smile rested on Falling Leaf's lips. "Why have you not gone to the house and found Margaret?" Meas asked, glad that he could talk once more in Lenape.

"It is too interesting here," Falling Leaf answered. "The birds sing so beautifully in these woods that I determined to find out what species they are. I watched and listened for all I was worth."

"Falling Leaf, since you watched the birds so closely, what did you see and hear?"

"I saw an oriole and heard her sing. I watched her carrying the lace to weave into her basket nest," teased Falling Leaf.

"Falling Leaf, quit your teasing and speak without the joke. Did I understand? Cool Water wants to go with me now?"

"Meas, there is no doubt she wants to go with you, NOW. Her song says, 'To live with thee and be thy love.' She is determined. Whether going off with you is simply the romantic notion of a young woman or the resolve of a strong spirit, I cannot tell.

"Meas, there could be some good reasons why Cool Water is a problem to keep here," Falling Leaf said thoughtfully. "It may be even dangerous for her to remain much longer." And then with a grin he added, "Do you notice her black hair and black eyes? Or are you too enthralled with her bare feet?"

"Falling Leaf, my eyes do see. I am not blinded by sweet feelings for her. My ears hear the cooing of the dove. But I am not drunk with passion. My mind still rules the heart. I am a Lenape man, not a boy. I want a good wife ... like my mother. I do notice the black hair and black eyes, but I also see the light skin. So what are you trying to tell me?"

"Meas, Cool Water is not born of English blood. My guess is that she is either Spanish or Italian. Judging by the way she sings and by her dreamy eyes, I'd have to go for the Italian."

"Falling Leaf, then tell me. Do you think this Italian dove would rock Lenape babies, tend the cooking fires well, and keep the flame of the spirit bright in my wigwam? Or would she soon tire of her duties and fling her desires upon some other wisp of wind?"

"Meas, I am not the Great Spirit. I do not know what lies ahead in her path. I do not know what Cool Water will become. Cool

Water has many good things about her—strength, fire, spirit, warmth, beauty—but who can tell what she will do when the trees fall upon her?"

"Aye, Falling Leaf, Cool Water is beautiful," Meas continued. "But a lily of the valley is also a thing of beauty with its tiny, tender white bells that droop so delicately from the stem. Alas, the outward beauty of the flower can be destroyed with only a snap of the finger.

"Strength of spirit is like the hickory sapling that cannot be uprooted by the fiercest storm, for the root is deep. If bent or bowed even to the ground, it will spring back straight and strong as ever, for the root is deep. If the stem be crushed by a fallen tree, a new shoot will spring forth, like unto the old, for the root is deep. Strength of spirit comes from the root buried deep within the heart.

> She's only a sapling, supple and sure,
> She's only a brooklet, outbound and pure.
> How will she bend? How will she wend?
> When the stick becomes a tree,
> When the brooklet reaches the sea,
> Then what will Cool Water be?
>
> Could a youth whose heart does bleed
> At the sigh of one poor slave boy's need,
> Could a maid whose heart does burn
> At the cry of orphans in their turn,
> Could a virgin whose heart's desire
> Is only to tend my hearth and fire;
> Could such a heart be untrue to me
> In my lodge by the Siconece?
>
> If the root within her heart
> Has grasped the truth throughout her youth,
> If the roots of kindness, good, and right
> Grow deep and long and strong,

Then no storm above can tear apart
The roots from the soil of her heart.
Such will Cool Water be
When the twig becomes a tree.

"Very well then, Meas. After such poetry, I understand that you are still settled on having the white dove. But how are you going to get her?" Falling Leaf inquired. "To have and to hold is different than to wish and to want."

"Falling Leaf, the Lenape way is for a man who wants a wife to treat with the girl's father for a quantity of wampum to be paid on the day of marriage."

"Meas, Josias Fendall does not care about wampum. He is not Cool Water's father. And I doubt if he could find a parson in all of Maryland or Virginia who would marry Cool Water to a heathen savage. And I can assure you that the first lieutenant of the state of Maryland will not attend a Lenape marriage on the Siconece to receive his wampum. These are hard things for me to tell a friend. But are you sure that you want to go through with this loony idea?"

"Falling Leaf, because the hunt is a long one does not mean that the hunter must give it up. Because the trail is faint does not mean that the skillful may not follow it. Let us hide the matter of Cool Water behind the cloud.

"Did you not tell me that Sachem Koketotoka wants me to open a trading post on the Siconece? Are you not carrying twenty-eight pounds of English wampum? Does Captain Big Field wish to smoke all the tobacco growing in the fields around us? Should we not find Captain Big Field and treat with him?"

"Aye, Meas, you are handsome right. The Dutchman in you wouldn't miss a good trade because of a heart murmur.

"By the way, Meas, did you see Cool Water's garden? And the garden grows so well—maize, beans, peas, squash, pumpkins, muskmelons, watermelons, cucumbers, sweet potatoes, and many plants such as I have seen only in Dutch gardens. Just the sight of it makes my belly sing."

"I saw the flowers—flowers that make my spirit sing," Meas responded.

"Come, Meas," said Falling Leaf. "We must find Governor Josias Fendall before you leave the ground completely."

Meas and Falling Leaf found Captain Big Field at the port not far from his manor. A small town was springing up around the port. Off to one side of the town, overlooking a scruffy pool of water before it dispersed into marsh, Governor Fendall strode purposely back and forth. He calculated the rise from the riverbank. He eyed the angle of the summer sun. He stepped off the distance to the well.

Governor Fendall was so intent on his survey, he failed to see his visitors approaching until they were upon him. Falling Leaf greeted Governor Fendall with a cheery "What's going on here?"

Governor Fendall stopped and smiled. "I'm planning a new courthouse. We're going to make it a two-story brick building with an arched entrance, glazed glass, wrought-iron hardware, sawn timber—the works. I think the site lends itself well to this project, and it will be a building we can all be proud of."

"Isn't this pretty far from St. Mary's City for a courthouse?" Falling Leaf queried.

"Ah, did you not hear? We have divided St. Mary's County in two pieces and named the new one Charles County.[23] With the large number of settlers coming into this area, we were getting many complaints that it was too far to the courthouse at St. Mary's City. The new courthouse for Charles County will be right here at Port Tobacco. It will be very convenient for all and," Josias paused, "I guess I can safely tell you, my Protestant friends and I will be able to control our affairs much better. That means, shield some things better from the eyes and ears of Lord Baltimore and the Catholics."

---

[23] By proclamation of Governor Josias Fendall in the name of Lord Baltimore on 10 May 1658.

"Don't you think this courthouse might be grander than the one they use in St. Mary's City?"

Governor Josias Fendall burst into a wide grin. "Could be. Times have been good in this region. As you have no doubt noticed, this area really grows tobacco, and Lord Baltimore is taking in ten shillings on each hogshead of tobacco shipped out of the province. So he has money to spend.

"Actually, Lord Baltimore wants to reduce the tariff to only two shillings per hogshead, but so far I have kept that bit of news from the planters. It's kind of a useful tool, you know. Nobody likes to pay taxes, and if taxes cause wrath against a Catholic lord in a faraway land, it's not all bad. Depending on whether England goes Catholic or Protestant, royal or parliamentary, the Protestants here may be able to gain control once more. You kinda have to sail with the wind, you know.

"Enough of my windy blow on politics. Falling Leaf, what brings you and Meas to Port Tobacco?"

"Business. Meas has had some dealings with the Dutch merchants in New Amstel, and he is interested in trading with you for your tobacco crop. Or do you plan to smoke it all?"

Governor Fendall laughed. "I don't know which is the bigger joke, Meas buying my tobacco crop or the governor smoking the whole crop. Maybe we should take a tour of the manor and talk about things some more."

"Yes. Yes, Captain Josias, if I may call you that. Let's do take a tour of the manor. But first, maybe we could stop by the house for a drink and some refreshment before traveling in the midday sun. How's that for inviting oneself?"

"Yes, do call me Captain Josias. I like that name among friends. As for the refreshments, we'll have to see what the women can come up with on the spur of the moment. Let's head for the house."

The trio strode easily along in step—Captain Josias on the left,

Falling Leaf in the middle, and Meas on the right—on the wide grassy road to the house. Falling Leaf continued his friendly banter with Captain Josias, but Meas maintained his usual quietness.

"Captain," Falling Leaf started out, "Meas can outtrade a Dutchman. You'd better make sure you have your pants on tight when you trade with him. And it's all fair and square."

"Falling Leaf, you can rest easy. Meas will be the first of them Indians that can best me in a trade. I tangled with some pretty mean traders before I came to Maryland at age thirty with eighteen servants. Don't pity me too bad."

"Captain Josias, how long ago did you come to Maryland? Have you traded with any Indians before?" Falling Leaf wanted to know.

"Falling Leaf, I have been in the country for only four years. I have not traded with any Indians. What is the need? They seem to be a very worthless, passive lot. They are hopeless drunks. They can't read or write. They don't know the Gospel. Now you tell me Meas is a trader!"

Falling Leaf laughed. "Ah, Captain Josias, I see you're too sharp for me. You see right through my simple jokes.

"I see acre after acre after acre of tobacco all along this river," Falling Leaf went on. "Is it all yours?"

"No, it's not all mine. Some of it belongs to Judge Hatch, my father-in-law. Together we own a pretty good chunk of land.

"This is how it came about. Lord Baltimore has all this land King Charles gave him ... before the King lost his head, of course.[24] All the land Lord Baltimore claims, and he will have every square foot he can, does him no good unless he has people to farm it and pay him quit rents.[25] To attract settlers to Maryland, Lord Baltimore gives 1,000 acres to a settler for every five servants he can bring with him.

"Judge Hatch and I together managed to bring eighteen servants along over, at least the way we count servants. So we picked out

[24] King Charles I was beheaded in 1649.
[25] A rent paid in lieu of required feudal services (i.e. so many days of labor for the ruler).

2,000 acres,[26] give or take a few hundred, of some of the finest land in Maryland. The climate is pleasant, the water is good, and the soil grows fine tobacco.

"Everything is so pleasing here in Charles County that one adult man can produce one hundred bushels of maize, twenty bushels of beans and peas, and 1,000 pounds of tobacco ..."

"Captain Josias," Falling Leaf cut in, "are you going to smoke all this tobacco?"

"You and your jokes," Captain Big Field laughed. "Let us go inside now and relax in the shade while the sun burns off some of its midday power. I will check with Mary and see what kind of refreshments she can manage for us."

Much to the surprise of Captain Big Field, the dining table was already set for four people. Silverware and china plates decorated with sprays of roses and violets awaited them on the woven tablecloth. Three wine goblets stood ready in front of three dinner plates, but in front of the fourth stood a large glass filled with water. Mary greeted the two guests and invited them to sit around the table with her. Meas took the spot with the water glass. Falling Leaf sat across from him, while Captain Big Field took the spot with the wine bottle beside it, and Soft Heart sat across from Captain Big Field. All bowed their heads, and Captain Big Field asked the blessing.

As soon as Captain Big Field finished his prayer, he popped the cork on the wine bottle and poured wine into each of the three goblets. Then as Mary, Falling Leaf, and Captain Big Field touched their goblets together, Captain Big Field said, "To the health of our guests and a fine tobacco crop." Meas watched.

As soon as the ceremony was over, Captain Big Field continued talking about tobacco. "As I was saying, one hand can produce about 1,000 pounds of tobacco ..." Meas listened.

---

[26] Josias Fendall was granted 2,000 acres of land in Charles County on August 23, 1656.

Cool Water entered the dining room and served the table one dish after another—maize bread, butter, molasses, cheese curds, squash, cabbage, carrots, cucumbers—and finished the meal off with watermelon. Cool Water refilled Meas's glass with water, but she kept her eyes and hands busy with her work.

While the others ate, Captain Josias plodded on, telling his guests how to plant tobacco, how to raise tobacco, how to harvest tobacco, and how to market tobacco. But he always kept coming back to the one big problem with tobacco—labor. "Just about the time I get a servant trained on how to grow the crop, his time of service is up," he complained. "When a servant's time is up, he can get a grant for fifty acres of land, take a hoe and a knife, and raise tobacco as easily as I can. To solve this problem I've bought several slaves ..."

Soft Heart interrupted him. "If you would stop talking and start eating, you might catch up with the rest of us," she suggested. But her gentle rebuke didn't stop Captain Big Field. "With slaves and a few good years, I might even be able to double the size of my plantation to 4,000 acres ..." On and on he went.

When Cool Water placed Captain Big Field's watermelon serving on his plate, he stopped his tobacco oration, put his arm around her, and drew her tight against him. "What a fine meal Maria has made for us," he said. "I tell you, this Maria is a jewel—a gardener, a cook, a singer, a bea..."

Soft Heart half rose to her feet, her face pale and her lips drawn tight. She pointed her finger straight at Captain Big Field and hissed, "Let go of her, you, you ..."

"Ah, calm down now, Mary," Captain Big Field urged as he relaxed his hold on Cool Water. "I was only complimenting her on the fine meal she fixed."

Cool Water blushed and glanced at Meas. He caught the hurt and the fear in her eyes. Then she disappeared out the door.

The four of them finished their watermelon in silence.

Some shouts from outside and a rapid pounding of feet on the porch floor broke the silence. "Master Josias," a boy cried, "a horse has his gut hanging out!" Captain Big Field bolted for the door.

Meas and Falling Leaf jumped up to follow him, but Soft Heart raised her hand. "Sit down," she begged. "I want to talk with you."

Meas and Falling Leaf resumed their seats, but Soft Heart rose from her chair and suggested, "Maybe we could visit better in the sitting room. That way Cool Water can clear the table and do the dishes."

The three of them made their way to the sitting room. Soft Heart closed the door. Soft Heart and Falling Leaf seated themselves on chairs. Meas faced the two and seated himself cross-legged on the floor.

Soft Heart put her face in her hands and tried to regain control of herself. Meas and Falling Leaf waited.

Some time passed before Soft Heart dried her moist eyes and began to speak. "I hope you two can help Maria and me. But I want to tell you about Maria first.

"Josias and I, my mother and father, and our sixteen servants sailed from England to Maryland in the winter of 1654. After nearly three months of bobbing up and down and blowing this way and that, everyone aboard was anxious to get to St. Mary's City.

"We had already entered the Chesapeake Bay when a ship flying a Dutch flag hailed us. Before we knew anything was amiss, the captain of the Dutch ship had lashed his boat to ours. We got a close-up look at the ship—patched sails, torn rigging, holes in the sides, rusty cannon, and the meanest lot of sailors imaginable. How they could ever sail the ship in that condition defies imagination. Those rogues swarmed on board brandishing their swords and pistols.

"The captain was a man with a large bulbous nose and a bushy Blackbeard."

Falling Leaf raised his hand slightly. Soft Heart stopped and Falling Leaf asked, "Did the first mate on this ship have a long scar on the side of his neck?"

"Why yes, he did. Do you know this Blackbeard?"

"Yes, I have some acquaintance with both Blackbeard and Neck Scar. In fact, I believe it was only last week I happened to be close by when they were both at the confessional. I lie not. The sins of those two are many."

"Really? And when I get through, you'll know of several more of their sins. Blackbeard told Josias he was a privateer employed by the Dutch to protect Dutch shipping in English waters. And for a small fee he protects Maryland and Virginia merchants using their own ships from the high tolls and tariffs taken on British vessels.

"Josias is a pretty good trader, and he made a bargain with the black-bearded scoundrel. Blackbeard sold Josias two young girls he kept in his cabin for one pound sterling each and then let us go."

Falling Leaf let out a low whistle. "How low down can a person get?" he exclaimed.

"When a man sells his soul to the devil, he'll stoop to anything," Soft Heart continued. "Josias thought it a good deal. We had two more servants worth four hundred acres of land and a way to bypass British tolls and tariffs on future tobacco shipments for only two pounds.

"But the girls. The poor wretches had nothing except the wish to forever blot from their memories the past—the storm, the fight, the abuse by the devils. Neither Margaret nor Maria had a spark of hope left in them, not even the desire to live."

"Did Blackbeard tell you anything about Margaret's and Maria's past?"

"Very little. I wasn't sure I could even believe what he did tell us. Blackbeard claimed he rescued the two from a sinking ship in the Caribbean. It is more likely they were stolen to be sold as servants in Virginia ... after Blackbeard got through with them. The girls know nothing of their real parents, but were raised in the Caribbean. They spoke Spanish when they first came.

"My heart went out to those orphans. From that day on I took those two girls in my care and raised them as my own two daughters. Young people are strong, and both of them responded well. I taught them many things needed to survive in this wilderness—to cook, to garden, to wash—and some things needed for happiness—to read, to sing, and to love. In time, the girls came to love and trust me.

"As you saw on your last visit, both girls blossomed into attractive young ladies, and there was no end of servants and suitors desiring marriage, especially with Margaret.

"Then Josias began to notice Margaret and to pay her special attention. After that, Josias would not agree to any marriage proposal for her. I stood equally determined that I would never allow two women under the same roof vying for my Josias's attention. So I did a desperate thing. Without Josias's consent, I sold Margaret as a servant and put her on a ship to New Amsterdam. May God have mercy," Soft Heart whispered and made the sign of the cross.

"Josias seemed to accept Margaret's disappearance quite well, but now he is paying attention to Maria. And this time, it will not be possible for me to sell her. If Josias himself does not sell her, she will be only an escaped servant or slave, and as such, she will forever live in fear of being caught and punished as a runaway.

"So what can we do to get Maria away from here?" Soft Heart looked at Falling Leaf and waited.

"Soft Heart, for that is what Meas calls you and the name fits you well, I want to talk this over with Meas before I give you an answer."

Falling Leaf switched to Lenape and explained to Meas the details of the story. He didn't need to explain much to Meas, for although his English was limited, nothing had escaped his eyes.

"Soft Heart," Meas asked, "what Cool Water want?"

"Cool Water wants to go with you to Swanendael," Soft Heart answered.

"Soft Heart think good or bad Cool Water live with Meas?"

Soft Heart hung her head. "Meas, I hardly know what to think. My own lot would certainly be easier if Josias would agree to letting Maria go. But I'm afraid it would be such a strange world for Maria—wigwams, language, religion, friends, foods—everything. She's only sixteen. All the changes might overwhelm her."

"Yes," Falling Leaf agreed. "If Cool Water goes with Meas, there would be no turning back. She could never return to Maryland. Both the Catholics and the Protestants would want to cut her throat. I tried to talk Meas out of this idea, but he seems determined to have Cool Water."

Both Soft Heart and Falling Leaf looked at Meas and waited and waited. Captain Big Field slipped back into the room and sat down quietly beside Soft Heart.

At last Meas rose to his feet. His black eyes stared into the distance as though he were seeing far beyond the wall and the three listeners. Cool Water came and stood at the door. Meas began to speak.

> I speak slowly in the council of older and wiser ones than I. Our life is like the sun that rises at the dawn, climbs higher and higher across the sky until it shines in full brilliance at noon, and then begins to sink toward the horizon.

As Meas spoke, he slowly raised his hand, pointed to the eastern horizon, then traced the path of the sun across the sky until it fell below the floor in the west.

> There is naught that man can do to change the course of the sun, for it is a settled thing that it must sink below the horizon.
>
> Sometimes one's life is a long summer day. Other times a life is but a short winter day. But every life must sink into the darkness of the grave. Mengwe and Dutch, Susquehannock and Swede, English and Nanticoke, Spaniard and Lenape, all

alike must end their journey across the sky and descend into the grave.

Freemen, lords, sachems, sailors, servants, slaves, priest or Protestant, Catholic or clergy; when the sun sinks into the earth, the spirit of every one must depart from the body.

At the sunset all are equal.

Seeing then that at sunset we are all equal, why should we fight and kill and steal and hate one another? Why should the Lenape hate the English? Why should the English hate the Lenape? Is there no way to smell the fragrance of life together while the sun still shines on our spirits?

I and my people, the Lenni Lenape, will show you that way. For hundreds of years, generation after generation, we have built our wigwams in the Land of the Dawn. It is our homeland, and we, the Lenni Lenape, are the grandfathers of many other peoples who have gone out from us and who now surround you—Nanticoke, Pampticoke, Powhatan, Piscataway, Shawnee.

Our grandchildren, as well as the Susquehannocks and the Mengwe,[27] have designated the Lenape as the "woman" among all the nations. Understand then, it is the task of the "woman," the Lenape, to reason with nations who war one with another so they may stop their killing and honorably bury the hatchet deep underground.

Today, as a Lenape, blood brother of Sachem Koketotoka, grandson of Eesanques, of the nation of Mattahorn and Tamenend, I tell you it is not good that Englishmen spill the blood of Englishmen upon the waters of the Chesapeake.[28] It is not good when Englishmen drain the blood of Indians

[27] The Mengwe were called Iroquois by the French.
[28] An Englishman and prior owner of Kent Island, Captain William Claiborne and his forces fought a sea battle with the forces of Governor Calvert on 23 April 1635. The battle was fought at the spot where the Pocomoke River empties into the Chesapeake Bay.

upon the soil of their own homeland. It is not good when Indians tear the scalp from white men who would drive them from that same land.

Sachem Josias Fendall, tell your people, "We, the Lenape, will take the palefaces down into the river and scrub the evil blood out of their veins. And when they come up out of the water, the Lenape will adopt them as Real Men.[29] Then they may mingle their blood with ours, not on the killing fields, but in living flesh and blood."

Come, Great Sachem, the light of day still shines upon our spirits. The sun has not yet set for you and me. Let us dwell together in this beautiful homeland ... in peace, and ... in love.

"Come, Cool Water, stand by my side." Cool Water moved slowly toward him. Meas held out his hand and she took it. "Meas and Cool Water will show others the way," Meas continued. "Cool Water, the Lenape will scrub the bad white blood from your veins, and you will be of the Lenape nation until your sun sets and the spirit departs from your body. Your papooses will carry the strength and dignity and power of the Lenape in their veins in the Land of the Dawn the Great Spirit has given us.

"And when the sun sets on Meas, the Great Spirit shall say of Meas: 'He lived in love and peace in the Land of the Dawn.' "

Meas turned and faced Cool Water. He took her other hand in his and gazed down upon her. "Sing now?" he asked. Cool Water nodded and burst forth in song. Meas sang with her.

Captain Big Field quietly slipped his hand over and touched Soft Heart's hand. She laid her hand in his, and a bit of color returned once more to her cheeks.

> But could youth last, and love still lead,
> Had joys no date, nor age no need,
> Then these delights my mind might move,

[29] *Lenni Lenape* means "real men."

CQ204

"Could youth last, and love still lead."

–Meas and Cool Water

To live with thee, and be thy love-e-e-e.

The duet ended, but no one moved. It was Captain Big Field who broke the magic of the moment. "We must treasure this moment forever in our memories." Then he added, "At least until the sun sets for each of us."

———

Somehow the hour had gotten late. Meas, Falling Leaf, and Captain Big Field had toured Sachem Big Field's plantation.

Meas had seen the ghosts of girdled trees lurking amidst the tobacco patches where Captain Big Field had destroyed the forest to make way for the tobacco. Meas had seen the black slaves toiling. Meas had seen the Indian slave boy. Meas had seen the indentured servants. Meas had seen the horse with the gut hanging out, the victim of a neighborly dispute over the horse's trespassing.

Now the three men—Lenape, Swede, Englishman—sat on the edge of the porch floor while the mosquitoes began their nightly ministry. Each of the three puffed occasionally on his own pipe while each pondered his thoughts of the day.

Meas started it off. "Captain Big Field," he asked, "if you could own as big a field as you would wish, how big a plantation would you want?"

Falling Leaf translated and Meas waited.

Captain Big Field hedged. "That depends on a number of things. What would it cost to buy? How long will I live? Can I get labor? But just for anyhow, to answer your question, let's say 20,000 acres."

"But," Meas persisted, "if you were to get 20,000 acres, how would you get them?"

"Under the present conditions, I suppose Lord Baltimore would have to grant them or sell them to me."

"Captain Big Field, tell me: who is this Lord Baltimore? I have never seen him. Falling Leaf says that this Lord Baltimore has never seen the beautiful bay or the rivers flowing into it or the people who have lived here long before this lord ever saw the light of day. Why do you give him gifts so he will allow you to live on the land?"

"Meas, I must tell you. Years ago the King gave the land around the Chesapeake Bay to Lord Baltimore. Now Lord Baltimore can make laws, levy taxes, raise armies, and appoint the governor and other officials. Lord Baltimore can do anything he wants with Maryland."

"But Sachem Big Field, how did the king have the right to give this land to Lord Baltimore? The king has never been here either. Did you not say the king is now dead?"

"True. True. The King has lost his head. But God gave the King this land. God decides who will have the land. If God chooses to give the land to a Christian nation—peoples with great sailing ships, wheels, compasses, flint, books, records, prophets, iron tools, duffel cloth, and guns—the ungodly heathen must yield to His will. Thus you see, God chose to give the land to the King, and he gave it to Lord Baltimore."

"Now you are making fun of me, Captain Big Field. You think I am only an ignorant savage."

Even in the Lenape tongue, Captain Big Field could notice the anger rising in Meas's voice.

"There are many kings—France, Sweden, England, Spain, Netherlands—and they all say the same thing. God gave us this land. Hah! How can you be so childish? God did not give the land to any king. The Great Spirit gave the Lenape this land centuries gone by, and we have been here to live in it and to care for it.

"How can you say we are a heathen people? We worship the Great Spirit. We do not destroy the land, plant weeds, and ruin the soil so it will grow nothing for years. It is the Christian nations who war and plunder and kill and rape and who would drive us away rather than live in peace with us and with one another.

"Sachem Fendall, do you believe this childish tale, 'God gave this land to the king'?"

"Aye, Meas," Governor Josias Fendall responded, and his voice took on the hardness of the battle-tested first lieutenant of the state of Maryland. "There is another thing besides religion that settles which king or which lord owns the land. It is called a gun. He who is the strongest will take the land."

Meas stood up, laid his pipe aside, and began a discourse to the night that even Tamenend would have applauded:

So it is the gun that decides who will possess this land, is it?

Then you admit that your god has nothing to do with who owns the land. Is that true? Tell me it is not true. Or does your god favor the English over the Lenape, the Nanticoke, the Pampticoke, the Powhatan, and the Piscataway because the English are more cruel and ruthless? Is the trader who makes the Lenape drunk and then steals from him blessed of your god because he was stronger?

I am thankful that I do not know such a god. The Great Spirit the Lenape know smiles on those who do right. He punishes those who do evil.

And if it is only the gun then that makes it right to steal another's land, is it also the gun that makes it right to kidnap an Indian child and enslave it? Or to steal a black man and woman and carry them far away from home in chains? Does might indeed make right?

Do the tomahawk and the scalping knife and the gun indeed determine who will live free along the Siconece and who will perish enslaved along the Potomack?

It is not so, Captain Fendall. I have seen the newborn fawn totter on its spindly legs and make its way to its mother's teat. No one taught the fawn where to find its treat. The Great Spirit put that instinct within the fawn.

Just so, when the Great Spirit created man, he gave him an instinct so that no one needs to teach man what is right and wrong. He who would be free cannot flee from the spirit in his heart. He cannot hide from that inside. Good and evil cannot together bide unless it tear apart the sinews of the heart.

No, Great Sachem Fendall. Do not tell me that a gun decides what is right and wrong along the Potomack or along the Lenape River. He who kills and steals and binds with rope must live in hatred, fear, and dread. But he who trades in kindness, love, and right will fill his heart with happiness and peace instead.

So, Great Sachem Fendall. If you grow 20,000 pounds of tobacco, you cannot smoke it. If Lord Baltimore owns the whole Chesapeake, he cannot drink it. What good does it do either one of you to war and strain and toil for gain when in the end you're dead?

Meas stopped. The singers of the night took up the chant. The frogs blew their chests in and out, "Get ahead. You're dead. Get ahead. You're dead. Get ahead. You're dead," they croaked. The katydids scraped the edges of their wings together and cheered with screeching waves of "Wh-e-e, wh-e-e, wh-e-e." The chorus continued on and on while the trio smoked in silence.

"Meas," Captain Big Field said, speaking first, "there is much truth in what you say. Men cannot buy happiness by doing evil. And in the end we are all dead.

"But right and wrong is not always black and white. Sometimes it is easier to turn hard questions over to the pastors and priests than to torture our own spirits. I choose not to bother myself with too many infernal broodings about past decisions. My choice is to look ahead. Move forward. Let us leave this heavy subject.

"Meas, did Falling Leaf not tell me that you wished to trade with me? What do you wish to trade? In this whole area we have many needs, but not much to trade besides tobacco."

"Oh, Captain Big Field, Falling Leaf is right. I did come hoping to trade with you. But I am only a poor man and have not much to offer Captain Big Field. Besides, I am a poor trader who cannot calculate well and must beg that you will be gracious in your dealing with me. I have only twenty-eight pounds to trade."

"Indeed! Only twenty-eight pounds of tobacco is a small sum. It will not buy much. Do you not have some beaver that you might be able to have ready by next spring when the trading ships come by? The demand for beaver has gone down, but we might still sell them at a discount. Right now, everything is figured in terms of tobacco."

"No, Captain Big Field, I am afraid the skins of our village are already sold for this coming year. Sachem Koketotoka made a bad trade last year, and now our village is obliged to the Dutch next year. I cannot offer you any skins."

"Ah, the Dutch. Crafty merchants, that bunch. I deal with them. You have to watch them close or they will hamstring you and take everything you got. Was any liquor involved?"

Captain Big Field tapped the porch floor. "Let's see, what else could we come up with to trade? No beaver. Only twenty-eight pounds of tobacco."

"Oh, Captain Big Field, there is a mistake. It is not twenty-eight pounds of tobacco that I trade but twenty-eight pounds of English wampum."

"Twenty-eight pounds of what?" Captain Big Field nearly choked on his smoke.

"Twenty-eight pounds of sterling silver," Falling Leaf added.

"Twenty-eight pounds of sterling silver!" Captain Big Field gasped. "How in the world did Meas ever come by such a hoard? Oh, never mind. We can talk now! Meas, what do you want?"

"Captain Big Field, I have not tried to hide my affection for your servant girl. She reminds me of my mother. I would like her to live with me along the Siconece. Would twenty-eight pounds of silver be enough to purchase her?"

"Well, Meas, I told you earlier, everything on the plantation—cows, horses, hoes, hogs, hogsheads, wages, servants, cloth, dresses, hats, shoes, suits—everything is bought and sold in terms of how many pounds of tobacco it will buy. So we need to convert twenty-eight pounds ster-r-ling to pounds of tobacco. Let us do some figuring. One pound of ster-r-ling silver," and Big Field rolled the word *ster-r-ling* over his tongue like honey, "equals 160 pounds of tobacco. So your twenty-eight pounds ster-r-ling would be equal to," and Big Field paused to do some arithmetic, "30 times 160 equals 4,800 minus (2 times 160 equals 320) or 4,800 minus 320 equals 4,480 pounds of tobacco. That's right," Big Field said confidently. "Meas, your twenty-eight pounds ster-r-ling equals 4,480 pounds of tobacco.

"I have just purchased a new manservant for 2,000 pounds. So, yes, I would be willing to let you have Maria for the same price, 2,000 pounds of tobacco."

"Captain Big Field, it gladdens my heart that you are willing to sell Cool Water. But is it not true that a maidservant does not cost as much as a manservant? Could a maidservant not be bought for one-half the price of a manservant?"

"Aye, Meas, sometimes one can buy a maidservant for less than a manservant. However, Maria is not an ordinary servant. Mary has taught her many skills such as you saw demonstrated at the dinner table. In many ways she is worth far more to the plantation than a manservant. She is young and strong and attractive. Really, she is worth more than a manservant. But since I offered her to you for only 2,000 pounds, I will stick to my word."

"If the Captain is demanding such a high price for Cool Water, would he include all her clothing and a few other goods she has become attached to so she will feel at home on the Siconece?"

"Certainly, Meas, a servant is entitled to take all her clothes and personal items such as looking glasses, trinkets, books, pillows, and such like with her. What do you have in mind when you say 'a few other goods'?"

"Captain Big Field, it is kind of you to agree to let Cool Water take her personal items with her, and to be willing to include a few other goods to make her feel at home on the Siconece. I have seen that her clothes are few and rather worn. I would desire that Cool Water have a set of new frocks and aprons of blue linen, two neckcloths, and two bonnets. Then for special occasions I fancy that she might enjoy ten yards of the lighter newer woolens, Kersey and Penistone, as I believe they are called, along with the necessary needles and threads to make them into whatever Cool Water wants. I believe she would like a new pair of sho..."

"Whoa," shouted Captain Big Field. He grabbed his sides and held them while he struggled to get his laughter under control. "Meas, you have long since used up any slack in the price we agreed on for Maria. Have you gone mad? What in the world do you want with such fine clothes for Maria? Are you not taking her to live half-naked among the heathen on Whore's Creek? Such clothes are worn by Christians."

"Captain Fendall," Meas answered gravely, "can Cool Water not be civilized as you describe it? Is she not Christian now? Can she not wear civilized clothes and still be Christian? I like her clothes. She shall have the new clothes. There is still much tobacco to trade.

"There are other things I want for Cool Water. You have taught her to garden well with many plants that are strange to me. But the food is familiar to her. And the flowers around the garden will make her spirit sing. It would seem only a small cost for you to send seeds along with Cool Water so that she may have a garden on the Siconece with foods and flowers in it just like the ones she grows for you.

"Cool Water must also have the Indian slave boy, to whom she has grown attached, to help her in the garden just as I helped my mother in the garden. They will need two of the metal hoes just like..."

"Whoa, Meas." Big Field was laughing again. "You're being silly.

There is not that much tobac..."

"There is yet lots of tobacco," Meas continued. "Cool Water will need pots and pans and kettles to cook the food in and pretty dishes and glassware, such as she uses at your table, with which to serve the food and drinks. There must be a shiny wooden table on which to place the plates and silver and glass. Cool Water must be civilized.

"Cool Water needs one cow, from which she can make butter, curd, and drink. She will need a pail and churn and..."

"Meas, stop," laughed Captain Big Field. "There is no more tobacco. You are not even trying to keep track. I suppose you are going to ask for a horse next."

"No, Cool Water can do without the horse," Meas continued. "I will not insist on the horse. But a yearling heifer and a young bull. Yes, I am keeping track. When Captain Big Field calculated the value of the English wampum, he said one pound buys 160 pounds of tobacco. I know one pound of English wampum buys 250 pounds of tobacco. My twenty-eight pounds of English wampum buys 7,000 pounds of tobacco. There is still much tobacco.

"Captain Big Field, there is one more thing I must have if we are to complete this trade. I cannot walk the cow across the Chesapeake, nor can I carry all the other goods I have bought on my back. You have many friends and ship captains who sail these waters. Would you not be so kind as to have one of your ship captains deliver my order to the Siconece before the spring month comes?"

"Oh, Meas. You wear me out.

"Yes, I can include the shipping. The very picture of you walking your cow across the Chesapeake tickles my whiskers and moves my heart with pity. I must help you," and Captain Big Field burst out laughing.

"The very idea.

"Meas, I cannot keep track of everything you ordered, but I suppose it's a deal."

"Oh, Captain Big Field. That is no problem. I keep very good track. I know it all. Yet there is one thing I just happened to remember. My gun is not much. It is broken. It will not fire. Could you not include one good gun for me of the highest quality? And maybe some powder and ball?"

"No, Meas. That is too much. One gun too much. I cannot do it. Maybe I can help you get your gun fixed and let you have some powder and ball. Would that work?"

"No, Captain Big Field. I do not like my gun. It is a cheap gun and poorly made. I want a good gun. Surely the Captain has an extra gun around the plantation that he would let me have. Does he not?"

"No, Meas. I would really like to help you out. But the gun is too much. There is no tobacco left. I cannot include the gun in the deal."

Meas reached his hand into the bag of silver coins and stirred them. They jangled noisily in the darkness. Then he said, "I really wanted to trade with you, Captain Big Field, but I guess it is not possible. It makes my heart heavy to think that I may lose Cool Water, but if you cannot include the gun I will have to take my English wampum elsewhere."

"Meas," Captain Big Field said slowly, "I have done some more calculations, and maybe there is enough tobacco so that, after all, I may include the gun, powder, and ball."

"Oh, most gracious Captain Big Field. My heart sings. It is most kind of you to see beyond the value of tobacco and to see what joy and pleasure this brings to my heart. I shall be grateful to you as long as the rivers run and the sun shines. But I must still cry out to you for pity. You must look down on me and see that if I am to be civilized, then not only must Cool Water wear the clothes of a civilized Christian. I also must wear the clothes of a civilized Christian. And the thought has come to me that maybe you would have a spare hat, shirt, stockings, suit, and shoes so that I, too, might become civilized."

It was too much. Falling Leaf rolled on the porch floor laughing.

He tried to translate for Captain Big Field. It would not come out all at once. Captain Big Field started laughing too. He laughed because Falling Leaf laughed. Then Captain Big Field laughed because he understood what Meas had said. The tears came to his eyes. He pushed his hands harder against his sides.

Meas did not laugh. "What is joke?" he asked. "I make deal." The two roared even louder.

Captain Big Field wiped at the tears streaming down his face. "What sport!" he exclaimed. "Meas, I can't remember that I have ever enjoyed such mirth. Why, it's just as if I blew whole fields of tobacco up in smoke and enjoyed smoking every bit of it. Of course, you shall have my suit of clothes, hat, stockings, and shoes. It's a deal."

"Okay," Meas said. "Here is deal: I give you two pounds English wampum. You give me gun, powder, ball. In spring month Captain Big Field and Soft Heart bring—seeds, cow, Indian boy, Cool Water, clothes, tools—everything to Siconece. I marry Cool Water. Give you twenty-six pounds sterling."

Meas stood up and held out his hand to Captain Big Field. "Shake hand," he commanded.

Captain Josias Fendall, Sachem Big Field, Governor of the State of Maryland rose and took Meas's hand. Meas gripped the hand firmly. "It's a deal," Meas said.

"It's a deal," Captain Big Field responded.

Meas tightened his grip on Big Field's hand and drew him closer until he could see his eyes in the dark.

"You no touch Cool Water," he warned.

"I no touch Cool Water," Captain Big Field promised.

Narrated by Glikkikan

Owechela smiled. "What do you think, Glikkikan? Could Meas run a trading post?"

"It seems like he got everything he wanted," I answered.

"Owechela, why did Meas want the white man's clothes? Why did he want to be civilized? Did he not show Captain Big Field that the Lenape were a better people than any of the Christian nations?" I asked.

"Aye, Glikkikan, good questions one and all. I see that you seek the truth.

"The tale of Meas is not yet ended. Listen well, Glikkikan. As Meas said, 'Because the trail is faint does not mean that the skillful may not follow it.' Listen to the story and follow the trail. Perhaps you will find the answers to your questions, and ... the truth."

Chapter 4 — 1658-1659

Meas—the Defender

As told by Owechela

In early spring *The Dove*,[28] an English trading vessel, sailed into the mouth of the Siconece and lashed itself fast to a makeshift dock. Meas himself waited next to the place of the sacred pole and the spot where his mother lay buried. Tiny white flowers bloomed profusely around the spot, nodding their tender white bells in joyful swells.[29]

Two hundred Lenape watched quietly as Falling Leaf, Meas, Meoppitas, and Sachem Koketotoka greeted the ship and its passengers. Sachem Big Field climbed over the edge first. Sachem Koketotoka and Sachem Big Field exchanged solemn greetings.

When the formalities had ended, the crew rolled three carefully packed hogsheads[30] over the side and down the plank onto the dock. Eager hands rolled them up the hill onto the grass. A windlass lifted

---

[28] The smaller of two boats bringing the first settlers to St. Mary's City in 1634. A replica of *The Dove* sails the Chesapeake today. Contact <www.stmaryscity.org> to see the ship.
[29] Lily of the Valley probably brought over from Holland.
[30] A cask used for shipping tobacco, forty-two to forty-three inches in length and twenty-six to twenty-seven inches in the head.

a cow in a net, then swung her helplessly over the edge of the boat before dropping her gently onto the dock. Next came a yearling heifer and then a bull calf. A small Indian boy jumped over the edge and ran down the plank to stand beside the cattle and the hogsheads. Last of all, Cool Water stepped over the edge, walked down the plank, and stood waiting beside the other merchandise, her eyes down and her head hung in respectful obedience.

"That's everything," said Captain Big Field. "Now I have delivered everything. Even my suit is in one of the casks. You already have the gun. Some additional powder and ball are also in the casks. Where is the twenty-six pounds ster-r-ling? Meas, that is the deal, is it not?"

"Where is Soft Heart?" Meas asked.

"She could not come because of the children," Captain Big Field explained. "Soft Heart sends you her greetings and wishes you much happiness."

"Can you not stay with us for the ceremony?" Meas wondered.

"No," Captain Big Field said, lowering his voice, "the ship cannot wait and I must accompany it to New Amstel. You see, our last year's tobacco crop is on board, and I will have to do some hard trading with Hinoyossa." Captain Big Field let out a hearty laugh. "Of course, after trading with Meas, I should be able to slice off one of Fat Pig's hams and he'd think it was all a joke. Meas, where is the ster-r-ling so I can be on my way."

"I must talk with Cool Water a few moments first," Meas stalled. Meas slipped over to her and she raised her black eyes in question. "Is everything in the casks?" he asked in Lenape.

"Yes," she answered in Lenape, "I packed it myself."

"Did Captain Big Field touch you?"

"No, Captain Big Field did not touch me."

"Is Soft Heart well?"

"Yes, I think so, but her heart is sick."

"And what about Cool Water? Is she well?"

"Oh, Meas," she said, looking up at him through tears in her eyes, "Cool Water's heart is singing, but she's terribly scared."

Meas patted Cool Water lightly on the head and reassured her, "My white dove will be all right. Everything will be all right."

Meas gave Captain Big Field the twenty-six pounds sterling and the Lenape watched as *The Dove* flitted out into the bay.

As the sails and the white flag with the red crossbars disappeared over the Lenape Bay, a great shout went up from the crowd standing on the bank. "We carry the Spirit of Tamenend in the Land of the Dawn. We carry the Spirit of Tamenend in the Land of the Dawn. We carry ..." On and on the cry rolled as the Lenape faced the east.

The women gathered around Cool Water and started to pull and push her toward the bank of the Siconece. She looked helplessly at Meas. He nodded. Six women led her to the river's edge and carefully undressed her. The chant continued as the six took Cool Water into the river and scrubbed her from head to toe. They brought her once more to the riverbank and surrounded her while some combed the tangles from her long black hair. Others began to dress her in soft leggings of deerskin and moccasins with tiny silver bells attached, and a long dress made of intricately woven white swan down and feathers. A wide black belt with a single string of wampum in the middle girdled her waist. A brilliant red linen cravat sat snugly around her neck with the crossed ends draped on her chest. A silver band, sprung across the top of her head and ending in front of each ear, held her black hair in place. The women placed a wreath of ivy leaves interwoven with those tiny white bell flowers on her head. They slipped two gold bracelets on each wrist. Last of all, they fastened around her neck a glittering chain with the copper medallion that had belonged to Meas's mother dangling from it.

When the women had finished their task, they turned Cool Water to face the chanting crowd standing on the hill above. Then the women stepped back from her in a sort of "V" with Cool Water at the point. The women faced her, placed their left hands on their hips, bent toward her, and held their right hands out palms upward.

Meas raised his arm. Cool Water raised her arm. The chanting stopped.

A bevy of unmarried girls converged on Cool Water. They chattered excitedly and led her away toward the village. The crowd again descended on the rest of the trade goods Meas had bought.

Meas opened the hogsheads. A swift blow or two with his tomahawk burst the locking bands on the lid. Meas lifted each item from the cask for all to see, then gave it to someone standing nearby. Item by item, Meas repeated the task until all three casks were empty and most of the crowd was carrying some treasure. Then Meas handed the rope of the cow to Koketotoka, the rope of the heifer to Meoppitas, and the rope of the bull to the Indian boy.

Meas took the lead, and the procession followed him back to the village. Meas led the way to a new wigwam standing by the edge of the village. He directed that the cattle be tied to trees where they could chew on early grass. But all the rest of the items he stowed inside the wigwam. When the last treasure had arrived and the carriers had gone, Meas seated himself on a mat by the wigwam. Another mat lay on the ground beside him.

The entire village stirred with fires and cooking. Each home prepared some meat of its own. Gradually, the entire village reassembled at the new wigwam, each carrying a present of meat. When all the guests had arrived, they stood in respectful silence while a group of lighthearted maidens led Cool Water to Meas and seated her on the mat beside him.

Koketotoka faced east and prayed the ancient prayer of the Lenape. The guests seated themselves on mats they had brought with them.

Cool Water rose and served Meas his dinner. Then she went about gaily serving dinner to all the rest. All admired the splendid woman Meas had taken for his own. Many commented in Lenape, not realizing that Cool Water understood. "She will make Meas a good wife."

After Cool Water had finished serving, she once again seated herself beside Meas and ate her own meal. Then the two rose together and sang their duet in English. The song was barely finished when other songs in Lenape started ringing out. A drum picked up the beat, reed flutes and Jew's harps joined in. The singing and dancing began.

Cool Water and her Indian servant boy raised a wonderful garden that first year. Like others in the village, they planted large fields of maize, beans, squash, and pumpkins. Meas helped with the tillage and planting, placing the various seeds in the black soil at the times and in the manner Cool Water wanted. In addition to the staple crops, they seeded the additional plants—peas, muskmelons, watermelons, cucumbers, sweet potatoes—and flowers Meas had bought from Charles County, Maryland. Meas and Cool Water chose the fields close to his mother's grave and not far from the fabled Fountain of Youth.

Cool Water tended to the milking of the cow, the churning of butter, and the curd making. She found the waters of Tired Moon Pond much better than the saltwater of the Siconece for cooling the milk. In addition, the cattle could drink freely from its fresh waters.

Further southwest from the Fountain of Youth and an easy walk from the Siconece, Tired Moon Pond nestled itself in a three-sided swale among the fields and trees. Soggy ground on the southwest end wandered off until it lost itself in distant higher ground. Tired Moon Pond lay shaped much like the head of a giant horned cow when the crow looks down upon her. Each horn of the pond curved gently back toward the other, encasing a beautiful meadow and a few scattered trees on the high ground inside the loop. The high ground extended through the opening between the horns of the pond toward the south.

Because of the cows and their constant need of care, Meas decided not to follow the seasonal migration of Koketotoka's villagers. He and the Indian boy built a log house at the southeast corner of the pond. Even with its wood floor and glass windows, it was no match for Captain Big Field's house. But Cool Water moved in gladly and made the rude building her home. Now she could store her precious "English dishes" and "Christian clothes" safely.

Meas traded the melons, peas, potatoes, milk, cheese, and curd with the other villagers for the promise of maize at harvest.

It was a good season and the harvest plenteous. Meas and Cool Water and the Indian boy were able to fill six hogsheads with shelled maize[31] besides having an ample supply for their own winter use. Others in the village likewise experienced a surplus of maize. Meas was able to secure additional hogsheads, and when the maize was all shelled, Meas had sixty hogsheads of shelled maize packed and waiting in a rude shelter he had built to house it.

Two Tongue Boyer sailed in on a small sloop laden with trade goods. His ship stopped at the makeshift pier. From there, Two Tongue paddled on up the Siconece in a small boat to Koketotoka's village. Koketotoka sent for Meas and Meoppitas.

Two Tongue made it plain that he had many kettles, many clothes, traps, knives, many other useful tools, powder, ball, matchcoats, bracelets, bangles, medals of all kinds, and rum. "Would the headmen of the village not like to come down to the ship and look at his goods?"

---

[31] Expected yield of shelled Indian corn: 15 to 20 bushels per acre. Eight bushels per hogshead.

"No," Meas said, "we do not want to trade right now. You well know that we have no skins or beaver to trade at this time of year."

"I understand," Two Tongue assured the three headmen. "That is no problem. You can trade for what you want now, and you can pay after the trapping season is over."

"We will wait till we have the skins and beaver before we trade them," Meas said firmly. "And then we will trade our skins with whoever gives us the best price."

"Meas, I see you have mastered one part of trading well," Two Tongue said agreeably. "Goods can always be bought cheaper with wampum than on credit. Really, I did not come to trade for skins and beaver. I was hoping that you had some extra maize that you might trade. I saw many maize fields all along the Siconece as I came. The Dutch know this soil produces the finest crops. And I have often heard that the Sickoneysincks are the best growers of maize anywhere along the Delaware. Surely you have some surplus maize that you would like to trade, do you not?"

"Ah-h-h, as you say, Two Tongue, this part of the Land of the Dawn is the most favored of all. From Canaresse to Cape Henlopen and west to the Chesapeake, the land is unexcelled. I know this land and its people well, for during my Vision Quest I lived its glories.

"Yes, we have had a good crop this year," Meas replied modestly, "and there is a small surplus. But right after harvest is not a good time to sell maize. We shall wait until later in the winter when the maize is used up and people are hungry. Then we can trade better."

"Maybe this year[32] is different," Two Tongue went on. "The Dutch settlers at New Amstel have been very sick. In fact, continued sickness curbed the settlers so far down this summer that all labor in the fields was abandoned. Shiploads of settlers arrived without bringing any supplies. Many are fleeing to Maryland. There is no maize in New

[32] The year was 1658.

Amstel. I am sure I can get you a good price for any maize you have."

"If the settlement is in such distress, perhaps we should share some of our maize with them," Meas offered. "We must help them in their hour of need. To do less than share with our friends would be unkind and cruel."

Meas stopped to ponder the situation. Two Tongue Boyer waited and waited. Koketotoka, Meoppitas, and Meas sat impassive. At last Meas continued, "Perhaps I have thought of a way. If Two Tongue would not be offended, I would like to show him my new gun."

Two Tongue agreed that he would like to see Meas's new gun. Meoppitas hurried to Meas's blockhouse by the pond to fetch it. In due time he returned and handed the gun to Meas. Without a word Meas handed the gun to Two Tongue. Two Tongue looked carefully at the gun and ran his hand expertly over the stock and along the barrel. "It is one of the best," he said admiringly. "You cannot buy such guns in Maryland or Virginia. They must be imported from Europe. Does it shoot true?"

"Aye, on the mark. Notice. The sight on the end of the barrel is different from most. It makes it easier to see the mark. The fire pan and flint are improved and will fire every time. This gun will not break as easily as our old ones.

"The hunting season is nearly upon us, and every hunter in the village would like to carry such a gun. Do you have such guns on the ship?"

"No-o-o. I do not have any guns like that on the ship. Even my own is not of such quality. There is another problem. Even if I can get such guns, I am not sure that Director Alricks, Jitter Hen as you call him, and Commander Stuyvesant, whom you know as Strutting Turkey, would allow me to sell guns like that to the Indians."

"Very well then, we have nothing to trade. My heart cries that the Dutch settlers must suffer want when the Lenape have maize. But I guess Jitter Hen and Fat Pig can find maize in Maryland among the Christians there. And as far as guns go, I suppose guns are like a flock of geese. If there's one goose around, there are surely more somewhere nearby."

"Meas, you mentioned Fat Pig Hinoyossa. Let me talk to him and

CQ205

Three barrels of maize for one good gun.

see if he can work something out. He's a ready trader. How much maize do you have to trade?"

"If you have enough guns, we will have sixty hogsheads of good shelled maize to trade,"[33] Meas answered. "And certainly we will need powder and ball in good supply. It should be worth one gun for each two barrels of maize, thirty guns of good quality."

"I do not know what Fat Pig might say, but I am sure he will not do two barrels per gun. Maybe three barrels per gun, twenty guns of good quality," Two Tongue countered. "Whatever you do, don't trade the maize till you hear back from me."

And that's the way the deal was left dangling when Two Tongue sailed his sloop back out into the Lenape Bay.

In less than one month Two Tongue returned. "Fat Pig can do three barrels per gun," he said triumphantly. "Do you still have the maize?"

"We still have sixty barrels of maize. If the guns are of good quality and the powder and ball are ample, I will take his offer," Meas agreed.

And so it was that one evening at dusk at the beginning of the hunting month, Meas saw a battered but well-armed ship flying the Dutch red, white, and blue flag meet Two Tongue's sloop in the deep water near the cape. They were together only briefly before the warship disappeared in the sea. Then Two Tongue's sloop sailed up to the makeshift dock on the Siconece with twenty fine guns. Early the next morning, the sloop struggled out into the bay laden with sixty barrels of maize.[34]

Meas put all the new guns in charge of Koketotoka. "You decide which brave gets a gun," Meas told him. "All I want is that I get to trade all the skins and beaver taken. I will get the Lenape the best price possible. If any brave gets a gun, I get to trade all his pelts. That

---

[33] Sixty hogsheads or barrels times eight bushels per barrel equals 480 bushels of corn. One acre could produce 20 bushels of Indian corn, so the 480 bushels represented the yield from 24 acres.
[34] Approximately 13.5 tons of corn plus the weight of the hogsheads.

is our agreement."

The first papoose came in the frog month. Meas could not have been prouder of his son. He doted on Cool Water.

Meas adopted Cool Water's Indian servant boy as his own son. The village priest named him "Kill Weed."

The rifles made a difference, and the hunt turned out well. Falling Leaf helped Meas with the sales of the pelts the hunters brought to him. Meas was able to pay good value for the pelts and when the bargaining was completed, he would throw in an extra looking glass, a sparkling pendant, or a shiny ornament "just for the wife."

Not all the pelts came to Meas and Falling Leaf. Several hunters returned from the hunt by way of Teotacken's village to the north. Two Tongue met them there. When the rum was all gone and the trading all done, Teotacken's village lay in ruins. Men and women lay carelessly about, dirty and unkempt. Fights broke out amid good friends. Children hid in the woods for fear of what their crazed drunken parents might do to each other and to them. When soberness returned to the village, Two Tongue was gone with all the pelts and had left only a few supplies and worthless trinkets in return. He "traded" the good guns for cheap guns.

The guilty hunters finally slunk back to Koketotoka's village like whipped dogs with their tails between their legs. Wives, children, and friends suffered the disappointment quietly. They knew what had happened. Koketotoka ignored them. And when Koketotoka called the village council together, the transgressors were not invited.

The fallen ones sulked about, fingering their cheap guns and muttering threats against Two Tongue.

"Get over it," Meas ordered. "Don't do it again. Now you must work doubly hard. Catch and dry the shad. Plant the maize. This is a good land, and if you work hard, we shall yet have something to eat and something to trade this winter."

HOMELAND IN MY HEART

The heifer and the cow calved on the same day in the beginning of the fawn month. They both had heifer calves.

On the same day the cows calved, an Indian messenger brought word to Koketotoka that Hawk Bill Beekman[35] and Fat Pig Hinoyossa[36] were summoning all the headmen from Siconese to Canaresse to treat with them. The place of meeting was to be at the boat dock on the Siconece. The ship would arrive in six days with lots of gifts on board.

By the sixth day[37] hundreds of Lenape from the region—Siconece, Quistin, Boempies Hook, Peskamohot, Kwickenesse, Seckatackomeck—had gathered and camped around the edges of the maize fields between the boat dock and Meas's blockhouse on the edge of Tired Moon Pond.

During the day, young men and boys held contests—jumping, running, rowing, wrestling, tomahawk throwing, marksmanship with bow and gun—while crowds watched and cheered.

Women worked to cook large kettles of succotash and savory meats. In between they watched the contests, cheered the games, and visited one with another. Cool Water could understand the Lenape quite well now. All the women treated her with kindness and as if she had been one of them all her life.

The headmen held interminably long council meetings around a fire on the north slope of Tired Moon Pond. Meas, Meoppitas, Koketotoka, and their near relations—Mocktowekon, Sawappone, and Mettomemeckas—along with Teotacken came from the Siconece. Katenagka, Esipens, and Sappataon came from Quistin. Pochoeton, Quegkamen, and Hoatagkony came from the land near Canaresse. Mameckus and Hockarus came from Peskamohot. Matapagsikan came from the land of Seckatackomeck. Sixteen headmen and sachems sat

---

[35] William Beekman, commissioner for the Dutch West Indies Company.
[36] Vice director under Stuyvesant for the Dutch West Indies Company.
[37] The treaty date was 7 June 1659.

together at the council fire.

In the evening, orators, Meas as the best of them all, entertained the crowd with stories of the past—Poconguigula, the Great White Bear, Strong Friend, Tamenend, Big Belly, Mattahorn, Strutting Turkey, Mengwe, Turn Coat, Alligéwi, and Eesanques, good manitos and bad manitos. Even young children sat fixated and crowded as close as they could get to the orators. Sometimes the young ones knew ahead the details to come and would gleefully help the storyteller along. Older ones shouted approval of great feats or groaned in agony during sad parts. The storytelling often lasted far into the night.

Into this festive setting, around noon of the sixth day, a grand sloop flying the red, white, and blue Dutch flag entered the Siconece and tied up at the makeshift dock. The sloop fired two of the great guns when it left the bay. Again, when the ship was moored to the ramshackle pier, two of the great guns fired once more, their muzzles pointed in the direction of the gathering crowd.

As soon as the guns fired, twenty Dutch soldiers clambered overboard and charged up the high bank to the knoll overlooking the field. An officer carrying a Dutch flag set the flag's pole on the ground and held it there. The twenty soldiers stood with their guns ready.

Next Fat Pig Hinoyossa, Hawk Bill Beekman, and Two Tongue Boyer, followed by several other Dutch officials, climbed the bank and stood near the flag. Two Tongue Boyer left the Dutch officials and walked forward to meet the waiting Meas. "Where are the other headmen?" Two Tongue asked. "Did you not receive Fat Pig Hinoyossa's summons to treat with us here?"

"We have received your notice," Meas answered. "Sixteen headmen await your coming to treat with them at a council fire next to Tired Moon Pond."

"The headmen must come to the ship to treat with the Dutch. This is the appointed place of meeting," Two Tongue declared.

"No," Meas insisted. "The single voice of the Sickoneysincks' Council is that those who would treat with us must come to our fire without their guns. We will not sit under Dutch guns to talk while in our own homeland."

After Two Tongue returned to the waiting Dutch headmen, it took quite a while before they slowly began to move toward Tired Moon Pond, beyond the sight of the soldiers and the reach of their guns. The Lenape headmen and sachems sat patiently waiting the arrival of their guests.

When the guests came, they were properly welcomed with long and kindly speeches. They were given savory venison, beans, greens, herbs, maize, oysters, crab, shad, salmon, and cool drinks of waters and teas. The Dutch officials watched the ongoing contests and the games.

Evening was fast approaching before the Dutch officials could gather at the Lenape council fire to conduct business. Teotacken lit the calumet[38] and passed it around the circle, with each one taking a puff. After the calumet had completed its lengthy tour, Teotacken invited Fat Pig to share the nature of his business. Two Tongue interpreted for Fat Pig.

"Today I thank you for your welcome and the kindnesses the Sickoneysincks have shown to us. I, Alixander Hinoyossa, along with," and here Fat Pig bent his powerful torso slightly in the direction of each one as he introduced them, "Willm Beekman, Jacob Jacobsen, Hendrick van Bylevelts, Jan Broersen, our skipper Michel Poulussen, Pieter Alrichs, and our interpreter Alixander Boyer are honored to attend your Sickoneysinck Council Fire.[39]

"These honorables represent the Honorable director General

---

[38] The CAL-yew-met was a tobacco pipe having a bowl made of soft red stone and a long reed for the stem, usually ornamented with many feathers. It was smoked as a symbol of peace, as a mark of welcome to strangers, and for other ceremonial purposes.

[39] These proceedings took place on June 7, 1659, and an English translation of the lost Dutch document is recorded on pages 288-289 of Weslager, C. A., *Dutch Explorers, Traders, and Settlers in the Delaware Valley, 1609-1664*.

Stuyvesant and the councils of New Holland as beings fully
empowered by the Right Honorable West India Company of
Amsterdam to act on its instructions and in its best interests.

"You are well aware that the Right Honorable West India Company
has traded with the Sickoneysincks of this area for many years. You
probably do not know of the Company's far-flung connections with
New Amstel, New Amsterdam, and Amsterdam in the Netherlands.
These towns I mention are only a few of the great cities joined
together by Dutch ships and merchants. Because of these connections
we are able to get you the best prices for your peltries, skins, and
maize. We want to continue to trade with the Sickoneysincks and all
the Lenape along the South River.

"In order to continue this trade with you and to make it easier to
protect this trade from rival nations, such as the English, we wish
to build a fort on the same spot where Swanendael once stood.
Thirty years ago, a Dutchman, Gillis Hossitt, bought this same land
from your fathers—Aixtamin, Oschoesien, Choqweke, Menatoch,
Awijkapoon, Hehatehan, Nehatehan, Atowesen, Ackseso, Maekemen,
Queskakons, and Eesanques. Queskakons and Eesanques even went
to New Amsterdam and before Peter Minuit, the director of the West
India Company at that time, and fixed their marks on the agreement
of sale. Your fathers received from Hossitt 'good Mrchandize, as
Cloath, axes, adzes, Corralls with severall more such like Mrchandize
well worth Bevers,' and your fathers declared 'they had full
satisfaction' for the payments they received.

"Nevertheless, even though the Right Honorable Company bought
the land from your fathers, it again wishes to purchase these same
lands from you. The Right Honorable Company is now offering
you many trade goods for 'all the land between Cape Hinlopen and
Boempies Hook lying in the South River of New Holland, stretching
two or three days' walking up into the country or about thirty miles.'

"So that it may be clear to you and to your children, and that there be again no future wars, it must be understood that 'you do transport the said parcel of land free and without encumbrance and do desist hereby your rights and properties forever, without reservation of any right, part interest or dominion therein, obliging yourselves to keep this your transport irrevocable and to perform the same according to law therefore provided. Furthermore, you do promise that when these lands shall be possessed and cultivated, then as well, man and beast shall dwell and live in unity and peace; and if by accident any damage should happen, such shall be communicated unto the upperheds or sackemakers, and they will take care that reparation shall be made.'[40]

"So, headmen and sachems of the Lenape gathered here today, do you wish to treat with the Right Honorable West India Company and sell this land again in return for the numerous gifts and merchandise offered by the Right Honorable Company?"

Teotacken thanked Fat Pig for coming to the Siconece. Teotacken said the council would consider his offer and give him a reply tomorrow when the sun stood straight overhead.

The Dutch officials returned to the ship and sailed out into the bay for the night. The council continued far into the night. Every one of the sixteen headmen had his chance to speak. Between speeches, long periods of silence prevailed. When the morning light began to roll back the darkness, Teotacken rose, faced the east, and prayed the ancient prayer of the Lenape. The council chose Meas to give the answer to the Dutch, and then all retired to their own camps.

In the morning the Dutch sloop returned again to the dock on the Siconece. Officials, soldiers, and sailors fretted about on the shore until the sun stood straight overhead. The Dutch officials made their way to the banks of Tired Moon Pond and waited until all sixteen members of the council appeared. Teotacken took care of the opening

[40] Land description and sale conditions taken from translation of recorded treaty.

formalities, then called on Meas to give the answer of the council.

I, Meas, son of Eesanques's daughter, have been called upon to give to the Right Honorable Dutch West India Company the full answer of the united council of the Sickoneysincks gathered here on the bank of the Siconece River.

You have asked to buy from us as the rightful owners the land between Cape Henlopen and Boempies Hook for two or three days' journey inland.

You are right. We are the rightful owners of this fair land. The Great Spirit gave us this land hundreds and hundreds of years ago. It belongs to us and to our children to share its fruits and enjoy its bounty.

You have also taught us that thirty years ago we "sold" this same land to Gillis Hossitt and therefore to the Right Honorable West India Company. In this you are mistaken.

We do not know what the paper said that Eesanques and Queskakons put their mark upon. But we know exactly the words of the treaty our fathers made with Gillis Hossitt and Peter Minuit. "You may live with us in peace and share this good land as long as the sun shines and the Siconece runs to the sea."

Your fathers broke this treaty. They would not live peaceably among us and treated our fathers and mothers as dogs and slaves. Our fathers slew those evil men on this very soil. To this day the twenty-five arrows shot through the dog and the bones of thirty-two dead men David de Vries buried should serve as a warning to the Dutch that they dare not break the vows they make to us.

You say your fathers paid cloth and axes and adzes and wampum and merchandise as a trade for our homes and maize fields and hunting grounds. As if our fathers sold their lives for a few beaver and several strings of wampum. Our fathers' heads were not empty. They would never have agreed to such an empty bargain. The gifts your fathers gave to our fathers were only pledges assuring that your fathers would dwell in peace with our fathers.

You say that you want to build a fort here to protect us from the English. Your lips speak only vain words. Even a child knows that you want to force us to trade only with Fat Pig and Two Tongue. We wish to trade with whoever will give us the most wampum or tobacco or goods or sterling.

We do not want traders to come among us with rum and then steal our peltries and maize. We do not care if they are Dutch, English, French, Spanish, or Swede. Let this be a warning to you. If you bring rum into our villages, we will stave the ends in and drive you from our villages.

You say that you wish to bring settlers to this fair land. We will share the land with settlers who come, if, and only if, they live peaceably among us. But the Dutch are like blue jays that shriek and cry amongst themselves, yet in an unguarded moment they dart in and devour the eggs and young of other birds. We will watch any settlers who come.

You say you want to treat with us. We do not understand the words you tell us. They are strange words. The paper talks only to you. Two Tongue may not tell you what we say. Two Tongue may not tell us what you say. We do not know. Two Tongue has lied and stolen from us before. Why should we believe him or trust him now?

Fat Pig Hinoyossa, if you wish to treat with us, we will treat with you. You may come and live among us if, and only if, you live in peace. We will continue to hunt and fish and to plant our fields as we have always done. You may build a trading post next to the boat dock to aid us in our trading, but you may not interfere with our trading. Drink your own rum, but do not bring it here. If you do not wish to abide by these terms, then go away. Do not return to the Siconece. Give your gifts to another.

Fat Pig Hinoyossa, I warn you. Remember Swanendael.

I, Meas, son of Eesanques's daughter and son of Gillis Hossitt, have spoken.

Meas turned and looked at each of the other fifteen members of the council. "Have I spoken well?" he asked. And each one answered, "Aye, very well."

Narrated by Glikkikan

"Owechela, why did Teotacken make the Dutch wait around so long for an answer?" Glikkikan asked. "The Dutch probably knew very well what they wanted when they issued the summons for the Lenape to gather on the Siconece."

"You have to understand, Glikkikan, that one of the hardest things for a Schwannek to do is to wait. They are always in a hurry to do everything: to sail, to come, to go, to buy, to sell, to fight, to make peace.

"Schwanneks have no time for proper ceremonies, to think, to visit, or to just sit and enjoy the moment and the gift of life. A Dutchman, especially, is like a squirrel who always scampers about burying another acorn and never taking the time to eat one.

"The waiting at a council fire at first disturbs the Schwanneks, then angers them, and finally destroys them. They cannot wait.

"Teotacken made the Dutch wait, not to harm them, but because that is the proper way to conduct a Lenape council fire."

"Owechela, did Fat Pig make a treaty with the Lenape at the Sickoneysinck Council Fire on the Siconece?" I asked.

"Yes, he did make a treaty, and sixteen headmen and sachems put their marks upon it. But what the paper talked, only the Dutch knew."

"Don't you think," I pressed, "Fat Pig would have been afraid to make the paper talk one thing and promise the chiefs something else?"

"No, Glikkikan, I do not think Fat Pig was afraid to do exactly that. And who knows? The paper may have said exactly what Fat Pig said it did, but maybe the Dutch understood it one way and the Lenape did not understand it at all. Besides, there were the gifts."

"Owechela, why would the gifts change the treaty?"

"Well, there were lots of them. Pretty glittering things like adornments for the women—bracelets, anklets, earrings, and medals— just like the ones Meas's mother loved so well. There was lots and lots of brightly colored light-woven cloth. The women loved the gifts. There were two matchcoats[41] for each of the headmen of the council. And when the Dutch ship sailed out into the Lenape Bay, it left three ankers of rum perched on the dock."[42]

"Really?" I exclaimed. "Did not the chiefs knock the ends in and drain the poison into the Siconece as Meas said they would?"

"Glikkikan, I wish I could tell you Teotacken and Koketotoka staved in every barrel. But that is not the way it happened. Too many Lenape craved the stuff, and long before any of the chiefs arrived at the dock, the rum had disappeared into the woods.

"Fat Pig did hear Meas's warning. Word got out. For several years the Dutch could not find settlers willing to stake their necks against a promise that they would live peaceably among the Siconese," mused

---

[41] A kind of mantle originally made from skins sewed together. Now made from a coarse cloth.
[42] One anker usually equals about ten U.S. gallons.

Owechela.

"It was a very odd, or could we say 'different' bunch, led by a dreamer, that showed up on the Siconece to settle there four years later.

"But there I go again, getting ahead of my story."

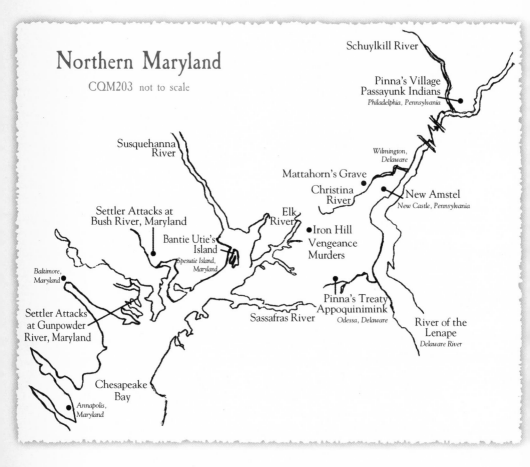

Northern Maryland

CQM203 not to scale

Schuylkill River

Pinna's Village
Passayunk Indians
Philadelphia, Pennsylvania

Susquehanna
River

*Wilmington,
Delaware*

Mattahorn's Grave

Christina
River

New Amstel
New Castle, Pennsylvania

Settler Attacks at
Bush River, Maryland

Elk
River

Bantie Utie's
Island
*Spesutie Island,
Maryland*

Iron Hill
Vengeance
Murders

*Baltimore,
Maryland*

Settler Attacks
at Gunpowder
River, Maryland

Pinna's Treaty
Appoquinimink
Odessa, Delaware

River of the
Lenape
Delaware River

Sassafras River

Chesapeake
Bay

*Annapolis,
Maryland*

Chapter 5 — 1661-1663

Meas—the Interpreter

As told by Owechela

The Right Honorable West India Company went ahead and built a rude fort on the old Swanendael site. The site lent itself well to commerce. Ships of sizable burden could sail up to the fort built on a point of land where high ground jutted out of the marshes to meet the river. Across the river a long narrow band of sand dunes separated the river from the bay and the sea all the way to Cape Henlopen. To the south and west lay the maize fields and forests. Small ships and canoes could bring Lenape and their cargoes down the Siconece to the fort.

Meas liked the spot. Outside the fort lay his mother's grave surrounded by the tiny white flowers brought from Holland. Meas loved to take Cool Water and the papoose and sit there remembering the stories his mother had told him. He told those stories to Cool Water and Kill Weed. The papoose listened too.

Meas pretty well had the use of the fort to himself. Fat Pig sent an occasional ship by to check on things and to trade with Meas whenever Meas had something to trade or needed supplies. At times, a few Dutch soldiers would come for a stay and occupy the fort.

One of these Dutch soldiers, Harmen Cornelisen, showed keen interest in the Indian trade.[42] Whenever Harmen could, he traveled with Meas to the Indian villages and assisted him in every way possible. Meas liked Harmen. Harmen's quiet and friendly manner put chiefs, women, and children alike at ease. Harmen said little, but his sparkling blue eyes observed everything—trees, flowers, plants, Lenape habits and customs, birds, wigwams, wildlife, the earth. Harmen saw it all and he liked the Siconece very much.

Harmen learned a few of the Lenape words, but he could do better talking with Meas and Cool Water in his limited English. Meas watched Harmen pat the puppy, let the calf suck his fingers, and gently hold Cool Water's newest papoose. "How can you be so gentle with the littlest of creatures and still be a Dutch soldier bent on killing the enemy?" Meas teased.

"I guess I missed my calling," Harmen answered while his eyes studied the fit of one joint on the cabin corner. "I make a very poor soldier," he said as he carefully cradled the papoose with his bony fingers. "I hate this marching, drilling, fighting, obeying orders. Should I dangle my scalp in front of white and red savages for a few paltry guilders each year—guilders Strutting Turkey refuses to pay? Even now my wife in New Amsterdam is suing the Amsterdam Council for my back wages. I hate this soldiering."

"Yes, Harmen, you do have too fine a head of hair to risk having it lifted for only a beaver or two. But how much would you take for your scalp?"

"You have a point," Harmen chuckled. "To me, my scalp is priceless. However, you should see my brother Pieter's head of hair. It's a virtual haystack. My scalp rates worthless compared with his."

[42] Harmen Cornelison was posted to Fort Sekonnessinck in 1660. Records also show him in Manhattan in 1662.

"I'm not interested in buying either your scalp or your brother's," Meas said reflectively. "Right now I'm trying to figure out what I should call a jolly, kindhearted soldier who can barely bring himself to kill a mosquito?"

Meas's eyes moved over the walls of the cabin. For a time he watched Cool Water's nimble fingers shelling beans.

At last Meas spoke. "Harmen, among the Lenape, you shall no longer be called Harmen. You shall be called Weak Gun, for the strength of the gun hides not in powder and ball, but in the heart of the soldier who wields it."

"Ah, Meas, you have rightly judged. I have no heart for this soldiering business. 'Twas only an excuse to see the world and to leave Holland. What I would really like to be is a trader like you, Meas. Right here on the Siconece."

Now it was Cool Water's eyes that twinkled mischievously. "Oh, Weak Gun," she said as she took the papoose back from his large hands into her small ones. "Anyone can become a Lenape and stay here. We will take you down in the Siconece and scrub all the bad blood out of you. Then you will be one of the People of the Dawn, one of the Real Men. Then you can stay right here on the Siconece and be a trader just like you wish."

Weak Gun's eyes flitted from a corner log joint to catch a glimpse of Cool Water's face and then hurriedly settled back to a special knot in the wall. "Could you really scrub all the bad Dutch blood out of me?" he asked.

"I did not say all the 'Dutch blood' out of you," Cool Water responded lightly. "I said all the 'bad blood.' It is not a nation that makes our blood bad, but a spirit that makes our blood rot. I have Italian blood in me, maybe some Spanish or Indian. Meas's father was a Dutchman, but Meas is good and kind, not like Fat Pig, Strutting Turkey, and Two Tongue. But we both carry ..."

Cool Water stopped. She saw that Weak Gun didn't hear her any longer. His sparkling blue eyes were fastened on Meas and his mouth hung open.

Meas nodded. "It's true. My father was none other than Gillis Hossitt of Swanendael."

Meas's trading volume grew. More and more of the Lenape brought their skins and maize to Meas and trusted him to get for them the needed supplies. He always traded kindly for the Lenape, trying to get the Lenape the best deal possible.

Falling Leaf also sailed up the Siconece to trade with Meas on various ships flying the black and gold Maryland flag. "Aren't you afraid Fat Pig will catch you?" Meas asked.

Falling Leaf laughed. "Not really," he replied carelessly. "Fat Pig trades with Virginia and Maryland planters all the time. Fat Pig doesn't care which flag the ship flies that he trades with. He's not all that loyal to the Dutch or to the West India Company either. The important thing is that you trade with Fat Pig. He knows that if you trade with me, sooner or later, he'll get a cut out of the deal, probably on both sides of the trade.

"And, really, at the moment, Fat Pig can't do much about this little trading fort on the Siconece. Great Heron Baltimore gave Fat Pig quite a scare." Falling Leaf started laughing again. This time he couldn't stop. Meas waited while enjoying his friend's lightness of spirit.

Finally Falling Leaf got ahold of himself and went on. "You remember, Meas, that Captain Big Field told us how Great Heron wants every foot of land and water he can claim. The land from the Potomack River and around the Chesapeake Bay as far north as forty degrees latitude is not enough, although Great Heron's lordly eyes have never seen the Chesapeake waters nor has he ever set one of his lordly feet on the dark soil around it. Great Heron wants to swallow New Amstel and the Hoerenkill as well."

Again, Falling Leaf paused to laugh before going on. "Only three months after Fat Pig Hinoyossa and Hawk Bill Beekman bought the Hoerenkill, Captain Big Field sent Colonel Nathaniel Utie accompanied by his brother, a cousin, and a servant on a mission to New Amstel.[43] Meas, you have to know this Colonel Utie to picture what he did to Jitter Hen Alricks and Fat Pig Hinoyossa, not to mention Hawk Bill Beekman. The best I can think of to describe Colonel Utie is a bantam rooster, crowing for all he's worth and just itching for a good fight.

"Well, Colonel Bantie Utie and his cousin, Major de Vrint, rode into New Amstel on sleek, spirited horses. They wore full battle gear—shining back and breast plates, overlapping tassets,[44] and plumed helmets. The sun glinted off their swords and polished gun barrels. Bantie Utie strode into Fop Outhout's Inn and introduced himself as a ranking officer in the service of His Majesty, the King of England, and a personal emissary of Lord Baltimore. He demanded the best rooms, the best meals, and the best wines available, and urged that nothing be spared in the care of his horses.

"Next Bantie Utie and his interpreter, de Vrint, strutted around town for three days. They counted eight soldiers[45] and one hundred houses, noted the sorry state of the fort and the defenses in general, and warned the townspeople that they were trespassing on Great Heron's territory. Bantie Utie told the people that if they would vacate the town, they could live in Maryland under his lordship's government. Otherwise, he would be forced to drive them out and plunder their homes.

---

[43] September 6, 1659.
[44] A series of connected iron plates protecting the thighs.
[45] For reasons unrelated to Utie's coming, a number of soldiers had already fled to Maryland.

"Meas, can you imagine the fearful state of mind Jitter Hen Alricks was in by this time? By the time Bantie Utie demanded an official hearing, Jitter Hen nearly collapsed. Bantie Utie ordered Jitter Hen, Hawk Bill, and the council to vacate the town immediately or declare New Amstel subject to Great Heron's government. Bantie Utie threatened that if officials did not vacate or submit, he himself could not be held responsible for any blood spilled because Great Heron had the power to make war without consulting anybody.

"Meas, if you had been Jitter Hen, what would you have done with Bantie Utie?"

"Falling Leaf, that is an impossible question," Meas answered. "I care not for either Jitter Hen or Great Heron or Bantie Utie. Let me ask you a question. If a Dutchman steals an Indian's gun and then a Marylander steals the gun from the Dutchman, whose gun is it?"

"Meas, I suppose I would have to say the gun still belongs to the Indian."

"And how will the Indian get the gun back, Falling Leaf? Will the Marylander give it back to the Indian if the Indian shows the Marylander it belongs to him? No. Will the Dutchman help the Indian wrest the gun away from the Marylander so the Indian may have his own gun again? No. I will tell you what will happen. If the Indian steals his own gun again from the Marylander, both the Marylander and the Dutchman will shoot the Indian. Is it not so?

"Anyway, go on with your story, Falling Leaf. What did Jitter Hen do?"

"Meas, Jitter Hen begged Bantie Utie to give New Amstel three weeks' time to consider his demands. Bantie Utie avowed that Maryland had five hundred men under arms just waiting on orders to march against New Amstel, but he 'reluctantly' agreed to hold things up for three weeks. Then Bantie Utie left town.

"Even before Bantie Utie vanished into the woods, Jitter Hen had a report on the way to Strutting Turkey Stuyvesant in New Amsterdam. I can well imagine Strutting Turkey let out two extra gobbles and two extra snorts the day he got the report. Strutting Turkey sent sixty soldiers pronto to New Amstel. He ordered the commanders to arrest Bantie Utie as a spy and send him to Manhattan in chains if he ever stepped out of the woods again. Strutting Turkey sent two special envoys to meet with Sachem Big Field at St. Mary's City and to protest Bantie Utie's warring ways when Holland and England were at peace with each oth—"

"But Falling Leaf," Meas broke in, "help me understand. What was the squabble about? Did not Strutting Turkey take Christina from the Swedes even though the Swedes were there first? Should Strutting Turkey have been surprised if Great Heron plucked New Amstel from him because Great Heron had more soldiers and guns? Why even argue about which king claimed the land first or who settled the land first or who supposedly bought the land from the Indians first?

"If right and wrong has nothing to do with who owns the land anyway, why didn't they just declare war and fight it out? Or better yet, why couldn't they just live in peace together with each other and the Lenape? What was wrong with the Schwanneks?"

"Meas, I will tell you the truth. One blinded by greed and power has a simple job to convince himself that what he does is right. And if one is sure he is right, it helps quiet the sting in his spirit for doing what he knows is wrong."

"And Falling Leaf, if Strutting Turkey and Great Heron both have convinced themselves that New Amstel and the Siconece and all the land in between belongs to them, then they will fight?"

"Aye, Meas. They will fight."

"Aye, Falling Leaf. If Strutting Turkey and Great Heron will fight, then the Lenape must also prepare to fight."

"Meas, I cannot disagree. But to end my hilarious tale which you do not find amusing, I will tell you what happened only three months after Bantie Utie tormented Jitter Hen Alricks. The sun set for the last time on Jitter Hen Alricks,[46] and Fat Pig Hinoyossa took his place as sachem of New Amstel."

Narrated by Glikkikan

"Owechela, do you think Bantie Utie really thought he could scare the Dutch into moving out of New Amstel?" I asked.

"No, Glikkikan, Bantie Utie knew the Dutch would not just pack up their bags and sail away. I think Bantie Utie was all guff and huff and puff and bluff. He sure put on a good show. The trouble was that Great Heron and Big Field were not bluffing. They meant to drive the Dutch from New Amstel."

"Owechela," I asked excitedly, "if Great Heron and Big Field meant to drive the Dutch out of New Amstel, then what about the Lenape on the Siconece? Did Great Heron intend to drive them out too?"

"Glikkikan, when a great fire roars through the fields and forest, all the animals are driven before it. All are alike before the fire.

"In Maryland, Captain Big Field led a new uprising against Great Heron, and Bantie Utie sided with him. The revolt failed, and Big Field almost lost all his fields and was ordered driven from Maryland. Great Heron softened Big Field's punishment and allowed him to keep his fields at Port Tobacco, but Big Field could never be one of Great Heron's councilors or captains again.

"Glikkikan, do not think because Great Heron and Big Field spat

[46] Jacob Alricks died 20 December 1659.

in each other's faces, they disagreed about who owned the Land of the Dawn. No. No. They both agreed that the Siconece and New Amstel and all the land in between belonged to Maryland. Their fight was over whether Great Heron or Big Field would get the gifts[47] from it each year. Neither Great Heron nor Big Field cared a spit for the Lenape, the Nanticoke, the Choptanks, or the Susquehannocks.

"The same thing was true of Fat Pig and Strutting Turkey. They wanted the Land of the Dawn and would fight anyone to get it ... including the Lenape."

As told by Owechela

The dugout entered the Siconece from the Lenape Bay and paddled its way by the dock at the fort. Shortly past the dock five Lenape braves in war paint sprang out and quickly hid the canoe in the undercover. The canoe carried no trade goods and the braves were strange to the area. Two of them slipped off into the fields in search of Meas.

The braves found Meas and Cool Water checking the maize fields. They seemed to have no trouble finding Meas or picking him out. They knew the one they looked for.

The messenger held out the string of wampum in front of him so Meas could see it. "This is the message of the wampum," the brave began.

I, Sachem Pinna of Pickhattomitta and of the Passayunk[48]

---

[47] Taxes were a very difficult concept for Indians to comprehend.
[48] *Passayunk* means "in the valley." Passayunk was probably a Lenape village located between the Schuylkill and Delaware Rivers in present-day Philadelphia, Pennsylvania.

Lenape, to Meas of the Siconece[49] Lenape. Greetings.

Brother, I saw your face at Mattahorn's funeral.

Brother, the birds of the forest sing of your oratory. The birds sing of your exploits among the Dutch and the English. And the birds have sung to me of your goodness to the Lenape.

Brother, Falling Leaf brings word to me that you have taken a wife. May you be blessed with many sons and daughters, and may you and your descendants prosper in the Land of the Dawn.

Brother, I know that you speak the English tongue. The Marylanders have begun a war with us, and now Great Heron's brother has commanded me to treat with him at Appoquinimink.[50] I wish you to be my tongue at the meeting.

Brother, before we go to treat at Appoquinimink, I wish you to come to a Passayunk Council Fire at Pickhattomitta. There we will teach you the events of the war. Oconiccka (o-co-NEE-ka) will bring you to Pickhattomitta and return you to the Siconece after we treat at Appoquinimink.

Meas reached out his hand for the wampum. "I am honored to accept Pinna's invitation," he said, and took the wampum from Oconiccka. "Your journey here has been a long and tiring one. Would Oconiccka wish to fill his stomach and rest his eyes before beginning the return journey? I would wish you to taste some of Cool Water's beans, maize bread, and butter while you are here. May your memories of your time on the Siconece always be pleasant ones."

"It is true that the journey has been a three-day journey," Oconiccka replied. "And the way back will be a five-day journey with much paddling. I would like to accept your kind offer, but our business is

---

[49] Siconece is a river. The Siconesse Lenape were people who lived in the region of the Siconece River.
[50] Near present Odessa, Delaware.

urgent and dangerous. We are at war. Many Marylanders will shoot at any Indian that just walks by. Perhaps some of our journey will have to be at night. Pinna bade us begin the return trip as soon as you are ready to travel, so we must decline your kind offer until we return in a time of peace. But I have heard much of the Fountain of Youth on the Siconece. Would it be asking too much to imbibe its magic before beginning the return journey?"

Meas urged Oconiccka to drink deeply of the fabled water, told Cool Water and Kill Weed to keep a constant vigil against coons in the maize fields, hugged his two-year-old son, and then followed his escort back to the waiting canoe. Meas took his place among the paddlers, and the canoe raced along the Siconece and out into the bay.

Meas enjoyed the trip through the Lenape Bay and then up the Lenape River, past Boempies Hook, past New Amstel, and past the scattered Swedish, Finnish, and Dutch farms fanning out from the settlements. The fall days bred blue and green vistas with tinges of red, orange, and yellow leaves accented by sparkling sunbeams. Meas traveled the Lenape River while it sported its finest dress.

Pinna awaited Meas at Pickhattomitta. Pinna fed him choice meats, berries, and vegetables in abundance. He gave him a mat to sleep on in his own wigwam. As the village sachem, Pinna carried the responsibility of caring for official guests, and Pinna's wife and daughters saw to it that Meas lacked nothing a Lenape chieftain could have desired.

Meas met with the Passayunk Council the next day. The council went through the proper ceremonies welcoming Meas to their circle. Then Pinna rose and addressed the council:

> Counselor Meas, I have asked you to come and be my
> tongue when meeting with the Sachem of Maryland.
> Therefore, I want you to know the truth of events that have
> brought us to this present state of war. The Passayunk Council

at this special fire witnesses that my tongue tells only the truth.

Counselor Meas, you know well that for many years the Mengwe have committed murders against other nations with whom the Lenape were at peace. Then the Mengwe left a club indicating it was the Lenape who murdered and scalped. When the Eries or the Cherokee sent an avenging party out to attack the Lenape, the Mengwe joined the avenging party in their attack against the Lenape. In this way they brought many nations against the Lenape with whom the Lenape really had no quarrel.

Counselor Meas, now the Mengwe are at it again. The Mengwe bring raids against the settlers in Maryland. The settlers in Maryland cannot tell the difference between Mengwe, Susquehannock, or Lenape. To the Marylanders, all the Indians are heathen savages.

In the spring month of this season, Mengwe killed a Marylander's wife and plundered his house. Four days later, Mengwe came again and shot five cows, a steer, and some hogs.

Several days later Oconiccka and three other Passayunk Lenape traveled along Gunpowder River. Without provocation, the Maryland planters shot one of the four Lenape, overturned their canoe, and dumped all their goods including three guns into the river. The remaining three Lenape fled homeward on foot.

At Saquesehum[51] the three braves met four Marylanders returning home from New Amstel. The braves killed all four of the travelers and took their clothes, shoes, and packs. Oconiccka gave one of the hats to two Susquehannocks

---

[51] Known as Iron Hill near the present Delaware-Maryland border.

traveling to New Amstel. Oconiccka and the other two promptly fled home to Passayunk.

One of the two Susquehannocks proudly wore the gray hat to New Amstel, where suspicious citizens promptly threw them in jail. Fat Pig questioned the two carefully. He realized the two Susquehannocks knew nothing of the murders and released them, but he did learn from them that Oconiccka had given them the hat.

Fat Pig sent for Oconiccka. I and twenty other Passayunks went with Oconiccka to New Amstel. Fat Pig told us he received wampum from Bantie Utie, but when Fat Pig gave us the message of the wampum, his face was the face of the coon in the roasting ears. This is the message of Bantie Utie's wampum:

> I vnderstood from Mr. Hollingsworth that four men belonging to this Province were murdered by the hand of some of your Indian neighbors. And further, that upon his accusacon yow had Comitted them to Guard, I sent this Expresse to yow to be informed of the true State of the matter. It is not our Custome to putt vp the injuryes of Indians, nor to bury the blood of Christians in forgettfullnes & oblivion, Therefore I request yow to deliver me the Indian Prisoners that I may deale with them according to our Justice in like cases. I am now at Spesvtia, and there shall remayne till I haue provided for the safety of the people and the honor of our nacon and there shall Expect an answere from you.[52]

Counselor Meas, I told Fat Pig of the unprovoked attack and murder of the Passayunk brave by Marylanders. Furthermore, I told Fat Pig of another attack by Marylanders upon Passayunk Indians that took place within a few days,

---

[52] Archives of Maryland Online, Vol. III, "Proceedings of the Council of Maryland, 1636–1667," p. 415. Minor adaptions made.

maybe even before the killing I have just described to you.

Two canoes carrying nine Passayunk Lenape braves paddled down Bush River. A boat carrying several Marylanders came out on the river and asked those in the canoe what they were doing. The other canoe pulled up to the shore where a vicious dog attacked one of the braves. The brave shot the dog in self-defense. The white men in the boat immediately shot all five braves in the canoe. One of those five was my own brother. In all the shooting that followed, the Lenape did succeed in killing one white man and wounding another.

Fat Pig listened closely to our account. Then Fat Pig said, "Great Heron and Bantie Utie have thrown down the tomahawk to Strutting Turkey. Bantie Utie has warned us at New Amstel that he will not be held liable for any blood spilt if Great Heron's soldiers attack us. I do not want war with anyone—Great Heron, Lenape, Piscataway, or the Susquehannocks. I want to trade with all of them.

"But if Great Heron makes war upon the Lenape, I do not blame the Lenape for shooting back. I will not turn Oconiccka and his friends over to Bantie Utie."

Those were the words of Fat Pig. Fine words they were. Fat Pig passed out gifts to us as a sign of his friendship. And as we departed for Passayunk, he loaded two ankers of rum in our canoes.

Counselor Meas, what think ye? Shall we pick up the tomahawk Great Heron's brother throws at our feet and fling it back at him, or shall we bury it?

Sachem Pinna resumed his seat. Old men, sachems, and young braves sat quietly awaiting Meas's answer. Meas smoked on his pipe until the last embers died out. Then he turned the pipe over, knocked the ashes on the ground, and rose to his feet.

Sachem Pinna and all noble Lenape gathered around this council fire at Passayunk. I am but a green sapling with tender bark. My trunk remains slender and shows not the thickness purchased by many years of age.

Besides that, the question Pinna has set before me is one at which I must aim my arrows with the greatest of care. For to miss the mark on either side could easily mean that the Lenape will be driven from the Land of the Dawn. Perhaps the mark lies beyond the distance for my bow to reach. Nevertheless, I will string my bow and shoot.

Sachem Pinna, the war thrust upon the Passayunk Lenape is not a new war. Ever since the Schwanneks have come to our lands, they have all been intent on taking our land.

At first, the Schwanneks are timid. The Schwanneks say they need only a little land to plant some herbs on or to set their chair upon. Soon more Schwanneks come. With white-winged canoes, Schwanneks spread out into every river and valley, taking over the fields and forests and streams. Soon they do not ask if they may hunt or fish on OUR lands. They tell us we may not fish in the rivers and bays. They tell us we may not farm OUR fields. They tell us we may not hunt in OUR forests. And if the Schwanneks do not succeed in killing us first with strange diseases, or in stealing our wills and our goods with rum, the Schwanneks will soon tell us we may not build OUR wigwams in the Land of the Dawn.

"Ah," you say, "the Schwanneks are not all the same."

Sachem Pinna, that is true. Schwanneks are different. Dutch trade as greedily as a hog slurps rum. Virginians spring with the suddenness of a panther. New Englanders dive with the swiftness of an eagle, and Marylanders hunt with the ruthlessness of the wolf. The Schwanneks are all different.

Yet the Schwanneks are all the same. To the Hog, the Eagle, the Panther, and the Wolf, the Lenape are but a harmless Hare darting in and out of the bramble bushes. The Lenape are but prey for all of them.

Sachem Pinna, let a Lenape but tread carelessly upon a Schwannek's hole in the ground and the Schwanneks come boiling out as hornets bruising for a fight.

But let the Schwanneks attack the Lenape, and the Lenape will act as flocks of black ducks trying to hide in the marshes. If pressed upon they will burst into flight in an effort to escape, only to be permanently driven from their haunt or slaughtered upon their return.

Sachem Pinna, at this moment the Lenape dare not make war upon the Schwanneks, for they would be as small children fighting with sticks and rocks against warriors with guns and tomahawks.

Our bows and arrows will not reach the enemy. Our cheap guns rust and our powder is wet. Worst of all, the Spirit of Tamenend has departed from our people. Hunters and warriors sell their wills to any Schwannek for only a keg of rum. Our villages crumble and die from disease, drunkenness, and darkness. The light in the spirit has gone out.

We must rekindle the fire in our spirits. We must restore the Spirit of Tamenend to the Lenape. We must retake the Land of the Dawn. We must remand the demons in the rum back to the gaols of the Schwanneks. We must retouch the heart of the Great Spirit and tap the strength of Tamenend, Eesanques, and Mattahorn to carry us past the dangers of the moment.

Sachem Pinna, today the Lenape have no choice. We are scattered. We are shattered. Today we are weak. Now is the season to make peace. But the Lenape must begin at once to plant and till the seeds of war. And the next time the red moon rises over the River of the Lenape, the Lenape shall be prepared to fight.

Sachem Pinna, the words of Meas are ended.

Meas resumed his seat and waited. Sachem Pinna again rose to his feet.

Counselor Meas, again we are thankful you have come to Passayunk to attend our council fire. Your words of caution show your knowledge of the past, an awareness of the present, and call for action in the future. We shall heed the words of truth you speak.

Yet I would point out to you that when we meet with Great Heron's brother at Appoquinimink, our position is not entirely one of weakness. Remember that Great Heron has also attacked Fat Pig and Strutting Turkey. The Dutch will be only too glad to have us on the same side with them in any war with Great Heron. The Lenape will not buy peace at just any price.

Counselor Meas, will you go with me to Appoquinimink and be my tongue so that we may make a just peace with Great Heron's brother?

The fire[53] at Appoquinimink was a small one. Only Counselor Meas and Sachem Pinna of Pickhattomitta were present to represent the Passayunk Lenape while Governor Philip Calvert, Scribe Henry Coursey, and Councilor John Bateman represented Great Heron and his province of Maryland. The meeting took place in a local house

[53] Meeting and subsequent treaty took place 19 September 1661.

with Governor Calvert flanked by Scribe Coursey and Councilor Bateman on one side of the table. Directly across the table from Governor Calvert sat Sachem Pinna. Behind Pinna, and a bit to his left, stood Meas. At one end of the table, a yellow-and-black-checkered flag hung from its floor stand.

Sachem Pinna began the conference with an opening statement. He thanked the governor for coming to Appoquinimink to make peace. Pinna recounted the stories of the two Marylander attacks on the Passayunk Indians and the vengeance killing of the Marylanders. Then Pinna went on:

> Governor Calvert, seeing then that the English have slain divers men belonging to the Passayunk Indians now under my command, and among them my own brother, in revenge of which divers English have been slain by those Indians, yet I do believe all those outrages were committed by the English without order from the governor and council, so I assure the governor and council that those revenges were taken by my Indians without my or any of my great men's knowledge. Therefore, I desire that all might be forgotten and that from henceforward my Indians might live in peace with the English.

To which Governor Calvert replied, "King Pinna, as I desire peace, I desire justice also. You will deliver up the Indians that killed John Norden and Sepherin Hack with his companions to be proceeded against according to their deeds."

Sachem Pinna answered thus:

> Governor Calvert, the English began this war. They first killed one of my men as he and those with him were peaceably coming by their plantation, overset their canoe out of which they lost three guns, afterward pursued them into the woods and there shot at them. My Indians fled having lost one

man and their goods. On their way home they met the said Norden and Hack and companions. Contrary to the advice of an old man of the company who stood weeping and trying to persuade the others to speak with the great men of the English first, they did kill Norden, Hack, and his companions, saying that the English would have war and they should have it.

Since that time, the English have set upon two canoes of Indians and killed five of them, among them my own brother. Notwithstanding all this, I am willing and desirous to make peace with you, even forgetting the blood of my own brother.

To which Governor Calvert responded, "King Pinna, since the time of the murders, Indians have killed eleven head of cattle and twenty head of hogs. We demand that you pay the settlers for these losses.

Sachem Pinna answered:

Governor Calvert, it is certain that it was not my Indians who killed the cattle and hogs. My Indians fled immediately after they were shot upon. You should know that the Mengwe have made attacks similar to the ones the Marylanders have experienced for many years. Mengwe purposely kill and plunder trying to incite the Marylanders against the Lenape and the Susquehannocks. It is the Mengwe's design that the Marylanders will attack the Susquehannocks and the Lenape. Are you so simple that you cannot see their evil deceit?

Do you want to continue the war you have started? In the attempt to make peace, I have offered to overlook the murder of my own brother whose blood cries out to me from the ground. I can do no greater thing. But if that is not enough for you, you shall have your war and I shall avenge the blood of my brother.

Do not be mistaken. The Passayunk Indians will not fight

this war alone. All the Lenape scattered along the the River of the Lenape will rise to defend the Land of the Dawn against the Schwanneks.

The Susquehannocks also know that the Mengwe are doing the killing. They will help us fight Maryland.

You also know full well how Great Heron Baltimore and Bantie Utie have threatened to drive the Dutch from New Amstel. Strutting Turkey Stuyvesant and Fat Pig Hinoyossa will be glad to help the Lenape fight Great Heron.

Governor Calvert, if you do not wish to forget the blood that has been shed and wish to insist on payment for cattle and hogs my Indians did not kill, Maryland shall have war and plenty of it. The choice is up to you.

Governor Calvert's reply was not long in coming, "King Pinna, I did invite you to this place to make peace and not to make war. The record of events you have given agrees in the main part with the testimony I have received from those present on Patapsco River and Bush River where the murders and plundering took place this past Easter. From what I have learned, the Cinigoes[54] were making raids in that area at that time, and it could well be that their aim was, as you say, to set Maryland against the Susquehannocks and the Lenape. Maryland will not be taken in by such deceit.

"Maryland wants to make peace. But to prevent such tragic incidents from reoccurring in Maryland, we must have your pledge to abide by certain terms of conduct. I propose the following:

1. If any Englishman finds a Passayunk Indian killing either cattle or hogs, it shall be lawful for the English to kill the said Indian.

---

[54] A name for Senecas or a subtribe of the Mengwe. One of the tribes of an alliance known to the English as the Five Nations or Iroquois.

2. If any Indian kills any Englishman, the said Indian and all the company of Indians that consented to the murder shall be delivered up to the English to be proceeded against according to the laws of Maryland.

3. If any Indian comes near the house of an Englishman, he shall be bound to halloo, and upon the appearance of any English, he shall throw down his arms and shall suffer his arms to be in the English possession until his departure.

4. If any Indian meets an Englishman in the woods, he must immediately throw his gun on the ground and present a pass showing that he may travel in Maryland."[55]

Sachem Pinna answered this way:

Governor Calvert, these are not the articles of peace, but the terms of surrender. You are not so daft that you do not know that no Indian would ever be safe under such terms.

Governor Calvert, under your first proposal, all the Englishman has to do is to 'say' that he saw an Indian killing a pig and *boom*, the Indian is dead. No Englishman will ever punish him for killing the Indian. And what happens if the Englishman's hog destroys the Indian's maize or invades the Indian's wigwam? It must then be lawful for the Indian to shoot the owner of the hog.

Governor Calvert, under your second condition, it is a known fact that no Indian accused of murder and delivered up to the laws of Maryland would escape death. You must also promise that any Englishman who murders an Indian and all who agreed to the murder will also be turned over to the Indians to be dealt with according to our customs.

Governor Calvert, your absurd third and fourth conditions

---

[55] The treaty was completed on September 19, 1661. Weslager, *The Delaware Indians*, p. 142.

can never be agreed to, for they always leave the Indian at the less than tender mercy of the Englishman. My own brother's blood warns me of the Englishman's lust for blood. The Englishman must be the one to throw down his gun first.

Great Heron's brother responded kindly to the objections of Pinna. Then the Maryland sachem ordered his pen and ink man, Coursey, to take the discussion into mind and draw up a peace treaty between the people of Maryland and the Passayunk Indians. Several times, the three Maryland headmen conferred while Scribe Coursey wrote down the words.

Governor Philip Calvert summarized the words of the treaty for Pinna. Pinna put his mark on the treaty, and the three Maryland headmen signed it.

Councilor Bateman had just finished signing his name to the treaty when Meas stepped quietly up to the table. His powerful frame towered over the bent form of Scribe Coursey. Meas said nothing, but held out his open hand. "Do-o-o y-yo-u-u wa-wa-nt th-th-e tr-tr-eat-ee?" stammered Scribe Coursey. Meas only nodded his head and continued holding out his hand.

Three mouths fell open, and three sets of eyes stared at Meas in disbelief. Governor Calvert recovered first from the shock. "Meas, what do you want to do with the treaty?" the governor asked.

"Governor Calvert, I will get my wife to read the treaty to me," Meas answered. "I will see if it says the same words the governor spoke to Pinna."

"Meas," and Governor Calvert struggled to control his voice which wanted to pitch from squeak to boom. "It is impossible for us to give the treaty to you. The treaty belongs to Maryland and Lord Baltimore. His lordships would be very angry if he did not hold the treaty. Do you really have a wife who can read English?"

"Aye, Governor Calvert," Meas said sociably. "The former governor of Maryland, Captain Josias Fendall, raised my wife as a Christian. Cool Water reads English very well." As Meas spoke, he edged a bit closer to the table and suddenly snatched the treaty from the astounded Scribe Coursey.

Meas held the paper in front of him and studied it closely. "Ah, yes," he said. "Is this not the mark of Pinna? So the paper belongs to Sachem Pinna and Great Heron both. Both of them should have the paper." Meas tapped his brow. "Yes, yes," Meas continued, "that is the answer. We shall have two papers. I will hold the one paper while Scribe Coursey makes another one like it. I will watch the trail of his quill and see that the turkey tracks are the same on both papers. Then Pinna can put his mark on the second paper and the three Maryland headmen can put their signs on the new paper. Great Heron shall receive the new paper, and Pinna shall have the first one."

Meas moved around the table and stood beside Scribe Coursey holding the treaty carefully where the scribe could see it. Scribe Coursey looked quizzically at both Governor Calvert and then at Councilor Bateman. Both men refused to meet his eyes. Scribe Coursey shrugged his shoulders, took up a clean sheet of parchment, dipped his quill in ink, and began to write.

Two large canoes left Pickhattomitta in the waning days of the autumnal month and drifted down the Manayunk River. Pinna sat in the bow of the lead canoe and Meas in the bow of the other. At the River of the Lenape, the canoes veered to the east, and six sets of powerful arms in each canoe propelled the canoes upstream. The canoes swung side by side and the race was on. The crisp fall morning air stirred each brave to exert himself. The ripple of his muscles, the rhythm of the paddles, the racing of the canoes through the water—all excited the heart to push forward.

Three miles upstream, the River of the Lenape turned boldly to the north. At the bend, Pinna raised his paddle and pointed to the east. "Look!" he shouted to Meas. "Fort Nassau." Meas never broke his stroke with the paddle, but he glanced at the crumbled remains of the old Dutch trading post and fort, the fort Strutting Turkey dismantled to use in building and arming Fort Casimir.

Three miles further, the River of the Lenape bent to the northeast. In another three miles, Pinna lifted his paddle and pointed to the west where a small stream entered the river. "Look! Tacony Creek," he called. "And, of course, Shackamoxon, the place of the Great Council Fire of the Lenape." This time Meas lifted his paddle in salute as did five others in his canoe.

In another five miles, Pinna once more lifted his paddle and pointed west. "Counselor Meas," he called. "Look! Pennypack Creek." Meas smiled. Now he understood why they called the sachem Pinna.[56]

Two more miles and Pinna called out again, "Look! Counselor Meas. Rancocas Creek to the east, and, soon to come, Poquessing Creek to the west."

Four miles further Pinna cried "Look!" yet again. "Neshaminy Creek where Mattahorn humbled Strutting Turkey."

In the next two miles, the River of the Lenape narrowed considerably, and a large island butted out into the river. The two canoes eased off to quieter water along the island and stopped next to each other. All were glad for a rest.

"Look!" Pinna said to Meas. "This is Matennecunk Island, the best and largest island in the Lenape River.[57] Several years before Gillis Hossitt bought Swanendael, the Dutch built a house and trading post on this island. The Swedes drove the Dutch out for a time, but now

---

[56] *Pinna* means "look" in Lenape.
[57] Known today as Burlington Island and about 300 acres in size.

none other than Fat Pig Hinoyossa claims the island. Fat Pig lives on this place with his seven children. We are going to paddle around Matennecunk, and I want you to see the glories of Fat Pig."

The two canoes began moving again up along the east side of the island while Pinna continued his tour.

"Look at the dykes surrounding the low areas of the island. When the river rises during wet periods, these dykes prevent flooding of the crops. Meas, these soils are so rich that they can grow thirty-five bushels of maize to the acre instead of the twenty bushels per acre you harvest along the Siconece. Other crops grown in his fields and gardens do equally well. The tools his servants use in the fields are all of iron and of the best quality.

"He husbands many sheep, cattle, hogs, and horses. He has lots of servants to care for the animals and his family. Many of them are black-skinned. And Fat Pig has built houses for his servants or they live in corners of his own great house.

"Fat Pig's house is the grandest house on the Lenape River. Only at Drunk Island are the houses equal to Fat Pig's. The walls of his house are built of clay bricks and it is roofed with clay tiles from Holland. The openings are filled with glass to let the light in and keep the rain out. The floors are of wood so that they stay dry in the wettest of seasons..."

Pinna continued his glowing description of Fat Pig's island paradise until he had expanded every detail known to him. Then Pinna lapsed into silence. The canoes rounded the top of Matennecunk and started drifting southward with the current as the island slipped quietly by them. Matennecunk had almost vanished when Pinna spoke again.

"Fat Pig has everything the Schwanneks seem to want. Yet he is not happy. He always wants still more. People do not like to trade with him because the trade must always be in his favor. He will never do a favor for someone else. I am told he constantly refuses to accept

Strutting Turkey as his chief. Other Dutch do not like him either, because Fat Pig is always number one. His slaves hate him and do his bidding only out of fear. He in turn must live in fear that the slaves will run away or perhaps even kill him. Or perhaps a greater warrior may come who will kill him or throw him in prison. Fat Pig, too, yields to the demons in the rum. Often." Pinna again lapsed into silence.

"Pinna," Meas began, "I, too, have seen the same thing with the Schwanneks. It is as you say. No matter how much they have, they always wish for still more. Take Great Heron. He claims all the land around the Chesapeake Bay, yet he attacks the Dutch because he wants still more. Therefore he cannot live in peace. Instead, he must fight his neighbors and live in constant fear that someone else may take the land from him. He cannot be happy."

The canoes glided smoothly southward until they came to Neshaminy Creek. Here they turned and paddled up Neshaminy Creek until they came to the village of a young Lenape chieftain named Tamenand.

Tamenand took Meas and Pinna into his own lodge and entertained them with the best of his provisions. The villagers bent to give their best to the visiting braves, and runners went out to other villages informing neighbors of their special guests.

Outside Tamenand's lodge, Tamenand himself lit a small fire and seated himself and his two guests before it. The circle around the fire kept growing as local sachems arrived to pay their respects to Sachem Pinna and Counselor Meas. At dark, Tamenand lit the peace pipe and passed it around the circle. When all eight had smoked, Tamenand laid the pipe aside and invited Pinna to give the reason for his visit. By now the entire village and the visitors crowded in close to the fire— aged men in the first ring, braves next, boys, and then women and children at a respectful distance.

Sachem Pinna rose and spoke distinctly that all might hear. He thanked Tamenand and all present for receiving them so kindly. Pinna said the purpose for their coming was to report to Tamenand, to the visiting sachems, and to everyone present on the peace treaty just concluded with Governor Calvert of Maryland.

Sachem Pinna told how Counselor Meas had served as his interpreter at the meeting. Sachem Pinna carefully recounted the events of the war between the Marylanders and the Passayunk Lenape. He discussed in detail the arguments over the terms of peace. Then he excitedly told how Meas wrested the treaty itself from Scribe Coursey. Pinna held the precious paper up for all to see. Great shouts of "Bravo!" cleft the forest night, and many a brave cast an admiring glance at Meas. When the shouts had stilled, Sachem Pinna explained that now the party would travel on to Siconece so that Cool Water might read the words of the treaty to Pinna and see if Great Heron's brother spoke true words. Again, shouts of "Bravo!" rang out, and, at that instant, no one could have blamed any Lenape woman who might have envied Cool Water.

Sachem Pinna said he wished many Lenape to hear the story of the treaty and told how he planned to tell the story often on the way to the Siconece. Then Pinna concluded, "Our spirits must not flag or fail. Every buck, doe, and fawn must carry the Spirit of Tamenend on in the Land of the Dawn. Open your eyes that you may see Tamenend's spirit in Meas from the Siconece."

The villagers dispersed for the night, but the headmen continued sitting around the fire. Occasionally, one of the sachems would throw out a few pungent thoughts to hang in the air like wood smoke above a campfire on a still night. Nothing big, nothing demanding an answer.

When morning light first began to push its promise along the eastern horizon, Sachem Pinna, Sachem Tamenand, and Counselor Meas were already standing with right arms outstretched to the east.

As one man, the three chanted the ancient prayer of the Lenape:

> Great Spirit,
> Maker of the sky, the earth, the sun, the moon,
> Keeper of the spirits of the fish, the birds, the animals, the trees, the
>   stones.
> Guardian of the Four Winds,
> Thank you for bringing light again to the People of the Dawn.
> Thank you for sending fire to warm our houses and cook our food.
> Thank you for bringing water to inspire the ground and to quench our
>   thirst.
> Thank you for the ground to grow the maize and the deer to give us
>   meat.
> For the ancient song of the Lenape,
> For the everlasting sun that rises this day,
> We three, headmen of the Lenni Lenape, thank you.

When the three had finished the chant, each one took a small pinch of tobacco from his pouch with his left hand and sprinkled it on the ground before him. Then the three stood motionless with their right arms raised and two fingers pointing toward the horizon.

When the sun cracked the horizon, all three dropped their arms. Tamenand turned to the other two. "I have received a word," he said. "I will go with you to the Siconece."

Later that morning, as the sun neared the point where it would once again begin its descent, three canoes left the village and headed south down Neshaminy Creek and out into the Lenape River.

Paddles dipped and flashed in unison as the three canoes followed each other down the river. Again, Pinna's cries of "Look!" rang out as the canoes whisked southward, greeting each in turn: Poquessing Creek, Rancocas Creek, Pennypack Creek, Tacony Creek and Shackamoxon, abandoned Fort Nassau, the Manayunk River and

Passayunk, Tinicum Island and Printztorp, and finally Christina Creek.

Pinna's canoe turned into Christina Creek. The other two canoes followed. The cadence of the paddles slowed, and no one spoke. Well up the Christina, Pinna pointed to a spot on the river's north edge. All three canoes grounded at the spot, and braves lashed the canoes to trees. Then all eighteen Lenape solemnly followed Pinna's lead up the worn trail through field and forest till they came to a small fenced spot. The entire party seated themselves in three rows on the east side of Mattahorn's grave. Meas, Pinna, and Tamenand sat at one end of each row. Each Lenape faced the grave and the west. No one moved. No one spoke.

After the squirrels had again romped and chattered in the trees close by the grave, Meas rose, climbed inside the fence, and examined the carved pole he himself had helped set at the head of Mattahorn's grave. Then Meas faced the silent Lenape and paid tribute to Mattahorn by recounting the story of Mattahorn's life. When Meas had finished, every head bowed in awe and respect.

Meas stood by the grave until the sun bowed into the horizon. In the ensuing twilight, the group quickly made its way back to the canoes and on a nearby knoll set up camp for the night. Meas, Pinna, and Tamenand sat smoking around a small fire by themselves while the braves busied themselves with the few necessary duties for a traveling Lenape band.

"Sachem Pinna and Sachem Tamenand," Meas began after complete darkness had settled over the camp. "Much has taken place in the six years since we buried Mattahorn. The Dutch grow rich. The English all around us grow in numbers. The Lenape shrink like a new shirt being washed for the first time. Yet Mattahorn's spirit towers over the Lenape in the Land of the Dawn.

"I have seen the silver tortoise Mattahorn held in his hand as he lay in the coffin. That medallion embodied not only Sachem Mattahorn's spirit, but also the Spirit of Tamenend. Might it be possible to find the silver tortoise taken from Mattahorn's grave? If found, might not the silver tortoise be used to revive the flagging spirits of the Lenape and to remind our children and our children's children of the Spirit of Tamenend in the Land of the Dawn?"

Sachem Pinna spoke next. "Counselor Meas, I, too, have seen the silver tortoise you speak of. It truly captures the Spirit of Tamenend, Eesanques, and Mattahorn. The silver medallion would doubtless be a great symbol for the Lenape, and, if found, should not be returned to Mattahorn's grave. It should be kept for a sign to the Lenape."

"But, Counselor Meas, you know the tortoise has been stolen from Mattahorn's coffin, along with the wampum belts that caressed the Great Sachem. We know a Schwannek stole these things, for no Indian would ever have disturbed Mattahorn's grave. I do not believe a Schwannek would dare to sell the wampum belts or the silver tortoise anywhere in the Land of the Dawn. The risk of being discovered would be far too great. Doubtless the tortoise is now resting in some king's palace across the great waters. To find it is as hopeless as finding a feather blown away by a hurricane."

Now it was Sachem Tamenand's turn to speak. "I think Sachem Pinna is right on one thing. If found, the silver tortoise should not be returned to the crumbled coffin. If found, the Lenape must hold the silver tortoise as a symbol above the Land of the Dawn that it might ever stir our spirits and strengthen our wills.

"But I am looking at a different side of the tree about where the silver tortoise might be found. I think it quite likely that the one who robbed the grave still holds the silver tortoise and the turtle wampum belts as well. The tortoise is only a small amount of silver. It would not be worth much to any trader who might melt it down. It would have little value to any king whose bed is covered with silver and gold. But to the Lenape, the silver tortoise is priceless. The thief knows all this. Therefore, I think the thief holds the tortoise until he thinks the time is right to sell it.

"And who else would want the wampum belts? They are worthless to the Schwanneks unless the Indians will trade beaver and pelts for them. However, 'tis true the wampum belts could easily be torn apart and restrung so that one could never tell the wampum shells came from Mattahorn's coffin. The only clue would be if some trader offered too much wampum."

Meas responded, "Sachem Pinna. Sachem Tamenand. We will hide our words deep underground. But let us seek the silver tortoise ...

"Perhaps the Great Spirit will lead us to the trail of the one who holds the silver tortoise ...

"I believe there is one who trades among the Lenape who would be evil enough to steal from a Lenape chieftain's grave ...

"Perhaps I may dangle some bait before him and see if he strikes at it."

Other canoes loaded with Lenape braves arrived at the campsite long before the travelers were ready to depart. Local sachems came to pay their respects to Pinna, Tamenand, and Meas. The three took great care to smoke the peace pipe with the visiting sachems, and then to report to everyone present on the peace treaty just concluded with Governor Calvert. And Pinna concluded his story by holding up the treaty and giving his rousing call to the Lenape:

"Our spirits must not flag or fail. Every buck, doe, and fawn must carry the Spirit of Tamenend on in the Land of the Dawn. Open your eyes that you may see Tamenend's spirit in Meas from the Siconece."

And so it happened a number of times on the unhurried trip down the Lenape River. A canoe would appear in the Lenape River, and some messenger would hail the travelers. In the name of the local sachems, Pinna would be invited to give his report. Messengers came from both sides of the Lenape River. Word traveled from village to village much faster than the canoes of Meas, Pinna, and Tamenand could get there.

One golden fall day rolled into another while Pinna led his party southward. The coloring of the leaves turned ever brighter. Each night the moon grew brighter and fuller. On the night the moon broke the horizon in the east at the same time the sun dropped out of sight in the west, the canoes rushed into the dock on the Siconece.

Hundreds of Lenape camped in the fields and forests to the southwest of the fort. Koketotoka and Teotacken welcomed hero Meas home with long speeches, enlarging on his past feats—the trade with Fat Pig for the Virginia bondmen, the trade with Two Tongue for the rifles, and the best-loved story of all, the purchase of Cool Water. That night Cool Water wore the tribal heirloom, the swan-feather dress she wore on her wedding day. And when the crowd clapped and clapped at the end of Koketotoka's tale, she danced lightly forward and kissed Meas.

Then it was time for Pinna's treaty story. A great hush fell over the crowd while Pinna told how Mengwe had first attacked a Maryland settler on Gunpowder River, killing his wife, five cows, a steer, and a number of his hogs. Naturally, the Marylanders wanted revenge. So Marylanders attacked four Passayunk Lenape passing peacefully by, overturned their canoe, dumped their goods and three guns in the river, and killed one of the four Lenape in the canoe. The war was on.

Pinna spared no detail of the war, including the murder of his own brother. He went over how Governor Calvert demanded that he deliver Oconiccka and his friends to Maryland for punishment and how Governor Calvert wanted him to pay for cattle and hogs killed by the Mengwe.

Pinna laid out how he himself had offered to forget the death of his own brother and make peace if Maryland also would forget the deaths suffered at the hands of Oconiccka and his friends.

Pinna showed point by point how Governor Calvert demanded terms of peace which would make it unsafe for any Indian to live or wander anywhere in Maryland. "I called them terms of surrender," Pinna shouted, "not a peace treaty at all. I threatened Maryland with war by the Lenape, the Susquehannocks, and the Dutch before Governor Calvert brought forth a treaty acceptable to me. Then I, Pinna, Sachem of the Passayunk Indians, put my mark upon it."

Pinna held the vaunted treaty high. Great shouts and cheers raced back and forth until the chant started: "We carry the Spirit of Tamenend in the Land of the Dawn." Over and over the chant rolled from the throats of the Lenape throng while Pinna held the precious paper aloft.

Pinna lowered the paper and the tumult quieted. "We would not have this paper here today if Meas had not acted boldly," Pinna continued. "If it were not for Meas, only the Schwanneks would know what the white man's wampum says. But because Meas wrested the paper from Scribe Coursey and forced him to copy the turkey tracks on another paper, the Lenape can also know the pledges made at Appoquinimink.

"Now, because of the cunning and bravery of this grandson of Eesanques, which you have heard much about tonight, and every bit of it rings true, you shall hear in the Lenape tongue the message Great Heron across the Great Sea shall hear in his tongue.

"I am now proud to present to you two who carry the Spirit of Tamenend in the Land of the Dawn: Meas and his wife Cool Water, the hope of the Lenape. They will tell us the words of the peace treaty."

Again great cheers and shouts broke the stillness and again a chant: "They carry the Spirit of Tamenend in the Land of the Dawn."

Meas and Cool Water stepped from the shadows into the full moon's lustre. Meas raised his hand. The crowd quieted.

"Listen to the words of the treaty Pinna has put his mark upon." Meas translated each sentence into Lenape after Cool Water read it to him in English. Together they gave the sense of the whole treaty with no comments or explanation.

This is the treaty written exactly as read by Cool Water:

Articles of peace and amity concluded betwixt the honorable Philip Calvert Esqr Governor Henry Coursey Secretary and Mr John Bateman Councellor on the behalfe of the Lord Proprietary of this Province of Maryland and Pinna King of Pickhattomitta on the behalfe of the Passayoncke Indians on the other parte

(vizt)

Imprimis that there shall be a perpetuall peace betwixt the people of Maryland and the Passayoncke Indians

2^{ly} It is agreed betwixt the abouesaid partyes that in case any English man for the future shall happen to finde any Passayoncke Indian killing either Cattle or Hoggs that then it shall be lawfull for the English to kill the said Indian.

3^{ly} It is agreed betwixt the abouesaid partyes that in case any Indian or Indians shall happen to kill any English man for the future (which God forbid) that they the said Indian with all that company of Indians with him which consented to the said murder shall be deliuered up to the English there to be pceeded against according to the lawe of this Province.

4^{ly} It is further agreed betwixt the abouesaid partyes that in case any English man shall happen to run amongst the Passayoncke Indians that the said Indians bring them to Peter

Meyors and there for every English man that they shall deliuer they shall Receive one Matchcoate.

    The marke X of Pinna

    Signed and Deliuered this

    19th of September 1661[58]

Meas and Cool Water finished reading the treaty and retreated into the shadows close to Pinna. Pinna sat in stunned silence. "These are not the words I agreed to," Pinna said quietly to Meas. "I am but a fool. Can you say something for me lest the people tear me limb from limb?"

"Aye, Sachem Pinna. I will speak. Take heart. The lies of one do not make a liar or a fool out of another." Meas stepped once more into the full moon's light, and his words rang with sparkling clarity through the still night air.

Sachems, friends, neighbors, and kin. As your cries of carrying Tamenend's spirit tell us, this night we are bound together by more than blood, by more than tongue, by more than home, by more than friendship. This night we are bound together by a spirit, the Spirit of Tamenend! We cannot bring the great Tamenend back from the clouds when we see his image as the lightning flashes across the sky. Nor can we wait on him to lead the way when tempestuous winds would destroy us. But we can nourish Tamenend's bold spirit in our bosom and not fear to take the first step. We must take the first step. We have no other choice except to cower in submission before evil spirits. We may blame the Schwanneks for swindling us with forked tongues, for stealing our goods, for subjecting us to drunkenness, or for shooting us. The Schwanneks are not the problem. It is the evil spirits within us

---

[58] Archives of Maryland Online, Vol. III, p.433.

CQ206

Meas lifted the treaty aloft that all
might watch it burn.

that destroy our own wills and that cause us to whimper and whine in self-pity. Let us slay these evil spirits and cast them into the Great Sea and pray that the tide will never again wash them up on our own shores. Let us spring forward with the courage of Tamenend and take the first step, and the second, and the third—or the thousandth one—in the Land of the Dawn.

You have heard the twisted words of the treaty.

Meas held the treaty paper up again that all might see. He bent over the fire, held a corner of the paper in the glowing coals until the precious document burst into flame. Meas lifted the paper aloft that all might watch it burn. Then Meas burst forth once more:

Brethren! Listen! Sachem Pinna denies that he ever agreed to such words. Sachem Pinna never agreed to surrender the life of any Indian in exchange for the life of a pig. Sachem Pinna never agreed to bind any Indian and turn him over to the Schwanneks that they might slay him. Sachem Pinna never agreed to forget the murder of his own brother in exchange for one colored matchcoat. This night you bear witness to these words.[59]

You saw me burn the paper of lies. The Spirit of Tamenend will not allow us to be slaves to lies and injustice. While the Lenape yearn for peace, we must prepare for war. While the Lenape delight in love, we must prepare to fight.

We must prepare because we are not ready now. We are many small peoples. If we fight now, the Dutch will chew us

---

[59] The following astounding note confirms the author's belief that the Indians never knowingly agreed to the terms of this treaty. "On September 13, 1661 [Pieter Alricks] was sent with two Chiefs of the river Indians to Maryland to negotiate a Treaty of Peace with these Indians. The Indians deserted but Alricks met the Governor and Council of Maryland at Col. Utie's house and the Treaty was agreed upon." Admiral Goldman, "Pieter Alricks," unpublished manuscript in Delaware Historical Library: Wilmington, Delaware, 1949.

village by village and barrel by barrel. The Lenape must unite before we fight. The Lenape bands must be wound together as many small strands intertwined make a ship's strong rope. The Spirit of Tamenend must twine together our wills and give us strength.

We are not ready yet. If we fight now, Great Heron, with a few shakes of his long neck, will swallow the Lenape as he has gulped down the once noble Nanticokes[60] to our west. Great Heron "treated" with Sachem Unnacokasimmon. Every year Sachem Unnacokasimmon must pay four arrows to Great Heron. Sachem Unnacokasimmon asked his people to tie a white cloth around their left arms so Marylanders could tell their peaceful intent. That was not enough. Now Great Heron demands that when a Nanticoke meets a Marylander, the Nanticoke must throw down his gun to the ground. The Nanticoke hide like swamp rats in their own land. Will the Lenape bow to a similar fate?

No! No! We must prepare to fight. Our sachems must talk with each other at Shackamoxon. Every Lenape brave and headman must stave in every barrel of rum that comes to his village. We must obtain guns equal to the guns of any Schwannek, and we must learn how to use them well. If we love peace, then we must prepare to fight.

We seek peace. We, the Lenni Lenape, the Real Men, will not suffer truth to fall undefended in the Land of the Dawn. This night I call on every Lenape warrior to pick up the fallen Spirit of Tamenend and hold his spirit in your heart. Be strong of heart and fixed in will. Prepare to fight that truth and right may prevail. Prepare to fight that those who will not live peaceably

[60] *Nanticoke* means "the tidewater people." These people lived on the eastern shore of the Chesapeake Bay. They originated from the Lenape, hence the Lenape called them Grandchildren.

among us shall be driven from the land.

The Spirit of Tamenend calls us to step forward, not in fear and weakness, but with courage, wisdom, and strength. And this night we call on the Great Spirit to shine the light of the full moon on the path for us to follow in the good land he has given us.

The words of Meas are ended.

Narrated by Glikkikan

"Owechela," I said excitedly, "Meas really did have the courage of the bear to snatch the treaty away from Scribe Coursey, didn't he?"

"Yes, my son," Owechela replied tenderly. It was the first time Owechela had ever called me son.

The many days and moons spent together must have tightened the yearning in the old chief's heart for one to come after him.

"Glikkikan, you must understand. Meas's courage sprang not from the strength of the bear, but from the cunning of the wolf. Meas could speak and hear the tongue of the English. Cool Water could follow the trail on the paper as Meas could follow the trail upon soft earth. To Meas, the turkey tracks could be made to tell the truth. Knowledge gave Meas boldness.

"Meas's boldness did not break forth in brash and foolish acts that some would imagine to be courage. Instead Meas counseled the Lenape not to fling themselves boldly upon the Schwanneks, but to prepare to attack with the united strength of the wolf pack."

Owechela's answer did not satisfy me. I pressed Owechela further: "If learning the tongue of the Schwanneks is so important, then why do not many more Lenape learn it?"

"Son, I do not know the answer to your question," Owechela said gravely. "I only know that speaking English gave Meas power. My dream would be that perhaps you will learn many tongues. Perhaps your children will learn to read and follow the trails on paper. Should the Lenape learn the ways of the Schwanneks? Or should we drive the Schwanneks out of the Land of the Dawn?"

The old man's eyes stared into space. "I dream that a man of peace will arise among the Lenape. Once I was young. Now I am old. Yet I have never seen that the fruits of war tasted of ought but sorrow and pain.

"Ahhhh. The fruits of war look so tasty when viewed green upon the tree—revenge, justice, plunder, peace. Yet when the fruit ripens and the blows of the tomahawk fall, when the knife tears away the scalp, when the gun cracks and the warrior falls, when the women wail, when the orphans cry for lack of meat, 'tis only the bitterness of the unfrosted persimmon that we taste.

"There is no victor in war save misery and death."

"But Owechela, did not Meas do the right thing to prepare the people for war that they might defend their homeland? Should the Lenape allow the Schwanneks to lie and steal and murder while truth and justice lay dead in their coffins? Did not Pastor Campanius teach us that it is hard for a weak man to extract justice from a strong man?"

"My son," Owechela answered, "it does seem at times that to prepare for war, as Meas urged, is the right thing to do. I only say that I have never seen the fruits of war taste as sweet as the promise.

"Glikkikan, I warn you that many things do not turn out the way we expect them to. This is very true in war—the enemy does the unexpected, the weather brings a freak storm, the manitos disrupt the battle.

"Take what happened on the Siconece—Meas thought the danger

would be from new settlers whereas Pinna thought the danger would come from Great Heron. Great Heron feared the Protestants, Fat Pig, and Strutting Turkey. They were all wrong.

"Listen well, Glikkikan. The tale of Meas, the hope of the Lenape, goes on."

Chapter 6 – 1663

Meas—the Sage

As told by Owechela

Meas spotted the ship as it tacked directly to the inlet where the Siconece emptied into the Lenape Bay. The ship, flying the red, white, and blue Dutch flag, continued on to the decrepit dock and the abandoned trading fort.[58] As soon as the ship had anchored and a plank was let overboard, men hasted off the ship and climbed the bank of the Siconece.

Meas watched from the shadow of nearby trees. He counted twenty-five men and sixteen women and children, forty-one in all. Most of them walked unsteadily, but with a bit of persistence and help they managed to make it to the top of the riverbank. There all the men fell on one knee and laid their hats in front of them while the women bowed their white-capped heads. Their leader prayed. When the prayer ended, the group sang together.

The songs pleased Meas. They were much like the songs Cool Water sang for him and the papooses, not jarring and raucous songs, but songs soothing to the spirit.

[58] The ship, *St. Jacob*, arrived at New Amstel 28 July 1663 after dropping the settlers off at the Whorekill.

Meas slipped in closer to the ship. The singing ended, and all hurried back down the bank to the ship where the sailors were already busy piling goods on the rickety dock. Men, women, and children scrambled to retrieve their precious goods—strange tools of all kinds, clothing, kettles, dishes, provisions—and carry them to higher ground. When the passengers agreed that all their belongings were off the ship, the sailors unlashed the ropes and the ship sailed on out into the bay.

When the ship's sails had dropped over the horizon, Meas left the cover of the trees and walked boldly toward the group standing amid the remains of the fort. One of the group gave an instant "halloo" and ran to meet him. "Meas," he shouted, "I have come back. It is I, Weak Gun."

Meas strode forward to meet Weak Gun. Both raised their right hands and touched lightly. Meas stroked his own left arm three times. Weak Gun returned the sign. "You have come," Meas answered. "And who are all these with you?"

"Come," Weak Gun invited. "Both my brother and sister have come along, and I am anxious for them to meet you. We have been on the ship for two months, and everyone is thankful we have arrived safely. And now we have found you so quickly, or should I say, you have found us? My brother Pieter has spent years in England and speaks English very well. From now on we will be able to speak very well with you."

"With me and Cool Water also," Meas added.

After the words of greeting, Meas and Weak Gun made their way in silence to the group huddled by their goods. Weak Gun spoke to the group in Dutch while Meas stood by impassively.

Then Weak Gun's brother stepped forward. Meas knew instantly he had to be Weak Gun's brother Pieter. He had the same dreamy sparkling eyes, the same thin frame. And on top of the now bared head, a stack of unruly hair strayed in every direction.

Pieter stepped forward, held out his hand to Meas, and said in English, "Meas, we come as friends. We have cast ourselves upon these shores and lie prostrate before you. We bring no great guns, no soldiers, no flags.

"We have only the love of God in our hearts, the skills of our hands, and the hope of a better life here on the Siconece.

"One and all in this small band have vowed to work together in this beautiful land to build a fair and just society. Meas, will you and your people help us?"

Meas looked into the dreamy, sparkling blue eyes of the leader and glanced at a reflection of his own soul. There shone the vision, the dream of life, not as it was, soiled by heartbreak and hatred, but life as it should be, glistening with fairness and justice and love.

Meas stood enchanted by the vision put forth so ably by Pieter, the leader, the prophet, the dreamer. He liked the vision, the dream. He liked the sparkling eyes, the kindly manner, and the dreamer. Meas held out his hand. "Dreamer," Meas said, "the Lenni Lenape will share the Land of the Dawn with you."

Meas stroked his left arm three times.

Dreamer repeated the sign.

Meas held up his hand. "I would ask of Dreamer a favor," he said. "This place is Swanendael, the Valley of the Swans. The outlines of the Sickoneysinck fort you see mark the outline of the Dutch settlement established here thirty and two winters gone by. My mother brought me often to this place and to the spot outside the walls where her father was slain. My mother rests on that same spot today.

"Dreamer, I heard your songs of peace. Would you take your band to my mother's grave and there sing songs of peace for her?"

Dreamer spoke to the group in Dutch. Then he turned to Meas and said, "Yes, we will be glad to honor your mother with several songs and a prayer. Show us to the grave."

HOMELAND IN MY HEART

Meas led the way to the spot at the far end of the fort where the sacred pole with the copper plate showing the tawny cats had once stood, the spot where Eesanques had crumpled in a pool of blood, and the spot where his mother lay buried. Meas pointed to the shallow hollow of sunken earth and stood facing east while Dreamer stood beside him. The group formed a semicircle around the two, Meas and Dreamer, and began singing sighing, wistful songs.

Meas's head bent forward, and tears rolled down his cheeks. Dreamer slipped his arm around Meas and allowed it to rest lightly on Meas's shoulders. When the singing stopped, Meas begged for more. This time the tempo of the music picked up. The lilt of the music and the smiles on the faces of the singers talked of joy and peace and hope.

When the singing stopped, Dreamer, still holding his arm around Meas, prayed: "Almighty God, Creator of the heavens and the earth, the giver of light and the dispeller of darkness, today, in this small part of your vast worlds, we honor and praise your mighty name. We worship you as the One who molded creatures, great and small, from the dust of the earth and breathed into their nostrils the breath of life, and then we honor you as the One who gathered of that same dust, formed it into your own likeness, and gave that likeness the breath of life and a living spirit. Today, at this grave, where lie the remains of Meas's mother, every one of us is reminded that our bodies must some day yield to your holy touch and return to dust. As you have snatched the breath of life from Meas's mother, so you will draw the breath of life from each of us. Just now, beside this grave, we pray that you would comfort Meas's heart. Bring healing and peace to his spirit. Almighty God, this day we submit our bodies to your decree and trust our eternal spirits to your divine judgment. In the name of Jesus, your Son, we pray, Amen."

All stood quietly after the Amen. Meas raised his head and looked at the group around him. Meas saw faces weary and worn with travel, but also bright, cheerful, and alive with hope. "Dreamer," he said, "the sun rushes toward his bed. What will these people do for food and for the night?"

"I do not know how or when," Dreamer responded, "but God will provide. Jacob, when he was a pilgrim and stranger once slept under the stars with a rock for a pillow. God's angels went up and down the ladder and cared for Jacob, and God stood at the top of the ladder and spoke to Jacob ..."

Weak Gun laid his hand on Dreamer's shoulder. "Could we talk a moment?" he asked in English. Three of the men drew aside from the group and consulted together for a time. Then Dreamer motioned for Meas to join them.

"Meas, we are glad for your friendship," Dreamer began. "We have great hope that you will help us settle here on the Siconece."

Weak Gun again laid his hand on Dreamer's shoulder. "Yes, yes," Dreamer said brightly, and then went happily on. "God has brought us to this lovely place."

Weak Gun squeezed his large hand tightly on Dreamer's shoulder. "Er, er," Dreamer stalled under the powerful grip. "Meas, from now on I am to be the interpreter," Dreamer said humbly, and he stepped back behind the other two while meekly placing his left hand on top of his right hand.

The tall, strong Dutchman with reddish hair held out his hand to Meas. Dreamer translated. "I am Helmanus Wiltbanck. I married the sister of these two brothers, Harmen Cornelisen Spycker and Pieter Cornelisen Plockhoy."[59] Meas touched hands briefly with Helmanus, and then Helmanus came right to the point. "As you can see, we plan to settle in this area on land purchased from the savages four years ago. We are anxious to look around and choose our site so we can begin

[59] Harmen is the former soldier known to Meas as Weak Gun. Both *Spycker* meaning "nail" and *Plockhoy* meaning "haystack" were nicknames not associated with the Dutch familial name. Meas gave Pieter the name of Dreamer.

building our homes. Harmen is familiar with the Siconece and has picked several likely sites we want to choose from. Meas, will you show us around?"

Meas stood tall and straight before the three Dutchmen. His face showed not a trace of emotion. "Friend Wiltbanck, you have come to a good land. We wish to smoke the peace pipe together. I and my people will share with you as guests from our wigwams. But it is evident that you do not understand the land or our customs. You do not understand the treaty the Lenni Lenape made with the Dutch four years ago. It must take several days before we can light a council fire and give you an answer to your question. Until we have lit the fire, you may bring your people next to my cabin at Tired Moon Pond and camp there. Or you may camp here at Swanendael until we have your answer ready. What will your choice be?"

"Meas, we do not wish to sit around and smoke the stinking sot-weed. The season is already late, and we have much work to do. If we are to have housing for this band before winter sets in, and if we are to get the winter crops planted, we must make every day count. We could even say we must make every *hour* count. We must choose our site immediately and begin work tomorrow.

"Meas, could you not show us around today, and then you can have your powwow while we build?"

"So you do not have time to smoke the peace pipe?" Meas asked. "Therefore, I shall name you No Smoke Wiltbanck.

"No Smoke, you bring no wampum and no gifts for Koketotoka and Teotacken to back up your words of peace. You have no time to smoke. Neither do I have time to show you around.

"No Smoke, unless you make a peace treaty with Koketotoka and Teotacken, I can show you no spot among these trees and fields where it is safe for you to build your houses. I have been very plain with Fat Pig Hinoyossa. All settlers who come to the Siconece must live peaceably with the Lenape or we will make them like the settlers of Swanendael.

"No Smoke, think hard. Would you like to leave your heavy tools here and walk to Tired Moon Pond for the night, or would you rather camp here while I light the council fire for Koketotoka and Teotacken?"

No Smoke, Weak Gun, and Dreamer talked among themselves before No Smoke gave Meas an answer. "Thank you for your offer of Tired Moon Pond. Harmen tells us it is truly an enchanting place. But I think it best if the band stays together here and guards our stuff. However, Pieter and Harmen have decided they would like to go with you for the night."

Meas bowed slightly toward No Smoke. "You need have no fear of harm to you and your goods as long as you remain near the fort. You are now guests of Teotacken, Koketotoka, and Meas. When the council fire is ready, we will send a messenger for you."

Meas, Weak Gun, and Dreamer began the walk south along the Siconece through scattered maize fields and towering trees toward Tired Moon Pond. "Oh, Brother Harmen," Dreamer exclaimed, "the Promised Land is more wonderful than you described it. The words I wrote describing the land to the settlers cannot tell enough. Now mine eyes have seen the flower of New Netherland, the noblest of all lands, with its limitless abundance.

"Birds obscure the sky, so numerous in their flight. The animals roam wild ... fish swarm in the waters and exclude the light ... Look at the river and the bay alive with fish—halibut, mackerel, bass—filling the inlets with their silvery flopping bodies. Look at the millions of ducks.

"Look at the primeval forests of towering oak and pine, the lacy cypress near the water, the drooping willows in the swamps. The land teems with bears, foxes, beavers, eagles, and unknown creatures in unbelievable abundance.

"See the clearings sporting profuse bouquets of flora and wild fruits. Look at the black dirt so rich that seed trusted to its bosom must yield an hundredfold.

"Look at the bogs lush with reeds and flowers I have never seen before. These bogs could be drained and farmed as we have done in Holland. Truly Governor Hinoyossa spoke the truth.

"The land is wide open. If we could only have gotten one hundred men to join us instead of just the twenty and five. The land needs many, many people. Let the redeemed settlers of our society so live and work together that even the barbarous and savage peoples may share in the abundance of the land. Let the poor of Europe flock to this land of limitless abundance so that they may all share of its goodness."

"Friend Dreamer," Meas said, "the land truly is a good land. I know it well. You do not need to convince me that the land flows with abundance. But where are the poor savage peoples with whom you wish to share this abundance?"

"Meas, are you not one of these poor savages? Would you not like to have more food and more clothing and better housing? Would you not like to know a God of love so that your people would not be so cruel and constantly warring with each other and the settlers?"

"Friend Dreamer, I and my people are known as the Lenni Lenape. We are content with the bounty we dip from the streams, the fruits plucked from the fields, the meat and honey lifted from the forest. We sit content before our fires and rest easy in our wigwams. Our clothes do not bind or cumber our movements. I and my people want nothing.

"Friend Dreamer, it is the Schwanneks who come to our land that never have enough.

"Schwanneks never have enough land. They will kill, lie, and steal to get more.

"Schwanneks never have enough beaver. French, English, Swede,

and Dutch fight that they might have ALL the beaver. Schwanneks
set one Indian tribe upon another so that one nation may buy beaver
cheaper.

"The fields of the Schwanneks are never large enough. They would
destroy all the trees and our hunting grounds to plant tobacco.

"Friend Dreamer, it is not only that the Schwanneks are not
content. They are also cruel and savage.

"Schwanneks brew the rum and bring it to our villages. Indians do
not brew the poison that makes stupid fools of us.

"Schwanneks brought both the large and the small pox to us.[60]
Before the Schwanneks came, we did not suffer from these deadly
scourges.

"Schwanneks tear Indians, Blacks, and Whites from their homes
and enslave them in distant lands. The Lenape never make slaves of
others. Instead, the Lenape adopt strangers and accept them as one of
their own blood.

"Schwanneks have not brought plenty and love to our homeland.
Time and again, Schwanneks have sown only scarcity, sickness, sorrow,
and strife in the Land of the Dawn.

"Dreamer, tell me. Who is savage and cruel among us? Do I not
speak the truth?

"Dreamer, tell me. Do your dreams bring more than sweet talk to
the Siconece? Or shall we suffer anew if we allow your band to dwell in
our land?

"Dreamer and Weak Gun," Meas continued, "let us lay aside these
troubling thoughts till the night crowds in upon the fire. Tonight we
may return to these thoughts and sort through them closer. Perhaps
we may glean some truth from them that still eludes us. For now, let
us enjoy Tired Moon Pond and the milk and honey Cool Water will
have for us."

---

[60] *Large pox* denotes the venereal disease "syphilis." *Small pox* denotes "smallpox," caused by a virus now
eradicated, which has killed more people than any other disease.

Weak Gun let out a cry of delight when a glimmer of light sparkled off the waters of Tired Moon Pond. He ran forward till he could see Meas's cabin set by the southeast corner of the pond.

Cool Water stood on the land bridge on the south side and petted the dark red cows as they sidled past her onto the island. In six years' time, her one cow, one heifer, and the bull calf had grown to a herd of six cows, three heifers, two young bulls, and four spring calves.

Two white swans, a cob and a pen, and four gray cygnets swam about on the long north loop of the pond. The swans readily upended, reaching their long necks below to gather in hidden delights.

Ducks swam busily about in the reeds or quacked noisily as they suddenly burst into flight.

By the time Meas and Dreamer caught up with Weak Gun, the evening sun lit every object in its reach in a golden hue. Behind every golden object the sun touched, dark shadows cast their enchanting spell on the scene. Meas, Dreamer, and Weak Gun stood dazed by the splendor. For a time, even Dreamer had nothing to say as all three quietly rested their spirits in the peace around them.

" 'Tis a scene worthy of painting by Flinck, Steen, Van Goyen, or Vermeer," Dreamer murmured. "I believe Vermeer could paint it best, for he captures the light and shadow perfectly. But then Van Goyen works more with landscapes, so maybe I would favor him for this scene. Sad to say, neither one of them is here to see the picture, and I cannot paint the scene upon a canvas. But perhaps with words I can tap the beat of the heart upon the mind. Something like this:

> I left the Netherland by the ocean strand,
> I rode the path of the sea,
> To search for a promised land,
> Where all might free and equal be,
> Here by the Siconece."

The three men continued their walk around the east end of Tired Moon Pond, crossed the outlet brooklet, and made their way to the cabin. Weak Gun and Cool Water needed no introduction. They greeted each other warmly. "Cool Water," Weak Gun said, "this is my brother, Pieter Cornelisen Plockhoy." Weak Gun pointed to Pieter's unruly pile of hair and laughed. "Haystack," he said. "*Plockhoy* means 'haystack.'"

Weak Gun pointed to himself. "Harmen Cornelisen Spycker," he said and laughed again. "I guess Haystack is no worse than Nail for a nickname. Anyway, I'm proud to claim him for my brother. We're both sons of Cornelis.

"Cool Water, do us both a favor. If you count us true friends, call us only by our Lenape names. I am Weak Gun, a gentle soldier whose gun will not fire at the most inopportune times. And Meas has named my brother Dreamer, Friend Dreamer. Friend Dreamer, like myself, carries only kindness in his heart and dreams in his head. Cool Water, would you do that for us?"

Cool Water looked into the sparkling, friendly eyes. She liked this gentle man. There was something about him that drew her to him. Maybe it was the intense feeling that Friend Dreamer himself liked everyone else. "Sure, Weak Gun," Cool Water answered. "I shall know no other name for your brother save Friend Dreamer. In fact, I have already forgotten any other names for either of you. Now you two make yourselves comfortable while I prepare the evening meal. Meas has gone to make some arrangements for tomorrow. When he returns, I will have the meal ready."

Cool Water was true to her word. Honey, fresh warm milk, maize bread, and an ample kettle of succotash were ready for the guests when Meas returned. Before each helped himself, Friend Dreamer prayed:

> Lord of heaven and earth, thank you for bringing us safely across the mighty waters to the fatness of this favored land. Thank you for the kindness of these friends who have set this food upon the altar and shared it with two weary pilgrims. Bless this home with peace. In the name of Jesus we pray, Amen.

The three men sat in a circle on the ground and ate in silence while Cool Water stood attentively ready to serve them. By the time they finished the meal, darkness had crept in, and the mosquitoes were swarming upon their hosts. Meas rubbed bear grease liberally on his bare skin, then passed it on to Weak Gun and Friend Dreamer. They followed his example.

Meas rose and said to his guests, "Now let us move about a bit and pick a choice spot, perhaps on yon side of Tired Moon Pond, where we can pick up our thoughts of the afternoon."

The three walked slowly back to the spot of the evening beauty and seated themselves carefully, Meas cross-legged on the ground, the other two on an old log with a tree behind their backs.

Again Meas rose, gathered a few small sticks, and placed them between his seat and the logs. With his flint, he soon had a tiny blaze going. Meas resumed his seat, took out his pipe, loaded it with a mixture of two-thirds tobacco leaves and one-third sumac leaves, and kindled the leaves with a hot stick from the fire. Then he puffed contentedly away for some time before offering the pipe to Friend Dreamer.

"Meas," said Friend Dreamer, "I thank thee for thy kindness, but I pray thee will not be offended if I decline the smoke. I understand not the custom, and smoke is not pleasant to my lungs."

Meas handed the pipe to Weak Gun. Weak Gun readily took the pipe and expertly drew and puffed for some time before returning the pipe to Meas.

Meas carefully turned the pipe over and tapped the ashes upon a stick extending out from the fire.

"Weak Gun, tonight the moon is tired and falls early upon his bed. His slender form reclined high above us ere the sun descended to his hiding place in the west. Now the moon trails closely upon the path of the sun; soon the sun and moon will lie in bed together.

CQ207

They saw the world,
not as it was, but as it ought to be.

–Meas and Friend Dreamer at the Soul Meet

"Weak Gun," Meas went on, "perhaps you are also tired and would like to recline. Friend Dreamer has much to tell Meas in a tongue difficult for you to understand. We will not be offended if you wish to drift off to the southeast corner of the pond for the night."

Weak Gun took his cue and trailed off in the faint light along the edge of Tired Moon Pond. When he was gone, Meas spoke once more. "Friend Dreamer, a black walnut falls from the tree. Hidden within a husk and a thick hard shell dwells a living kernel rich in taste. But before I may taste the kernel, I must strip away the husk and with great effort crack open the thick shell to secure only a tiny meat. So it is with truth. The husk and the shell come easily before the eye, but the kernel must be obtained with effort.

"Friend Dreamer, this afternoon, upon the path, I spoke to you of some of the cruel things the Schwanneks have done to the Indians. Yet you must know that not all white men are Schwanneks. I have pale-faced friends who would never harm us—Falling Leaf, Weak Gun, Cool Water—and although I never met him, our record tells us Pastor Campanius was such a man. In fact, such palefaces treat all men fairly and justly.

"Friend Dreamer, I read your heart that you and your band are also unlike the Schwanneks. You bring no great guns nor long knives nor soldiers to defend yourselves from the savages. The ship sails away. You pray to the Great Spirit. You sing songs of kindness and peace. You see beauty and dream of fairness and justice.

"Friend Dreamer, at New Amstel I have watched the blacksmith's hammer beat upon the glowing iron to bend or flatten it into many different shapes. No one walks off a ship unshapen by the blows of the past upon his life. Tell me of your past that I may see what sort of design the past has wrought upon you."

"Sage Meas," Friend Dreamer began, "truly I have been formed by the past, and I will delight in telling you my story. I was born in

Zurik-Zee in Netherlands. *Netherlands* means 'a land below the sea.' Practically the whole of Netherlands has been a conquest of man over the sea.

"Sage Meas, imagine, if you can, all the marshes of the Siconece with dykes walling off the sea and its saltwater from the land. Imagine tall towers standing along the dykes holding revolving sails that use the strength of the wind to lift the water over the dyke and dump it into the sea. Then picture the black fertile soil of those flatlands covered with sheep and black-and-white-spotted cows grazing lush grass. Add to that fields of grain, green in winter and golden during harvest. Picture tens of villages of brick with tiled roofs spread over those lands. Canals crisscross those lands, with ships bearing burdens and people from village to village and to the sea. Picture it in your mind, if you can. Then you will have seen the land of my birth."

"Friend Dreamer, I can see the land you picture. My mother told me stories of Holland. I have seen the dykes on Fat Pig Hinoyossa's island in the South River. I have seen the tower and the revolving sail at New Amstel."

"Sage Meas, in my lifetime, the Netherlands or Holland or the land of the Dutch, whatever name you choose to call it, has become the wealthiest, the strongest, and the best-regulated country in the world.

"Sage Meas, Dutch farmers till the soils and produce abundance from the land. Dutch craftsmen in the villages and cities make all sorts of tools and merchandise. Dutch shipbuilders build the best ships, and Dutch sailors and soldiers sail them to every known land. Dutch chartmakers draw the best charts and maps of land or sea found anywhere. On the other side of the world where the sun is shining right now, a Dutch sailor, Abel Tasman, found a land he named New Zeeland. Still another Dutchman, Willem Janszoon, found a land in the same part of the world as New Zeeland; he named it New Holland.

"Sage Meas, Dutch merchants trade not only in New Amsterdam

and on the South River and the Caribbean, carrying goods back and forth to Europe, but also in places still farther away such as Cathay, Arcadia, and India.[61] And I must confess that the Dutch trade many slaves from Africa."

"Friend Dreamer, I have seen the marvelous Dutch ships. I know much of Dutch traders and soldiers. And I also know how the Dutch sell slaves, many black, some red, some white."

"Sage Meas, there is more than meets the eye in what has made the Dutch special. A whole palette of Dutch painters. Drost, Hals, Van Goyen, Rembrandt, Flinck, Steen, Vermeer, and a hundred others have captured upon canvas a new way of looking at life.

"Sage Meas, it was this new way of thinking about things in an ordered way that helped Dutchmen make important changes in the design of ships and buildings. This new way of thinking about things meant that men wrote down their ideas and tested them instead of just going by their feelings. For instance, you have oft observed the moon and you could confidently tell me, 'Tonight he is tired and will go to bed early.' Because of past experience you also know that the moon will go to bed later and later each night until he is round and full, when he will stay up all night."

"Friend Dreamer, I have watched the moon. I know much about his habits."

"Sage Meas, do you know that the moon causes the ocean tides to go in and out twice every day? We know this is true because over hundreds of years thoughtful men wrote down records about the habits of the moon and the tides. Then men guessed at what caused the seas to come in and go out. Many of their guesses were silly, and testing proved them false. But continued testing of ideas has proved that the moon causes the tides. Today, because Dutch chartmakers know the habits of the moon, mariners can look at their charts and

[61] Cathay, known as China. Arcadia, known as Indonesia.

tell exactly when it will be high or low tide at any time of the year."

"Friend Dreamer, I know how the sea comes in to the Siconece and goes out again. It has not bothered me to understand why the sea does so anymore than to understand why it rains."

"Sage Meas, the new way of thinking about things encouraged men to test their ideas, and prove them, instead of just guessing or simply trusting their own feelings. It also encouraged men to challenge the ideas and beliefs of rulers to see if they were true rather than bend their necks in abject submission.

"In testing their beliefs, some men discovered that there was a higher standard of truth than the word of the pope or the king. One Dutch priest named Menno Simons found a teaching in God's Book that said, 'No man can build on any foundation except Jesus Christ.' To Menno Simons, that verse meant that the teachings of God's Son, Jesus, were stronger than the decrees of the pope, the king, or the Dutch Reformed Church."

"Friend Dreamer, Cool Water has read to me from the Book. All the Christians make much ado about 'the Book.'"

"Sage Meas, my parents followed the teachings of Menno Simons that he took from God's Book. In earlier years, those in Holland who followed the teachings of Menno Simons were hunted, captured, thrown in stinking gaols, stretched on the rack, and burned at the stake or sold into slavery. By the time I was born, Mennonites in Holland were considered more as 'strange' and 'weird' than as threats to society. Mennonites were allowed to stay in the land."

"Friend Dreamer, I have heard that the Schwanneks kill many men in battle. I did not know that Christians also torture prisoners and burn them at the stake."

"Sage Meas, when I became a man, I decided to follow the teachings of God's Book in the way the Mennonites taught. Jesus taught that God loves all men—red men, black men, and white men—and that we should do good to all men, even returning good for evil. Because all men are the creations of a single God, they should behave as brothers toward each other. To take a gun or knife and kill one's fellow man is wrong."

"Friend Dreamer, the Lenape also believe the Great Spirit made us. We do not kill our brothers."

"Sage Meas, all men should not kill, but Jesus taught more than that. Jesus also taught that created brothers should not set some men up as lords to make servile slaves out of others. Jesus said, 'He that would be great among you should be the servant of all.' That means that rulers must not take a whip and chains and force other men to do their bidding. If men do right and good, then rulers should protect and encourage them.

"Sage Meas, all kinds of slavery are wrong, not just the binding of one's body to another. There is also the forced bondage of the spirit. All men should be free to choose who they will trade with, which master they will serve, where they will live, and which religion they will follow. Under Jesus' teaching, all men have been set free from the chains of slavery."

"Friend Dreamer, on the Siconece we are free. The Great Spirit tells us it is wrong to make slaves of others."

"Sage Meas, God's Book also tells us, 'Blessed is he that considereth the poor, the Lord will deliver him in time of trouble; the Lord shall preserve him, and keep him alive, and he shall be blessed upon the earth.' At another place in God's Book, it teaches that those who have much goods should deal fairly and justly with the poor and the orphans and the widows and help them in their suffering. This I wanted to do.

"Sage Meas, I saw the great disorder among men in the world; evil governors or rulers, covetous merchants and tradesmen. Lazy, idle, and negligent teachers have brought all under slavery. These men of the world try to see who can have the most servants and not do service to others. Instead of trying to ease men's burdens, as if there were not trouble enough in the world, these men still make the burdens heavier with new devices as if their design were to vex and grieve poor people with their excess and riot."

"Friend Dreamer, you speak true words. Fat Pig Hinoyossa behaves in just such a manner."

"Sage Meas, it is not just governors and men of the world who act in this manner. Even the so-called spiritual persons or clergymen persuade poor people to believe that they take care of their souls so the poor will more willingly drudge for them. The clergy convinces the poor that they love the soul which they cannot see, while at the same time having no compassion on the body which they do see. This is lies and deceit."

"Friend Dreamer, say on. Again you speak true words. My friend Falling Leaf tells me Bent Stick Grasmeer is just such a parson."[62]

"Sage Meas, true Christians are as well touched with the miseries of the body as with the miseries of the soul. I saw the excellency of the true Christian love compared with the folly of those who consider not to what purpose the Lord of heaven and earth hath created them. I saw that in the world, in society, no one loved the poor enough to care for them.

"Sage Meas, in my thoughts I came to the place where I saw that people of 'the world' could not stand us, and we being unable to better them, must reduce our friendship and society to a few in number and maintain it in such places as are separate from other men, where we can without hindrance love one another and mind the wonders of God, eating the bread we earn with our own hands, leaving nothing to the body but what its nakedness, hunger, thirst, and weariness calls for. So I purposed in my heart to do something to make the poor in these and other nations happy by bringing together a fit, fusible, and well-qualified people into one household government

---

[62] Wilhelmus Grasmeer, a minister in the Dutch Reformed Church.

or little commonwealth.

"Sage Meas! In this little commonwealth, everyone may keep his property and be employed in some work, as he shall be fit, without being oppressed. This is the only way to rid these and other nations from idle, evil, and disorderly persons, and from all such as have fought and found out many inventions to live upon the labor of others."[63]

"Friend Dreamer! Your little commonwealth sounds just like the way the Lenape live now. All men are free to do fit work and yet no ruler oppresses them."

"Sage Meas, I found few persons in my native land who wanted to help me do what they called 'your wild dreams.' The Dutch have a saying: 'Mother poverty is the bride of dreamers.' The saying must be true, for I am a dreamer and I am poor. Yet it is also true that dreams bring richness to the soul. How poor are they who have no dreams to nourish them!"

"Friend Dreamer, the Lenape often seek for the manito to speak to them in dreams. The Vision Quest of a young man is held sacred throughout the rest of his life."

"Sage Meas, looking round about me, where to begin my little commonwealth, I found no better object in Christendom than the Lord Protector and the Commonwealth of England. I resolved for a while to leave my family and native country, fearing if I should not manifest to the magistrates in England what was upon my spirit, that they, having much to do with other affairs, might through the subtilty of the clergy, as in other nations, easily be deceived.

"Sage Meas, in England I wrote letters to the council explaining my plan. The Lord Protector Cromwell himself heard me several times with patience. Then, as all men must, Lord Protector Cromwell died. His son Richard ruled England only a short time until the dead King's

---

[63] The preceding paragraphs contain direct excerpts from two pamphlets by Peter Cornelis-son, Van Zurik-zee, and published in London in 1659.

sons, Charles and James, returned to England.[64]

"Sage Meas, during this time I wrote letters to Parliament explaining my plans for a little commonwealth and published thousands of these letters for the public to read. Richard showed no interest in my schemes, and when King Charles II returned, he offered no help at all to start any communes. My ideas for helping the poor, just and fair government, freedom of worship, and stopping slavery only inflamed the King against me and many others with similar thoughts. I considered returning to Holland and my family, but resolved not to give up yet.

"Sage Meas, then King Charles II commenced a campaign to suppress opponents. Powerful men and dissenters alike, on one pretext or another, went to the Tower in London to cool their heated minds and maybe lose their hot heads. The King's supporters dug up the Lord Protector Cromwell's body from his grave inside the church and dragged his corpse through the streets of London. They hung his rotted body on a pole in a public square for a day, lopped off his head, impaled it on a pole, paraded the head around London, and finally stuck the head on a spiked fence of the King's palace where it hangs to this day."

"Friend Dreamer, the Lenape would never touch the grave of a dead man, be he friend or foe! This is the work of godless savages who respect nothing, not even death!"

"Ah, Sage Meas, you are right. 'Tis the way of the world. Men who do not fear God act in such a way." Dreamer hung his head in thought for a while before his tired voice went on.

"Sage Meas, I nearly lost the vision in the throes of London. I returned to my homeland bereft of the dream and any earthly means to start a little commonwealth. But in Amsterdam God acted. He

---

[64] Lord Protector Cromwell died 3 September 1658. Charles II returned from France and ascended the throne on 29 May 1660, thus restoring the English monarchy.

moved men so that what seemed impossible to me became possible, and today I and twenty-four other men arrived here to set up a little commonwealth in this favored land.

"Sage Meas, when I arrived back in Amsterdam, tired, penniless, and sad, I read the glowing reports that my brother Weak Gun was sending home about the land of the Siconece. Then Governor Hinoyossa returned to Amsterdam and persuaded the Amsterdam rulers to buy all the South River from the West India Company. Governor Hinoyossa then informed the rulers that four years ago he had bought all the land on the Siconece from the savages. Governor Hinoyossa urged the rulers to settle this land as quickly as possible to keep the Marylanders from grabbing it first.

"Sage Meas, the rulers of Amsterdam agreed with Hinoyossa and were so anxious to find settlers that they actually loaned one hundred guilders to each man who would agree to come over. Passage for women and children would be free. Besides that, the Amsterdam burgomasters agreed to let us set up our own government and pay no taxes for twenty-five years. Neither will we be forced to pay tithes to support an official preacher.

"Sage Meas, it was almost too good to be true. I told the burgomasters I could find one hundred men to take up such an offer. I could not imagine who among the poor and distressed would not want to take up such a chance to better their lot. I found only twenty-four men and myself willing to come immediately. So we have banded together and come to set up our little commonwealth on the Siconece, a place where true Christians may know a bit of Christ's kingdom on earth, a place where there will be fairness, justice, and peace."

"Friend Dreamer, I share your beautiful dream of fairness, justice, and peace on the Siconece. But it is only a dream and perhaps you shall awake to find it gone.

"Friend Dreamer, we plant the maize, but sometimes the crows pluck up the seeds. We plant the maize, but weeds grow as well as the maize. We till the maize, but sometimes the rains do not fall. Sometimes the rain falls and drowns the maize. At other times the maize nears harvest and then the coon, bear, or deer may rob us of it. The dream of much maize may not always be. Sometimes the children cry for maize.

"Friend Dreamer, we build a weir in the stream to catch the fish. But if there is a stake missing or there is a hole that we do not notice beneath the water, all the fish will find it and escape. Perhaps a hole you do not see lies open in your little commonwealth."

"Sage Meas, again your wisdom shines as the stars on this summer night. The truth is that only God knows what may happen. But a place of freedom from slavery, a place of righteousness, love, and brotherly sociableness, a place of peace is a noble dream, and I love to admire it. Even if my little commonwealth fails to transmit the world to our posterity in a better condition than we first found it, the world will still be the richer for having seen my vision. And I, I will have the joy of knowing I have given this little dream to the world."

The rest of the night passed quietly betwixt the sage and the dreamer, each to his own thoughts and to his own dreams. But at the first hint of morning light shoving the darkness westward, Meas arose and faced the east. Standing there above the glassy waters of Tired Moon Pond and the cabin to the right, surrounded by quiet fields framed by towering still trees, Meas lifted his right hand and pointed skyward above silent sand dunes and the whispering ocean beyond. Meas chanted the ancient prayer of the Lenape in his own tongue:

> Great Spirit,
> Maker of the sky, the earth, the sun, the moon,
> Keeper of the spirits of the fish, the birds, the animals, the trees, the stones.
> Guardian of the Four Winds,
> Thank you for bringing light again to the People of the Dawn.

Thank you for sending fire to warm our houses and cook our food.
Thank you for bringing water to inspire the ground and to quench our
    thirst.
Thank you for the ground to grow the maize and the deer to give us
    meat.
For the ancient song of the Lenape,
For the everlasting sun that rises this day,
I, Sage Meas of the Lenni Lenape, thank you.

When Meas had finished the chant, he took a small pinch of tobacco from his pouch with his left hand and sprinkled it on the ground before him. Then he stood motionless with his right arm raised and his two fingers pointing toward the horizon.

When the sun peeked over the horizon, Meas lowered his arm and turned to Friend Dreamer. Friend Dreamer knelt, also facing east, and offered his own prayer in the Dutch tongue. When Friend Dreamer had finished, he rose and faced Meas.

"Would you be so kind as to translate your prayer for me?" Dreamer asked. Meas carefully translated the chant to English. Dreamer listened.

"Sage Meas," he cried in wonder, "you pray to the same Creator God that the Christians pray to. Can it be?" Friend Dreamer shook his head. "Can it be that they serve God with sincere hearts, even though they know not the Christ? Can it be?" he asked for the third time, not of Meas, but of himself.

"Friend Dreamer, it is not a hard thing that the Great Spirit who makes birds of every color should also make white men as well as red men. Why would it take two Great Spirits to make men of varied skins?

"Friend Dreamer, let us leave our lofty thoughts in the clouds and tread upon the ground to yon cabin across the pond. I see that Cool Water has already taught Weak Gun to do her bidding. Look how he milks the cow and gathers wood for the fire. He is a good man.

"Friend Dreamer, I think that now you and Weak Gun should return to the fort and to your people. When the sachems arrive at the council fire, I will relay your request to them and explain the things you have taught me. When our answer is prepared, we will send for you and Weak Gun and No Smoke to come to the council fire.

At noon that day, Meas lit the ceremonial council fire on the same spot where he and Friend Dreamer had lit their council fire the night before. Soon after the lighting of the fire, sachems and headmen accompanied by warriors began arriving from other Lenape encampments. Some came from the west on foot trails. Others followed streams and rivers by canoe until they paddled in the Siconece and arrived only a short walk from Tired Moon Pond.

By evening, all sixteen sachems and headmen present at the making of the treaty with Fat Pig Hinoyossa four years earlier sat around the council fire. Meas, Meoppitas, Koketotoka, and their near relations—Mocktowekon, Sawappone, and Mettomemeckas—along with Teotacken came from the Siconece. Katenagka, Esipens, and Sappataon came from Quistin. Pochoeton, Quegkamen, and Hoatagkony came from the land near Canaresse. Mameckus and Hockarus came from Peskamohot. Matapagsikan came from the land of Seckatackomeck. Teotacken lit the calumet and passed it around the circle from one headman to the next. Each man in the circle puffed as long or as little as he wished before handing it to his neighbor. When the calumet finally returned to Teotacken, he rose and welcomed each headman, by name, to the council fire on the Siconece.

Next Teotacken bid each headman tell the general condition of the gardens, fields, and animals in his clan. How was his wife and family? Was there any sickness? Had there been any visitors? Had the headman traveled lately? Had he had any notable hunting or fishing event? Had the headman had any dreams he wished to share?

After Teotacken had finished his lengthy welcome and instructions, he resumed his seat, and one by one the headmen of the villages took their turns rising and giving their reports. Each one spared no detail he felt worthy of reciting. Meas told of the coming of the settlers to the Siconece and shared Friend Dreamer's vision of fairness, justice, and peace.

The night was nearly spent when the last headman finished speaking. Teotacken again lit the calumet and passed it around the circle. Then all sat in silence until the first rays of light began to brighten the eastern sky. Teotacken and fifteen others rose and faced that light while lifting their right arms to the horizon. As one man they chanted the ancient prayer of the Lenape, and as one man they sprinkled the tobacco offering on the ground before them. As one man they remained motionless until the sun crept above the horizon.

Again, the headmen resumed their seats around the council fire. In silence they pondered the reports and the tales of their brethren. No doubt some reveled in the glory of past hunts. Others felt the caresses of loved ones, while others pondered the meaning of dreams, and still others thought of forty-one strangers camped at the old fort.

Two squirrels scampered around the trees near the council. One of them grew bold enough to dart within the silent circle and calmly eat a nut. Then chattering and scolding, he again withdrew to join his playmate.

Gradually, silently, the entire circle of men began to think about the forty-one guests camped at the abandoned fort. Teotacken arose. "Brethren," he said, "I will tell you my dream:"

In my dream I saw a small pine cone blown along the ground by

East Wind. "Sit upon it," West Wind commanded. I sat upon it and sprang up quickly, for it pricked my seat. "Burn it," North Wind ordered. I threw the cone upon the fire and it flamed up quickly, for an instant. The fire consumed not the cone, and the heat from the flame did not warm me. "Plant it," South Wind whispered. I pressed the cone into the earth. Lo, forty-one shoots sprang forth.

In my dream I smiled. The dream was good. While I still smiled, the locusts arose out of the ground and chewed off every sprout. Then I awoke.

Teotacken again took his seat, and another long period of silence ensued. Each councilor carefully considered the meaning of Teotacken's dream.

Koketotoka spoke next:

I, too, have dreamed. In my dream I saw a small colony of ants building a home on a bank of the Siconece. Herein lay a marvelous thing. The ants had no chief or ruler, yet each ant worked diligently to bring in stores for the good of all. The ants harmed no one; they dwelled in peace.

Then I saw a large dog the size of yon red bull wander along the Siconece. The dog had an ugly face as though someone had smashed his nose back into his brain. Teeth as sharp as a steel knife protruded from each corner of his lower jaw. His teeth were like unto the tusks of a boar hog. I could see that the dog wore a bright red jacket. The dog was so terrifying, I broke into a profuse sweat until my body was covered with wetness.

The dog turned sideways and cast about as though he searched for something. Then he found the anthill. The dog stood triumphantly astride the anthill. The dog began to dig, and the earth flew in every direction until the entire ant house lay uprooted and spread out beneath him. Then the dog left.

As my dream continued, I saw the ants again rebuild their house.

Again they harmed no one. They dwelt in peace with their neighbors. Many, many moons later, the same dog returned to the Siconece. If it were possible, on this visit the dog appeared more terrible than the first time he came. This time the dog wore a jacket with black and yellow stripes, like unto the stripes of the hornet.

Again the dog found the anthill. Again he stood astride the ant house. Then he lifted his left leg and peed on the anthill, pee filled with lies, hate, greed, and all kinds of evil. Then I awoke.

Koketotoka sat down. Sixteen councilors pondered the meaning of Koketotoka's dream. The summer sun stood high in the sky. Men perspired. No one moved. No one disturbed the councilors. A shower came bringing coolness. Still no one moved.

At last Meas rose to speak. "Fellow councilors of the Lenape on the Siconece," he began. "We as Lenape may know some about our past. We can never know all about the past, for the truth is always colored by the one who remembers it.

"We know some about the present, for it is real to us. We touch the earth and feel it. But the earth feels differently to every person. So how are we to tell how the earth feels to our friends or to our enemies? We cannot tell why one man kills another. Even if the killer tells us his reason, it may be only the shelter behind which he hides the truth. So we who die can never know all about today.

"And the future belongs to the Manito alone. Man knows nothing of tomorrow, for the greatest among men will die, perhaps tomorrow. What the Manito chooses to reveal to us about the future through dreams is the Manito's gift to us.

I, too, have dreamed a dream. In my dream I saw a Great Black Heron alight on the western shore of the Chesapeake Bay. This great bird immediately began snatching fishes and frogs from the Chesapeake and dashing them down its gullet. The more the bird devoured, the more it grew until the bird swelled to such a size that it could place one foot on each shore of the Chesapeake Bay. Towering there, high above the water, the bird cast its yellow eyes eastward to the Land of the Dawn.

Then with lightning-like thrusts of its long neck, the Great Heron snared fishes and frogs from all the land between the Siconece and New Amstel. Fish and frog alike tried to hide from that piercing stare. But there was no escape from the evil eye and the long neck. Terror reigned in the Land of the Dawn.

Next, a gray dove lit upon the branches of a tree along the Siconece. I was greatly perplexed in my dream, for the dove cooed as a dove should. But the dove's feet were like the claws of an eagle, and he flew with a long sword hidden upon his back.

When the Great Heron poked its head below the clouds to look at the new visitor to the Siconece, the dove jumped on the head of the heron and grabbed it in his eagle claws. The dove flew a great wide circle back over the Chesapeake Bay. Holding the Great Heron's head firmly in his talons, the dove began to climb up through the loop he had made of the heron's neck. Higher and higher the dove climbed until he tied the long neck of the huge heron in a great knot stretching into the clouds.

Then I awoke.

Meas sat down again. Once again, sixteen councilors seated around a small fire on the north side of Tired Moon Pond reflected on what the Manito wished to reveal to them. What was the meaning of the three dreams? Or what were the multiple meanings of the three dreams? Were the dreams one and the same? Or did each dream reveal a separate mystery?

The sun began to fall from its noontime zenith while sixteen councilors weighed the intriguing mysteries of the dreams. Not a single councilor doubted that the Manito had spoken directly to them. The only question was, What did the dreams mean?

Teotacken raised his right thumb slightly and pointed toward his left. The councilor on his left rose to his feet and gave his idea of the meaning of the dreams. Sometimes the speaker wandered further than a bowshot from the subject, but no one stopped him or even expressed concern at the time being wasted.

When the speaker had finished with all he wished to give, he resumed his seat and the councilor to his left rose and gave his views. Each councilor continued thus until the councilor on Teotacken's right at last rose to speak. The sun had already gone to bed, and the pale light of a summer evening presided over the Siconesse Council when the fifteenth councilor sat down and Teotacken rose to speak.

"Fellow councilors," Teotacken began. "Surely the Manito has spoken to us. He has given us the gift of future truth, but he has wrapped it in a cloud into which we are not yet able to peer with our eyes. As events come and the moons pass, I am sure that those who live shall know the meaning of these dreams. Today, we do not understand many parts of the dreams. However, the Manito has given us what we need to know for the decision that faces us today: What shall we do with the forty-one strangers camped at the old fort?

"First of all, the Manito tells us these forty-one strangers camped here are people of peace. This is borne out by what we see with our own eyes. They bring no great guns. They fly no flags or set sacred poles to mark their boundaries. The strangers are few in number and have no soldiers close by to drive us out. These people are our friends."

After these words, every councilor let out a hearty "Eigh."

"Next," Teotacken continued, "the Manito tells us that the great danger on the Siconece comes not from the forty-one strangers, but from dogs and herons from beyond our land. We must warn these settlers of coming danger. Perhaps these settlers do not know of the wrath to be poured upon them."

Again the councilors agreed to Teotacken's words with a hefty

"Eigh."

"Therefore," Teotacken went on, "let us make a treaty of peace with these people according to the very same words we made with their countrymen: 'If they will live in peace among us, we will share the land with them as brothers.'"

And all the councilors shouted, "EIGH!"

Teotacken recessed the council until all was in readiness to resume the council again the following day.

Preparations could not be completed before late afternoon the next day. Of course, no one tried to hurry them. "Things will happen when they happen" was the old Lenape adage that ruled the councilors. And such a mindset was not to be tampered with even for the impatience of one so noticeable as No Smoke Helmanus Wiltbanck.

The messenger brought the wampum belt and a set of deerskin gloves to the Old Company Fort early in the afternoon and announced that the Siconesse Council was now ready to treat with No Smoke, Weak Gun, and Friend Dreamer at the council fire above Tired Moon Pond. The three Dutchmen almost beat the messenger back to the council fire and found only a few hot coals in the fire and not a single councilor present.

No Smoke tried sitting on a stump and soaking in the grandeur like Weak Gun and Friend Dreamer so easily did. It didn't work. He arose. Like a sentry he paced back and forth from one end of Tired Moon Pond to the other. Still, not one councilor appeared.

On one tour of duty, No Smoke neared the two brothers relaxing in the shade. "Brother, come join us," Friend Dreamer called to him.

No Smoke Wiltbanck nearly exploded. "You two are no better than the savages. I say like the Bible says, 'If you won't work, neither should you eat.' It's no wonder the savages are so poor. They lie around all day and smoke pipes all night. And if you two think you're going to make a living in this wilderness working only six hours a day in your little commonwealth, you'd better think again." No Smoke threw up his hands and marched off once more toward the swamp on the west end of Tired Moon Pond.

The birds stopped their chirping and stirring about before the council fire again flamed up brightly and all sixteen councilors seated themselves comfortably around the fire. Now the circle included twenty men—the sixteen councilors, the three guests, and Falling Leaf. Falling Leaf stood easily at Teotacken's right and slightly behind the sachem. Teotacken opened the council by introducing Falling Leaf to the guests as "a strong spirit, a son of Mattahorn, and a gifted interpreter."

"We trust Falling Leaf," Teotacken said, "and tonight he will make our true words known to you."

Teotacken then welcomed the three guests to the Siconesse Council and explained to them the proper ceremonies of a Lenape council. Teotacken invited No Smoke, Weak Gun, and Friend Dreamer to be one with them in the council and explained that he wanted none of them to feel like a dry fish while attending the council.

Then Teotacken lit the calumet, took several puffs, and passed it around the circle. Each councilor and each of the three guests puffed as much or as little as he wished. When the calumet returned to Teotacken, he laid the pipe aside and directed several others to give welcoming speeches. At last, Teotacken again arose and addressed the guests.

Travelers, strangers, visitors. I am not yet sure what to call you. I do not wish to call you Schwanneks, for as of yet you have done us no harm. As of yet I cannot call you friends, for one may not be a friend to another if the one refuses to be a friend. We would hope that ere night has fled before the stealth of dawn, we may fall upon each other's neck, we to call you friends and you to call us brothers.

Strangers, you have come from a strange place. You bring strange thoughts. You bring strange customs.

Strangers, you do not wish to learn peace and contentment from us. Instead, you expect to teach us to learn your ways of worry, hurry, and war.

Strangers, you have come here to settle in this land. I am sure that Fat Pig Hinoyossa has told you that the Dutch bought the land from us and now it is yours to do with as you choose.

Strangers, I must tell you that you do not know what you are doing. If you see a child ready to pluck a hot coal from the fire, will you not reach out and stop him? If that same child wishes to play with a rattlesnake, will you catch it and give it to him? No. No. Any caring adult will teach the child, that he may not be harmed. In the same way we must teach you of the danger along the trail that you follow.

Strangers, the council has carefully considered what you do and the snakes coiled along the path you follow. The council has asked Sage Meas to instruct you in the wisdom of the Siconesse Council.

Strangers, listen well to the words of Sage Meas.

Meas and Falling Leaf rose and stepped to the east end of the circle. Gradually, the circle shifted into an oblong pattern. Aged men and women began gathering in rows behind the councilors. Lenape men in the prime of life, young men and maidens, boys and girls, mothers

"We carry the Spirit of Tamenend in the Land of the Dawn."

—Meas and the Lenape

CQ208

and papooses, visitors from surrounding villages, and last of all the strangers from the Old Fort found their spots on the grass-covered hill. Like maize popping up after a spring rain, the crowd suddenly appeared from the paths, streams, forests, and fields around Tired Moon Pond.

A light rain refreshed every blade of grass and every flower with glistening beauty, and then the evening sun once more burst out upon the gathering throng. Meas and Falling Leaf stood side by side, splashed in sunlight and adorned with smiles as they watched the Lenape come to them. High above Meas and Falling Leaf the arch of a rainbow spanned the sky reaching from Swanendael in the north to Cape Henlopen in the south.

Meas slowly raised his right hand and held it aloft. The crowd quieted. Suddenly Meas shouted, "WE CARRY THE SPIRIT OF TAMENEND IN THE LAND OF THE DAWN." At first the cry came back to Meas like a distant rumble of thunder. But each time Meas repeated the cry, the feeling and power coiled into the response. The overcharged cry snapped and sizzled until the crowd sent its thunderous call crashing back to Meas, "WE CARRY THE SPIRIT OF TAMENEND IN THE LAND OF THE DAWN."

Soon Meas no longer gave the starting cries, yet the chant surged forward in full-throated power. Meas dropped his arm while he and Falling Leaf listened. "So it must have been 1,000 years ago," he mused to Falling Leaf.

Again, Meas raised his arm and held it aloft until the towering waves of the chant stopped surging toward him. A hush fell over the crowd. Not that the power of the chant disappeared when the waves subsided, only that the power surged in tremendous currents beneath the calm surface. Sage Meas—seer, storyteller, and spokesman for the Lenape peoples in the Land of the Dawn—held out one hand toward the people as though he were inviting each one to clasp it and stroll with him for an evening's walk.

My people, guests, and all who hear me this day. 'Tis not a light thing to carry the Spirit of Tamenend in the Land of the Dawn. And we might ask, "What is the spirit that pulsed through Tamenend and pushed him to so boldly take that first step?" Come with me that we may traverse the trails our fathers trod. As we cross and recross their worn paths, perchance we shall hear the spirits of the ancient ones calling out guidance and wisdom for us today. Perchance we shall discover anew the beat of Tamenend's spirit among us.

My people. Guests. Children and grandchildren of the Lenape nation. The Great Spirit, as he did seven years ago, has once again cast upon our shore a group of helpless strangers. These strangers totter about on the beach like a newborn fawn trying to find its mother's teat for the first time. Like the fawn, these strangers are spotted with innocence and do not know of the wolves, eagles, and panthers that would prey upon them.

My people. Seeing that these strangers, like orphans without father or mother, cannot know the danger of the red coals, but may instead tumble into the fire, we, the Lenape sachems at this council fire on the Siconece, have chosen to instruct these innocent children in the learning and lore of the Lenape people.

My people. Guests. Children and grandchildren. Hear then the Parables of Tired Moon Pond:

The Parable of the Man Who Wanted to Be King

A long time ago a Schwannek came to the Siconece. "I am king here now," he told the whale.

The whale blew a great spout of water into the clouds. "Can

you do that?" asked the whale.

"No, I cannot blow so much water so high," the Schwannek answered, "but I am king here now and I can kill you if you will not obey me."

The whale reared his great flukes high into the air and brought them down upon the water with such a smack that he upset the Schwannek's boat. Then the whale dived deep and hid in the bottom of the Great Sea.

Next the Schwannek discovered a huge school of herrings swimming in from the ocean to the Lenape River. "I am king here now," he shouted to the tens and tens of thousands of herrings as they swam past.

"What does a king do?" the herrings asked as the school flowed past the Schwannek.

"The king directs mindless herrings so they do not stall in a tangled mass and swim in circles," the Schwannek replied.

"Then we do not need a king," the herrings answered. "We have never had a king. We swim very orderly without one." So the thousands and thousands of herrings swept on past the Schwannek.

Next, the Schwannek looked up at the white fluffy clouds. "I am king here now," he called out to the clouds. The clouds danced high above the Schwannek, swinging, shifting, scudding from one partner to another, lifting, dropping, catching, twirling, laughing, and singing. The clouds paid no attention to the Schwannek.

"I am king here now," the Schwannek shouted at the clouds.

This time the clouds rolled their eyes downward and gave their hips an extra shake before politely asking, "And what shall we do for the king? Shall we stop our winging and swinging and singing and shed tears of sorrow that now a king has come to the Siconece?"

"No," the Schwannek roared back to the clouds. "Do not stop dancing. Now you must dance with me. I am the king."

The clouds turned dark and ugly while they bent their swollen eyes toward the Schwannek. "Oh, King. When we are sad we cry," the clouds answered. The tears of the clouds began pouring down on the Schwannek. And more and more fell.

"STOP IT!" the Schwannek roared to the clouds. The clouds dashed into one another and the lightning flashed. The thunder grumbled. The clouds poured their tears upon the Schwannek until he jumped into his white-winged canoe and sailed away from the Siconece never to be seen again.

Once again the whale sent his spout soaring into the clouds.

Once again the herring school swam joyously up the Siconece.

Once again the clouds could swing with East Wind and West Wind. Once again the clouds could hold each other close and smile down upon Tired Moon Pond.

The Parable of the Man Who Would Not Look Up

Another Schwannek came to the Siconece. "I am lost," he told a Lenape sachem. "I cannot tell which way is east and which way is west."

"I will help you," said the sachem. "The sky is clear tonight. I will show you the North Star. When you see the North Star, you will always know which way is east and which way is west."

The sachem pointed to the North Star. The star shone brightly and steadily.

But the Schwannek would not look up. "I do not believe in the North Star," said the Schwannek.

The Parable of the Man Who Walked on Water

A Schwannek came to a Lenape council fire by Tired Moon Pond. "I will show you how to walk on water and then you will give me Tired Moon Pond," said the Schwannek.

The Lenape council laughed at the Schwannek. *No one knows how to walk on water,* they thought, but wanting to please the Schwannek they put their marks on his paper. The Schwannek gave the Lenape each a matchcoat and several ankers of rum. Then he left.

One bitter cold winter day the Schwannek returned. "I have come to show you how to walk on water," he boasted, "and to claim Tired Moon Pond for my own."

"This is not water. This is ice," a sachem protested.

"There is water under the ice," said the Schwannek. So saying, the Schwannek strapped a pair of runners on his feet and went skimming over the ice.

"Bravo! Bravo!" cried the watching Lenape.

The Schwannek flipped around and skated backwards as he waved at the cheering Lenape.

"Faster! Faster!" yelled the Lenape.

The Schwannek strained every muscle to fly backwards over the ice until he struck the edge of the pond and crashed his head into a tree.

"Now Tired Moon Pond belongs to him," said the sachem.

The Parable of the Warrior

Still another Schwannek marched off a ship at Swanendael. His muscles bulged with strength. He stood head and shoulders above the tallest Sickoneysinck. He was a fearsome warrior eager to conquer and kill.

But the Schwannek never knew the Siconece, for he never heard the buck snort, nary a warbler sing, nor the honk of geese winging overhead. The Schwannek warrior had plugged both his ears with clay.

And the Schwannek warrior never saw a rainbow, for he was color-blind.

The Parable of the Governor

A Schwannek governor came to a Lenape council fire and commanded, "Follow me."

"Where are you going?" an old sachem asked.

"I do not yet know," the governor answered. "But after you get out of my way, the path shall become clear to me."

The Parable of the Contested Field

Four Schwanneks wrangled over who owned a certain field.

"The field is mine," said a Schwannek wearing a red and blue hat. "The field is mine because a long time ago a man wearing a red and blue hat sailed past this field in a boat and claimed the field for my country."

"That's silly," shouted the second Schwannek wearing a blue and gold hat. He picked up a club and waved it at the first Schwannek. "The field is mine. I bought the field from the savages. The savages planted this field long before your captain ever sailed up the river."

"Hold on," shouted a third Schwannek wearing a red, white, and blue hat. The third Schwannek unsheathed his long knife. " Give way!" he shouted at the second Schwannek. The third Schwannek made a pass at the second Schwannek with his long knife. "The field is mine. The savages gave the field to me. Besides that, I was the first white man to plant the field. It is undoubtedly mine."

"Take it easy," a fourth Schwannek wearing a black and gold hat ordered. He pointed a pistol at the head of the third Schwannek. "The field is clearly mine," he growled. "The king, before he was beheaded, bless his soul, gave the field to my father before my lordships passed away."

The Parable of the Forbidden Song

One spring the crows flew by Tired Moon Pond and talked to the cardinals. "We like the trees and the pond and the fields where you live. We see that you use only a few of the trees to perch in and to nest on. We will build two nests here this year."

"Very well," said the cardinals. "It is true that the sky is big here and the trees are many. You may nest here if you do not sing. We have many fine voices among the birds here around Tired Moon Pond and your voices are a bit coarse. We cardinals must ask that if you come, you agree not to sing."

"We will not sing," agreed the crows, and they bobbed their bodies back and forth in unison.

But the crows were a nasty lot. They made no effort to quiet their raucous cawing. And when the young crows started practicing their caws, the racket around Tired Moon Pond became unbearable.

Again the cardinals talked to the crows. "You promised not to sing if you nested here," said the cardinals to the crows.

"Oh, we have kept true words," said the crows. "We do not sing. We caw." And the crows laughed loudly while they cawed noisily.

Of course the cardinals were not happy with the deceit of

the crows. They asked the owl if he would help them talk to
the crows. The owl agreed and stirred himself in the middle of
the day to meet with the crows.

The crows laughed at the owl. "The stupid cardinals should
have known that *cawing* is not *singing* when they treated with
us." And the crows began to make fun of the owl, calling him
a "blind old buzzard" and screaming nasty threats at him.
The loud insults of the crows soon drew hundreds of crows
to the owl. They dived at him, tried to peck his eyes out, and
harassed him until the poor owl found his own hollow tree
once more.

After the crows had driven the owl from the sky, the crows
ordered the cardinals to meet with them. "With all your
complaining, you are stirring up all the birds around Tired
Moon Pond," they croaked. "This is the crime of excitement,
and if you are found guilty, you may be choked to death," the
crows told the cardinals.

"However, we will not just turn you over to the hawk for
choking. First you must be given a fair trial according to crow
law."

On the appointed day, the crows tied up the wings of the
cardinals, dusted their bright red feathers with soot, and cast
them at the base of a juniper tree on Cape Henlopen. A stout
raven perched on a snag jutting out the top of the tree. Twelve
crows clung to one gnarled limb below the raven. On the
ground, two pelicans waddled back and forth in front of the
cardinals. Whenever the pelicans opened their pouch bills, the
smell of rotten fish spewed out over the cardinals.

"The cardinals stand accused of *insidious excitement*," the
raven declared. "Today the twelve crows in the choir must
decide if the cardinals are guilty or not guilty of *insidious*

excitement. Proceed!" the raven ordered.

The pelicans opened their gaping mouths. Crows quickly tossed in a kettle of fish.

"Does the choir find the cardinals guilty?" asked the raven. All twelve crows bobbed up and down in agreement.

"Now," said the raven, "the full penalty under crow law for *insidious excitement* is death by choking. But due to my concern for fairness, I will reduce the punishment for this first offense to—" the raven hiccuped before finishing—"no singing around Tired Moon Pond. But be warned, from here on, any songbird caught singing at or near Tired Moon Pond will be choked to death at once."

The Parable of the Goose's Air

One fall a goose began flying in a great circle over Tired Moon Pond. Day after day she climbed into the sky and began her endless journey.

"Lady Goose, what are you doing?" asked the owl.

"I am guarding my air," the goose replied. "You see, O Wise One. If other geese fly across Tired Moon Pond, they might damage my air. I cannot allow that."

"Wh-o-o-o? Wh-o-o-o gave you the air?" asked the owl.

But the goose did not hear the owl. She honked and honked and honked as she beat the air in her endless patrol over Tired Moon Pond.

The Parable of the Calabash Nut

Two gray squirrels spied a walnut the size of a calabash growing on the tree in which they nested. "Wow!" chattered

Daddy squirrel as he flung himself from limb to limb and raced around the nut. "I wonder how big that nut will get."

Mama squirrel perched in a nearby crotch and snapped her tail back and forth. "You had better calm down," she said, "or you'll knock the nut down before it's done growing. We had better warn the papooses not to go out on that limb or the whole limb might break off and the nut crash down on top of them and kill them."

Every day Daddy squirrel climbed to the limb above the huge nut and sat there watching it grow. Then before he scampered off, he would lean down and put his ear against the nut while he thumped it with his front paws. "I believe it's going to be a good nut," he whispered to Mama squirrel. "Maybe we shouldn't tell the neighbors about the nut. They might get jealous."

"What makes you think I can't keep a secret?" scolded Mama squirrel.

The calabash nut fell to the ground. "That is the largest nut I ever grew," said Daddy squirrel. "We must show it to the neighbors."

"Are you crazy?" said Mama squirrel. "The neighbors might eat the nut. It's our nut. It grew on our tree."

Daddy squirrel dug a hole for two nights while no one was looking. He and Mama squirrel pushed the heavy nut into the hole and buried it.

Two moons later they dug up the nut. It was filled with rancid sap.

The Parable of the Spectac'lar Fight

A bustling trumpet vine climbed into the heights of a giant

pine. Two thousand blooms spilled out from the vine. A hummingbird flitted by, then hovered o'er a bursting flower that he might slip a furtive tongue within an orange dress and thus caress a lick of sweetness from its tenderness.

A second hummingbird found the florid vine. He swept past hundreds of enticing beauties that winked and whispered of pleasures held within. With haste he stirred that he might hurl himself upon the other bird. The tiny birds engaged in a spectac'lar rage—buzzing and diving, flashing and whirling, whizzing and scolding, whirring and soaring.

While the two birds thus fought in dizzying fury, two hundred thousand ants, without one cross word, followed one by one on up the vine, tiptoed inside those teasing dresses, and licked the sweetness from two thousand flowers.

The Parable of the Hidden Sun

Three Christians traveling home from church meeting on a clear sunny day fell to discussing the morning sermon, "How to Tell East and West."

"The parson was not real clear about which way was east and which way was west," said the tall Christian as he strode easily along, "unless the parson was standing inside the meeting house."

"That is all fine and dandy," said the limping Christian as he leaned hard on his cane. "But how does that help me since most of the time I am a long way from the meeting house? How do I know east and west?"

"That is easy," resumed the tall Christian. "Listen for church bells. When you hear the church bells, you will know exactly where the meeting house is located, and from that you can always tell east and west."

"It's not quite as easy as you make it sound," chimed in the third short Christian as he pumped his legs busily, trying hard to keep up. "It seems to me that east and west are wherever one thinks they are. For depending on where one stands, the sound of the bell may come from the east one time and from the west another time."

"I agree," said the limping Christian. "Where the meeting house stands cannot tell us east from west. Unless we define the terms first, we can never agree on what is east and west."

"If you allow every man to decide for himself what is east and west," replied the tall Christian, "there will be great confusion among the people. The pastor must teach what is east and west, and heretics who disagree must be cast out of the meeting house."

"I guess I'll have to agree with the parson," sighed the short Christian. "Maybe we can't really know east from west."

The limping Christian smiled sociably. "I think the parson was right," he declared. "Sometimes it is hard to tell east from west."

The sun beat down mercilessly on the trio, and the three stopped to rest under a shade tree. The tall Christian removed his hat and wiped beads of perspiration from his face. Then he replaced his hat and smiled down upon his two companions. "See what I mean," he said. "When no one knows how to tell east from west there is confusion."

He that has ears to hear, let him hear.

Worthy strangers, you have come to the Siconece to build houses and to plant crops. You have also come to claim the fields and forests as your own and to drive us away.

Worthy strangers, perhaps today you say, we want only a little land to set our chair upon. We wish only a small plot to grow our herbs on. We have heard those words before. Many times. They are lies. Tomorrow the whole land will be covered by roosting pigeons, and there will be no place for us and our children to hunt and fish or to plant our maize.

Worthy strangers, Fat Pig Hinoyossa has lied to you. We sold him no land. None. Let me tell you the exact words of our treaty with Fat Pig Hinoyossa: "If you wish to treat with us, we will treat with you. You may come and live among us if, and only if, you live in peace. We will continue to hunt and fish and to plant our fields as we have always done ... If you do not wish to abide by these terms, then go away. Do not return to the Siconece. Give your gifts to another."

Worthy strangers, there is another reason we cannot and will not sell the land to you or to anyone else. We did not make the land. It does not belong to us or to you. The Great Manito made the land and the air and the water. It belongs to him.

Worthy strangers, do you float your sacred poles in the ocean and declare, "This sea is mine and mine alone"? Do you hang your poles from the clouds and proclaim, "The air is mine and mine alone"? So why do you plant your sacred poles in the corner of a field and dare to say, "This field is mine and mine alone"?

Worthy strangers, I would beg that my words do not weary you, for you must hear me on. Can a dolphin sell the water he plays in? Can a woodpecker sell the tree he dwells in? Can a buck sell the land over which he roams? Neither can a Lenape sell his homeland.

Worthy strangers, give up this evil thought of the

Schwanneks that one man or one nation must own the earth. The Schwanneks fight and kill and steal and enslave others that they might "own the land." They lie and twist the truth. They give gifts to ease the pain of a tossing heart within while grasping for still more land without.

Worthy strangers, the Schwanneks have deceived themselves. They cannot see that a little land is never enough and that even a large land does not satisfy the spirit. For every evil seed—theft, lying, deceit, war, unkindness, murder—the Schwannek sows in his quest for more land, a vine—hate, fear, guilt, rage, jealousy, despair, distrust—springs up within the Schwannek himself until the vines entangle and then strangle his very spirit.

Worthy strangers, may I picture the folly of the Schwanneks in yet another way? The Schwannek yearns for ever more land—50 acres, 100 acres, 200 acres, 2,000 acres, or 10,000 acres, or the whole Chesapeake Bay—to be flung upon his back that he might bend under its weight and be crushed to a miserable life of toil and strife. Why must the Schwannek bear such a burden? Can he not see that no matter how much earth he carries on his back, he will have to lay it down and add to it two handfuls of dust from his own body?

Worthy strangers, let me teach you a better way. You may use the land as friends and brothers with us. You may build your houses and plant fields, and we shall fish and hunt and plant fields as we always have. Together we may use the land and be borne along in one canoe by the fatness and goodness and beauty of this our homeland.

Worthy strangers, you must remember. Since we have not made the land, but only use it for a time, we must tread softly upon the earth that the Manito be not displeased with our

coming and going. For the Manito may watch how we walk
upon the earth and frown upon our spirits in the path of the
sky.

Worthy strangers, I speak for the united council of the
Lenape on the Siconece. We will treat with you and call you
friends and brothers if you will live quietly and peaceably
among us. Never again shall you call us savages, and never
again shall we call you Schwanneks. Your good shall be our
aim, and our happiness shall be your desire. Dogs and herons
may come to the Siconece and do you harm. But neither we
nor our children shall ever cast one evil eye toward you. Our
love for you shall continue as long as the sun shines and the
rivers run down to the sea.

Friend Dreamer, No Smoke, and Weak Gun. From this day
forward the Lenape shall no more call you and your people
strangers and wanderers, but friends and brothers. The moon
and the sun have heard my words.

Friends and brothers, you are no more pilgrims. As friends
of the Lenape on the Siconece, you may build your houses and
plant your crops on the land from the Swanendael Fort at the
mouth of the Siconece to the banks of Tired Moon Pond.

Friend Dreamer Cornelisen, on these lands you may rear
your little commonwealth in the sky where your king shall
be named Kindness and your parson shall be called Peace.
To you, Friend Dreamer, I give the herd of red cattle grazing
the shores of Tired Moon Pond—six cows, three heifers, two
young bulls, and four spring calves. Every time you drink of
their milk and taste of their curd and meat, may you always
remember the covenant of love you have made with your red
brethren, the Lenape on the Siconece.

No Smoke Wiltbanck, this night I bequeath to you the suit,

the shoes, and the hat of the former governor of Maryland, Captain Big Field Fendall. This man's garments shall be your own. And each time you wear Captain Big Field's fine clothes, may you remember the teaching I held before you this night: If you touch the earth lightly, it will nourish you. But if you beat heavily upon it, the earth will bind up your spirit.

Weak Gun Cornelisen, to you I grant my gun. This is a trusty gun that always fires and shoots true. May the gun always remind you of the trust we have placed in you this night. Trust that you will do us good and not harm. Trust that you will stand beside the Lenape on the Siconece as true brothers.

Friends and brothers, it was this same trust that gave Tamenend the courage and the boldness to take the first step. For he trusted that the Land of the Dawn, a land he had never seen, would one day belong to his children's children.

Friends and brothers, people of the Lenape nation, children, grandchildren, and all who hear me this night. Together we shall carry the Spirit of Tamenend in the Land of the Dawn.

The entire crowd rose to its feet and shouted, "Bravo! Bravo!" Meas walked up to Friend Dreamer and they touched hands lightly. Meas stroked his left arm three times. Friend Dreamer returned the Lenape expression of special warmth. Meas did the same with Weak Gun and No Smoke. Every member of the Lenape council likewise repeated the sign with each of the three.

A drumbeat started. Flutes stirred the air. A gentle chant began, "We carry the Spirit of Tamenend in the Land of the Dawn." Two great concentric circles formed, encircling the council fire, the flutes, and the drums, with the men and boys on the outside circle facing the women and the girls on the inside circle. Lenape and guests intermingled in the two circles.

The circles began to move in opposite directions. Moccasins, bare feet, and booted heels tapped the earth and moved with the rhythm of the drum. The measured chant continued, "We car-ry the Spir-it of Tam-e-nend in the Land of the Dawn." The ladies gave the first cry. The men followed with their heavy voices. Then all together chanted the line, "We car-ry the Spir-it of Tam-e-nend in the Land of the Dawn."

The tempo picked up. Feet tapped faster and bodies swept hastily by one another. The flutes started a tune and the voices of the singers began to follow the flutes. Older men and women dropped out of the circles followed by children and less hardy spirits. The circles drew tighter and closer until only the young and strong whirled and sang. Now the notes fell rapidly upon one another, no longer forming words. Instead the voices of men and women called out only "las" that fell together on blended notes.

A spell flowed out from the circling singers over the watching crowd. Not one could move. Not one wished to move. The Spirit of Tamenend rustled over the waters of Tired Moon Pond and whispered, "Tonight there is peace in the Land of the Dawn."

Narrated by Glikkikan

Owechela started coughing again. He had been coughing a good bit lately. Sometimes he spit up a spot or two of blood. He tried to hide the blood from me. But the blood and the coughing worried me.

I pushed Owechela to hurry on with the story as the days grew shorter and the nights longer there above Neshaminy Creek.

Owechela really wanted to tell me everything he knew, but I could tell he was growing weaker.

"Glikkikan," he said, "in eight moons, during the month of roasting ears,[65] the whole village will journey down Neshaminy Creek and follow the Lenape River to Passayunk on the Manayunk River. At this festival, boys from many villages will tell the story of the Lenape people. None of them can tell the whole story, so each of them must tell only a favorite part. Maybe you should think some about which story you want to tell."

"Owechela," I told him, "that is a hard choice. The way you tell these stories, they are all fascinating. But I love Sage Meas. I can hardly wait to find out the meaning of the dreams of Teotacken, Koketotoka, and Meas. And whatever happened to Weak Gun, No Smoke, and Friend Dreamer? And did Meas ever find the silver tortoise stolen from Mattahorn's grave?"

"Glikkikan, listen well to the unfolding tale of Sage Meas."

[65] The month of August because the corn ears are ready to be roasted.

The Spirit of Tamenend

As told by Owechela

F riend Dreamer and his band scampered busily about at
Swanendael building a large meeting house and dining area
they named Peace Hall. Peace Hall, combined with a temporary
shelter for lodging and other personal needs, gave them much more
comfortable surroundings than they had had for months aboard the
St. Jacobs. Actually, the band of forty-one souls had the main structure
under roof by the time the Siconesse Council had called for them.

"We don't have time to dawdle and smoke pipes," bellowed red-
haired No Smoke Wiltbanck, and he pushed every able hand from
dawn to dark. No Smoke always came up with a job for everyone, even
the smallest children among them. "Idleness is the devil's workshop,"
No Smoke preached.

All fell to the job assigned them with zest, for the people had a
mind to work, and after all, no one wanted the devil busy within him.
Friend Dreamer smiled and happily chipped in at whatever task No
Smoke assigned him.

Now that the treaty with the Siconesse Council had granted Friend
Dreamer's band use of the land as far south as Tired Moon Pond,

HOMELAND IN MY HEART

No Smoke began laying out a miniature Dutch town with individual dwellings and shops just north of Tired Moon Pond. The axes rang while skilled craftsmen whittled and sawed and fitted the beams and boards into neat barns and houses. No Smoke set up a crude forge outside the fort, and the smith began at once to mend tools and fashion new ones.

The women tended the fires and cooked the fish, meats, maize, squash, pumpkins, beans, and all manner of herbs Meas brought to them.

And the Dutch women knew exactly what to do with the milk from those little red cows. Some days they heated the milk in one of their large copper kettles, added the rennet,[66] and then drained off the whey. The women salted the curd and pressed it into rounds of delightful cheeses which they aged in a dark cellar where water oozed up from the ground. They fed the whey back to the cattle.

On other days they skimmed the cream from the top of the bucket after the milk had set for a day and turned slightly sour. The women placed the cream into a narrow wooden keg with a hole in the lid. A boy plunged a dasher up and down until he churned the agitated cream into butter. Men craved the taste of the pungent buttermilk drained from the butter, but the women hoarded the acrid liquid to be used in baking fluffy corncakes.

Cool Water watched everything the Dutch women did with their dairying, baking, and sewing. Cool Water helped what she could, but she was best at caring for the herd of little red cattle. She could milk faster than any Dutch woman, flashing the milk in steady streams into the singing bucket as she pulled and squeezed the teats in alternating rhythm.

Meas, too, watched the busy Dutchmen. He wandered unhurriedly from worker to worker, stopping to watch what each one did. When he knew everything that was going on, he would drift over to his

---

[66] The lining of the fourth stomach of a calf that causes the milk to curdle.

mother's grave and seat himself upon the ground there. Often, Friend Dreamer would leave his job and also come to sit with Meas.

Many times they passed long periods in silence. At other times they shared their dreams and the secrets of their hearts. Often No Smoke would stride briskly over to the two and mutter something in Dutch. Friend Dreamer would always respond cheerily with a "jah, jah," and then continue his visit with Meas. No Smoke would shrug his shoulders and hurry on to the task at hand.

During one of these daytime reveries, Meas spoke. "Friend Dreamer, I hate to trouble your pleasant thoughts, but I have a question that bothers my sleep. I see many worker bees buzzing busily about bringing pollen and nectar back to the honey tree. In the hive the bees transform the pollen and nectar into comb and honey so they may have food to rear the young and stores for the winter. But, Friend Dreamer, where are the stingers of the bees? How will the bees drive off those who would destroy the hive and rob the honey?"

"Sage Meas, 'tis true. We are defenseless Christians. We do not wield the tomahawk, knife, and gun to kill God's children, even in our own defense. We follow the example of Jesus Christ, God's Son who suffered and died rather than fight back. Jesus told His followers, 'If my kingdom were of this world, then would my servants fight.' Jesus did not fight even though He could have called in ten thousand angels to destroy His enemies. Neither should we fight.

"Sage Meas, we are people of kindness and love and peace. Our weapons are truth, justice, and righteousness. With these weapons God's children shall conquer the world.

"Sage Meas, if we are on God's side, there is no power that can overcome us. Now tell me, do you think the Lenape will break their pact with us and cause us harm? Everyone feared that the savages would eat us alive. Instead, God has miraculously blessed us with your help and friendship.

"Sage Meas, why would anyone else want to harm our little commonwealth? We build. We do not tear down. We plant. We do not steal another's goods. We set men free to do their own choosing. We do not make slaves and force other men to do our bidding. We are people of peace. We do not fight and kill. Why would anyone wish to harm us?"

"Friend Dreamer, I do not know why anyone would wish to harm you. I do know that if you live in peace here on the Siconece, no Lenape will harm you. But I must warn you that according to Koketotoka's dream, the Red Dog is coming to attack you. Beware the Red Dog!"

Less than two moons after the peace treaty with the Dutch settlers, during the autumnal month,[67] a large ship flying black and yellow flags entered the bay and anchored some distance from the Swanendael fort. A smaller vessel put out from the large ship and quickly pulled up to the dock at the old fort. The smaller ship brought a letter:

> To Pieter Cornelius Plockhoy van Zerikzee and the Mennonite settlers from Amsterdam:
> Baron Charles Calvert, governor of Maryland, and the son of Cecelius Calvert who is the Second Lord Baltimore of Baltimore and the sole owner of the province of Maryland by royal patent would be pleased to visit the settlement on the Whorekill. I and my twenty-six attendants await your further desires.
>
> ~Baron Charles Calvert

When the large ship sailed into the harbor and docked at Swanendael, all was in readiness for the special guest.

No Smoke was dressed in Governor Fendall's old suit, boots, and hat. Friend Dreamer, Weak Gun, and Sage Meas stood side by side to

---

[67] Around the end of September 1663.

greet the governor and his retinue.[68]

Friend Dreamer gave the welcoming speech in which he told the story of how God had made it possible for his small group to come to this beautiful land and begin a little commonwealth, a little commonwealth that would extend fairness, justice, and equality to the poor and despised of many nations. Furthermore, this community would be an example of freedom both in matters of body and conscience. There was to be no servile slavery named amongst them, and every man was to be free to come or go "as he willed."

At this outburst, Meas watched the governor fidget while a number of eyes in his escort rolled upward. But the uneasiness of the guests bothered Friend Dreamer not a whit. He soared upward to still more lofty heights of his inspired vision.

"God has smiled on this little commonwealth and even blessed it with the undeserved love and kindness of the savages," he sang.

Then Friend Dreamer reached his hands toward the sky and cast his face upward. "This is none other than the peaceable kingdom of Christ on earth where the wolf and the lamb shall lie down together." Friend Dreamer stood in a trance while a hush fell over the packed room. Then Friend Dreamer burst into a short prayer and closed it with, "In the name of Jesus we pray, Amen."

And all the people said, "Amen." A lone voice started a hymn, and other voices joined the chorus. Slowly the song moved along as voices of the men and women blended together in four-part harmony.[69] When the song ended, all was once again still.

No Smoke Wiltbanck and Friend Dreamer led Baron Calvert and his entourage on a slow tour of the settlement. No Smoke relished explaining every detail of the young settlement to his interested

---

[68] The attendants and servants of a prince on a journey.

[69] It is uncertain whether the Dutch Mennonites would have used four-part music at this date. Given the artistic expression and progressiveness of the Dutch Mennonites, along with the natural practice of singing parts when unaccompanied by instruments, it seems plausible that these Mennonites would possibly have sung in four-part harmony.

observer. They traveled as far as Tired Moon Pond before returning to Peace Hall for lunch.

Friend Dreamer directed the guests to be seated at the tables. The governor found himself served on Cool Water's fine English dishes. Dutch ladies in sparkling white caps and aprons bustled about with tasty meats and juicy vegetables. The Dutch ladies offered the guests their best corn bread and their sharpest cheeses. The governor brought out French wine as his part of the repast.

The young baron of only twenty-six winters proved to be an astute guest. "Where are the defenses of the colony?" he asked. "You know how the savages wiped out Swanendael and have threatened to kill any settlers ever since. Why did the Dutch abandon the fort and leave you unprotected? Would you not like the protection of Maryland?"

"No, we would not want the protection of Maryland," Friend Dreamer responded. "The savages, as you call them, have been very peaceful and kind to us. We have found them to be less cruel than many 'Christians.' "

The governor changed the subject. "You are Dutchmen. Yet I am served on English dishes. I see the Red Devon English cattle and not the black and white Dutch Holsteins. I see an English suit, boots, and hat on Director Wiltbanck. How did you come upon so many English goods so soon after walking off the *St. Jacobs*?"

Friend Dreamer smiled. "Our Lenape brother, Meas, had the red cattle and the suit before we arrived. He gave these things to us as a part of the treaty the Lenape made with us."

"Very interesting," commented the governor. "And where did the savage get the cattle and the clothes? Do you not know that some savage probably killed a Maryland settler and stole the cattle and the clothes and the dishes?"

"No, no, your honor," Friend Dreamer replied. "You completely misjudge our brother Meas. Meas was a trader and he bought the goods fair and square from none other than the former governor of

Maryland, Captain Josias Fendall. Meas also bought the governor's stepdaughter and married her. Meas and Cool Water live in the blockhouse you saw by Tired Moon Pond."

At the name of Josias Fendall, the young governor spluttered, "The treasonous thief. He tried to steal the whole province of Maryland from my Lord. And you say this heathen Meas married Fendall's Christian stepdaughter? Were they married in a Christian church?"

"Your honor," Friend Dreamer replied in a soothing voice, "I wish that you would stop referring to Sage Meas as a heathen and a savage. The Lenape perhaps have a higher standard of right and wrong than many so-called Christians. For instance, they do not keep slaves. They share their goods generously with one another. I wish you could have heard the Parables of Tired Moon Pond that Meas told on the treaty night. He has much that 'Christians' should learn. But in answer to your question, Meas and Cool Water were married here on the Siconece according to their custom. Do you not think that God honors their marriage?"

"Pieter Cornelius Plockhoy von Zerikzee," the governor exploded. "Now I know you are a heretic. You would say that a heathen who does not believe in Jesus Christ and the Holy Mother of God can be saved. Furthermore, you would suggest that the heathen should teach us. And then you accept as a brother a heathen savage living in fornication with a Christian woman. Now I fully understand why the Dutch call this place the Whorekill. It must be full of evil women and their illegitimate children."

Friend Dreamer's eyes lost their sparkling glow and narrowed into gleaming slits filled with righteous wrath. "Just one correction, sir," he said coldly as though slapping an eight-year-old boy's mouth. "It was the Dutch *men* who made whores of Indian women. It was *not* Indian men who made whores of *Christian women*. Remember that when you call Swanendael Whore's Creek."

"And you should remember also that Maryland was founded as a haven for Catholics," the governor spat out, "and not as a hideout for heretics."

Friend Dreamer said nothing more.

At last Governor Charles Calvert continued. "It is true that Maryland tolerates Protestants and even welcomes other unhappy people to our settlements as long as they believe in Jesus Christ and do not abuse people of other beliefs. Such abuse even includes calling someone an Anabaptist, for which a fine of ten shillings is levied upon the railer. If the railer cannot pay, he is publicly whipped and held without bail until he satisfies the one he defamed. So I suppose there is room in Maryland even for Anabaptists[70] such as you.

"I can see that you are certainly a hardworking, industrious people who will strengthen Maryland. And to have good relations with the savages, er, er, Indians, is of benefit to all. We should not squabble, but work together.

"Maryland would like to welcome you as able settlers. Maryland's quitrents are far lower than the tithe extracted by the Dutch on all commerce and lands. Would you not like to swear fealty to our Lord Baltimore and his government in exchange for land and greatly reduced rents?"

"Governor Calvert," Friend Dreamer responded, "the city of Amsterdam has granted us a twenty-five-year exemption from all tithes and taxes of any kind. Furthermore, we are bound by our word to repay to the city of Amsterdam the 2,500 guilders loaned to us to found this colony. Thank you for your interest in our little commonwealth, but we must abide by our agreement with the Dutch."

Cool Water listened to the governor's tirade while she waited on his table. Decked out in her white cap and white apron, she easily passed for one more Dutch Mennonite.

On the other hand, as soon as he properly welcomed the governor,

---

[70] Meaning "rebaptizer." A broad designation indicating those who practiced adult baptism and which included Mennonites.

Meas dropped from the governor's sight and eased out among four of the governor's black slaves. They greeted Meas freely and without fear, accepting Meas as one of their own.

"What ya'll thank of Massa all powded n puffed n decked out wi such purty fethas?" one of them asked. And another added to the question, "Now ain't he a dandy?"

Meas looked hard at his questioners before answering. "I guess one could say the Guvne's rit gud lookin," Meas said, mimicking the black speech with ease. "Skunks iz awful purty too," Meas went on, and he rolled his eyes upward in a perfect imitation of their manners. "Bu I sho-o wouldn' play wid em, an speshly wen dey go wi de tails up in de ai."

All laughed heartily at Meas's joke. After the joke, the blacks readily shared news from far and wide picked up from the slave web. "Da smallpox is done sta'ted aga'n over in Ma'yland," one of them reported. "Da Nanticokes is dyin' like flies. Won't be long till it comes over dis a-way. Once it starts, da evil spirits spreads it. Cou'se it doan bother black folks none, at least not black folks dat as been brought over from Africa."[71]

"And why doan hit botha da black folks from Africa?" Meas asked.

"Well, us dat come from Africa has got da jinx on da smallpox. When we was little fellas, da witch docta scratched our arms and rubbed some evil pus in da blood. Den he say some prayers ovah da spot, waved his hands roun' a while, screamed a few times and we was done. Da spot got sore for a few days, and den da scabs fell off and lef' a scar. It shew dough work. We ain't nevah had da smallpox since, and we ain't nevah gonna git da smallpox. Dat witch docta's charm worked." Proudly they showed Meas the scars on their arms.

"What happens to the chillun bo'n in dis country?" Meas asked of his black friends.

---

[71] Carrell, Jennifer Lee, *The Speckled Monster*, Dutton, New York, NY, 2003, pp. 174, 177, 419, 422. The evidence heavily supports prior inoculation of African slaves for smallpox when it was still unknown in this country.

"We ain't never foun' da spell to stop smallpox heah. If da young uns gits it, dey dies. We be real ankshus bout dem young uns. We be real ankshus to get on to New Amstel town and den on back home and see 'em.

"Ya know why we a visitin heah and why we goes to New Amstel town?" The slave held his hand against one side of his mouth and rolled the whites of his eyes. "De Guvner be real ankshus to slide deeze Dutch towns in his back pocket," he whispered. "Ya mind my wurd, or ya'll be lik us," and the slave shook his finger knowingly at Meas.

Meas withdrew to his haunt by his mother's grave and watched as the twenty-six attendants gathered up their pompous master, his horses, and his luggage, and loaded him back on the ship. After the ship had sailed out of sight, Friend Dreamer made his way to the grave too.

"Sage Meas, what think ye of our guest?" Friend Dreamer inquired.

"Friend Dreamer, I like not the Little Heron hatched from an egg of the Great Heron. Little Heron wears the plumage of a turkey, but his eyes are the cold eyes of a hawk waiting to kill. Twenty-six buzzards circle Little Heron waiting to feast on his prey. I like him not."

"Sage Meas, I wonder if Little Heron might be the Antichrist spoken of in Revelation. He is evil while claiming to be good. Do you think Little Heron is the Red Dog you warned me about?"

"No, Friend Dreamer, Little Heron is not the Red Dog. Little Heron is the Black and Yellow Dog that will come many moons after the Red Dog has visited the Siconece. Beware the Red Dog first."

A long silence followed. Then Meas again spoke. "Friend Dreamer, if the smallpox came to Swanendael, would this evil strike your people the same as it does other Schwanneks ... and the Indians?"

"Aye, Meas, smallpox is in the hands of God. Smallpox falls, like the rain that God sends, upon both the just and the unjust. But as I explained to you during our soul meet at Tired Moon Pond, the

Dutch have a new way of thinking about things we do not understand, a way of testing ideas to see if they are true or false. We should do the same with smallpox.

"Sage Meas, let us think about smallpox. Some things we know. Some things we do not know. Maybe we will have some ideas about smallpox that can be tested. Mayhap God will bless us with knowledge rather than the curse of ignorance.

"Sage Meas, if the smallpox falls upon our band, we know there are two groups of people who will not suffer from it. If anyone ever had the smallpox before in his lifetime and survived its horrors, that person will never again suffer from this sickness. Usually, anyone who survives the ruptured pustules of smallpox bears the scars all over the face and body for the rest of his life. These people are marked for life.

"Sage Meas, we also know that there is another group of people who have no marks or scars on their bodies and yet do not fall ill with the smallpox. These people are the milkmaids, the girls and women who milk the cows. Because their skin has never been damaged by the ravages of smallpox, there is an English saying, 'Pretty as a milkmaid.'[72]

"Sage Meas, what we do not know is why milkmaids do not get smallpox. Not everyone who ever milks a cow is spared. But somewhere there is a connection between women and cows and being spared from smallpox.

"Sage Meas, in our band almost all the adults have had smallpox sometime and survived. The children are few in number, but they will likely meet with smallpox, and we pray God will be merciful to them, for many children die."

"Friend Dreamer, I talked to four black slaves of Little Heron. They all showed me a mark on their arms where the witch doctor had cast out the evil spirit of smallpox. They assured me they will never get

---

[72] This common saying led Edward Jenner, an English physician about thirty years later, to speculate that milkmaids were immune to smallpox because of their contracting cowpox. He conducted experiments that proved his theory correct. His practice of using cowpox to inoculate one safely against the scourge of smallpox led to the eradication of the disease in the 1970s.

smallpox. Is your God strong enough to cast out this evil smallpox spirit for the Indians?"

"Sage Meas, you bring us many medicines and salves that bring healing among us. You advise us how to cure snakebite or upset stomach and when not to eat certain poisonous foods. Do these medicines bring healing because they cast the evil spirit out that is causing the sickness? No. These cures work because you and your ancestors have found that they restore health to the body. And even though you may not understand *why* it works, experience has taught you that a particular remedy will bring healing.

"Sage Meas, healing is as simple as setting a snare for a rabbit. If the rabbit sticks his head in the snare, he will be caught. There is no evil spirit in the snare. Neither do I believe an evil spirit lurks in the smallpox. The fact that we do not understand the illness and cannot see the killer hiding within it does not mean that an evil spirit tortures the sick or that God punishes the afflicted for sin."

"Friend Dreamer, then what should I do that my children and my people be not destroyed by the smallpox? For smallpox rages as a fire in dry grass when it strikes an Indian village; it kills all the young and the old, the weak and the infirm. The strong barely survive to tell of its horrors, and in some cases whole villages die.

"Friend Dreamer, is there no hope?"

"Sage Meas, may God be merciful to you. And, Sage Meas, watch the red cows."

Meas watched the red cows closely. His eyes followed the herd as they grazed and then lay down, contentedly chewing their cuds. He observed how the cow seemed to dance about and kick lightly at the spring calf when it first suckled, as though the sucking hurt her. He watched closely when Cool Water pulled up her stool and put her head in the cow's flank. He listened to the music of milk streaming against the bucket sides. Then he saw the occasional sores on the cows' teats. Here was a pock filled with pus; at other sores the pocks were dried up and scabbed over.

"Cool Water," Meas asked excitedly, "what are the pocks on the cows' teats?"

"The cows often get those little sores on their teats in late summer or fall," Cool Water answered, showing little interest or concern. "Once every several years I get pocks on my hands, but after the pocks dry up and go away, the sores don't bother me anymore."

"Did Kill Weed ever have any of those sores?" Meas asked next.

"Yes," Cool Water replied. "Kill Weed got the pox the first fall he came to the Siconece when he often helped me milk. But they have never bothered him since."

That same day Meas sent for Kill Weed. When Kill Weed arrived at Tired Moon Pond, Meas gathered up Cool Water and the two papooses and settled down beside the herd of red cattle. While the others watched, Meas took his knife and scraped the skin on his arm at the same spot where Little Heron's slaves had shown him their marks. Then he scraped some pus from the sore on one of the cows' teats and rubbed the pus lightly into the blood that seeped from the scratch on his arm. Meas repeated the same operation on Kill Weed and on each of the watching papooses.

Eight days after Meas scraped the cow's pus into the wounds, a pustule erupted on the wound of each one along with a general feeling of sickness. The papooses fussed and tried to scratch their sores. Meas wrapped their arms with cloth, as well as his own. Kill Weed's sore remained small and bothered him only minutely. Meas felt the worst of the lot.

With his own reddened, erupted pustule standing open, Meas began hunting the villages of the other Siconesse headmen—Siconece, Quistin, Boempies Hook, Peskamohot, Wickenesse, Seckatackomeck. At each village Meas told the story of the governor's slaves and how they never feared smallpox anymore. He told Friend Dreamer's story of the pretty milkmaids and how they were no longer afraid that smallpox would attack them and mar their smooth skin. Meas explained how he had taken the pus from the cow sore and placed it upon his own scratch. Then he took off his cloth and showed them his own sore, his own badge of courage, and his own defense against the dread smallpox.

After Meas had finished telling his story, he always offered to scrape a tiny bit of pus from his own sore onto a scratch of anyone who wanted one like it. If the village medicine man scowled, no one dared step forward and ask for the pus. Even someone as well known and respected as Sage Meas could not cross the local medicine man.

At Boempies Hook and Peskamohot, the local medicine men came to Meas after dark and asked for "the scratch." At Quistin, Wickenesse, and Seckatackomeck a few women brought their children to Meas at night and asked to be "scratched."

On the Siconece, Sage Meas was the medicine man. Even so, only Koketotoka braved "the scratch" and ordered his family to do likewise. Everyone else held back. After all, they reasoned, why would anyone make himself sick? One goes to the medicine man to be healed, not to be made sick. If the smallpox comes, then we will go to the medicine man and ask him to drive off the curse and the evil spirits.

By the time Meas returned to Tired Moon Pond, his pustule had dried up, scabbed over, and fallen off. All that remained was the pockmark on his arm, just like the one the slaves had shown him. His papooses also bore the pockmarks on their arms and played cheerfully with no sign of illness.

Then the smallpox struck. No one knew how it had come to the scattered villages and spread its curse upon them, but some accused Meas of having brought the dread curse to the villages.

On the Siconece, the killer slunk into Meoppitas's wigwam first and struck him down. Suddenly Meoppitas fell to his mat with an extremely high fever, a terrible backache, a pounding headache, chills, nausea, and convulsions all at once. Koketotoka sent for Meas, and Meas came to help care for his brother. Meas stayed with Meoppitas for three days and nights and watched him in his stupor. Meoppitas cared not for food and at times refused even drink.

Others came to the wigwam to visit Meoppitas. Before the visitors left, they often asked Meas to "scratch" them. He always declined saying that he did not know where to get any more of the pus. "Besides," he added, "I doubt if it would do any good anyway. It takes days after the 'scratch' before the pustule breaks out. Neither do we know for sure that I and my children won't get smallpox."

"If you won't 'scratch' us, at least cast out the smallpox evil spirit and put a charm on us," they begged. But Meas refused.

Seeing that Meas would do nothing, Koketotoka called for Teotacken.[73] Teotacken came to Meoppitas's wigwam. Teotacken had no such scruples as Meas suffered about casting out the smallpox evil spirit. Casting out the evil spirit was exactly what Teotacken intended to do.

Friends packed into Meoppitas's wigwam till there was little room left. Teotacken danced beside Meoppitas while tapping a small handheld drum. He bowed and cavorted in rhythm with his beat while he sang to the Lenape spirits and asked them to grant him the power to heal.

During the dance Teotacken raised and lowered his voice in cadence with the drum. At regular-spaced times, Teotacken ceased dancing and blew a reed whistle while shaking a rattle over Meoppitas. Then Teotacken prayed for the strength to cast the evil from Meoppitas's body.

Next Teotacken brought out two eagle feathers and passed them back and forth the full length over Meoppitas. Then Teotacken pulled

[73] Teotacken's power was so well known that nine years earlier the Lenape at Christina had asked Governor Morning Light to furnish them a boat so they could fetch Teotacken from the Siconece to Christina. The Lenape believed Teotacken could carry off the evil spirit in a Swedish ship anchored at Christina.

a hollow bone of an eagle's wing from his medicine bag and held it aloft for all to see. He made a fist and tapped his hands against his lips before he ratcheted his screams up into an ear-splitting crescendo. Suddenly Teotacken fell mute, and the wigwam filled with silence.

Teotacken bent down and placed the eagle bone in Meoppitas's mouth and sucked. Teotacken rose in triumph and blew a pebble into his hand. He held the stone forth for everyone to see and exulted, "I have taken out the smallpox evil spirit, and Meoppitas is healed."[74]

Sure enough, the next day, the fourth day since the fever had begun, the fever subsided and Meoppitas felt better. Again he took food and drink. But on the fifth day, flat red blotches began to creep across Meoppitas's cheeks and forearms. Slowly, the blotchy rash spread over his chest, back, abdomen, and legs. Meoppitas scratched at the rash trying to relieve the annoying itch. Meas gathered leaves and herbs and made a type of salve he applied to the rash. Meas wrapped Meoppitas loosely in cloth in a vain effort to stop the itch.

The fever returned along with the backache. Meoppitas groaned in agony as his head pounded with the tempo of his pulse. As the throb of every heartbeat exploded in pain, Meoppitas thrashed about with his mind slipping in and out of delirium. On the eighth day after the attack began, Meoppitas's flat red lesions elevated into clear blisters that slowly filled with pus. His pustules became so thick they appeared to run together as one giant oozing sore. His face swelled into a mass of pimply flesh twice the size of his normal face.

The pus-brimming ulcers spread into Meoppitas's mouth and throat until every sip of drink or bite of food felt to him as though he was swallowing a hot coal. Meas tried to ease his brother's agony, but there was little he could do. A sickening odor of rotting flesh drove everyone except Meas from the wigwam. At last Meoppitas died, and his suffering ended. Meas and Koketotoka buried him. Then Meas returned to Tired Moon Pond once more.

---

[74] The ritual used by Teotacken is based on an account given in Robertson, R.G., *Rotting Face—Smallpox and the American Indian*, Caxton Press, Caldwell, ID, 2001, p. 51.

The killer struck again on the Siconece and again and again. There was no warning until the horrifying and painful fever, chills, and nausea set in all at once. Only a remote few of the Siconece clan escaped the smallpox onslaught, and fewer than half of the Lenape survived in a weakened state.

Meas's and Koketotoka's families remained untouched.

Teotacken died.

At Boempies Hook and Peskamohot, where the local medicine men had come to Meas after dark and asked for "the scratch," all escaped. The medicine men in those areas had prevailed upon their people until all had been scratched.

Smallpox blinded Friend Dreamer's only son.

The death and the suffering was terrible. But worst of all, smallpox forever destroyed the strength and vitality of the Lenape on the Siconece. Like a stout oak split by a mighty wind, the trunk could never be restored. After the smallpox, the Spirit of Tamenend flickered only briefly and then went out. There was no more courage. There was no more hope.

Friend Dreamer's band continued their fevered building and planting of the fields. Meas and Cool Water melded ever more closely into the little commonwealth. Gradually, even No Smoke Wiltbank felt at ease with Meas snooping around and yet not lifting a finger to help with the work. In No Smoke's mind, Cool Water made up for Meas's laziness with her diligent ways.

Weak Gun took over all of Meas's trading with the Indians.

Meas continued his retreats by his mother's grave and the long chats with Friend Dreamer.

In the spring month, Cool Water gave birth to a blue-eyed, light-haired son.

In the planting month, thousands and thousands of locusts crawled out of thumb-size holes in the ground, shed their skins, and sat themselves on trees, where they began making strange whirring noises. During the hottest part of the day, the noise waxed so intense that two people could scarcely hear each other talk.

Meas showed Friend Dreamer how to throw the locusts into hot coals and roast them lightly before tossing them into his mouth. "These locusts come out of the ground every seventeen years," said Meas. "They furnish us plenty of good eating while here, but they do not stay long. In only two moons the locusts will crawl into the rivers and streams and the fish will swarm to feed on them. We might just as well get our fair share now," and Meas tossed two more roasted locusts into his mouth.

Then Meas continued. "Friend Dreamer, the locusts are not a good sign for you. In Teotacken's dream, the locusts arose out of the ground and chewed off forty-one sprouts. As you can see, this is the year of the locusts. Either the Red Dog will come to the Siconece this year, or he will not come for seventeen more years. Beware the Red Dog."

"Sage Meas," Friend Dreamer asked, "what do you think we should do?"

"Friend Dreamer," Meas replied, "I do not know what you should do. I only know that the Lenape will not harm you. I also know that if you will not fight to defend yourselves from the Schwanneks, the Lenape will not come to your aid."

True to Meas's word, the locusts marched into the streams toward the end of the summer month. Roasted ears of maize replaced roasted locusts.

Meas and Cool Water both noticed a new vine the settlers had planted around the edge of the fields. The vines eagerly climbed ropes the settlers dangled from tall trees, ropes longer than two times the height of a man. "For what is the vine used?" Meas asked of Friend Dreamer.

"The plant is called a hop," Friend Dreamer answered. "In the second year, the vine will produce flowers used in the brewing of beer. Fat Pig Hinoyossa has opened his own brewery in New Amstel, and he pays a good price for hops."

"Friend Dreamer, do you not know the curse that beer and rum[75] are to the Lenape? So many sachems have spoken out against the rum trade with the Indians that the Dutch have declared it illegal to sell the poison to the Indians. But Fat Pig Hinoyossa just laughs, and his traders bring it to the Indians anyway. Koketotoka and I had warned Fat Pig repeatedly that if he brought any more of the stuff to the Siconece, we would stave the ends of the casks in.

"Fat Pig did not believe Koketotoka would actually drain the liquor instead of drinking it. Last winter when so many suffered from smallpox, Two Tongue Boyer[76] showed up at Koketotoka's village with two ankers of rum and some trade goods. Koketotoka caught Two Tongue with the rum and tomahawked both ends of both casks so that none of the rum could be saved.

"Two Tongue flew into such a rage he shot Koketotoka in the arm. Koketotoka jumped Two Tongue and knocked him senseless. When Two Tongue came to, he offered Koketotoka a palm-size silver medallion with an exquisitely carved tortoise as a ransom for his life. But Koketotoka disdainfully allowed Two Tongue to keep the medallion. Then he ordered Two Tongue to leave the Siconece at once and never to return.

"Now I would like to find Two Tongue and wring his neck. The silver medallion he held in his hand before Koketotoka is none other than the one stolen from the grave of Mattahorn. And I must have it. For the silver medallion matches the copper medallion given me by my mother."

"Sage Meas," Friend Dreamer said softly, "you have often instructed me, and rightly so, for you pointed me to the truth. Now I must teach you.

---

[75] Beer—a fermented alcoholic drink often made from barley or other grain. Rum—a liquor often distilled from sugarcane and molasses.

[76] Alexander Boyer undoubtedly died before the end of 1661. He could not possibly have been the culprit mentioned in this account that took place in early 1664. However, he represents unscrupulous traders who willingly did everything here credited to Two Tongue Boyer.

"Sage Meas, you have suffered many wrongs, both you and your people. But do not let the longing for a silver medallion bring bitterness to your soul and blood upon your hands. God's Book tells us:

> Be at peace with all men. Never take your own revenge,
> beloved, but leave room for the wrath of God, for it is written,
> "Vengeance is mine, I will repay, says the Lord."

"Sage Meas, God will bring punishment upon Two Tongue Boyer. But let God do it. For if we fill our hearts with hate and bitterness, we can never know the love of God or the peace that passes understanding.

"Sage Meas, no matter how much we hate or how many we kill, we can never force someone to love us. And neither will we ourselves love those we kill. And if we do not love our fellow man, we will never love God. Again, God's Book tells us, 'The one who does not love does not know God, for God is love.'

"Sage Meas, let us sit still and see what God will do to give you the medallion, and, 'let us pursue peace with all men, without which no one shall see the Lord.' "

"Friend Dreamer, my ears are open to your words. But my heart must yet listen. For the Schwanneks ... would drive us from our homeland. And we Lenape, the Real Men, should we love them and expect their God to deliver us from their cruelty and injustice? This thought is too big for my heart."

The thought troubled Meas. As in the days of his Vision Quest, he spent many days and nights by himself, roaming the forests, the fields, the marshes, the beaches, and seated on a singular high sand dune along Cape Henlopen. Meas liked his perch on Cape Henlopen with its sweeping view of the ocean to the east and south, the bay to the north, the marsh to the southwest, and the smoke from the cook fires to the west and northwest. He could not see Tired Moon Pond, but he knew exactly which smoke rose from Cool Water's fire.

From his perch on Sea Shell Dune, Meas watched the ships slipping by as they made their way from north or south and sailed in and out of the Lenape Bay. He knew the types of ships and the flags they flew, for he had traded with many of them.

Now Meas studied their comings and goings. At the end of the autumnal month, Meas spied two warships entering the Lenape Bay from the north. Both of the warships sported English red and blue flags fluttering from every mast. He noted how the large ships struggled with the shifting sandbars of the Lenape Bay as they carefully made their way northward.

After the two ships had sailed out of sight, Meas dropped down the sand dune, crossed the windswept barrens, and made his way into the marsh. There he picked up his canoe and paddled north past Tired Moon Pond until he came to the Swanendael fort. In his usual quiet way, he eased past the busy workers of the commune till he came to his mother's grave. He seated himself on the grass and waited.

Friend Dreamer found Meas there, seated himself on the grass, and waited. In due time Meas said, "Friend Dreamer, the Red Dog has come. I watched him sail north toward New Amstel. He will surely return to the Siconece."

Friend Dreamer smiled. "Sage Meas, all is in readiness. We have labored and built. We have planted and gathered. We have dwelt in peace and love. God has blessed our little commonwealth. We shall await the coming of the Red Dog." And Friend Dreamer burst into a verse of song.

Meas waited till Friend Dreamer finished his song and the lengthy prayers that followed. Then Meas left Friend Dreamer in his trance and slipped off to his canoe and back to Tired Moon Pond.

Meas moved rapidly now with firm purpose and a quiet resolve. "The Red Dog has gone to New Amstel," he told Cool Water. "He will surely return to the Siconece. I shall be ready when he returns."

Meas selected eight large pine trees close to Tired Moon Pond. He slashed through the bark until a sticky white layer the size of two hands shone clearly in the opening. At the bottom of each gash Meas fashioned bark funnels leading into small homemade wooden buckets he placed at the base of each tree. When he was done, pitch began oozing from each gash into the buckets.

"Where is Kill Weed?"[77] Meas asked of Cool Water. "I must have him to help me." Kill Weed came. Meas showed Kill Weed the slashed pine trees and the buckets he had placed below them. He taught Kill Weed how to make more buckets. "Make extra buckets," he ordered Kill Weed. "Whenever a bucket fills with pitch, replace it with an empty one and bring the full one to Sea Shell Dune on Cape Henlopen. I will be waiting for you there."

Meas took the first buckets of sticky pitch, returned to Sea Shell Dune, and resumed his vigil. Two days later, he watched the same battered ship that had brought the prize guns to him approach the cape from the south. The ship flew the red, white, and blue Dutch flag. Meas set fire to three of the buckets. Wind whipped black smoke from the burning pitch westward.

On the ship a mirror flashed bright sunlight at Meas three times. Meas picked up his mirror and three times flashed a bright beam at the ship. Before rounding the cape, the ship began dropping its sails. A small boat put out from the ship and headed straight toward Meas. When the boat reached the shore, Meas climbed aboard and the sailors returned to the mother ship.

Blackbeard waited for Meas in the main cabin. "Ah, Sachem Meas, we meet again," said the privateer in his gruff voice. "Perhaps this time on more friendly terms?" he questioned. Blackbeard held a loaded pistol comfortably in one hand while he talked. His other hand rested on the hilt of his sword.

Meas said nothing, but withdrew his pipe from his pouch and slowly loaded it with tobacco. He lit the tobacco and smoked thoughtfully. Blackbeard poured a glass of rum and he, too, pondered the

---

[77] Kill Weed was the Indian slave boy purchased, along with Cool Water, from Josias Fendall and later adopted by Meas.

situation while he sipped. When the cabin had filled with smoke and Blackbeard's glass had been refilled, Meas asked, "Blackbeard, do you remember the two girls you gifted to Captain Josias Fendall?"

A slow smile spread over Blackbeard's weasel face. "Aye, Sachem Meas. I remember the girls. How did you learn that I had anything to do with them?"

Meas waited before replying. "Captain Blackbeard, I married the younger of the two girls. Cool Water's the name." And then Meas continued puffing on his pipe.

" 'Twas a sad situation," Blackbeard offered.

"Perhaps Captain Blackbeard would like to make amends for his cruelty," Meas suggested.

"And what did Sachem Meas have in mind?" Blackbeard countered.

Meas leaned forward and stared intently into Blackbeard's eyes. "Captain Blackbeard, I have known for five years that a Schwannek stole a silver medallion from Mattahorn's grave. Although I suspected several different Schwanneks, I had no way of knowing what they might have done with it. However, this past winter, Two Tongue Boyer had a fracas with Koketotoka over some spilt rum. Koketotoka bested Two Tongue, and Two Tongue offered Koketotoka the silver medallion as a ransom for his life."

Meas paused, and Blackbeard asked, "Did Koketotoka take the medallion and let Two Tongue go? Or did he just kill him and keep the medal anyway?"

Meas went on. "Koketotoka did neither. Koketotoka will not kill a disarmed foe or steal booty from one at his mercy. To do so is no better than to steal beaver from an Indian when he is drunk. Koketotoka ordered Two Tongue to leave and never to return to the Siconece.

"Captain Blackbeard, I have often refused to trade with Two Tongue and Fat Pig, and when they did trade with me, I made them pay a high price. Now both Fat Pig and Two Tongue hate me, for I have warned them repeatedly that if they come to the Siconece, they must come without soldiers and without rum. We must be free to trade with whomever we wish to trade.

"Captain Blackbeard, Two Tongue hates me. And now he wishes to take revenge on Koketotoka as well as on me. Two Tongue will stop at nothing. I care not for revenge or pursuit, but I must have the silver tortoise. The one side of the silver medallion is a perfect match for the copper medallion given me by my mother."

"Sachem Meas, you know that to find Two Tongue and extract from him the silver tortoise will be very dangerous. Short of a raid on New Amstel itself, an impossible task for me, I cannot conceive how he might be captured. How much can you pay for the silver medallion? Almost anything is possible if there is enough money in it."

"Captain Blackbeard, I will pay you nothing for the silver tortoise. But I would remind the captain of a certain night on the Nanticoke River when he offered great riches in exchange for his life. And a certain Lenape Indian allowed both Blackbeard and Neck Scar to escape. Will you not honor that debt?"

Blackbeard laughed. "Hah! Sachem Meas, you jest. Do you speak of honor with one such as I? Can a dog know honor?"

"Sachem Meas, dogs know not honor. You say you will not pay me one farthing. Nevertheless, because the Almighty beats heavily upon my heart, I would deliver the silver tortoise to you.

"However, Sachem Meas, even if God Himself were to fight on our behalf, would He not expect us to aid Him in obtaining the medallion? Surely you would not be here if you expected a seagull to bring you the medal. What is your plan?"

" 'Tis true, Captain Blackbeard. I have thought much about the silver tortoise. Here is my thought. Two English warships have gone up the Lenape River ten days ago. The English ships will no doubt swallow New Amstel for Great Heron. As soon as the English have gulped down New Amstel, the ships will come to the Siconece to swallow Swanendael. Thirsting for revenge, Two Tongue will play into our hands. Willingly or unwillingly, he will come to the Siconece with those ships.

"Captain Blackbeard, I will signal you when the English ships come, but then you must decide what to do."

"Sachem Meas, for me to attack a British warship is risky. To attack two of them is foolhardy. Nevertheless, the one who chooses the time and the place of battle may catch un unwary foe.

"Sachem Meas, I believe you surmise correctly that the English have come to take New Amstel. Other ships have already informed me that an English fleet of four warships has already mastered New Amsterdam and Strutting Turkey Stuyvesant. Now you tell me the English have dispatched only two of the four warships to New Amstel. Perhaps fate will smile upon us and the English will send only one ship to take the undefended fort at Swanendael.

"Sachem Meas, I will keep my ship well hidden south of the Lenape Cape. You must signal me with two fires as soon as the English ships come. And perchance only one ship comes, you must light four fires. Then stay on the cape. If I conquer, I shall bring the silver tortoise to you."

Captain Blackbeard sprang up and held out his hand to Meas. "On my word of honor," he roared as he tottered out of his cabin onto the main deck. "Take this Indian back to the cape," Blackbeard bellowed. And every sailor within hearing jumped to do Blackbeard's bidding.

Two days later, at midmorning, Meas spied a lone English warship sailing boldly up to the wasted Swanendael fort.[78] Meas lit the four flares and waited till he saw the bright flashes from the distant ship. Then he sped down the dune and across the flats to his canoe and paddled north on the Siconece until he could see the hull of the ship in the distance.

Meas hid his canoe and moved as a phantom among the grass, maize stalks, bushes, and trees until he neared the field where one hundred wide-eyed, half-drunk, red-coated soldiers in threadbare breeches and

---

[78] The raid on the Whorekill probably occurred sometime in October of 1664.

shabby boots assembled. Meas stopped when he stood close enough behind them that any soldier would have been an easy mark for an arrow from his bow.

The drums began to beat, and fearsome yells rang through the air. The lines of soldiers marched forward, guns loaded and ready. The lone figure of Friend Dreamer stood waving a white flag directly in front of the advancing columns. The columns stopped. The drums quieted.

"Are not the countries of England and the Netherlands at peace?" Friend Dreamer shouted. "Then what mean these weapons of war? Have you come to attack friends who have done you no harm? We are a people of peace, a part of the peaceable kingdom of Christ.

"We work with our own hands to bring plenty to all. We bind not the hands of others with chains nor beat them with whips that they must serve us bread.

"In our little commonwealth, we allow every man to bow his own heart to God in his own way and do not insist that he be Mennonite, Reformed, Catholic, or Protestant.

"We plant. We build. We harvest. We share. We do not steal from others in the name of God or the king. So I would ask of each soldier, What evil have we done that you come to us with swords and guns?

"Today I call on each soldier to lay down your weapons that God might not hold you guilty of shedding innocent blood.

"Today we have no guns or knives or cannons which we will raise against you. The weapons with which we fight are the weapons of righteousness, truth, and the Word of God.

"Today God calls on each of you to do justice, to love mercy, and to walk humbly with your God. Today you may ignore that divine call to you. Today it lies in your power to kill, to rape, and to steal. But I must tell you that no command of king or priest can make those evil acts right before God. And if you do such acts, your soul will never escape God's justice.

"Today I warn you that it is a fearful thing to fall into the hands of a living God."

Friend Dreamer dipped his white flag and bowed his head slightly at the waiting soldiers. The soldiers hesitated. Some lowered their guns. Drumbeats resumed. Captains barked commands. The soldiers failed to move. The drumming stopped.

Two Tongue and the commander strode briskly forward to where Friend Dreamer stood holding his white flag. But instead of parleying with Friend Dreamer, the commander turned and shouted to his troops.

"This man who spoke to you plotted with Oliver Cromwell against his Royal Majesty. His Majesty, Charles II, has not forgotten such sedition and will root it out in every remote corner of his kingdom."

"Hang him," a soldier shouted.

"With your own ears," the commander went on, "you have heard this man say that orders of the King may be disobeyed at will. This is treason."

"Hang him! Hang him!" several more soldiers shouted.

"You should also know," the commander continued, "that this hotbed of sedition and treason on Whore's Creek shelters a heathen savage living with a Christian woman. Such whoredom and heresy must be rooted out."

"Root them out! Root them out! Root them out!" screamed the soldiers, and several of them discharged their guns into the air.

When the noise had subsided, the commander continued: "These Dutch Anabaptists defy the King and refuse to pay customs belonging to the Crown. As enemies and pirates, these seditious heretics must be reduced to total submission."

Everything broke loose. Cries of "Hang the traitor!" and screams of "Hang the heretic!" and great shouts of "Root them out!" mixed wildly with gunshots. A crowd surged toward Friend Dreamer. Strong, rough hands grabbed Dreamer by the ankles, jerked his feet and legs out from under him, and raced toward the edge of the field. Soldiers kicked him, clubbed him with their gun butts, and fired guns into the ground beside his head.

Friend Dreamer clung tightly to the white flag until soldiers snapped it from his grasp and tied his hands behind his back. They hoisted Dreamer high in the air while another soldier stood on the backs of his comrades and tied one of the hop-vine ropes in a slipknot around his neck.

Dreamer looked out over the shouting, unruly mob as though from a distant land. "Father, lay not this sin to their charge," were Dreamer's last words before the soldiers dropped him, and the noose tightened around his neck.

The commander and Two Tongue watched the body swing. A lone arrow whizzed through the air, pierced the rear of the commander's boot, and burrowed through sinews and muscles to lodge firmly within his foot. The commander screamed in pain, but no one heard him.

Drums beat rapidly. Guns fired. Frenzied soldiers ran off yelling, "Root them out! Root them out!" Dazed settlers fled as crazed soldiers charged into the old fort and south along the road to the new settlement. Settlers who escaped left everything and ran. Soldiers caught those who hesitated. The women and girls they raped. The men they tied up and sorely abused.

When a cluster of soldiers tore into the stillness of the cabin by Tired Moon Pond, they found Cool Water busy caring for her youngest papoose. "It's the English whore," they shouted. "The commander has offered a special prize for her." Strong arms pinned Cool Water to the wall while others tied her wrists together. Ten soldiers took her and the light-haired papoose outside.

Other soldiers raided the cabin and the area around it. They carried out the English dishes, the table, every piece of cloth, every cooking utensil, every knife, every hoe, every axe and every adz, every bucket, every article of clothing, every bracelet, every head of cabbage, every barrel of maize, all the dried meats and fish, every fur and skin, every pipe and all the tobacco. Everything of value the soldiers could tear loose or move they set down some distance from the cabin. They rounded up nine red cattle and began marching them toward the ship. When all the loot was clear of the cabin, they fired it and guarded it till fire rose in one immense burst of flame to consume it all. Cool Water did not look back, but hugged the papoose tightly and plodded forward.

Other soldiers plundered every house, shed, and building in the settlement. Soldiers carried off every round of cheese, every pat of butter, every vegetable and grain harvested and stored, every dish, cloth, blanket, shirt, and shoe, every hoe, every tool, and every loose nail. Everything of value they carried to the ship.

The soldiers fired only Meas's cabin and Peace Hall. The rest of the buildings they left standing.

As soon as Meas had shot his arrow into the commander's foot, he slithered away from the bedlam to better cover and raced for his canoe. With the canoe he paddled hurriedly along, keeping as close to the shelter of the west bank of the Siconece as possible. Deep in the marsh, Meas left the canoe and pushed on overland till once more he stood atop Sea Shell Dune.

Meas scanned the sea to the east. Blackbeard had moved his ship far out to sea where he could easily block the warship's exit from the Lenape Bay. Yet from the crow's nest, Blackbeard's lookout could also detect whenever the English warship put up sails and the raid on the Siconece was over.

Meas swung his eyes to the north. He could see the warship and the old fort. Out over the Lenape Bay angry dark clouds spewed rain downward in wind-whipped torrents. The storm appeared to move westward toward the old fort. Meas studied the storm. Would it strike the fort and the warship, or would it move to the south and miss

Cape Henlopen entirely? Or might the storm just hang there until it spent itself? He had watched many a similar storm on the bay, and he could never be sure what they might do. Storms took orders from the manitos and not from men.

Meas pivoted to the west toward Tired Moon Pond and the spot where smoke from Cool Water's fire often rose. A great cloud of smoke drifted upward from the exact spot. Meas stared at the smoke for a long time. His eyes misted over.

Again, Meas swung his eyes to the north. He watched as the powerful warship eased out into the bay and turned to the north. To the south, Meas saw Blackbeard hoist sail after sail as his battered ship gave chase. Then Blackbeard's ship disappeared behind the cover of the storm.

Blackbeard burst from the cover of the storm under full sail. He caught the large English warship by surprise as it carefully nudged its way through the unfamiliar shallows of the bay. Blackbeard guided his ship adroitly through the familiar waters, always tempting the larger ship to turn so it could blast its pursuer with its cannons. It didn't take long before the warship made its fatal mistake and ran aground. Blackbeard eased into position from which his cannon commanded the enemy ship, but the enemy's cannon could not fire upon his ship.

The commander ran up a white flag. "What are your terms?" the commander shouted at Blackbeard.

"ALL the loot, ALL the prisoners, and I said 'ALL,' two hundred muskets, and Two Tongue Boyer," Blackbeard bellowed. "Strike your colors quickly or we shall argue with my cannons."

The commander brought down the English flags immediately.

"Now, Commander, clear the decks of all men," Blackbeard ordered. "And you yourself shall stand on the poop deck in full view of my musket."

The commander hobbled[79] up on top of the poop deck.

Blackbeard kept his musket trained on the commander while his battered ship sailed alongside the great English warship and lashed the two ships together. Blackbeard ordered the commander to his battered ship's poop deck and stood guard over him there while he himself directed the transfer of the loot.

Blackbeard mocked the "brave" English soldiers who earlier had pillaged a peaceful village. Blackbeard laughed while his own ruffians goaded the hapless soldiers as they offloaded their spoils onto his own ship. " 'Tis the justice of God," Blackbeard jeered. He taunted them further. "God will punish you for your sins even if He has to use the devil himself to do it."

It was too much. Weary soldiers wilted under Blackbeard's withering scorn and hurried to escape the lash of his tongue. At last the soldiers finished the task and slunk back below deck like wet rats.

"You have the two hundred muskets. You have ALL the spoils," said the commander. "I am most uncomfortable standing on this wounded foot for so long and would like to return to my cabin. Will you not now honor your terms and be gone?"

"Must I remind you that my terms included the prisoners and Two Tongue Boyer?" Blackbeard growled.

"I have neither prisoners nor Two Tongue Boyer on the ship," said the commander. "I cannot give you what I do not have. Now my wound tires me. Have you not had enough?"

Blackbeard looked at his vanquished foe. "Sir Commander, I fain would hear how your wound came about."

"Some skulking savage shot me with an arrow from the rear," the commander complained.

---

[79] The commander of this raid, Sir Robert Carr, arrived in Boston on 4 February 1665, complaining of a leg injury he had received on the Delaware that prevented his wearing a boot. In a later letter referring to the battle at New Amstel, Sir Robert also lamented that he had nothing to show for the battle in which he hazarded his life. Sir Robert Carr, still in poor health, left Boston for England in 1667 and died in Bristol without ever reaching London.

"Indeed?" Blackbeard asked. "How did the cowardly scamps get so close to your position and you not detect them? 'Twas only one arrow, you say?"

"I saw no other arrows. Everyone's attention at that moment focused on the battle in front of us. There was an awful amount of shooting and yelling going on. 'Twas just an accidental shot from one lone savage."

"Just one arrow? One lone savage? An accidental shot? Did your troops not pursue the lone savage and kill him?"

"The troops were out of control at that moment, and they did not even know I had been hit. If it had not been for Two Tongue Boy—" The commander stopped and blanched.

"Ah, yes," Blackbeard went on smoothly, "that is a good idea. I would speak with Two Tongue Boyer. Maybe he could clear up a few matters for us. Send for him at once. I will relay your commands."

Blackbeard called Neck Scar above to take orders from the commander and then quietly added a few words of his own before Neck Scar departed. Neck Scar went straight to the commander's cabin and soon returned with Two Tongue Boyer marching in front of him. Neck Scar stopped Two Tongue on the main deck and roughly frisked him, even requiring that he remove his boots. Nothing escaped the notice of Neck Scar's practiced hands. Then Two Tongue and Neck Scar climbed up to join Blackbeard and the commander on the poop deck.

Neck Scar eased around behind the two prisoners and flashed a silver medallion at Blackbeard. "Two Tongue," Blackbeard began, "the commander and I were discussing his wound, and we had a few questions we thought maybe you could clear up. The commander tells me there was only one arrow shot at the time of his wound. Is that right?"

"I saw only one arrow," Two Tongue replied cautiously, "but there was much confusion and noise all around us, and it is possible I did not see the others."

"From which direction did the arrow come?"

"From behind us, sir."

"Were you facing the same direction as the commander when the arrow found its mark in the commander's boot?"

"Aye, sir. I stood beside Sir Robert and faced the same direction he faced."

"If you were looking the opposite direction, you did not see the arrow until you saw it in the commander's boot. Can you think of any reason a lone savage might have wished to kill the commander or you?"

Two Tongue thought for a moment. "I can think of none, sir," he said.

"Then we shall have to jog your memory a bit further," Blackbeard declared.

"What sort of enemy was the army fighting so as to allow one single savage to creep up from behind and accidentally shoot the commander in the boot?"

"Sir, the soldiers were hanging a man."

Blackbeard continued his relentless pursuit. "And did you know the man the soldiers were hanging? Are you sure the man the soldiers hanged was the right one?"

"Yes, sir. The man they hanged was the right one. He was the man Lord Baltimore wanted killed. I met the heretic before on a trading trip to the Siconece."

"How did you find the man the King wanted?" Blackbeard asked.

"The soldiers had no trouble finding the heretic. He stopped the soldiers in the field by waving a white flag."

Blackbeard continued his patient grilling. "Is it correct that you came along with the commander to help identify this heretic and maybe a few others?"

Two Tongue hesitated. "Yes, there was also a savage living with a white whore the governor wished to punish, and I also had several old scores to settle with Meas."

"Two Tongue," Blackbeard's voice rose, "do you think it possible the arrow in the commander's boot was meant for you?"

Two Tongue cringed. "Yes, sir. I thought of that possibility. But if I was the intended mark, why did he miss? Was it just an accident?"

Blackbeard leaped at Two Tongue and grabbed him by the throat. "You fool!" he shouted. "You knew the man you hanged was only a harmless dreamer. You knew you were never supposed to bring rum to the Siconece. You knew Koketotoka let you keep the silver tortoise and ordered you never to come to the Siconece again. What you did not know was that the silver tortoise saved your life from that arrow. Now the silver tortoise shall cost you your life!"

Blackbeard tightened his grip on Two Tongue's throat till the flailing arms and legs stilled. Then he dragged the lifeless body to the back of the deck and he and Neck Scar pitched it into the Lenape Bay.

" 'Tis the justice of God," Blackbeard repeated solemnly.

Blackbeard turned once more and stuck his bulbous nose in the commander's face. "Now, Sir Commander," he said, "I want ALL the prisoners."

Cool Water trembled by the open hatch in the commander's cabin. "I'd rather die than spend another hour with that wretched beast," she murmured to her papoose. She shuddered and then vomited as past memories of time with Blackbeard tortured her. In her right hand Cool Water clutched a knife handle with the blade pointed toward her breast. Her left hand gripped the copper medallion that once hung from the neck of Meas's mother. Her ears strained to catch every word coming through the hatch.

The commander did not flinch but spoke directly into the captain's weasel face. "Very well, Captain Blackbeard. You shall have them ALL. But the captain might wish to note that the night has settled upon us, the wind has died, and my ship has floated free. Perhaps we shall have a long night together. And in the morning light your tub is no match for an English warship."

Blackbeard took two steps back from the commander. This time he spoke with respect. "Sir Commander, we shall forget the prisoners.

You may go now."

The two ships pushed apart. Blackbeard allowed his ship to drift away while the commander kept his warship anchored.

Nightmares wracked Cool Water's sleep in the commander's bed. Several times she screamed and flailed about before again gaining control so she could drop off into fitful sleep once more.

The next morning Meas was still waiting on top of Sea Shell Dune when Blackbeard's battered ship rounded Cape Henlopen. The ship slowed and lowered a small boat to the water. Meas met Neck Scar at the water's edge. Neck Scar held out the silver tortoise. "Blackbeard sends you this on his word of honor," Neck Scar said gruffly. He dropped the prized medallion into Meas's hand and then added, "Two Tongue will never trouble you again." Neck Scar bowed slightly, sprang back into the boat, and hastened off in pursuit of Blackbeard's ship.

Meas slipped the silver chain over his neck and allowed the silver tortoise to swing freely against his chest. He climbed again to the top of Sea Shell Dune, faced east, raised his arms toward the horizon and began to chant:

> Great Spirit,
> Maker of the sky, the earth, the sun, the moon,
> Keeper of the spirits of the fish, the birds, the animals, the trees, the
> stones.
> Guardian of the Four Winds,
> Thank you for bringing light again to the People of the Dawn.
> Thank you for sending fire to warm our houses and cook our food.
> Thank you for bringing water to inspire the ground and to quench our
> thirst.
> Thank you for the ground to grow the maize and the deer to give us
> meat.

HOMELAND IN MY HEART

For the ancient song of the Lenape,
For the everlasting sun that rises this day,
I, Sage Meas of the Lenni Lenape, thank you.

When Sage Meas had finished the chant, he took a small pinch of tobacco from his pouch with his left hand and sprinkled it on the ground before him.

Then Sage Meas turned and looked to the west. The morning sun touched the marshes, the fields, the forests, the rivers, and the streams with golden glory. Here and there a column of smoke drifted upward. Slowly Meas swung his eyes northward until they rested on the glimmering gold of the Lenape Bay.

Sage Meas flung his arms outward. "The Land of the Lenape," he shouted. "My homeland!"

Narrated by Glikkikan

Refreshed by a morning dip in Neshaminy Creek, I raced up the hill to Owechela's wigwam. In another month I would leave for the great festival at Passayunk on the Manayunk River.

I found Owechela seated outside his wigwam looking south toward Neshaminy Creek below and the rising sun off to our left. His eyes swept in an arc as he viewed the land before him. I slowed my pace and sat down reverently beside Owechela.

"Glikkikan," Owechela said, "the Land of the Lenape is a favored land. It is our homeland.

"Glikkikan, I have taught you the story of our people, and you have been entrusted with this knowledge. Yours is a sacred duty that must never be tossed lightly aside. Yours is the duty to hold high the flame of hope that inspired Tamenend.

"Glikkikan, Tamenend never saw the Land of the Lenape with his eyes. Tamenend possessed the land only in his spirit.

"Glikkikan, we see the Land of the Lenape with our eyes. Cast your eyes to the Four Winds—north, east, south, and west—and see. This land is a good land. It is our homeland.

"But Glikkikan, just to see the land with our eyes is not enough. Like Tamenend," Owechela paused and then hurled every ounce of strength he could muster into one phrase, "WE MUST POSSESS THIS LAND IN OUR SPIRITS."

The old chief rested. His breath came in hurried gasps. I looked into Owechela's tired black eyes. I wished I could breathe for him. A coughing spell shook him and then his breath came easier again.

"Glikkikan," Owechela continued, "do you carry the Spirit of Tamenend in your own heart?"

I wanted to tell Owechela yes with all my heart. But I wasn't sure I knew what he meant, so I said, "As much as I know how."

Owechela laid a hand on my shoulder and said, "Glikkikan, would you sit in front of me so I can lay my hands on your head?"

Of course I readily sat down in front of Owechela. Owechela laid his wizened hands upon my head.

"Glikkikan, I charge you that you shall always possess the Land of the Lenape in your own spirit and that you shall always do your best to pass that spirit on to your people. May you forever be true to the charge you bear, a charge passed down to you from the spirits of past sages—Tamenend, Eesanques, Mattahorn, and Meas.

"Glikkikan, never tire in the search for truth. Never trade the truth for wampum. Always hold the truth aloft that your people might share in its goodness."

Owechela took his hands from my head and fumbled about under his shirt. Shakily he lifted two chains from around his own neck and slipped them over my head. From the copper chain dangled a copper medallion with a tortoise climbing across it. The other chain and medal bore a perfect match to the first, only it was of silver.

Owechela again laid his trembling hands on my head. "Glikkikan," he said, and his voice quavered, "you know well the meaning of these two tortoises. They have been bought with blood and dearly paid for. They are priceless to you and to your people.

"Glikkikan, I am told that there is yet another chain and medallion, like unto these two, but it is made of pure gold. I have heard that it, too, has been bought with blood and dearly paid for.

"Glikkikan, I have searched for many years to find the gold medallion and have not found it. You must find it."

Chapter 8 — 1664-1682

Finale

As told by Owechela

Meas hurried back to Tired Moon Pond.

At the pond Meas found that Kill Weed cared quite well for the two young children. Kill Weed knew how to catch fish and where to find grubs. His trusty bow had brought down a rabbit and a squirrel. He dressed them and roasted them over the still-hot cabin coals. He found some gourds and hollowed them out for drinking cups.

Kill Weed built a rude shelter and soon had the boy and girl nesting in beds of soft pine needles and leaves. Without a word Meas fell to helping Kill Weed. Together they selected the right size saplings for wigwam poles. By evening the two builders had a rough framework in place for a wigwam and had started slitting bark slabs to cover the poles.

Toward evening Meas again left the young ones with Kill Weed and followed the trail through the settlement to the old fort. The houses in the settlement still stood, although doors hung open and all window glass had been taken or broken. Every building in and around the old fort—Peace Hall, the attached cook shed, and the nearby smithy—lay in ashes.

Friend Dreamer still hung from the tree. Meas cut the rope with his knife and carried the body to his mother's grave. Weak Gun found Meas sitting there with tears in his eyes. Together they sat side by side facing the body throughout the night.

When the first rays of light shone over the sea, Meas rose and stood so his arms reached out over the body toward the light and chanted the ancient prayer of the Lenape. He sprinkled tobacco on the ground and then stood there waiting until the fall sun rose over the distant edge of the sea.

In the sunlight Meas and Weak Gun set to work opening a grave right beside the grave of Meas's mother. Weak Gun found two hoes the soldiers had missed. Others began to arrive at the grave, bedraggled, weary, and hungry. Yet even in their plight, each one took a turn digging at the grave and at covering it after they rolled the body in.

Meas found a charred board and with Weak Gun's help began carving letters into the wood.

When the dirt lay mounded over the grave, the group sang several Dutch songs while the tears flowed faster than the words. No Smoke offered up a prayer in Dutch. The group watched quietly as Meas walked slowly from east to west across the grave and on out of sight. Then he returned to the grave and set up his board marker. It read:

FRIEND DREAMER

A LOVER OF TRUTH AND PEACE

After a respectful period of silence while the group waited around the grave, Meas rose and spoke to the group. Weak Gun translated Meas's Lenape to Dutch.

"Friends, the Red Dog Koketotoka warned you about has come to the Siconece. The Red Dog has ripped from you your beloved leader and has torn from me my wife and papoose. The Schwanneks have looted our goods and filched even the smallest trinkets. The

Schwanneks have destroyed Peace Hall and burned my own cabin. The Schwanneks have done all this under the white sign of peace. May the deeds done on the Siconece be a curse upon their own heads and smallpox upon their hearts."

Meas paused and looked at the distraught band. He saw the torn clothes, the drooping heads, and the listless eyes. Then Meas went on. His voice was soft and soothing as a balm rubbed gently into a deep wound.

"Brothers, we have suffered much. The Schwanneks have taken much, but much remains. You still possess the covenant of peace you made with the Lenape. I will go with No Smoke and Weak Gun to the village of my brother Koketotoka. He will share with you everything they have: maize and beans, knives and guns, hatchets and axes, skins and clothes, kettles and pans. As the Lenape earlier shared their homeland and their cattle and their goods with their Peace Brothers, they will now again share everything they have with their friends in their season of want.

"Brothers, the Siconece is a good land that the Great Spirit has given us to share with our brothers. The Lenape will teach you how to live from the bounty of the land if you will feel gently its pulse and not be overcome by greed. There is no need for any to suffer want while fish and birds and deer swarm around us.

"Brothers, the Spirit of Tamenend still hovers in the hearts of good men on the Siconece. His spirit is a spirit of hope and courage. Because of the hope within us that justice and truth will yet prevail over evil and lies, our spirits must not droop nor our hope die within our breasts. We must summon the courage of Tamenend to take a step forward."

Meas lifted the silver tortoise from his chest and held it aloft.

"Brothers, amidst all our grief a touch of justice has come to the Siconece. This day the Great Spirit has returned the silver tortoise to the Lenape people, and he who stole it from the grave of Mattahorn breathes no more.

"Brothers, hope springs forth within my breast that Cool Water still clutches the copper tortoise in warm and tender fingers as I also grip the silver tortoise in a living hand. The flame of hope burns strong within me that I shall find her, draw her to me, and bring her once more to the Siconece.

"Brothers, I go in search of Cool Water. No river is too long for me to paddle to its source. There is no sea so broad I will not sail it. There is no trail so faint I will not follow it to find her. I want not for courage. I will risk all for Cool Water.

"But perchance I lose my life in the attempt to bring Cool Water back, it is my will that you bring Cool Water and myself back to the Siconece and close the earth upon us here beside my mother and Friend Dreamer. And if our bones cannot lie here in peace, then rest assured that our spirits shall regularly visit this hallowed place. And if I return not with a living hand grasping this silver tortoise I lift before you, you shall entrust the silver tortoise to Chief Tamenand on Neshaminy Creek. Likewise, the copper tortoise Cool Water now clutches to her breast shall go to Chief Tamenand."

Meas held the silver tortoise still for a long moment before he laid it once more against his chest. Then he continued: "Brothers, remember my kindness to you. While I am gone, lend Kill Weed aid as he cares for my son and daughter. Be father and mother to them until I return.

"Brothers, I would also ask the company of Weak Gun on my journey. I may need his Dutch tongue and the ready gun of a trained soldier.

"First, Weak Gun and I will go to New Amstel and seek signs of Cool Water's trail there. If we find any upturned leaves or footprints, I shall pursue her. As soon as I can, I will send Weak Gun back to you with news and perhaps with more supplies to aid in the rebuilding of your anthill on the Siconece."

Meas smiled. "Koketotoka's dream of the Red Dog digging up the anthill also told us the ants would rebuild their hill. His dream was true. You will rebuild.

"Now I must go to Koketotoka and tell him what has happened and what is in my heart to do. Perhaps Koketotoka will also have a word of counsel for me before he prays and asks the Great Spirit to go with me on my journey."

Tall, redheaded, blue-eyed No Smoke Wiltbanck stepped forward and placed his arm around Meas. "Brother Meas," he said, "we share your loss and your grief. Cool Water means much to every one of us. If there is anything we can do to restore her to you and bring her back to the Siconece, we want to do it. You may gladly take Weak Gun Spycker with you. Keep him as long as you need him.

"And Brother Meas, thank you for every kindness you have shown to us. The Bible says, 'In the day of your calamity, a friend close by is better than blood kin far away.'[80] You have proven that proverb true.

"Brother Meas, we pray that the God of heaven will prosper your journey and grant that you may quickly return with your beloved wife and papoose."

Then No Smoke Wiltbanck led his forlorn, plundered band in this prayer while Weak Gun translated it line by line into Lenape:

> Our Father in heaven, help us to honor your name.
> Come and set up your kingdom,
>   so that everyone on earth will obey you,
>   as you are obeyed in heaven.
> Give us our food for today.
> Forgive us for doing wrong, as we forgive others.
> Keep us from being tempted
>   and protect us from the evil one.[81]
> In the name of Jesus Christ we pray, Amen.

[80] Proverbs 27:10.
[81] Commonly known as the Lord's Prayer and found in Matthew 6:9-13.

Dusk crept over the Dutch village of New Amstel as Meas and Weak Gun paddled their canoe up the River of the Lenape past a neat row of shuttered houses on the strand. The chill of late fall night air hurried their strokes as they paddled upriver to the north side of a sand spit jutting out into the Lenape River. On the sand spit and reaching back to the firmer land stood the ghost of Fort Amstel.

In front of the canoe a dyke with a water gate butted across the path of the canoe. In earlier days a small river had flowed out of a large marsh exactly where the water gate now blocked their path. This small river had helped create the sand spit where Strutting Turkey had built Fort Casimir.[82]

In the fifteen years since the building of the fort, the Dutch had built a network of dykes and gates that converted the marsh into choice farmlands. The dykes also served as paths to outlying settlements.

Meas and Weak Gun pulled their canoe ashore and headed for the open gates of the fort.

"Weak Gun," said Meas, "do you know this fort is haunted by evil spirits? It is the same fort where Falling Leaf tormented Commander Jacquet with the screams of panthers. Within these walls Commander Jacquet heard the fiends screaming and saw the ghouls dancing."

Weak Gun seemed unimpressed by the tales of a haunted fort.

"Meas," he said, "I have been in this fort many times, and I have yet to see the first ghost. Soldiers are not frightened by such tales. Nevertheless, because you have warned me, I shall keep my gun ready, and if a spirit is sighted, I will have no qualms about shooting one."

Weak Gun led the way into the familiar fort. "We shall tour the barracks first," said Weak Gun, and he stomped noisily into a long,

[82] Fort Casimir built by Governor Stuyvesant, on this point called the Sand Hook, was also known at different times as Fort Trinity and Fort Amstel. The site today is located at New Castle, Delaware.

low shed that stretched nearly the whole length of the fort.

Meas hung back in the shadows wary of the spooky confines. A number of low houses clutched their roofs tightly to their eaves and hid their ghosts in dingy cellars. Here and there a few buildings propped helmeted tile roofs above a second story and held their spirits in cobwebbed garrets. The palisades poked bony accusing fingers upward, enclosing the buildings in a huddle of guilt.

Meas could hear Weak Gun whistling in the distance as he continued his tour of the fort remains. Meas slipped along the walls of the houses toward the whistling. He pitched a small stone onto a tiled roof. It rattled and banged as it bounced several times on the roofs before falling to the earth below.

The whistling stopped. A piercing shriek rent the darkness and a tortured cry hung on the night air.

Meas pitched another stone on the roof. While the rock clattered noisily down the roof, he moved swiftly toward where the whistling had been.

Again the piercing shriek rang out followed by an eerie stillness.

Meas made out Weak Gun's tensed form in the darkness as Weak Gun carefully searched the upper room windows from which the cry rang out. Meas laid a cold hand on Weak Gun's nape. Weak Gun squeezed the trigger on his gun, sending the ball far out over the Lenape River ... and fainted.

Meas threw Weak Gun over his shoulder and raced for the fort gate. He shoved the canoe from the bank and dropped Weak Gun into it. With another heave and a leap they were off into the Lenape.

Meas hung close to the cover of the western shore. As soon as they were hidden from the fort, he splashed water on Weak Gun's face until his color returned and his senses revived.

"Oh," said Meas, "I see that I have named you well. Your gun goes off at the most inopportune times. I fear you shall bring the whole town of New Amstel down upon the fort. I rather hated it for I wanted to see who the screams were coming from."

Weak Gun grinned like a coon. "I am simple, Meas, but I'll not be taken in quite that bad. The screams were part of your joke."

"No, Weak Gun," said Meas, "I was as surprised as you were when the fiend screamed. But did not the fiend cry out in Dutch? What torture did it hang upon the sullen air?"

"Ah, I remember," Weak Gun said faintly. " 'I am ruined,' was its anguished cry."

"Then we shall return to the fort," Meas urged, "and we shall see what sort of body this spirit has. For every spirit rests in some form, be it a bird, a beast, a bush, a rock, the water, the wind, or a tree. And I suspect this spirit dwells in a Dutchman."

"Why do we not let the spirits fend for themselves and be gone from this haunted place?" Weak Gun asked. "Let us look for Cool Water among the living and not among departed spirits from the nether world."

"Weak Gun, the spirits may tell us more of Cool Water than the living can," Meas insisted. "For the spirits know not only of the living, but they also breathe the thoughts of the dead. We must return to the fort."

Meas and Weak Gun pushed their canoe into the tall rushes along the shore and waded west till they came to the foot dyke. This time Meas led the way and Weak Gun trailed close behind. Once on the foot dyke, the two headed south, single file, until they crossed the footbridge above the water gate. Then the two stopped.

"Weak Gun, do not load your gun," Meas ordered. "If Lenape must do battle with Schwanneks, guns are of little use. At close range and in the dark a tomahawk is far more effective than a gun or sword.

"But do not hurry to shed blood. As Ever-Be-Joyful said, 'Cold blood brings forth hot blood.'

"Weak Gun, I have laid my hand upon both the bear and the deer without them knowing of my presence. In the same way I may steal upon the Schwanneks with far greater ease than I did upon the bear or the deer. And I may slip away from Schwanneks as easily as a sparrow flits away from a bear.

"Weak Gun, hide your gun in the bushes. We do not want a war. We want only to recover Cool Water and the papoose alive."

While Meas talked, he studied the scene in the silvery light. The foot dyke tied directly into the north end of the strand where the row of houses perched on the river front. The fort, off to his left, squatted on somewhat lower terrain as it jutted out into the river. Off to his right lay a nearby farmhouse. Beyond the closest house slept other scattered barns and houses of Dutch farmers.

"Well, Weak Gun," Meas went on, "it looks as though your call to arms has not been heeded. Gunfire in a haunted fort alarms not the—"

A door opened at the nearby farmhouse and a lone woman carrying a candle moved hesitantly toward the fort and straight toward Meas and Weak Gun.

"Talk to her," Meas ordered.

"Halloo!" Weak Gun called out while the woman was still some distance away. "Who goes there?" Weak Gun demanded in Dutch.

The woman paused and snuffed out the candle before answering. "Barbarah van Sweringen. Make yourself known," she commanded as she edged back toward the house.

"Harmen Cornelisen Spycker," Weak Gun called out quickly.

"Spycker, do you travel alone?" Barbarah asked as she continued backing toward the cabin.

"Nay, Barbarah, I have a friend with me," Weak Gun answered.

"Spycker, what's your business here?" Barbarah flung out next, and then bolted for the house door.

But it was too late. Meas gripped her tiny wrist firmly as she reached out to open the door, and with his other hand he held a warning finger across her lips. Barbarah did not cry out or struggle. Somehow she seemed to sense that Meas did not wish to harm her.

Meas motioned for her to go back to where Weak Gun waited and then released his grip on her wrist. Barbarah hesitated. Then she reached her tiny hand out and clasped Meas's wrist. Meas led her back to Weak Gun, and together the three moved within the covering shadows of the fort.

There they stood in the pale light. Meas tapped himself on the chest. "Meas, sage of the Lenape." Meas tapped Weak Gun on the forehead. "Weak Gun," he said. "He is a bad soldier. He shoots at ghosts."

Barbara laughed shakily. "Do you understand English?" Meas asked. She nodded. Meas tapped her lightly on the forehead. He pondered. "Ah, yes. Think Fast," Meas said proudly. "Weak Gun call, candle out, talk much, run. To the Lenape you shall be known as Think Fast.

"Think Fast, Weak Gun and I are here searching for news of my wife and papoose. We happened across your path only by accident. We will not hurt you.

"But do tell us where you were going when you stumbled upon us. Why did you venture out into the night by yourself?"

Think Fast gripped Meas's arm tightly with both hands and her head sagged forward on his strong arm while the tears poured out. "I thought I heard a gun go off," she sobbed, "and I feared the worst. So I started out to check if maybe ... maybe he killed himself. But, oh, I'm so glad you're here."

She lifted her face and turned imploring eyes toward Meas. "Will you go with me to look?" she begged.

Meas nodded. Think Fast braced herself and wiped some of the tears on her sleeve. "If you will relight the candle, I will lead you," she said.

Meas lit the candle. Think Fast, still clutching Meas's wrist, led the way through the hodgepodge of structures within the fort and stopped in front of a two-story building. "We will go up the stairs to the old courtroom," Think Fast whispered. "There you will see his ghost."

Each worn step creaked and groaned as the three climbed up the single flight of stairs. Candlelight flickered unsteadily over the ceiling and walls as the three emerged into the former courtroom.

At the front of the dark room two eyes glowed as they reflected the meager candlelight. Think Fast moved directly toward the staring eyes. Weak Gun stayed at the stairway ready for instant flight, but Meas had no choice save to follow Think Fast toward the glowing eyes. Think Fast's fingernails dug deeply into his wrist.

Think Fast laid an arm around the shoulder of the seated specter and whispered, "Sir Garrett, you have a guest."

"Sir Garrett van Sweringen, clerk, commissary, schout,[83] and second councilor of the city of New Amstel,"[84] the man replied in a flat, hollow tone. His eyes did not move.

"Dear, our guest speaks English," Think Fast whispered.

"I can do that," said the same toneless voice. "What does he want?"

"Why does Sir Garrett sit in this ghastly chamber?" Meas asked.

Sir Garrett let out a pitiful wail. "I am ruined. I am ruined," he cried.

"You are not ruined!" Meas shouted loud enough to scare all the ghosts in the whole fort. "You are but a hollow log with its heart eaten out by worms. Seek beyond your own ragged bones and the rotting walls of this devilish place for strength."

"I am ruined," Hollow Log van Sweringen insisted in the same flat voice. "The English did it. You do not understand.

"My house on the Strand, lands, cattle, sheep, horses, servants, and Negroes are gone. Sir Robert Carr took it all and gave it to Captain John Carr. I am ruined."

"But Garrett, you have me and Elizabeth and Zacharias. Are we nothing?" Think Fast said softly. "Now no one can say that I married you for money."

"I am ruined," the flat voice continued. "You do not understand. Sir Robert Carr did protest often to me that he did not come as an

---

[83] Pronounced the same as scout. An official in the Dutch colonies similar to a sheriff.
[84] First councilor and captain of the military was Sir Alexander (Fat Pig) Hinoyossa.

enemy, but as a friend, demanding only in friendship what was the King's right in that country.

"I gave in to Sir Robert, and drawing my sword, I kissed its long, straight, splendid blade, and broke it across my knee. Rising as high as I could in my stirrups, I threw the broken pieces to the left and the right and shouted, 'Farewell, good blade, forevermore! Forged in honor, thou shalt never be drawn in dishonor. Thy steel was for the Netherlands, my hands are for van Sweringen.' "

Again the voice rose to a wailing cry, "I am ruined. I am ruin..." Hollow Log choked up and stopped.

Think Fast looked sadly up at Meas, and pointing at her own head, she made a slow circular motion. Then she said soothingly, "Garrett dear, to be ruined without fault is no disgrace. Does it not matter to thee that I gave up my home in France and everything else to go with thee? I am now as poor as thee and I care not a whit 'tis so if thee will only find thy heart and live with me."

Hollow Log gave no sign of hope to the tender appeal but continued on in his dreadful monotone. "I am ruined. You do not understand.

"What kind of a friend seizes one hundred sheep, forty horses, sixty cows and oxen, seventy Negroes, a brew house, a still house and all its equipment, all the produce of the land for the year such as maize and hay, and all the unsold cargo stored in the fort amounting to four thousand pounds sterling?

"The English took into their custody arms, powder, and shot in a great quantity, four and twenty great guns, and transported them to New Amsterdam.

"The English took the Dutch soldiers prisoners and gave them to the armed merchant ship who sold the hapless fellows in Virginia.

"Those may be the spoils of a war never fought, but what friend will plunder tools for craftsmen, plow gear, and other tillage tools; likewise a sawmill and nine sea buoys with a great quantity of iron chain–all this besides the estates of Governor Hinoyossa, Peter Alricks, and myself?

"I am ruined. I have nothing left. I am ruined. You do not understand."

Meas grabbed Hollow Log by the shoulder and shook him as a dog shakes a rat. Then he leaned over until his dark eyes looked straight into the staring blue ones. "Hollow Log," he said through clenched teeth, "I do understand. All my goods plus my wife and papoose were taken by the same Sir Robert Carr that plundered you. He hanged my closest friend who did him no harm.

"I, Meas, sage of the Lenape, do understand. And as long as your devoted Think Fast stands beside you and offers you herself, do not say ever again that all is lost or that you are ruined."

Meas relaxed his grip on Hollow Log's shoulder, and Think Fast released her grip on Meas's wrist. The staring eyes did not waver but only reflected the glow of the candlelight.

The wail began again, "I am ruin—."

Meas slapped a stinging blow to the side of Hollow Log's face. Then he reached down and pitched the still form over his shoulder.

"Think Fast," he said, "let us leave this troubled place to bats and to rats and to deranged spirits from the past. I go in search of Cool Water.

"Think Fast," Meas added as the three trotted back toward the small house, "Hollow Log will revive, but he will need a lot of rest and gentle food to heal his heart. If you would have Hollow Log regain the strength of the green tree, listen kindly to what he may say, but do not speak to him of the past or try to reason with him. Speak only of the present and of hope for the future.

"Let him sleep as much as he will. Make sure he gets no beer or rum. I will bring some herbs to you in the morning that will help ease his pain.

"Now, Think Fast, tell me. How may I find Sir Robert Carr?"

"Meas, I do not know in which direction Sir Robert Carr has

gone. Perhaps you should talk to Sergeant Godefro Meyer van Cloppenburgh. The sergeant minces no words when the strongest ones will do. If you go to him, you should be aware that in the past there has been no love lost between him and Sir Garrett van Sweringen. Yet I believe you can trust him.

"Meas, I trust you. I will tell you how to find Sergeant Godefro, but you must tell no one how you found him. Our Dutch web must be protected in this conquered land."

Meas followed Think Fast into the quiet house and laid Hollow Log on a rude bed. "May the Great Spirit bring healing to his sick heart," Meas murmured. He turned to go.[85]

Think Fast squeezed his arm, lightly this time. "Meas," she whispered, "may the God of heaven help you find Cool Water and the papoose. And as the French say, *Bon voyage.*"

"In hiding" would have been the wrong words to describe Sergeant Godefro. "A wounded bull waiting to attack the first thing that moved" would have been more apt.

First of all, the sergeant was a big man. Besides that, he had the disconcerting habit of leaning over and roaring right into your face. The sergeant never whispered. He meant to be heard and he meant to be obeyed.

Not that the sergeant was mean. It was just part of his nature to bellow, and now the English takeover provoked him to still greater volume.

Weak Gun and Meas had no trouble finding the sergeant camped within the maze of dykes and marshes to the north of New Amstel.

[85] In less than two years after the English takeover of New Amstel, Barbarah and Garrett van Sweringen, along with two children (likely with some help from Garrett's family), made their way to St. Mary's City, Maryland. After bearing two more children, Barbarah died in 1670. Garrett remarried and fathered eight more children by his second wife. Garrett van Sweringen built up a sizable estate at St. Mary's City, served a period of time on the Governor's Council and as sheriff of St. Mary's County. He died in 1698 at the age of sixty-three.

"That's him," Weak Gun assured Meas. "I'd know his lusty bawl anywhere."

As soon as Sergeant Godefro saw Meas and Weak Gun padding toward him, he quit shoveling, sprang up on the dyke, and moved boldly toward them. He held his shovel in readiness until he recognized Weak Gun. Then Godefro rushed to greet him.

"Harmen Cornelisen," Godefro bellowed into Harmen's face as his powerful arms nearly crushed Weak Gun in a bear hug. "What are you doing out in this marsh?

"Cornelisen, I thought you gave up soldiering and went to trading with the savages. Why are you carrying a gun out here in this marsh? Are you going to hunt your own furs?"

"I'm looking for the fearless Sergeant Godefro Meyer van Cloppenburgh," Weak Gun informed the sergeant. "We heard you a great way off. Sergeant, who were you shouting orders to? We expected to find the whole marsh full of soldiers."

The sergeant grinned. "Marsh rats and water snakes. Those critters listen well and fight like Dutch soldiers, which is to say they don't fight at all."

"Sergeant, you impugn yourself with such a base attack on the courage of Dutch soldiers," Weak Gun charged. "Sergeant, explain yourself."

The sergeant bent his giant frame down toward Weak Gun and stuck his face inches away from him. "There was nothing wrong with the Dutch soldiers or their sergeant," he sneered. " 'Twas Judas Hinoyossa and his councilors that sold us to Sir Robert Carr. Betrayers, murderers, traitors— that's what they are."

The sergeant pressed his face still closer upon Weak Gun and glowered. Weak Gun took a step backward. Sergeant Godefro relaxed just a bit and also stepped backward.

"Ah, pardon me," he muttered. "I know you didn't have anything to do with Fort Amstel. It's just that it makes me mad even to think about it. I have to blow a whale spout and make a show just to let the pressure off."

"Yes, I can tell you're about to blow apart," Weak Gun injected. "Maybe we could find a place to have a smoke, and then you could tell us what's eating you. Sergeant, do you think your dyke work will wait?"

"Wait?" Sergeant Godefro snorted. "I don't care if it never gets done. That'll make the savages happy anyway," and Sergeant Godefro cast a sideways glance at Meas. "The savages don't like when we drain these marshes," he said.

"Nor do the Indians like the Schwanneks stealing their land," Weak Gun added.

"Huh?" the sergeant huffed. "This land belongs to the Dutch. We got here first, bought it first, settled it first, bought it with our blood at Swanendael and Murder Creek. Stuyvesant and Hinoyossa even bought the land from the savages a second time. We got the treaties to prove it."

Sergeant Godefro leaned hard on Weak Gun and bellowed, "Cornelisen, from the source of the South River to Cape Henlopen for thirty leagues inland, this land belongs to the Dutch and the savages be—."

Without flinching or batting an eye, Weak Gun butted in. "Maybe you should tell that to the English," he said evenly.

The sergeant exploded. Invective poured from his mouth like pus from an opened wound. He cursed the savages, the English, and the Dutch.

Sergeant Godefro's face turned red. He clenched his fists to strike at Weak Gun. Meas sprang on Godefro, knocking the burly Godefro over backwards. In an instant Meas pinned the crazed man face-down on the dyke and firmly locked his two wrists together behind his back.

Meas held his grip tightly till the stunned Godefro regained his senses. Then Meas slowly released his grip, turned his back on the prostrate form, sat down on the side of the dyke, and lit his pipe.

Weak Gun helped Sergeant Godefro to his feet, and they, too, made themselves comfortable on the dyke beside Meas.

Meas smoked thoughtfully as he stared out across the marshland. He handed the pipe to Weak Gun. Weak Gun puffed on the pipe for a time before handing it to Sergeant Godefro. Sergeant Godefro puffed a short time before passing the pipe back to Meas.

Meas turned the pipe over and tapped it on the ground before he broke the silence. "Weak Gun, tell Big Bull we have seen Hollow Log van Sweringen, and I wish to know what has eaten the heart out of his log. Weak Gun, you can translate for me."

Big Bull was willing to talk. The volcano within him had been opened but had not yet spent its fury. A subdued voice didn't match his brusque speech, and his old roar soon returned. Big Bull fumed:

> Schout van Sweringen is a crook. He is the hatchet man for Hinoyossa. In fact, Hinoyossa's whole council is in it together.
>
> I'll tell you why I say that.
>
> Nine years ago Governor Stuyvesant brought the *De Waag* up the South River and rooted out the Swedes. That little war cost the West India Company too much money.
>
> Even with a choke-hold on the South River, the Company lost money. The Company had to sell the whole South River to rich burghers in Amsterdam.
>
> The South River still lost money for the burghers. Bantie Utie threatened to take over New Amstel for Maryland. Bondmen fled to Virginia and Maryland instead of completing their terms. Sickness depleted the settlers. The English and Swedes siphoned off the fur trade. The savages fought. Everything was going to pot on the South River.
>
> Then Governor Hinoyossa got full control. He paid off the savages. He got in bed with Maryland and Virginia. He talked hundreds of settlers into coming across. He got in on the African slave trade. Hinoyossa made deals with everyone. In

only one year's time Hinoyossa turned things around on the South River. The future looked bright.

Everybody knew Hinoyossa and his gang stole big time. Schout van Sweringen and Hinoyossa traded Amsterdam's galliot,[86] millstones, and brew kettle for tobacco credited to their personal accounts.

Hinoyossa ripped off the palisades from Fort Amstel to fire his still and his brew kettles. Then he charged the City of Amsterdam for new pales.

Thieving drunks they were, but nobody cared. Everybody was making lots of money.

I had my own house stashed full of trade goods. It was packed from top to bottom. I couldn't have gotten another thing in. The English robbed everything—cloth, linen, wine, brandy, Spanish wine, stockings, shoes, shirts, and other goods.

Let the good times roll was what everyone wanted.

Nobody cared what the gang did except the English. They wanted some of the loot too.

We heard the English took New Amsterdam. Hinoyossa mustered New Amstel and Fort Amstel. There were ninety burghers and farmers and thirty soldiers. The fort contained twenty-four cannon, large amounts of shot, powder, and guns. We had no fear we could not defend ourselves if the English came.

The English came. A large warship mounted with more than forty guns and an English merchantman loaded with soldiers sailed up the South River to Fort Amstel. Governor Hinoyossa met alone with the commander, Sir Robert Carr.

When Governor Hinoyossa returned to the fort, he

---

[86] A Dutch merchant ship with very rounded ribs and flattish bottom.

ordered me to load the cannons with shrapnel and to supply the soldiers with muskets and double side arms. Then the governor walked down the line and asked the soldiers, "Are you ready to fight?"

The soldiers all yelled, "As long as we can stand up!"

The next day, about eight o'clock in the morning, nearly one hundred and thirty English soldiers and sailors from the warship and the merchant vessel landed. They paraded around to the rear of the farmhouse at the back of the fort. Shrapnel would have torn them up.

At about three o'clock in the afternoon, the warship dropped down within musket range of the fort and fired cannon shots, mind you, over the roofs of the houses in the fort.

The warship now lay at very close range and the shrapnel from my guns would have busted her wide open. I asked the governor whether I should fire on the ship. He forbade me to do so. I shouted at him. He again ordered me not to shoot.

As soon as the ship's cannons stopped shooting, the English soldiers on land climbed over the rear wall.

Weak Gun, do you think Dutch soldiers are such poor shots they could not have killed one English soldier as he climbed over the wall? Or do you think the soldiers lacked the courage to shoot?

No! The Dutch soldiers had been ordered not to shoot.

The Dutch soldiers were betrayed. The English in their fury cut down at least three and wounded ten. The English soldiers suffered not one scratch.

As soon as the attack started, I saw Schout van Sweringen and Ensign Pieter Alricks, both of whom were of the Governor's Council, jump over the side wall and run away. The cowardly traitors!

The blood of the dead, the plunder, the soldiers taken as prisoners—all must be charged to Judas Hinoyossa and his council. This is treason, and I will swear to it in Amsterdam as soon as I can get there.[87]

"So what of Schout Hollow Log?" Meas asked. "Why does he suffer so?"

"As to Schout Garrett van Sweringen," Big Bull answered, "he despairs because the guilt of past misdeeds haunts him while his ill-gotten gains have been stolen by another. He suffers justly."

"But suppose he suffered unjustly. Would you risk your life to help him?" Meas persisted.

"But van Sweringen is a scoundrel," Big Bull insisted. "I cannot change the torture God sends upon him. Nor will I risk one little finger trying."

"Weak Gun," Meas went on, "tell Big Bull that after the English took Fort Amstel they came to the Siconece and plundered our goods, murdered your brother, and stole my wife and papoose.

"Can Big Bull tell us where Sir Robert Carr may be found?"

"I can and I will tell you where Sir Robert Carr is to be found," Big Bull roared.

"My friend Steffen Ottingh van Loo was formerly foreman of the farmhands at Bommelerweert.[88] Governor Hinoyossa made this island the nicest place on the South River. He drained the marshes and made fertile fields and gardens. Hinoyossa built his wife and seven children a grand Dutch mansion and furnished it with the best of everything from Europe. It was nice. My friend Steffen looked after it all.

"But again, I can't meddle with the justice of God. Steffen tells me that Sir Robert Carr, the man you seek, came up the river in a small boat loaded with soldiers and overpowered the inhabitants of the

---

[87] Sergeant Godefro Meyer van Cloppenburgh swore out his account of the Fort Amstel Battle in Amsterdam, Holland, on 16 June 1665.

[88] The Dutch name for Matennecunk Island presently known as Burlington Island, New Jersey.

island. The soldiers plundered everything, even the bedding from under the people's bodies, and carried it all away.

"I have good word that Sir Robert Carr has given the estates, fine houses, and servants of van Sweringen and Peter Alricks to his own officers, but Sir Robert Carr himself has returned to claim Bommelerweert as his own.

"Oh! the exquisite justice of God. The thief is plundered by a robber!" And Big Bull burst into roaring, sidesplitting raucous laughter.

"Go!" Big Bull bellowed as soon as he could again get control of himself. "You will find the King's thief at Bommelerweert."

Meas and Weak Gun retrieved their canoe and paddled north to Passayunk.

Meas smoked with Pinna and other local Lenape headmen. When their mini council fire burned out, four young men readied a canoe to carry Weak Gun back to the Siconece.

Weak Gun wanted to stay with Meas, but Meas was firm. "You must carry news back to the Siconece and help Kill Weed care for the children," he insisted. "Weak Gun, you must go. The Lenape spies tell me that Cool Water and the commander are both on the island of Matennecunk.

"At Passayunk, Shackamoxon, and on Neshaminy Creek I have many strong friends. Before the new moon, I shall come once more to the Siconece bringing Cool Water and the papoose."

At midmorning, three long canoes paddled out into the River of the Lenape. The canoe carrying Weak Gun turned south while the two canoes headed by Meas and Pinna turned north.

"Look," cried Pinna as he spread his arms out wide. "The River of the Lenape."

Meas held the silver tortoise aloft, and the sun glinted on its burnished surface.

"Look," Pinna shouted, "the homeland of the Lenape."

The paddlers stopped for a moment.

Towering green pines mixed with bare-limbed oaks, beech, chestnut, and poplar crowded upon the rolling hills. In the creases between the hills, creeks and streams eased their waters into broad marshes covered with cattails and tall grasses. In a jumble of land and water and grasses and trees, the marsh joined the river. Quacking ducks and honking geese thrilled the spectators.

Meas restored the silver tortoise to his breast.

The cool air of late fall stirred the paddlers to action. They dipped their blades into the water in perfect rhythm as they chanted:

> *From Passayunk to Matennecunk we go,*
> *Onward! Onward! Onward we row!*
> *Never stop, never drop,*
> *Till Cool Water rides in the bow!*

Dark water sped past the canoes as they pushed north. At Passayunk and the surrounding villages, one hundred braves began applying war paint.

At the mouth of Neshaminy Creek, Meas beckoned Pinna's canoe alongside. "Pinna," Meas directed, "go up Neshaminy Creek and find Sachem Tamenand. See if Sachem Tamenand will also bring one hundred warriors. Tomorrow afternoon, I will meet Sachem Pinna and Sachem Tamenand and their two hundred warriors on the south end of Matennecunk Island. Bring only knives, tomahawks, and bows. No guns."

The canoes glided softly away from each other. There was no more chanting now. "To Fat Pig's haunt we go," Meas urged.

Meas stowed the canoe in a well-hidden glade on the south end of Matennecunk. He divided four warriors into groups of two. "See, but do not be seen," he instructed. "Two of you work around the east side of the island and two of you work to the west side. One shall guard the canoe and observe all river traffic. I will seek Cool Water."

Meas faded into the fields and pastures, the dykes and ditches, the shrubs and the trees—all parts of the Dutch masterpiece Fat Pig had made of Matennecunk Island. Black-and-white-spotted cattle browsed on the fall pastures. Hogs rooted among the chestnuts and acorns in the woods.

Like a hunter stalking his prey, Meas moved cautiously toward the brick mansion on the east side of the island. Perched on a knoll, the two-story mansion with its two lower wings sweeping out to each side hovered over a surrounding cluster of lesser sheds and barns like a mother hen with her peeps fluffed about her.

Meas hid among the trees above a cleft where a small stream rippled toward the river. Three black-and-white-spotted cows lay in the nearby pasture chewing their cud. Meas watched.

Four chimneys belched smoke upward. Two large mastiffs lay chained to stakes near the front entrance. Pales and gates enclosed the entire yard around the mansion. Two red-coated lesser officers strode in from the dock to the east. A mix of servants, slaves, and soldiers rustled about tending to the evening chores.

Then Meas saw her! Cool Water, carrying a milk pail, made her way toward the resting cows. "OO-oo," Cool Water called, the first note higher in pitch than the second. She threw her voice again toward the woods, "OO-oo."

"OO-oo," Meas called faintly.

"OO-oo," Cool Water called loudly. A cow roused herself and rose to her feet. Then another and another.

"OO-oo," Meas echoed again.

Cool Water moved toward the cows, scratching one on the poll, slapping another on the rump, and giving another a shove against the neck. Slowly she drove the three cows away from the mansion and the watching eyes of her guards. She began singing softly while her keen eyes searched the trees.

> *But could youth last, and love still lead,*
> *Had joys no date, nor age no need,*
> *Then these delights my mind might move*
> *To live with thee, and be thy love.*[89]

Meas joined in the song and together they held the last high note till it collapsed. The cows stopped walking. Cool Water knelt beside one of the cows and placed her pail under the udder.

In a flash Meas knelt beside her and held her tightly to him. Cool Water laid her head on his shoulder and murmured, "I knew you would come, but it has been so long," she whimpered. "I tried many times to escape but he always held the papoose."

Meas kissed her lightly. "Everything will be all right," he assured her. "Tomorrow night I shall come to claim you and the papoose." Then Meas was gone as swiftly as he had come.

While returning to the hidden canoe, Meas killed a young pig. By the time the scouts returned, he had roasted pork ready for eating. "Tonight we shall taste the best of the land," he declared, and the six stuffed themselves with the tender meat.

When the six had finished eating, they put out the fire and drifted back toward the mansion.

The chill of late fall night air settled over the island as Meas and his band waited in the darkness. Lights went out in the houses, and beast and bird quieted.

Meas threw back his head and began a long plaintive howl. The other scouts added their voices to the wolf chorus as the pack howled about the island.

The mastiffs growled throaty growls while they prowled loose about the yard and leaped against the fence trying to break out. Smaller dogs

---

[89] Words written by Sir Walter Raleigh. Set to music by James G. Landis.

yipped and yapped excitedly until close-up growls and snarls drove them under whatever loose cover they could find.

Chickens smothered in the roost.

The horses crashed through the rail fence and raced across the bottoms jumping several ditches.

Cattle crowded in close around the buildings bellowing in fright and dirtying everything they crossed over.

Guinea fowl hollered from the trees.

Geese honked in alarm.

The wolves howled. At times it was the cry of the lone wolf in the distance while at other times it was the pack running together and closing in for the kill. Then again the plaintive howl bounced off the very walls of the mansion.

Before the first light Meas and his pack returned to the hidden glade and slept till noon. As the sun started its descent, the six awoke and gathered around a small fire.

Meas laid out his plan. "As soon as Pinna and Tamenand and their warriors arrive, we will divide into six bands. Five scouts will each take thirty warriors. I will take the remaining fifty with me.

"One band will secure the main dock and scuttle the galliot moored there. All small boats and canoes will be taken.

"Two bands will sweep around each side of the island and cut the dykes at every water gate.

"All bands will make sure no one leaves Matennecunk or arrives on the island. Once darkness arrives, all warriors must come to the mansion and cordon it off.

"Make sure you kill no one unless the Schwanneks kill first. I and my band will entertain the commander until darkness covers us."

Tamenand and his warriors ferried across the river from the west. Pinna's Passayunk warriors paddled furtively up the river to the island glade. As quickly as possible each scout slipped quietly away with his band, some in canoes and some overland.

Meas led his warriors to the woods where he had talked with Cool Water and dispersed them well beyond reach of rifle fire from the mansion. He sent an unarmed messenger to the front yard gate.

From his hand the messenger dangled the silver tortoise. "What do you want, savage?" shouted a soldier as he pointed his gun menacingly at the messenger.

"I have a message for the commander," the messenger replied in good English.

"The commander does not have time to meet with you," the soldier scoffed. The messenger made no reply but twirled the silver tortoise beneath his extended hand.

"Begone," the soldier ordered, "or I'll turn the dog on you."

The soldier had no more than spoken when a single shaft sped into the heart of the great mastiff. The dog rolled over without a growl.

The soldier stared at the dog, looked at the messenger to see what magic he possessed, thought about his own exposed position, and then retreated into the house. The soldier soon returned and ushered the messenger in to see Sir Robert Carr.

"Are you the commander, Sir Robert Carr?" the messenger asked.

"I am the commander of the English forces on the Delaware," Sir Robert answered.

"This is the message I bear: 'The Lenni Lenape have come to take Matennecunk Island. I, Sage Meas, will meet with you alone. We will meet at the stump ten paces from the front gate to come to an agreement.' "

The commander eyed the silver tortoise carefully and slowly nodded. "Tell Sage Meas I will come."

Sir Robert did come. Resplendent in his red uniform with his sword swinging by his white pants, the commander swaggered out to meet Sage Meas. Or it was as close to a swagger as an officer of the King could muster with a limp and one black boot missing.

Meas stepped boldly out to greet the commander, clad in his tan

long-sleeved shirt, breechclout, buckskin leggings, and moccasins.
Long black hair swung in a single waist-length braid behind him. A
knife and tomahawk hung from an embroidered leather belt. The
silver tortoise lay openly upon his shirt.

The commander seated himself upon the stump, and Meas seated
himself cross-legged before him. Meas lit his pipe and smoked calmly.
Then he handed the pipe to the commander.

The commander took several puffs and remarked, "I like not your
tobacco and sumac mix. If I had only thought to bring some French
wine along 'twould have lent an additional sparkle to the parley." He
handed the pipe back to Meas.

"Sage Meas," the commander began, "your message said that you
have come to take Matennecunk Island. What right do you have to
take Matennecunk Island?"

"Commander Lame Foot," Meas answered, "fives of hundreds
of years ago, the Great Spirit gave the Land of the Dawn to
Sage Tamenend and the Lenni Lenape. The Lenape and their
grandchildren have lived in the lands on both sides of this river,
the River of the Lenape, for hundreds of years. It is our homeland.
Matennecunk Island, like all the Land of the Dawn, belongs to the
Lenape."

"Sage Meas, the Land of the Dawn you speak of is a wild,
uncultivated land inhabited only by godless savages. King Charles II, a
good Christian king, has given all this land to his brother, the Duke of
York."

"Commander Lame Foot," Meas asked, "is this king you speak of
the son of the English king who was beheaded?"

Lame Foot sat up straighter on the stump and furrowed his brow.
"Aye, Sage Meas, it was a most unfortunate time of turmoil in England
when Parliament gained control and beheaded King Charles I. But
God has now restored royal blood to the throne of England in the
person of his son."

"Was the king who was beheaded the king who gave the land to Great Heron Lord Baltimore?" Meas pressed. "Did not Charles I give to Great Heron all the land west of the Lenape River from Cape Henlopen as far north as Neshaminy Creek?"

Lame Foot raised his eyebrows and studied Meas as Meas puffed on his pipe. "It is true," Lame Foot continued, "that Charles I did grant Lord Baltimore a large tract of land around the Chesapeake Bay as far north as 40° latitude. But it is a doubtful case as to whether or not it comes east as far as the Delaware River."

"Commander Lame Foot," Meas asked, "why is it a doubtful case that Great Heron Baltimore owns all the land on the west side of the Lenape River including New Amstel and the Whorekill?"

A trace of anger grew in Lame Foot's voice as he answered. "Sage Meas, it's really none of your business, but here is your answer anyway. Lord Baltimore and Governor Hinoyossa connived to defraud the King of duties and tariffs owed him. I decided to put a stop to this illegal trade and bring New Amstel under the power of the King."

Meas took his pipe from his mouth and pointed the stem at Lame Foot. "Commander Lame Foot, would it then be correct to say that you invaded lands belonging to Great Heron Baltimore?"

Lame Foot squirmed on his stump. "Sage Meas, I have rooted out the Dutch usurpers from the Delaware River. As I said, Lord Baltimore's claim is a doubtful case."

"Commander Lame Foot," Meas continued his thrust, "would you say it is wrong to take lands from an English lord that were rightfully given him by the King?"

"If the Lord's claim is indeed valid, then it would be wrong to take the land from him. But like I said, it is a doubtful case."

"Then, Commander Lame Foot, if it is wrong to steal from Lord Baltimore, is it not also wrong to take the land from the Dutch and rob them of their possessions?"

"Sage Meas, I tire of answering your questions. I am the officer of the King in charge of his affairs on the Delaware. I will listen to any reasonable request the savages may make, but I will not return Matennecunk Island to the savages."

"Ah, Commander Lame Foot, this very night you will want to give Matennecunk Island back to the Lenape. Matennecunk only burdens you.

"When a thief steals, he must always look over his shoulder and live in fear that someone else will rob him. He who plucks a flower and stomps it underfoot can never enjoy its beauty like he who views it on the vine. The thief can never live in peace to enjoy his stolen goods. And if the thief gives his life defending his stolen goods, then whose will his stolen goods be?"

"Sage Meas," Lame Foot objected, "you make me out no better than a common thief. I have come to claim only what rightfully belongs to the King and to drive the Dutch usurpers from the King's lands. I have not robbed—" Lame Foot stopped.

"Commander Lame Foot," Meas spoke kindly, but again he pointed the stem of his pipe at Lame Foot, "you have deceived yourself.

"Commander Lame Foot, all the claims by the Schwanneks against Matennecunk are a farce. The pretenses of the King of England to this island stand as bare as a naked tree in a snowy field.

"Whether you stole Matennecunk and plundered the goods of Hinoyossa in the King's name, or whether you stole Matennecunk in your own name, you have no more right to the island or the goods you took than any other thief has to his loot.

"If might makes it right to steal, then the strongest thug may steal, rape, lie, kill, and murder at will. But it is not so.

"Commander Lame Foot, all men, even Schwanneks, know that the taunts of fiends haunt the spirits of those who do such wickedness. The guilty cannot escape. No matter how hard the wicked may try, they cannot dodge the arrows of the Great Spirit."

"Sage Meas, my spirit torments me not for enjoying the spoils of the victor. God used me to punish the brigand Hinoyossa and his cronies. 'Twas a just war if ever there was one."

"Does not the commander's spirit bother him for hanging a pious man on the Siconece, a man who only held out a white flag and asked to live in peace?" Meas asked.

"Sage Meas, that man was a dangerous heretic who with skillful words incited the people against the King. He taught against owning slaves; he harped on raising up the poor; and that rabble-rouser you call a man of peace even refused to place his people under the protection Governor Calvert offered him. I tell you, Plockhoy swung justly by order of the King and at the pleasure of Lord Baltimore. I carry no guilt for his soul."

"Does not Commander Lame Foot's spirit trouble him for looting a peaceful village belonging to a nation that was not at war with the King of England? The settlers on the Siconece earned everything they had with their own hands and stole from no one. They were not crooks like Hinoyossa, Two Tongue Boyer, and Hollow Log van Sweringen."

"Sage Meas, I am amazed at what all you bring up. No, I am not burdened by guilt. The soldiers flew out of control and raided Swanendael on their own. It could not be helped."

"Commander Lame Foot, did not the soldiers load the plunder on your ship? Did not the soldiers steal my wife and papoose and bring her on your ship? How can you say the soldiers were out of control?" Meas pressed. "Perhaps your spirit lies stark and still within you."

"Sage Meas, I like not the stings of your venomous tongue. You seek to teach me right from wrong. I do not need the guidance of a heathen savage, but am well able to look after my own spirit. You should be the one who worries about burning in hell without the grace of the Christian God."

"Commander Lame Foot, your god lurks in darkness beyond the mind. By your god nothing is wrong, and by your voice you suffer no

"You have deceived yourself."

–Meas to Commander Lame Foot (Sir Robert Carr)

guilt for theft or murder or rape. You think your god will pardon every cruelty you do if you only say, 'I did it in the King's name.'

"Commander Lame Foot, it is certain you know nothing of the ways of the Great Spirit who puts an instinct within each person that smites him when he does evil. The Great Spirit would not have us kill and steal. He would have all men dwell peaceably together in the Land of the Dawn.

"You must return Cool Water and her papoose to me. I will not kill or plunder if you will only return my wife to me."

Lame Foot sneered. "Sage Meas, if you think you will convince me to turn over my slave and her babe by a little sermon on guilt, you will wait for a long time. The King's soldiers are well armed."

Meas rose to his feet again. "Commander Lame Foot, you may spurn my little sermon. Nevertheless, the demons of guilt shall prick your spirit and haunt your soul. No matter where you go you shall not escape the taunting shrieks and tortured cries of the demons that hound you.

"And if words do not stir you, I will aid the demons in what they inflict upon you.

"Do not the demons in your foot, sent there by my arrow, constantly torture you? When the pain seizes you, do you not see Friend Dreamer holding the white flag and speaking kind words of peace? When you toss upon your couch, do you not see Friend Dreamer swinging on a rope and hear the screams of the fiends in your spirit?

"This very night we shall again stir the demons of guilt until you give up Cool Water and her papoose.

"You have eleven soldiers and guns with you. I have two hundred Lenape warriors armed with bows, tomahawks, and knives. Lenape warriors fight best at night where they slip in and out unseen by the foe to deliver their deadly blows.

"Warriors have already sealed off the island, cut the dykes, and scuttled the galliot. No one will leave or come to the island before the morning light.

"Your slaves and servants will not fight for you. Moreover, your soldiers will not fight—."

Lame Foot butted in. "Sage Meas, I see that the sumac smoke is going to your brain. Even if you have two hundred savages armed with sticks and stones, you cannot overcome well-armed and well-trained English soldiers behind thick brick walls."

"Commander Lame Foot, your soldiers will not fight," Meas repeated. "Your soldiers are cowards and attack only men and women and children who will not shoot at them."

Meas resumed his seat on the ground again and smoked thoughtfully for a time. Then he spoke once more with an air of finality. "Commander Lame Foot, I have talked with Sergeant Godefro. Why did you bring your warship so close upon Fort Amstel when the fort's cannons could have sunk it? Why did the Dutch not fire upon the English soldiers as they climbed over the wall?" Meas asked.

Meas's black eyes fixed on Lame Foot's eyes until the commander looked away. "But I remember," Meas continued, "you tire of answering questions, so I will answer them for you.

"You bartered with Fat Pig Hinoyossa[90] for the lives of his soldiers and the plunder at Fort Amstel. Fat Pig believed your promise that you would spare him and his lands and goods. He ordered his soldiers and cannons to hold fire. You lied to Fat Pig and his council and robbed them as well."

"Sage Meas," Lame Foot broke in, "an officer of the King will not treat such slander lightly."

"I care not one whit for Fat Pig and his gang of thieves," Meas continued. "Run them off.

"From your phony war at Fort Amstel you came down the River of

---

[90] Alexander D'Hinoyossa, his wife, and seven children became naturalized citizens of Maryland in 1671. In 1672 he went to Holland and obtained a captain's commission in the war against France. The Dutch court-martialed him and accused him of leaving his post, faintheartedness, unwillingness to fight, and mutiny. He was beheaded 8 August 1672.

the Lenape to the Siconece. There, without warning or cause, you set
your soldiers upon a peaceful people that raised not one gun against
you.

"Do you really think such brave soldiers will die fighting for a king
four moons distant? Or will they fight for a commander close by who
would senselessly have them scalped?

"Commander Lame Foot, your soldiers will give themselves up.
Nevertheless, convince yourself.

"The attack will begin shortly after dark. I would do you no harm
and my warriors will not harm you unless you shoot one gun first. But
I warn you that I will require the blood of every one of you if the least
harm comes to Cool Water or her papoose.

"Commander Lame Foot, do you wish to give up Cool Water and
her papoose now? Or do you wish to hear the wolves again tonight?"

Without another word Lame Foot rose from the stump and limped
stiffly toward the mansion. He slammed the heavy front door shut
with such fury that the sound echoed through the halls and high-
ceilinged rooms. Then all was still.

Meas slipped away into the trees and conferred with Pinna and
Tamenand. Then he made his way to the sheds and shacks around the
mansion and mingled with the servants and slaves.

Each one went peacefully about his evening task. "Yes, last night
was a scary night with the wolves so close," one admitted, "but the
livestock are now calmed down again."

"The livestock have quieted," a slave added, "but the dogs started
barking again this afternoon. The spirits will dance again tonight, I tell
you. I'm gonna stay close by the fire."

"Cool Water," commented a thin young girl, "says her man's coming
for her tonight. He's gonna carry her back home and set her free
again. Wish I could go with her."

A plump strong woman rebuked her, "Girl, you don't know what
you're asking for. Them savages will scalp you, roast you on hot coals,

and then eat you." The woman lowered her voice, and Meas couldn't make out what she said until the fat woman shook her head and said, "Not me! I'll take my chances with the white devils instead of the red ones."

"No! No! It's not true," the girl responded. "Cool Water says the Indians don't have slaves. The men love their wives and their papooses and will do anything for them.

"Cool Water says anyone can join the Lenape. She herself was a slave of a pirate and then the governor of Maryland. Meas bought her freedom and married her.

"Me? If I had the chance, I'd run in a heartbeat. I'd rather be hungry and free than a concubine of any English captain."

The older woman winced. "All I can say is that the striplings have to learn the hard way when they won't take advice. A skinny snippet will swing just as pretty as a fat slave," the plump woman warned.

Meas shadowed the young girl. He followed her to the well to draw water and spoke to her there. "I am Sage Meas," he said. "I have come to fetch Cool Water and take her home to the Siconece."

The girl started.

"Would you like to come with Cool Water?" Meas asked.

The girl nodded. "I'd do anything to be free."

"I like your spirit," said Meas. "I shall name you Free Otter.

"Free Otter, do you know that you must fight to live free, but to die a slave requires only that you do another's bidding?"

"Sage Meas, I am willing to do whatever you tell me if I can only escape this devil's clutches. Will you set me free like you did Cool Water?"

"Free Otter, if I free you from Commander Lame Foot and the Schwanneks catch you again, they will most certainly hang you."

"Ah, Sage Meas, I will risk the noose to strike loose these cursed bonds. I beg you, take me with you and Cool Water."

"Free Otter, tonight when the wolves howl and the first shed goes up in flames, you must make your way across the field to the stream where the cows drink. Do not be afraid. Many warriors are there to protect you."

"Sage Meas, can a friend come with me? He is strong and well able to fight."

"Free Otter, your friend may also come, but do not come together. Slip away one by one. Pass the word on to the other servants and slaves, even the soldiers. If they will come out to the stream, no one will harm them.

"After the commander returns Cool Water and her papoose to me, all those who come out to the stream will have the chance to choose whether they wish to live free on the Siconece or continue to serve the English as slaves and bondmen."

"Sage Meas, I will spread the good news. Tonight, all who come to the stream—servant, slave, or soldier—will not be harmed, and then ... they can choose, bond or free."

Meas watched Free Otter speed gracefully off into the growing darkness. Two water buckets suspended from the yoke across her shoulders did not slow her high and hurried step.

A thick darkness settled over the river, the island, and the mansion. The circle of warriors tightened around the mansion and buildings. The lone mastiff prowled loose in the yard. Rifles poked out through cracks in the shuttered windows. Chickens and guineas refused to settle on their usual roosts. Livestock and dogs milled about in confusion.

The circle tightened still further, driving all livestock, fowl, and dogs toward the mansion. Warriors threw the yard gates open and the great mastiff charged outward. A tremendous blow on the head sent him howling crazily to the mansion porch where he huddled in terror while his blood puddled on the cement before the front door.

As the circle tightened, it drove every farm beast and fowl within the yard. Then the yard gates slammed shut once more.

Meas let out a long plaintive howl. The horses and cattle stampeded wildly around the mansion. Shrieks of pain rang out as trampled dogs and fowl scrambled to get out of the way of thrashing hoofs. The wolf cries chased the animals around and around the yard, seemingly nipping at the flaying heels as the horses, sheep, goats, pigs, and cattle ran.

Amused warriors shouted, shrieked, and whistled at the perfect bedlam.

A lone gun cracked. The horses crashed through the yard fence and fled into the night with the rest of the herd panting and grunting along behind them.

The wolves quieted.

A small fire flickered at the base of a stable. Then the flames roared wildly upward as they consumed the wheat sheaves stacked around it and spread into the thatched roof above it.

Again the wolves howled, filling the night with a barrage of demonic noise. In the eerie firelight, servants and slaves began sneaking off toward the stream.

Another shed closer to the mansion burst into flame. The cries of panthers and owls, along with shrieks from tortured spirits, joined the wolves in their cruel medley. And at the front of the mansion Meas shouted the ghastly cry of Hollow Log Sweringen, "I am ruined. I am ruined."

More fugitives stole from the mansion. Two soldiers left their guns behind and joined the escapees at the stream.

Meas grilled the soldiers separately. Then he sent one of the soldiers back to the mansion accompanied by a squad of four warriors and Free Otter.

One of the slave shacks blazed up to brighten the sky. Bricks from the chimneys rattled and banged down the tiles of the mansion roof. All the while the shrieks and shouts and screams continued.

The fires died down. Suddenly the noise stopped. A ghostly stillness lurked in the darkness.

A great explosion in one wing of the mansion shook the entire building. In the next moment one hundred screaming Lenape rushed in upon the crazed commander and nine dazed soldiers who threw their guns on the floor.

Meas waited outside until Free Otter emerged from the darkness carrying Cool Water's papoose. "The little one is safe," said Free Otter.

"Where is Cool Water?" Meas asked.

"She is still with the commander," Free Otter replied.

"Free Otter, stay in the shadows until I find Cool Water."

Meas dashed inside the mansion. "Clear the house," he ordered the warriors. "Bring all the captives out to the stump in front of the mansion."

A fire blazed now near the stump, furnishing plenty of light to all around. Commander Lame Foot limped haughtily along at the head of the line of humbled soldiers and hopeful captives. Cool Water trailed along behind Lame Foot.

When all had gathered in the road by the stump, Commander Lame Foot spoke. "Sage Meas, you must be aware that your band of lawless savages has attacked soldiers of the King of England. If you persist in this war, you should know that the King will send more and more soldiers until the savages are completely crushed. The King will show no mercy.

"Sage Meas, if you do not bow before the soldiers of the King, the King will unleash the settlers in Maryland and Virginia and New England against all savages. They will be only too glad to destroy you.

"Sage Meas, on the other hand, if you are willing to give up this rash attack, I am prepared to make generous terms of peace.

"Sage Meas, if you will give up your plundering and allow my servants, slaves, and soldiers to dwell here in peace, I will give you Cool Water and her papoose and the copper tortoise. We will say no more about the burned buildings, the damaged mansion, the sunken galliot, or the dead dogs and ruined livestock."

"Commander Lame Foot," Meas replied, "it is not for the vanquished to dictate the terms of peace. This afternoon you refused my offer to stop the attack if you would only return my stolen wife and her papoose. Now I will tell you the terms of peace.

"Commander Lame Foot, you will give up Cool Water, her papoose, and the copper tortoise at once. If you do not produce them quickly, my warriors will plunder and burn every building on the island. You yourself will be burned and beheaded after the manner of the cruelties inflicted by the English upon their foes. Friend Dreamer has instructed me well in how the King himself treats his slightest enemies.

"Commander Lame Foot, your servants and slaves who came out to the stream during the attack may choose whether they wish to live free with us or wish to live in fear with you. I make only one exception for the soldier you sent out as a spy. He must stay with you.

"Commander Lame Foot, the warriors will take whatever they wish of weapons and goods. The island now belongs to the Lenape.

"Commander Lame Foot, if you agree to these terms and pledge to stop your wars and live peaceably among us, Cool Water will draw with pen and ink the treaty that we make with you this night. You and two of your soldiers will put their marks upon it and I, Pinna, and Tamenand will also put our marks upon it.

"Commander Lame Foot, do you sue for peace or do you want more of war?"

"Sage Meas, you lay harsh terms of peace upon us. Will you not treat my soldiers and me as prisoners of war and allow us to keep our arms and our honor? Must we be sold as slaves and criminals?"

"Commander Lame Foot, you sold the Dutch soldiers as slaves to Virginia. They had no choice. You are bound by the chains you have forged upon yourself—greed, hate, lust, murder, and deceit. From these I cannot set you free.

"You freely lie and steal and kill. Do you speak of honor? You bend truth as a child bends a willow withe to any shape he so desires. Your twisted words weary me.

"Commander Lame Foot, get me the papoose and the copper tortoise at once. Put your mark upon the peace treaty. If you do not wish to live in peace in the Land of the Dawn, return to your own homeland and there pillage and rape and kill till you die. You may not dwell here."

Meas turned to Cool Water and held out his hands. She came trembling to him. "Meas," she said, "he still hides my papoose. Do not trust him."

"My dear," Meas whispered, "do not fear. I have the papoose," and he wrapped her tightly in his arms. She laid her head upon his breast.

Cheers of "Bravo! Bravo!" gladdened the air as two hundred warriors, four black slaves, six English bondservants, and one English soldier joined together in the shouts.

Slowly Meas released one arm from Cool Water and gently nudged her to his side with the other. Then with arms intertwined they uplifted their outside arms to the cheering crowd.

Gradually the voices stilled so Meas could speak.

"Fellow Lenape, to be free in the Land of the Dawn calls forth boldness and courage. Thank you for your help in freeing Cool Water and giving her back to me.

"Fellow Lenape, casting aside the chains the Schwanneks would throw upon us comes not by rest," Meas said, clenching his fist, "but by courage that rouses to action. You have shown that courage."

Meas dropped his hand to his breast and lifted the silver tortoise high. Firelight glinted from it as he twitched the silver back and forth.

"Fellow Lenape, never forget. To take one bold step forward as Patriarch Tamenend did does not assure us that we and our children may dwell in this treasured land. To be free Lenape in the Land of the Dawn we must tread upon its sacred soil with Tamenend's spirit in our hearts."

Still holding the silver tortoise high, Meas shouted, "WE CARRY THE SPIRIT OF TAMENEND IN THE LAND OF THE DAWN."

Two hundred Lenape warriors answered his challenge, "WE CARRY THE SPIRIT OF TAMENEND IN THE LAND OF THE DAWN."

Again and again the cry rolled across the island before it faded into the sighing of the winter wind as it rushed across Matennecunk Island and the divided River of the Lenape that surrounded it.

Some say that when the winter wind whistles over the frozen river and sweeps across the island one can still hear the faint cry, "We carry the Spirit of Tamenend in the Land of the Dawn."

***

Narrated by Glikkikan

The festival on Neshaminy Creek went on for fives of days. Hundreds of Lenape from up and down the river came for the games, the council fires, and the storytelling. For my part, I chose to tell the life story of Sage Meas. I tried to tell the story of his life exactly as Owechela told it to me.

It went well for me. The children as well as the old men sat in rapt attention for such long periods that my voice would nearly give out. Many of the old men had known Sage Meas and had heard him speak. They nodded their heads in approval many times while I spoke.

When I held up the copper tortoise that belonged to Meas's mother, everyone leaned forward and all became perfectly still. I passed the copper tortoise around that many might see it and reverently touch it.

When I held up the silver tortoise, everyone gasped. It was like the flash of close lightning before the thunder cracks. My throat tightened and tears came to my eyes. I had to stop.

One of the old shamans broke out with the cry, "We carry the Spirit of Tamenend in the Land of the Dawn." The huge crowd took up the chant. Many tears were shed that day, and I didn't feel too bad about my own.

By the time I returned to Owechela's wigwam high above Neshaminy Creek, he was very weak. "Tell me about the festival," he said.

Owechela listened carefully to my excited report. Then he asked, "Did you tell the Lenape what the Schwanneks did to the Susquehannocks? Did you tell the Lenape about the Black and Yellow Dog Koketotoka saw in his dream? Did you tell the Lenape of the dove with the claws on his feet that Sage Meas saw in his vision?[91] The Lenape must never forget these stories."

"No, Owechela," I answered, "I do not know these stories."

"Then I will tell them to you the best I can," Owechela promised. Many times, as he told me the stories, it seemed his mind wandered off. I wasn't sure he had the story straight, but he always remembered to ask me, "Did you get it?" Then Owechela would say, "Now you tell the story to me."

The first story I pieced together for Owechela was the fall of the Susquehannocks. Owechela wasn't sure of the time the Susquehannock disaster had occurred, but it had to be about ten years after Meas made the Lenape peace treaty with Commander Lame Foot.[92]

The new English government in New York, as the English called New Amsterdam, refused to turn over the settlers or the land along

---

[91] The clawed dove Meas saw in his vision was William Penn. William Penn finally thwarted Lord Baltimore's drive to take over all the settlements on the Delaware.

[92] The year was 1675, which coincides with Bacon's Rebellion in Virginia in 1676.

the Lenape River to Great Heron Baltimore. Instead, the Duke of York's appointed governor continued the Dutch way of stirring the Mengwe[93] against the Susquehannocks.

For years, Little Black Heron Baltimore[94] adopted the policy of former governors of Maryland and made peace treaties with the Susquehannocks, giving them papers and silver medals tied with black and yellow ribbons. The treaties pledged protection and friendship "as long as the sun and moon shall endure."

The Mengwe now continued their old treachery of murder and leaving false evidence at the scene. In this way they stirred the Marylanders against the Susquehannocks.

One summer morning at daybreak, the Mengwe urged a Doeg Indian[95] to attack a Virginia herdsman named Robert Hen. Then the Mengwe killed the Doeg and left both Robert Hen and the Doeg horribly gashed and torn on Robert Hen's doorstep.

If it had really been a war party of Doegs, they would most certainly have taken their slain warrior with them. But the attackers did not take the dead warrior with them because they were Mengwe.

Settlers on the way to church discovered the murders. On hearing of the bloody deed, Colonel Mason and Captain Brent quickly collected thirty men and set out in hot pursuit. The avenging force "followed" the trail twenty miles up the Potomack River and crossed the river into Maryland.

Any Lenape knows that a Doeg war party would have left no trail. But these Schwanneks "followed" the Mengwe ruse twenty miles, crossed the river, and came straight to two wigwams, the one filled with Doegs and the other with Susquehannocks. The Schwanneks shot down ten Doegs and fourteen Susquehannocks before they stopped firing.

---

[93] Particularly the Senecas, one of the Five Nations, or Iroquois.
[94] Charles Calvert, governor of Maryland and son of Cecilius Calvert, or Lord Baltimore II.
[95] Doeg Indians in Virginia were likely an offshoot of the Nanticokes on the eastern shore of Maryland, and both were considered Grandchildren of the Lenape.

The Schwanneks never offered any gifts or sadness for the slain Susquehannocks, but they feared revenge by the grieved parties.

Again, the Mengwe struck in Virginia. This time Maryland and Virginia massed two armies totaling one thousand men and marched to the Susquehannock Fort on the north side of the Piscataway River.[96] Surprised by the sudden attack, the one hundred Susquehannocks—warriors, old men, women, and children—living within the fort had no time to prepare for a siege.

Under a white flag, six of the Susquehannock chiefs came out of the fort to talk with the commanders and demanded to know the reason for the hostile array. The chiefs assured the commanders it was the Mengwe who had committed the outrages in Maryland and Virginia. The chiefs showed the commanders the treaties and the silver medals tied with the black and yellow ribbons.

The pleas of the Susquehannock chiefs were only the wind blowing on the rock. The Schwannek commanders knocked all six chiefs in the head.

When the Susquehannocks in the fort learned what had happened, they determined not to give in to such faithless treachery. The defenders repulsed all attacks by the Schwanneks. They made frequent and fierce sallies against the raiders. The defenders drove some of the attackers' horses into the fort and ate them for food.

Whenever the Schwanneks proposed talk or surrender, the Susquehannocks asked, "Where are our chiefs?"

After six weeks of the siege, the defenders destroyed everything of usefulness in the fort, left a few old men, and seventy-five others escaped into the night.

The Susquehannock warriors raged down the Rappahannock, York, and James Rivers, wielding the tomahawk, knife, and gun, till they

---

[96] The site of the fort lay directly across the Potomac River from George Washington's Mt. Vernon. One of the commanders of the expedition was Col. John Washington, the great-grandfather of General George Washington.

killed sixty settlers, ten for each murdered chief.

Then they paused and sent a letter to Governor Berkeley of Virginia:

> First: Why do you, a professed friend, take up arms in behalf of Maryland, your avowed enemy?
>
> Second: We regret that former friends have become such violent enemies that they pursue us even into another province.
>
> Third: We complain that our chiefs, sent out to treat for peace, not only were murdered, but the act was countenanced by the governor.
>
> Fourth: We declare that, seeing no other way of obtaining satisfaction, we have killed ten of the English common folk for each of our murdered chiefs.
>
> Finally: We propose, if the Virginians will make us compensation for the damages sustained by the attack upon us and withhold all aid from the Marylanders, to renew the ancient league of friendship. Otherwise, we and those in league with us will continue the war so unfairly begun, and fight it out to the last man.

Governor Berkeley made no answer to the Susquehannock cry for justice and the offer of peace. Neither did the Schwanneks ever punish any of the guilty or offer any tokens of grief for the cruel deeds.[97]

I asked Owechela if I had told the story of the Susquehannocks properly. He opened his eyes wide and looked hard at me as though it was hard for him to grasp my question.

"Yes," he said. "Yes," he said again, "I'm sure you did."

[97] This whole account is condensed from the *Historical Magazine*, Vol. I, No. 3, March 1857. Historical Society of Cecil County, MD.

After a pause, Owechela went on. "Glikkikan," he said, "it is possible to know the story and miss the lesson.

"Glikkikan, never trust a Schwannek. When it comes to the land, a Schwannek will do anything—cheat, lie, steal, and kill. A Schwannek is a slave of the land.

"Glikkikan, I hear the words of Sage Meas, 'If you touch the earth lightly, it will nourish you. But if you beat heavily upon it, the earth will bind up your spirit.' Only those who understand will be free in spirit."

Owechela closed his eyes again. "Glikkikan," he said, "now tell me the story of the Black and Yellow dog on the Siconece."

I told Owechela I would try.

***

Meas brought Cool Water, the papoose, four black slaves, six bondservants, and one soldier along home to the Siconece.

The former bondservants and the ex-soldier readily mixed with the free ways of the Dutch band and settled among them.

Free Otter and her strong man, along with the second slave couple, presented a special problem. Their skin was black. If they dwelt openly with the Dutch or English or Indians, they would be captured by slave traders and hauled off to Maryland or Virginia at any time.

Meas hid the black freedmen in the marsh. He taught them the Lenape way of living lightly from the abundance of the earth. Weak Gun traded the work of their diligent hands for cloth and spices to supply their meager needs.

Free Otter asked for nothing more. Four of them no longer bowed to the will of another. Now they owned themselves.

Word of the freed slaves spread. Whispered from ear to ear, "Free Otter," leaped from plantation to plantation like a wildfire driven by the wind.

Desperate slaves with nothing but hope to drive them endured hunger, nakedness, and peril. They risked hounds, beatings, terror, and death if caught.

Many did not make it. If caught, they were beaten, hanged, or sold. But if a runaway could make it into the marshes and whisper that sacred name, "Free Otter," an Indian "hunter" might guide him toward the Siconece. The "hunter" might point the slave to a canoe he could "steal" or drop a bag of parched maize or dried meat on his path.

At first only a few runaways made it to the Siconece, bruised, bleeding, and exhausted. Then tens came in a year's time.

Free Otter nurtured the newcomers back to health and told them about life as a free man. Each person must give up the desire for revenge and evade rather than punish pursuers.

"We do not want to start a war," Free Otter warned. "We only want to be free."

Meas spread the escapees out in the marshes and in haunts only he knew about. He taught inductees never to dwell in groups and to keep all visiting to short periods.

"When hunted, never mass. Always scatter," Meas instructed. "Schwanneks cannot bring horses into these places. They must come on foot.

"Bloodhounds cannot trail through water. They will be of little use to the hunter. But you also can set fierce dogs upon them.

"Learn your surroundings well. If you are followed, dash about in circles as the rabbit does, giving time for others to escape.

"If the hunter will not leave, trap him. I will teach you how to hang the nooses and how to use a windfall and how to place the poisoned spikes in the pit and how to set copperheads upon him.

"Let the hunter become the hunted. And if he still will not leave, it is your life or his. Kill him."

As a result of several fruitless pursuits and two slavers who never returned, few slavers dared venture into the marshes and haunts bordering the west side of the Lenape Bay.

The slaves on Maryland and Virginia plantations were not the only ones who heard of the runaway refuge on the Siconece. The Schwanneks who claimed to own the slaves traced rumors to the Siconece as the likely hideout.

Little Black Heron Calvert[98] spit fire when he heard the rumors. It rankled him that eight years after Commander Lame Foot took Cool Water and hanged Friend Dreamer, the Whorekill was still under the Duke's control. Now a slave hideout at the Whorekill?

Little Black Heron sent Brigand Jones[99] with eight armed horsemen charging into the Whorekill. They tied up No Smoke Wiltbanck and all his neighbors and kept a guard over them while they plundered the houses and made off with their goods.

In the autumnal month of the same year, Brigand Jones returned again to the Whorekill, this time with thirty armed horsemen. Brigand Jones held a pistol to the head of No Smoke, he being the village chief, and the Maryland wolfmen forced their way into the King's courtroom.

There Jones and his wolfmen ordered No Smoke and the settlers to make an oath that they would be true to Great Heron Baltimore. No Smoke, Weak Gun, and all the other settlers were not willing to take the oath.

The Jones Crow Court threw the settlers in prison, where they kept them without meat or drink for a day. Then they brought the prisoners again into the courtroom. Brigand Jones threatened the settlers: "If you do not take the oath to Lord Baltimore, we will carry you to prison at St. Mary's City and take all your estates here."

---

[98] Charles Calvert was governor of Maryland from 1660 till his father's death in 1675, when he became the Third Lord Baltimore.

[99] Following instructions of Lord Baltimore, Governor Charles Calvert issued a commission to Thomas Jones of Worcester County on 20 June 1672. Captain Jones's orders were to "muster military forces to subdue ... all enemies ... to encounter, fight with, overcome, and destroy or take prisoners ..." See Archives of Maryland Online, Vol. V, pp. 110-111.

Seeing no other way, No Smoke, Weak Gun, and all the other townsmen made the oath to Great Heron. Brigand Jones and his wolfmen again plundered the Whorekill and left Raven Jenkins, a surveyor for Great Heron, in charge of Great Heron's government. Then Brigand Jones and his wolfmen finally departed to the south.

As soon as the wolfmen were out of sight, Weak Gun asked Raven Jenkins if he could continue his trading under the new government. Raven Jenkins sent a letter to Little Black Heron.

Two months later, in the hunting month, Raven Jenkins handed Weak Gun a scrolled paper tied with a black and yellow ribbon.

Cool Water read the paper to Weak Gun and Meas:

> These are in the name of the right honble the Lord Proprietary to License and Authorize Harman Cornellinson Merchant to trade with any of the Indian or Christian Inhabitants of the Counties of Somerset Dorchester and Worcester within this
>
> Province for any Furrs Skins or other Truck usually traded for with the Indians and the same to transport and sell at his Pleasure provided that he Obey and Comply with the Act of Assembly made touchᵍ Indian trade ...
>
> Given under my hand & seal at Arms this 16ᵗʰ day of December in the fourty first year of the Dominion of Cecilius & cᵃ Annoq Domini 1672
>
> Maryland ssᵗ
By his Excellency the Capᵗ General

Weak Gun laughed. "Sage Meas," he said, "now I am legal. Great Heron puts a gun to my head and gives me a piece of paper. I trade honestly and fairly as I did before, but now neither Great Heron nor Little Heron will bother me."

"Weak Gun," Meas cautioned, "do not trust the paper. A paper is no better than the word of the one who made it. We already know that both Little Heron and Great Heron are only pretty skunks with the bite of the copperhead in their mouths.

"Weak Gun, Little Heron is the Black and Yellow Dog that Koketotoka saw in his dream. He is the one who will uproot and pee on the Siconece anthill. Beware of him.

"Weak Gun, I strain at the meaning of the license. It says you may trade with the Indians and the Christians. Who or what is a Christian?

"Is a Christian anyone who has a white skin? Are Commander Lame Foot, Little Heron, Brigand Jones, and Raven Jenkins all Christians because they have white skins?

"Weak Gun, can a Christian be found by the color of the blood in his body? The same red blood courses through the veins of villains as pulsed through Friend Dreamer's heart. The same red blood races through the breast of Free Otter and every black person who hides in our refuge. I see the cow, the deer, the possum, the hog, and the rat all bleed red blood. Are they all Christians?

"Weak Gun, who are the Christians you may trade with? May you trade with the black people in our refuge?"

"Sage Meas, you have raised a good point. The license does not define a Christian. Therefore, I will trade with all men as Christians." Weak Gun laughed again. "Sage Meas, I said all men. That includes women," and he winked at Cool Water, "but no cows and no spirits."

Weak Gun's trading prospered as the freedmen numbers in the refuge swelled into the hundreds. Meas and Free Otter made sure that the freedmen traded only with Weak Gun.

Weak Gun took Meas's warning. He stowed all his peltries, beaver, fur, and truck in a hidden cellar on Tired Moon Pond. Within the cellar Weak Gun also kept a heavy chest of coins, papers, and valuables locked inside. Only Meas knew its location.

The stash grew to a considerable size.

Eight months after Cool Water read Little Heron's trading license to

Weak Gun, the Dutch captured New York and New Castle[100] and sent officers to the Whorekill to demand that Raven Jenkins yield to the new Dutch government.

Raven Jenkins and all of Lord Baltimore's crows on the Whorekill fled. Two months later the Dutch returned once more to the Whorekill and again demanded submission to the Dutch government. The Dutch officials harmed no one nor plundered any of their goods. This time No Smoke and the rest of the inhabitants swore to be true to the Dutch government.[101]

Weak Gun continued his trading undisturbed by the new Dutch government.

The peace was short-lived.

This time Little Black Heron sent forty horsemen from across the Chesapeake crashing down on the Whorekill. They charged into the Whorekill with their swords drawn, fire in their eyes, and venom spewing out of their mouths.

"We will have this place for Merry-Land," Yellow Dog Howell[102] cried at Chief No Smoke Wiltbanck.

"We did not and will not defend this place against Indians, English, Marylanders, or the Dutch," No Smoke Wiltbanck calmly replied. "We live peaceably with all men."

"Take the place if ye be strong enough," No Smoke suggested. "No one will stop you. We be only defenseless Christians who obey our Lord Christ's command, 'Love your enemies.' "

"That is why we have come to the Whorekill," shouted Yellow Dog. "Since you will not defend yourselves, we have come to defend you. Though it cost the province of Merry-Land a million in tobacco, we will protect you."

---

[100] On 12 August 1673 the conquering Dutch commanders commissioned Captain Anthony Colve governor-general of the Duke of York's former province.

[101] About the middle or the end of October 1672.

[102] Captain Thomas Howell of Baltimore County commissioned by Governor Charles Calvert, 1 October 1673, "to raise forty men...to lead them away unto the said county of Worcester...to fight and overcome, kill, destroy, and vanquish..." Archives of Maryland Online, Vol. XV, p. 28.

The forty Yellow Dogs marched into the place, killed many of the cattle, and ate and drank with the people for eighteen days.

During their stay, the Yellow Dogs asked many questions of the settlers about the savages and the black freedmen. "Had the settlers seen any niggers? Where were the niggers hiding? Were the savages protecting the niggers? How did the niggers get supplies?"

"Who knows? How can you tell?" the settlers answered vaguely.

The Yellow Dogs learned little about the freedman refuge. Even when they made armed forays beyond the Whorekill, they found only a few weak Indian villages with no sign of Blacks among them. Of course, the Yellow Dogs had no stomach for hikes deep into the marshes without their horses.

But sometimes settlers did let slip the name of a wealthy merchant and Indian trader named Weak Gun who remained absent from his dwelling next to Tired Moon Pond.

"Does Weak Gun trade only with Indians and Christians?" the Yellow Dogs asked. Villagers only shrugged.

The supplies in the Whorekill ran out. The horses ate all the hay and the grain. The settlers had no supplies left. No Dutch soldiers showed up to fight. After his eighteen-day stay, Yellow Dog Howell gathered up his ravaging pack and left the town. "The town was too poor to support the army," Yellow Dog griped.

Everyone breathed prayers of thanksgiving. Their "defenders" were gone. Weak Gun returned, bringing a rich supply of winter furs to his lonely cabin.

Then the Yellow Dogs swept back into the Whorekill and surrounded the settlement. Each Yellow Dog knew his man. There was no hiding or escaping.

Yellow Dog Howell commanded the settlers to muster next to Tired Moon Pond and to be sure to bring their arms and ammunition. Yellow Dogs bound Weak Gun and began to question him about his trading. "Do you trade only with Christians and Indians? Where is your license? Where are your furs?" the hounds asked.

Weak Gun would only say that he traded honestly and fairly according to the laws of Maryland. Little Black Heron's soldiers took burning matches and held them to Weak Gun's fingers till he told them where his hiding place was. They rushed to the cellar, took all his furs, and broke into his chest and stole whatever they wanted.

Then Yellow Dog Howell's "brave" soldiers took all the guns and ammunition, all the boats, and everything else of value. They killed all the remaining animals, bound some of the settlers, and burned every house, building, and shed to the ground ... save one. God spared one barn for the expectant mothers to shelter in that terribly cold winter night.[103]

The Lenape wept at how the Schwanneks had treated their own countrymen.

Again I stopped and asked Owechela if I had told well the story of the Black and Yellow Dog on the Siconece.

Owechela lay still on his mat. Finally he pulled his blanket tight up around his neck and slowly opened his eyes.

"Glikkikan," he said, "never trust the Schwanneks. If they treat other Christians as they did our Friends of Peace, what will they do to the Lenape?

"Glikkikan, tell me once more what happened to Cool Water and Free Otter." Owechela closed his eyes.

I reached down and took his hand into my own and knelt there before him. Owechela smiled.

I couldn't keep back the tears as I told the story we both knew so well.

[103] Christmas Eve, 1673. The Maryland legislature awarded Captain Howell and his soldiers more than twenty thousand pounds of tobacco for their part in the cruelties of this raid. Archives of Maryland Online, Volume II, p. 416.

HOMELAND IN MY HEART

The Susquehannocks made good on their promise to Governor Berkeley. They rushed down suddenly upon Virginia Schwanneks killing men, women, and children and then disappeared into the fastnesses of bogs, marshes, and swamps. Even armed Schwanneks rightly feared ambush if they dared to follow the Susquehannocks.

A slave from a Schwannek planter at the head of the James River[104] escaped and made his way to the Siconece. A second slave from the same planter escaped and fled across the Chesapeake. The planter's overseer gave chase, hunted down the slave with dogs, and shot him. The slave died gasping, "Free Otter."

The overseer never made it back across the Chesapeake. The Susquehannocks got him.

An army of enraged Virginians one thousand strong marched to the Siconece. They spread out across the miles and combed the marshes together. Indians and blacks alike fanned out seeking desperately to escape.

There was no escape. There was no mercy.

Young and old, men and women, red and black—all fell under the murderous fire of the Schwannek killers.

Oh, there were a scattered few who eluded the army. Sage Meas knew the haunts too well. They could never trap him.

Sage Meas gathered up Cool Water in his arms and laid her to rest beside his mother and Friend Dreamer. He lifted the copper tortoise from her breast and laid it over his own chest, directly above the silver tortoise.

Free Otter, too, earned a place of rest in that sacred spot. Even today her spirit roams free over the Siconece.

Sage Meas fled the Siconece. He made his way to Passayunk and married Chief Pinna's youngest daughter, Sweet Water.

He traveled with Sweet Water far up Neshaminy Creek past the spot

---

[104] The plantation of Nathaniel Bacon, the leader of Bacon's Rebellion against Governor William Berkeley. The galvinizing cause of the rebellion was the indiscriminate killing of all Indians.

where the Little Neshaminy joins in and the double stream becomes one.[105] He followed the north branch of the Neshaminy till the stream became small enough one could jump across it on a summer day.

From Neshaminy Creek, Sage Meas led Sweet Water north up the hill to a spring where sweet cool water bubbled out of the earth and ran back toward Neshaminy Creek. He built a wigwam there on the rock-strewn soil, and there in Peace Valley, Sweet Water bore Sage Meas a son.

That son was my father.

⸻

I squeezed Owechela's hand. Owechela smiled peacefully. Without opening his eyes, Owechela whispered, "Glikkikan, always seek the truth. Hunt for the gold—."

I felt Owechela's hand go limp.

I knelt there all night. When the first rays of light pushed the darkness westward, I rose, turned to the east, lifted my hands, and chanted the ancient prayer of the Lenape.

> Great Spirit,
> Maker of the sky, the earth, the sun, the moon,
> Keeper of the spirits of the fish, the birds, the animals, the trees, the stones.
> Guardian of the Four Winds,
> Thank you for bringing light again to the People of the Dawn.
> Thank you for sending fire to warm our houses and cook our food.
> Thank you for bringing water to inspire the ground and to quench our thirst.
> Thank you for the ground to grow the maize and the deer to give us meat.

---

[105] *Nischam-hanne* means "two streams" or "double stream," signifying a stream formed by the joining of two branches.

HOMELAND IN MY HEART

For the ancient song of the Lenape,
For the everlasting sun that rises this day,
I, Glikkikan, orator of the Lenni Lenape, thank you.

When I had finished the chant, I stood motionless with my right arm raised and my two fingers pointing toward the horizon. In my raised left hand I held the copper and the silver tortoises. I remained there motionless until the flaming ball rose over the Land of the Dawn.

My heart floated like a feather borne along by a brisk breeze, and my spirit soared with strength over the Land of the Dawn.

Now, I too, carried the Spirit of Tamenend in the Land of the Dawn.

Now, I too, like Tamenend and both my grandfathers, Meas and Owechela, possessed the Land of the Dawn in my heart.

This was my homeland.

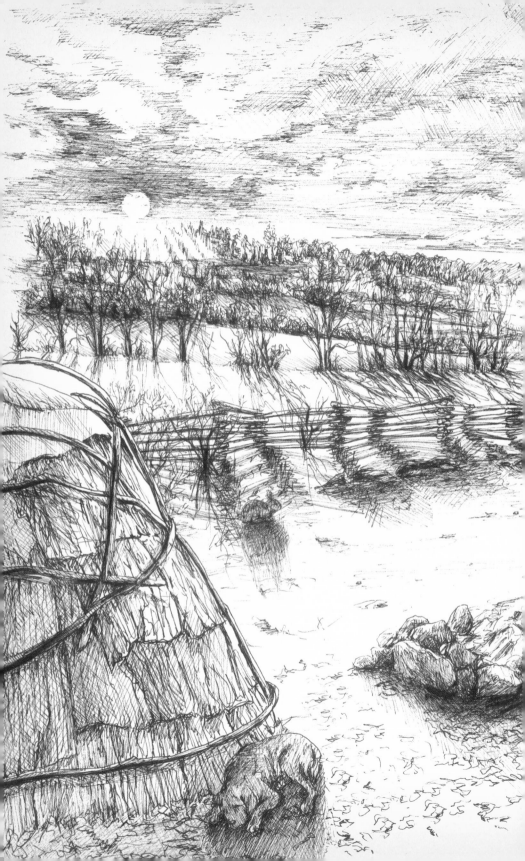

"Now, I too, possess the homeland in my heart!"

—Glikkikan in Peace Valley

CQ210

Cast of Main Characters

Bad Dog Hossitt—Gillis Hossitt, head of the first (1632) Dutch colony at Swanendael (Lewes, Delaware). Father of Meas.

Bantie Utie—Colonial Nathaniel Utie, a pompous Maryland officer sent to drive the Dutch settlers from New Amstel.

Big Bull Godefro—Sergeant Godefro Meyer von Cloppenburgh, a Dutch officer present at the overthrow of Fort Amstel by the English.

Big Field Fendall—Josias Fendall, Maryland governor, large tobacco farmer, and guardian of Cool Water.

Blackbeard—Edward Teach, self-styled Catholic privateer who raided shipping in the Caribbean and along the Atlantic Coast.

Commander Lame Foot—Sir Robert Carr, the English officer sent to secure English mastery of the Delaware River.

Cool Water—Maria, a pirated slave girl of dubious ancestry purchased by Meas and adopted into the Lenape tribe.

Ever-Be-Joyful—A grieving Lenape mother who helped bring about peace between the Lenape and the Cherokee.

Falling Leaf Cock—Lasse Cock, a Swedish lad whose life included trader, translator, Indian agent, and advocate.

Fat Pig Alexander Hinoyossa—An unprincipled Dutch soldier who became governor of all Dutch possessions on the Delaware.

Friend Dreamer Cornelisen—Pieter Cornelisen Plockhoy, a Dutch Mennonite visionary who led 41 settlers to Swanendael in 1663.

Glikkikan—A young Lenape boy being trained as an orator by his grandfather, Patriarch Owechela.

Governor Philip Calvert—Great Heron Baltimore's half-brother. He corrupted the treaty with Chief Pinna.

Great Heron Baltimore—Cecilius Calvert, Lord Baltimore II (1605-1675). A land-hungry lord who favored Catholics, but cruelly treated Indians, sects, and rival settlers. He never set foot on Maryland soil.

Hollow Log Sweringen—Garret van Sweringen, a Dutch nobleman deranged by the shock of the complete reversal of his fortunes.

Isadilla—The only son of a doting Lenape chief. When pushed beyond his physical limits, he turned into a robin.

Jitter Hen Alricks—Jacob Alricks (1603-1659). A wealthy Dutchman who came to the Delaware River in 1657 and was appointed the first city director of New Amstel. He appears to have been worrisome and insecure in his position.

Kill Weed—Cool Water's Indian slave whom Meas bought, carried to the Siconece, and adopted as his own son.

Chief Koketotoka—A drunken sot who had a spiritual revival and then ably led his people. Half-brother to Meas.

Little Heron Baltimore—Charles Calvert, Lord Baltimoe III (1637-1715). The heartless and vain governor of Maryland. A son of Lord Baltimore II, the proprietor.

Sage Meas—A Lenape orator/shaman who sought the meaning of Lenape life during the onslaught of the Schwanneks.

Meoppitas—A brother of Chief Koketotoka and a half-brother of Meas. He died of smallpox.

Sachem Mattahorn—A head Lenape chief who sought to preserve his people by allying the Lenape, Swedes, and Susquehannocks against the Dutch and Mengwe.

No Smoke Wiltbanck—Helmanus Wiltbank, the practical-minded leader of the 1663 Mennonite colony on the Whorekill.

Patriarch Owechela—An aged Lenape chief tells the story of his people to his grandson, Glikkikan.

Chief Pinna—Chief from Passayunk who treated with Philip Calvert and assisted Meas in the raid on Matennecunk Island.

Scribe Coursey—Henry Coursey, secretary and high councilor in Maryland who abetted the cheating of the savages.

Soft Heart—Wife of Governor Josias Fendall. Cool Water's guardian and teacher.

Strutting Turkey Stuyvesant—Peter Stuyvesant, an aggressive Dutch governor of New Amsterdam from 1647 to 1664 and conqueror of the Swedes on the Delaware.

Chief Tamenand—Friend of Meas who preserved the Spirit of Tamenend among the Lenape. Lived on Neshaminy Creek.

Oracle Tamenend—The Lenni Lenape leader who received the gift of the Land of the Dawn from the Great Spirit.

Shaman Teotacken—A highly regarded Lenape chief and medicine man thought to have great power over evil spirits.

Think Fast Sweringen—A French lady who sought Meas's aid in battling her husband's acute depression.

Two Tongue Boyer—Alexander Sander Boyer, a corrupt Indian trader and a regular interpreter for Dutch officials in Indian affairs.

Weak Gun Cornelisen—Harmen Cornelisen Spycker, a former Dutch soldier, special friend of Meas, brother of Plockhoy, and Indian trader.

Place Names

Appoquinimink—Near present Odessa, Delaware
Bommelerweert—Burlington Island, Burlington, New Jersey
Christina—Wilmington, Delaware
Fort Altena—Wilmington, Delaware
Fort Casimir—New Castle, Delaware
Hoerenkill—Whore's Creek. Today: Lewes, Delaware
Lenape Bay—Delaware Bay
Lenape River—Delaware River
Manahachtánienk—Manhattan Island, New York City
Matennecunk Isle—Delaware River, Burlington, New Jersey
Minquas Kill—Christina River, Wilmington, Delaware
New Amstel—New Castle, Delaware
New Amsterdam—New York City
North River—Hudson River, New York State
Odessa—Delaware, near Elkton, Maryland
Passayunk—Schuylkill River, Philadelphia, Pennsylvania
Port Tobacco—Near La Plata, Charles County, Maryland
Sea Shell Dune—Cape Henlopen, Lewes, Delaware
Shackamoxon—Kensington, Philadelphia, Pennsylvania
Siconece Creek—Lewes Creek, Lewes Delaware
South River—Delaware River: edge of Delaware, Pennsylvania, and
    New Jersey
St. Mary's City—Entry of Potomac River into Chesapeake Bay,
    Maryland: first capital of Maryland
Suppeckongh—Christina Kill, Wilmington, Delaware
Swanendael—Valley of Swans. Today: Lewes, Delaware
Tinicum Island—Due east of Chester, Pennsylvania
Tired Moon Pond—Blockhouse Pond, Lewes, Delaware

Fiction, History, and Truth

Beyond the historical name, we know practically nothing about Meas. He is a created character made to fit into the events and the times as I understand them. He is the hero of the story, reacting to historical events and circumstances in heroic ways. Without him there would not be a story, but a drab recounting of historical events. One could call this writing fiction.

Cool Water is wholly fictitious. Yet she helps to bring to life the strong economic, racial, religious, and political turmoil of the times in a way that no "straight history" could do.

Friend Dreamer Plockhoy is pure history and much of what is written about him comes from his own writing. The exact cause and date of his death is uncertain, although his hanging death by the soldiers is highly possible.

Most of the other characters are historical, and I fit them into the story true to the facts that are recorded about them. Sometimes I have added to their life things beyond the historical record.

The taking of Matennecunk Island and the slave refuge on the Siconece are wholly imaginary. We could wish they were true happenings, but there is no evidence to back it up.

What is written about Sir Robert Carr, his military exploits on the Delaware River and his occupancy on Matennecunk Island are true to what I could find about him. That is history.

The end of the slave refuge on the Siconece fits well with the indiscriminate killing of all Indians during Nathaniel Bacon's rebellion against Lord Berkley. That is history.

I believe that a writer of this kind of story can come closer to conveying the historical events and the times to the reader than a writer of "straight history," because he deals with feelings and thoughts and intents of the people involved. The storyteller deals with why people did the things they did.

This is not to say that writers of straight history do not slant the things they say or present limited facts in an attempt to lead the reader to wrong conclusions. For some writers, the truth is like a cloak they wear when it is convenient.

It is never my intent to mislead or deceive the reader. I have a great concern that while telling this story, I present the truth, not only in detail, but also in spirit. I may misconstrue a few details, but in the broad sense I aim to present to the reader a true understanding of colonial and Lenape history.

Yet as I wander through papers, books, and internet vastness in an effort to recreate people and places and events of three hundred years ago, I often grope through time and space and wonder, *Exactly, what is the truth?*

When hunting for the truth in events that happened three hundred years ago, it is never easy to know for sure what really happened. For one thing, the records are often scarce or nonexistent. For another, we seldom have both sides of a conflict recorded. The victor's tale is the one written down. Where we have more than one report of the same thing available, the various accounts often contradict each other or put an entirely different slant on what the observer saw.

Take this jingle, describing the natives, written by Richard Frame, a 1692 visitor to "Pensilvania"; [emphasis mine]

> Those that were here before the Sweeds and Fins,
> Were *Naked Indians*, Cloathed with their Skins ...
> Unless they are of *Esau's* scattered Seed,
> Or of some other *wild corrupted Breed*.
> They *take no care* to plow, nor yet to sow,
> Nor how to till their Land they do not know ...
> They neither do New Moons nor Sabbath keep,
> *Without much Care* they eat, they drink, they sleep;
> Those *Infidels* that dwelleth in the Wood,
> I shall conclude of them so far so good.

Here are excerpts from another description of the natives of Western New Jersey written by Gabriel Thomas. Gabriel Thomas lived in Pennsylvania and Jersey fifteen years before publishing this account in London in 1698.

> The first Inhabitants of this Countrey were the Indians
> ... for they *observe the New Moons* with great Devotion, and
> Reverence: ...
> Their chief Imployment is in Hunting, Fishing, and
> Fowling, and making Canows, or Indian Boats, and Bowls, in
> all which Arts *they are very dexterous and ingenious* ...
> Their Womens Business chiefly consists in *planting of Indian
> Corn*, and dress their Victuals, which they *perform very neatly
> and cleanily* ... In short, the Women are *very ingenious in their
> several Imployments as well as the Men.*
> Their Young Maids are naturally *very modest and shamefac'd:*
> And their young Women when newly married, are very nice
> and shy ...

I have read so many similar conflicting accounts of early America that sometimes I stand with Pontius Pilate in doubt and say, *"What is the truth?"*

For instance, I read the above jingle by Richard Frame and conclude that he wanted to picture the Indians as heathen savages worthy of destruction. Then settlers, in all good conscience, could kill the Indians and take their land. I read the above prose of Gabriel Thomas and think that he wanted to show how easy it was to get along with the natives so that prospective settlers would flock to "Pensilvania" and Jersey and buy land from his company.

I put all these conflicting accounts together and write down what I believe to be true. People call it fiction—historical fiction, because the history is told in story form. I call it "history with a heart and a face."

When I write Lenape history in story form—conversation; a beginning, a middle, an ending; conflict—I still want it to be true to life and to the historical record.

I have plumbed the depths of the internet, or should I say, trolled through the ocean enough to at least satisfy myself that what I have found will stand up to scholarly scrutiny.

I have searched enough to feel confident that even if new details arrive, as they surely will when thousands of readers check out the books, I am confident that, in the broad outline, the truth of what I have written will stand intact. Truth will stand the test of time.

As Owechela taught Glikkikan, "Glikkikan, we do not need to fear examining the truth. Truth is like a piece of gold that may be taken from our bosom and admired. If we polish it a bit as we hold it, it will only shine all the brighter."

A lie is not like the truth. A lie will tarnish and rust when examined. The closer the scrutiny, the uglier the lie becomes and the stronger the filaments of the web that bind the one who clings to it.

Those caught in the web of deceit they themselves have spun have told lies so often they no longer know what the truth is. They believe their own lies. As Meas tells Sir Robert Carr, "You have deceived yourself."

A love of the truth frees us from the fear of falsehood, the fear of being caught, the fear of disgrace, and the fear of punishment. As Jesus said, "The truth shall make you free."

The pursuit of truth turned the research and writing of The Conquest Series into a fantastic freedom adventure. Because I did not set out to force a character to support my own thoughts about the events he lived out, I was set free to find out what kind of man he really was and what made him do what he did.

That freedom excited my imagination and fueled the fires in the story. Real men came to life, and the surprises and insights Meas, Sir Robert Carr, Blackbeard, Cool Water, Josias Fendall, Free Otter, and the lordly Calverts gave me increased my interest in their story. As one editor said, "Like all good yarn-spinners, you have lived it yourself." Yes, I was there. It seemed real to me.

I hope that you will find the same zest and freshness in reading this history as I discovered when writing it.

Bibliography – Vol. II

Primary Sources

Adams, Richard C., ed. *Legends of the Delaware Indians and Picture Writing*. Washington D.C., 1905. (Kansas Collection, University of Kansas Libraries, Lawrence, KS, Microfilm).

Brinton, Daniel G. *The Lenape and Their Legends*. Philadelphia, PA, 1885. Reprinted: Lewisburg, PA: Wennawoods Publishing, 1999.

Carr, Lois Green; Menard, Russell R.; Walsh, Lorena S. *Robert Cole's World*. Chapel Hill, NC: University of North Carolina Press, 1991.

Harder, Leland and Marvin Harder. *Plockhoy from Zurik-see: The Study of a Dutch Reformer in Puritan England and Colonial America*. Newton, KS: Mennonite Board of Education and Publication, 1952.

Heckewelder, John. *History, Manners, and Customs of the Indian Nations*. Philadelphia, PA: The Historical Society of Pennsylvania, 1876.

Pritchard, Evan T. *No Word for Time, the Way of the Algonquin People*. San Francisco, CA/Tulsa, OK: Council Oak Books, 1997.

Sipe, C. Hale. *The Indian Chiefs of Pennsylvania*. Butler, PA, 1927. Reprinted: Lewisburg, PA: Wennawoods Publishing, 1994.

Weslager, C.A. *The Delaware Indians–A History*. New Brunswick, NJ: Rutgers University Press, 1972.

Weslager, C.A. & Dunlap, A.R. *Dutch Explorers, Traders and Settlers in the Delaware Valley 1609-1664*. Philadelphia, PA: University of Pennsylvania Press, 1961.

Weslager, C.A. *The English on the Delaware 1610-1682*. New Brunswick, NJ: Rutgers University Press, 1967.

Weslager, C.A. *The Siconese Indians of Lewes, Delaware.* Lewes, DE: Lewes Historical Society, 1991.

Weslager, C.A. *The Swedes and Dutch at New Castle.* Bart, New York: The Middle Atlantic Press, 1987.

General Sources

Acrelius, Israel. Translation and notes by Reynolds, William M., *A History of New Sweden; or The Settlements on the River Delaware.* Philadelphia, PA: The Historical Society of Pennsylvania, 1874.

Albensi, Bill. *Lenape* and *The Colony of New Sweden.* Wilmington, DE: Nopoly Press, Inc., 1987.

Barsotti, John J. *Scoouwa.* Columbus, OH: Ohio Historical Society, 1978. Original: Bradford, John. *An Account of the Remarkable Occurrences in the Life and Travels of Col. James Smith.* Lexington, MA, 1799.

Bronner, Edwin B. *The Founding of Pennsylvania, 1681-1701.* New York & London: Temple University Publications, 1962.

Carrell, Jennifer Lee. *The Speckled Monster.* New York, NY: Dutton, 2003.

Cohen, William J. *Swanendael in New Netherland.* Wilmington, DE: Cedar Tree Books, Ltd., 2004.

Coleman, Brooke. *The Colony of Maryland.* New York, NY: PowerKids Press, 2000.

Craig, Peter Stebbins, J.D. *1671 Census of the Delaware.* Philadelphia, PA: Genealogical Society of Pennsylvania, 1999.

De Valinger, Leon, Jr. "The Burning of the Whorekill, 1673," *Penna. Magazine,* 74, No.4 [October 1950], p. 476.

Donehoo, Dr. George P. *A History of the Indian Villages and Place Names in Pennsylvania.* Harrisburg, PA, 1928. Reprinted: Lewisburg, PA: Wennawoods Publishing, 1998.

Downie, John, *Peter Cornelius Plockboy: Pioneer of the First Co-operative Commonwealth, 1659*: Co-operative Printing Society Ltd., Manchester 4, 1931. Source: Irvin B. Horst, Sept. 1954, Mennonite Historical Library, E.M.U., Harrisonburg, VA.

Footner, Hulbert. *Rivers of the Eastern Shore.* Cambridge, MD: Tidewater Publishers, 1944.

Fradin, Dennis Brindell. *The Maryland Colony.* Chicago, IL: Childrens Press, Inc., 1990.

Frank, Albert H. *Transactions of the Moravian Historical Society.* Vol. 26: "Spiritual Life in Schoenbrunn Village," Nazareth, PA, 1990.

Grumet, Robert S. *The Lenapes.* New York, NY; Philadelphia, PA: Chelsea House Publishers, 1989.

Hall, Clayton Colman, LL.B., A.M., ed. *Narratives of Early Maryland, 1633-1684.* New York, NY: Barnes & Noble, Inc., 1910.

Harder, etc. *Delaware History.* Wilmington, DE: The Star Publishing Company, 1949.

Harrington, M.R. *The Indians of New Jersey, Dickon Among the Lenapes.* New Brunswick, NJ: Rutgers University Press, 1963. Original: Holt, Rinehart and Winston, Inc., 1938.

Heckewelder, John. *Narrative of the Mission of the United Brethren Among ... Indians, 1740-1808.* Philadelphia, PA: McCarty and Davis, 1820. Reprint: Arno Press, 1971.

Heckewelder, John. *The First American Frontier.* Arno Press and The New York Times, 1971.

Holm, Thomas Campanius, translated by Du Ponceau, Peter S. *Description of the Province of New Sweden.* Philadelphia, PA: McCarty & Davis, 1834.

Jacobs, Wilbur R. *Diplomacy and Indian Gifts, Anglo-French Rivalry Along the Ohio and Northwest Frontiers, 1748-1763.* Original: Stanford, CA, 1950. Reprint: Lewisburg, PA: Wennawoods Publishing, 2001.

James, Alfred Proctor and Stotz, Charles Morse. *Drums in the Forest.* Pittsburgh, PA: The Historical Society of Western Pennsylvania, 1958.

Jennings, Francis. *The Ambiguous Iroquois Empire.* New York, NY: W. W. Norton & Company, 1984.

Jennings, Francis. *The Founders of America.* New York, NY: W. W. Norton & Company, 1993.

Jennings, Francis. *The Invasion of America.* New York, NY: W. W. Norton & Company, 1975.

Jennings, Francis. "The Scandalous Indian Policy of William Penn's Sons: Deeds & Documents of the Walking Purchase," *Pennsylvania History*, Vol. 37 No.1, Jan. 1970, pp. 19-39.

Johnson, Amandus. *The Swedes on the Delaware 1638-1664.* Philadelphia, PA: International Printing Company, 1927.

Kraft, Herbert C. *The Lenape or Delaware Indians.* South Orange, NJ: Seton Hall University Museum, 1996.

Leasa, K. Varden. "Setting the Record Straight on Pieter Plockhoy." *Mennonite Historical Bulletin,* 3/1/04. <www.mcusa-archives.org>

Mancall, Peter C. *Deadly Medicine.* Ithaca, NY: Cornell University Press, 1995.

Mason, F. Van Wyck. *The Maryland Colony.* New York, NY: Crowell-Collier Press, 1969.

Mcintosh, John. *The Origin of the North American Indians.* New York, NY: Nafis & Cornish, 1844.

McLuhan, T. C. *Touch the Earth.* London, Great Britain: Garnstone Press, Ltd., 1972.

McNeal, Patricia. *Painters of the First Frontier,* compiled from *Westsylvania Stories.* Gettysburg, PA: Lord Nelson's Art Gallery, 2002.

Merrell, James H. *Into the American Woods.* New York & London: W. W. Norton & Company, 1999.

Myers, Albert Cook, ed. *William Penn's Own Account of the Lenni Lenape or Delaware Indians*. Wilmington, DE: The Middle Atlantic Press, 1970.

Olmstead, Earl P. *David Zeisberger~A Life Among the Indians*. Kent, Ohio: The Kent State University Press, 1997.

O'Neil, James F., comp. and ed. *Their Bearing Is Noble and Proud*. Dayton, OH: J.T.G.S. Publishing, 1995.

Paterek, Josephine. *Encyclopedia of American Indian Costume*. New York, NY: W. W. Norton & Company, 1994.

Plantenga, Bart. "The Mystery of the Plockhoy Settlement in the Valley of Swans." *Mennonite Historical Bulletin* 9/30/03. <www.mcusa-archives.org>

Robertson, R. G. *Rotting Face~Smallpox and the American Indian*. Caldwell, ID: Caxton Press, 2001.

Robson, Lucia St. Clair. *Mary's Land*. New York, NY: Ballantine Books, 1995.

Shoemaker, Henry W., comp. *A Pennsylvania Bison Hunt*. Middleburg, PA, 1915. Reprinted Lewisburg, PA: Wennawoods Publishing, 1998.

Sipe, C. Hale. *The Indian Wars of Pennsylvania*. Butler, PA, 1931. Reprinted: Lewisburg, PA: Wennawoods Publishing, 1995.

Smith, Craig Stephen. *Whiteman's Gospel*. Winnipeg, Manitoba: Indian Life Books, 1997.

Tantaquidgeon, Gladys. *Folk Medicine of the Delaware and Related Algonkian Indians*. Harrisburg, PA: Commonwealth of Pennsylvania, 1972.

Tate, Thad W. & Ammerman, David L., ed. *The Chesapeake in the Seventeenth Century*. New York, NY: W. W. Norton & Company, 1979.

Tehanetorens. *Wampum Belts*, Onchiota, NY: Six Nations Indian Museum, 1972.

Turdo, Mark A. *Common People, Uncommon Community Lenape Life in Moravian Missions*. Nazareth, PA: Moravian Historical Society, 1998.

Valinger, Leonde, Jr. "The Burning of the Whorekill, 1673" *Penna. Magazine*, 74, No. 4. [October 1950], p. 476.

Walker, Bryce, chief ed. *Through Indian Eyes*. Pleasantville, NY: The Reader's Digest Association, 1995.

Wallace, Paul A. W. *Indian Paths of Pennsylvania*. Harrisburg, PA: The Pennsylvania Historical Commission, 1965.

Wallace, Paul A. W. *Indians in Pennsylvania*. Commonwealth of Pennsylvania, 1961. Reprint: Harrisburg, PA, 1999.

Wallace, Paul A. W., ed. *Thirty Thousand Miles with John Heckewelder*. Published 1958. Reprinted: Lewisburg, PA: Wennawoods Publishing, 1998.

Wenning, Scott Hayes. *Handbook of the Delaware Indian Language*. Lewisburg, PA: Wennawoods Publishing, 2000.

Wilson, Dorothy Clarke. *Bright Eyes*. New York, NY: McGraw-Hill Book Company, 1974.

Witthoft, John. *The American Indian as Hunter*. Harrisburg, PA: Commonwealth of Pennsylvania Historical and Museum Commission, 1999.

Zeisberger, David. Archer Butler Hulbert and William Nathaniel Schwarze, ed. *David Zeisberger's History of the Northern American Indians*. Marietta, OH: Ohio State Archaeological and Historical Society, 1910. Reprint: Lewisburg, PA: Wennawoods Publishing, 1999.

Zeisberger, David. *Journals & Diaries of David Zeisberger*. Gathered by Earl Olmstead, Kent State, OH, 1988.

About the Author

by Fonda Joy Wadel

L ove for learning sparked early in my dad's life.

Raised on Pennsylvania and Virginia farms by a professor father and a home-loving mother, his world formed in a place where work and study intermingled. Reading and history lessons captured his young mind in class while farm chores educated his hands at home.

After graduating from high school in 1960, Dad chose agricultural work for three years. But the yearning for book learning propelled him on to college. For another year he sharpened English composition skills and reveled in Bible and history lessons.

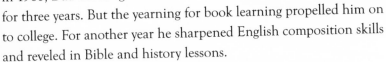

Dad enlarged his education with diverse experiences. For fourteen years he dairy farmed on Georgia plains. He taught high school students amid Pennsylvania hills. He wrote at a publishing house in the New Mexico desert.

From his West Virginia mountain home he edited educational newsletters and penned articles for farm magazines. Hobbies varied from chess games and singing to beekeeping, landscaping, and composting.

His agricultural, economic, and historical interests spurred travel to Central and South America, Europe, Africa, Australia, and New Zealand.

Dad prizes truth. He refuses to accept pat answers flipped to ethical questions. His beliefs demand Bible research, historical evaluation, and world-view consideration. He enjoys stirring minds through church periodicals, Sunday school classes, and Bible history lessons.

Dad's manifesto flies above the hearts of all seven of his children:

Drink knowledge. Hail adventure. Stand on truth.

About Christian Aid Ministries

C hristian Aid Ministries was founded in 1981 as a nonprofit, tax-exempt 501(c)(3) organization. Its primary purpose is to provide a trustworthy and efficient channel for Amish, Mennonite, and other conservative Anabaptist groups and individuals to minister to physical and spiritual needs around the world. This is in response to the command to ". . . do good unto all men, especially unto them who are of the household of faith" (Galatians 6:10).

Each year, CAM supporters provide approximately 15 million pounds of food, clothing, medicines, seeds, Bibles, Bible story books, and other Christian literature for needy people. Most of the aid goes to orphans and Christian families. Supporters' funds also help to clean up and rebuild for natural disaster victims, put up Gospel billboards in the U.S., support several church-planting efforts, operate two medical clinics, and provide resources for needy families to make their own living. CAM's main purposes for providing aid are to help and encourage God's people and bring the Gospel to a lost and dying world.

CAM has staff, warehouses, and distribution networks in Romania, Moldova, Ukraine, Haiti, Nicaragua, Liberia, and Israel. Aside from management, supervisory personnel, and bookkeeping operations, volunteers do most of the work at CAM locations. Each year, volunteers at our warehouses, field bases, Disaster Response Services projects, and other locations donate over 200,000 hours of work.

CAM's ultimate purpose is to glorify God and help enlarge His kingdom. ". . . whatsoever ye do, do all to the glory of God" (1 Corinthians 10:31).

The Way to God and Peace

We live in a world contaminated by sin. Sin is anything that goes against God's holy standards. When we do not follow the guidelines that God our Creator gave us, we are guilty of sin. Sin separates us from God, the source of life.

Since the time when the first man and woman, Adam and Eve, sinned in the Garden of Eden, sin has been universal. The Bible says that we all have "sinned and come short of the glory of God" (Romans 3:23). It also says that the natural consequence for that sin is eternal death, or punishment in an eternal hell: "Then when lust hath conceived, it bringeth forth sin: and sin, when it is finished, bringeth forth death" (James 1:15).

But we do not have to suffer eternal death in hell. God provided forgiveness for our sins through the death of His only Son, Jesus Christ. Because Jesus was perfect and without sin, He could die in our place. "For God so loved the world that he gave his only begotten Son, that whosoever believeth in him should not perish, but have everlasting life" (John 3:16).

A sacrifice is something given to benefit someone else. It costs the giver greatly. Jesus was God's sacrifice. Jesus' death takes away the penalty of sin for everyone who accepts this sacrifice and truly repents of their sins. To repent of sins means to be truly sorry for and turn away from the things we have done that have violated God's standards (Acts 2:38; 3:19).

Jesus died, but He did not remain dead. After three days, God's Spirit miraculously raised Him to life again. God's Spirit does something similar in us. When we receive Jesus as our sacrifice and repent of our sins, our hearts are changed. We become spiritually alive! We develop new desires and attitudes (2 Corinthians 5:17). We begin to make choices that please God (1 John 3:9). If we do fail and commit sins, we can ask God for forgiveness. "If we confess our sins, he is faithful and just to forgive us our sins, and to cleanse us from all unrighteousness" (1 John 1:9).

Once our hearts have been changed, we want to continue growing spiritually. We will be happy to let Jesus be the Master of our lives and will want to become more like Him. To do this, we must meditate on God's Word and commune with God in prayer. We will testify to others of this change by being baptized and sharing the good news of God's victory over sin and death. Fellowship with a faithful group of believers will strengthen our walk with God (1 John 1:7).